MIXED COMPANY

A novel by
Andy Horne

Carpenter's Son Publishing

Mixed Company

©2013 by Andy Horne

Published by Carpenter's Son Publishing, Franklin, Tennessee

Published in association with Larry Carpenter of Christian Book Services, LLC
www.christianbookservices.com

Cover Design by Debbie Manning Sheppard

Interior Design by Suzanne Lawing

Copy Edit by David Reynolds

Printed in the United States of America

978-0-9893722-8-2

DEDICATION

To my patient, encouraging, adventurous and multi-faceted wife, Sylvia

CONTENTS

Mid-May 2001

CHAPTER 1

Pretty in Pink

The hard-eyed, lean young man followed Randolph Cavanaugh from Minneapolis into Memphis on Northwest Airlines the evening before. There was no telling how or when the boy had picked up Dolph's trail, but today was going to be a tailing exercise for the kid.

The American Airlines flight to the Dallas-Fort Worth regional airport left Memphis at 6 am. Cavanaugh preferred early morning flights. That was the time many businessmen traveled to get in nearly a full day's work. Dolph was no different. Besides, morning weather is generally more stable with milder temperatures. Dolph didn't always dress like a businessman, but peculiarly this morning was wearing a bright pink jogging suit. His bulk and height made air travel in coach less than bearable in conventional business clothing. People stared at Cavanaugh, and why not? He was their oddity of the morning, an aging fat pink rabbit carrying a briefcase, the Wall Street Journal and a light suit bag.

The kid, dressed like a young professional, almost lost Dolph and his pink clothing at DFW's ground transportation, but somehow managed to catch up during the cab trip to Love Field, Dallas' more popular near city airport. Even considering Cavanaugh's heft, he could, when necessary, move quickly.

DFW travelers had lined up for taxis, and ahead of Dolph were parents with two small children in a tandem stroller. The children were laughing and chattering about the big man dressed in pink as the dad was trying to find out the cost to haul all of them to Fort Worth. Sensing a further delay while the parents loaded their kids and baggage, Cavanaugh went straight for the second cab in line and sped away. The young man was fifth in line, and an attendant blocked his effort to cut ahead of the others. Dolph looked back from his cab and saw the young man arguing with the attendant, waiving something in the attendant's face, probably his Bureau credentials. However, by the time Cavanaugh paid for his Southwest Airlines flight to Houston's Hobby Airport, he spotted the kid entering the Love Field terminal. The pink suit didn't blend in well, and Dolph correctly assumed the kid would accompany him on the flight to Houston. Dolph appreciated that some folks always focus on the irrelevant.

He deplaned in Houston at 9:30 am and again headed for ground transportation on the lower level. This time, the boy walked past Dolph and got his cab first. Cavanaugh saw him again pull out his wallet and speak to the driver, whose eyes moved from his passenger to the big man dressed in pink lumbering over to the next taxi. The driver, a young Black man whose dreadlocks cascaded down his neck, played like he was indifferent to all this.

Interstate 45 traffic was still heavy on this Thursday morning, but it was beginning to thin. They would be in the city's center in 17 minutes. Dolph looked back a couple of times and saw the boy's cab two cars back. As instructed, Cavanaugh's driver pulled in front of One Shell Plaza on the Smith Street side of the building, a white office tower on the west side of downtown. It was time to make things more challenging for the boy.

Houston's downtown tunnel system is a pedestrian labyrinth of commercial and retail activity set more than 20 feet below the streets. Connecting over 75 buildings with seven miles of tunnels, the system provides safe, convenient, year-round movement through the city's center regardless of the weather. A casual observer on the surface might think downtown was dead, but life teamed below. Each of the buildings connects to the system by a variety of elevators, escalators or stairways, large and small. It is a maze to the uninitiated; however, to Houston's 140,000 downtown workers and this day, a big pink rabbit, it was the briar patch.

Cavanaugh took 20 quick steps down into the system and turned left, picking up his pace to the next building, Two Shell Plaza, a less glitzy structure than One Shell. His options there were to go left to the Pennzoil building, straight to the Esperson buildings or up an escalator to the Walker Street level. He chose up and went a few steps east before turning north on Milam to Pennzoil. Back down into the system, he made his way under the Mellie Esperson building facing Walker Street.

There, off a little known alcove, was a doorway into a public men's restroom, a relic of the pre-tunnel basement. Adjacent to that doorway was a stairwell to the Esperson's south lobby and a set of elevators. Dolph was in the restroom only long enough to strip off the jogging suit and pitch it in the trash, adjust his tie and put on the pants and jacket from his suit bag. He stuffed the suit bag into his briefcase and then wheezed up to the lobby. A few steps and one turn down a hall took him to the Niels Esperson bank of elevators. Riding to the 11th floor, the elevator gently rumbled and rocked in its 73-year-old shaft. Two turns to the right brought him to a door marked "Private". As he stuck the key into the lock, he smiled at the last sight he had of the young man standing out on Walker Street. The kid was looking around and had to be wondering what happened to the pink suit. It had not been a good morning for the young FBI agent. It was 10:12 a.m. There was a lot to do before Cavanaugh could go home.

CHAPTER 2

Esperson Delight

The two Esperson buildings are unique architectural antiques of the Houston business community in design, history and longevity. Virtually all of Houston's old office buildings still standing have changed beyond their original image and purpose. None ever possessed the Espersons' artistic ambience. Only the Espersons remain as beautiful office structures.

The Niels Esperson building facing east on Travis Street, completed in 1927 at 32 stories, was then the tallest building in Texas. Built by his wife, Mellie, after Niels' death in 1922, the building remains a classic of Italian Renaissance design amongst its more modern, often ostentatious neighbors. In 1941, she completed the adjacent structure of 19 stories facing south on Walker Street bearing her name. The Danish immigrant and his mid-Western wife were significant public figures in pre-modern Houston, and the paired office buildings defined the city's skyline for decades.

Symbolic of the matrimony of the Espersons, many of Mellie Esperson's 19 stories connect to its taller companion, an important feature for at least one of its tenants.

Dolph Cavanaugh secured a long-term lease in the mid-1980s during one of Houston's few but usually beneficial economic down times. The 1,400-square-foot space he acquired had a secluded and private entrance on the Niels side, but his business entrance was on the Mellie, 1111. As with all the other building standard business names stenciled on solid dark varnished wooden doors, PCF Investment Company was in black lettering with gold trim.

The office waiting room, tastefully decorated with an oriental carpet, comfortable leather chairs, hand-carved wooden side tables covered with current business magazines and shaded lamps, suggested tradition, reliability and discretion. A portrait of Admiral John Fisher, First Sea Lord of the British Navy's Admiralty in the late 19th century and in the early years of the First World War, one of Dolph's personal heroes, adorned the wall opposite an opaque pass-through window. Entering Dolph's business domain encouraged reserved voices.

The working spaces inside were not much different in decor. Behind an open secretarial space containing two large desks, copy and fax equipment, a collation table and two five-drawer lateral filing cabinets, was a small kitchen on the left and Dolph's large, private office on the right. On one side of Dolph's personal office was a door into a small windowless bathroom with a shower, and on the other side, the private entrance from the Niels side of the building.

Dolph's private space replicated the feel of the waiting room except that it contained a portrait of Sam Houston, hero of the Battle of San Jacinto. Old Sam was another personal hero of Cavanaugh's, not for his military exploits, but more for the fact that Houston had come to Texas, then in rebellion against Mexico, with a down and out public status. A former U. S. congressman and governor of Tennessee, he got a second chance in life. With that opportunity, he became a victorious general, president of the new republic, and twice governor of the state. Sam last was elected governor in a hostile secessionist climate, and he later refused to sign the bill declaring Texas' withdrawal from the Union. Dolph's life to this point had been a string of unrecognized second chances without the kind of success that made men cheer and women feel proud. Still, life had been good to him.

Dolph went into the secretarial area and retrieved his mail, neatly grouped by the young woman who came in two, and on some occasions, three times a week. Her limited duties were to check on and sort, but not open, the mail, tend the few plants, list all telephone messages and replace any outdated waiting room magazines. She only had one door key, and that was for the front door. Mr. Cavanaugh's personal office door remained locked whenever he was away. When she was in the office alone, she was to keep the front door locked as well. Visitors never came to the office unless Dolph was in.

For the past 10 years Dolph had only hired female undergraduates from Rice University, or occasionally the University of Houston, for 15 hours a week at the handsome rate of $20 per hour. For students, the income was astronomical and the work undemanding and unlikely to interfere with their studies. These girls tended to be sweet, attractive and efficient. They were vaguely aware of the investment business legitimately conducted by Dolph, but clueless about Dolph's other commercial pursuits. Long ago, Dolph began following two special rules when it came to his office. He never conducted or recorded any of his shady "bidness" from that space, and he never molested the help; it was bad for business.

The office had two major purposes: lawful management of his earned assets and a place of transition from his other world of fraud schemes and money laundering. When he left the front door of PCF Investment Company, he was almost identical to several of the Esperson business tenants: reclusive, conservative, cordial, well-mannered and wealthy. He thought of the Esperson buildings as his personal Superman phone booth. Increasingly however, he wanted to detach from that other life beyond the back entrance of his office.

As he began going through the mail, focusing on the few bills that had come in, he picked up his telephone and dialed. Corrine's greeting voice always bubbled. "Hey, darlin', you've been gone too long. When are you coming home?" She always made him feel welcomed.

"I've missed you too. How'd you know it was me?"

"Country Boy, I always know when you call. Don't you understand that?"

For 27 years, he'd been asking the same question, she never once gave him a straight answer, and she wasn't going to start this morning. Country Boy was one of Dolph's nicknames from college. Corrine was ignorant of its origins but liked it enough for occasional use. Dolph stopped acknowledging the name several years ago, and never encouraged Corrine's usage of it.

"I just got in this morning, and I've got to pay some bills and return some calls. I've also got to make a little money, you know. I'm thinking I'll head out after lunch, but before the traffic picks up on 288."

The drive to Bay City would take a little over two hours if he didn't dawdle. He had really missed his wife. Dolph knew she was the best thing that ever happened to him.

"What are you doing today?" Not waiting for her answer, he volunteered his guess. "Going out to the shop?"

"I did that yesterday. I'm meeting the girls in 15 minutes for a little pool time and lunch at the Nouveau. You know we try to get together every Thursday until kids get out for the summer." She paused. "I'm jumping in my two-piece right now."

Corrine was a mother of two fine grown sons moving excitedly into her 48th year, and still looked like a million dollars. She was physically strong and healthy. Dolph lingered on a mental image of her getting ready for the country club.

"Baby, I sure am tired of going on the road. What would you think of me hanging it up for good?"

Corrine had heard this before, but now Dolph was saying it more often. Maybe he was serious.

"Well, we can afford it, and I'd like to find out what it would be like to have you around all the time. Let's talk this evening."

Dolph knew she was getting anxious to leave the house, but he was enjoying hearing her voice. She was always the better person in their marriage.

"You give me a report on the gossip when I get in, and tell that pampered tart Eloise hello for me. Have fun."

Dolph pulled out his three-ring checkbook and began writing checks and filling out deposit slips for oil and other lease payments as well as some real estate note receipts. Returning phone calls could wait until next week. After stamping the envelopes and reconciling his bank balances, he locked up his papers and then shredded and bagged his trash. The shredder turned all paper into little dots, not the strips made by conventional and cheaper machines. Long before identity theft became the widespread tool of ordinary crooks and techy computer geeks, Dolph had been an expert in the field. This expertise dictated exacting steps to protect both sides of his business identity. Careless and casual disposal of trash created many victims for fraud schemers and provided evidence for prosecutors to convict wrongdoers. With sufficient time and dedication, the strips could be pieced together by crooks and cops alike, but not the dots.

As Dolph left the office on the Mellie side, he dropped the mail in the wall slot and took a short walk to the locked men's room. Opening the plastic trash bag, he ran about a half cup of water into the bag, resealed it and tossed the shred into the waste can. The moisture would further muck up the shred.

At this time of day, there was no one in the halls. He took the elevator down to the fourth floor. From there, it was a 10-foot walk into the Esperson garage. He actually maintained three vehicles in other buildings on the tunnel system, but today he went to his 10-year-old Suburban. The weekend was coming up, and he wanted the comfort of the old truck while he was in Bay City.

CHAPTER 3
Bay City Texas

Bay City, established in 1894, the county seat of Matagorda County, is located southwest of Houston by about 80 miles. Surrounded by rice fields and grasslands for cattle, Bay City, population 18,000 and nowhere close to any bay, is about 25 miles from the Gulf of Mexico and a long way from anything regarded as important to today's so-called modern culture. Until construction began on the South Texas Nuclear Project west of town in the 1980s, almost no one visited Bay City except the annual migration of geese, their hunters and a few folks hoping to get away from life in the big cities. Despite its version of urban sprawl, Bay City retained its small-town flavor.

Big-city scandals other than marital or sexual rarely touched the area. Lying, cheating and stealing were often only on the petty level, livened occasionally by a little light killing. Even now, hardly anyone pays long or serious attention publicly to what one preacher delicately called the companion misadventures of the heart and the body. For example, years ago, when a young inebriated local lawyer imagined he was the Christmas gift to a county employee, who also may have been hitting the eggnog hard at the courthouse party, his conduct resulted in an indictment for aggravated sexual assault. The young man got probation, saved his license, but appropriately ruined his local reputation. When one of the two district judges for the county was casually asked if he attended the party, he proclaimed his absence, and in support of that position, said he had affidavits from two individuals that he was robbing a bank up in Dallas at the time of the celebration. Soon the lawyer left tow,n and the whole affair was forgotten.

Dolph always wondered why the law called that crime aggravated sexual assault. It seemed to him that such a terrible thing done to a woman shouldn't carry such a fuzzy title. It was rape, pure and simple; men that did that deserved to be called rapists and nothing less. A rapist, in Dolph's view, ought not to get probation under any circumstances, and a death penalty was appropriate in many cases.

Non-violent but ominous sounding financial crimes happened elsewhere, not in Matagorda County. The local weekly newspaper, if it reported anything at all on such matters, did so with a sparse and poorly edited summary taken from the big-city dailies. The poor editing had more to do with not understanding the offenses than the journalistic ineptitude common in all small communities. In some ways, Bay City may as well have been another planet. For Dolph Cavanaugh, Bay City was just a bigger and more pleasant phone booth.

* * *

The area had plenty of wealth, some old and much new, and was not without its dreamers. When the South Texas Nuclear Project came along, there were those who thought Bay City would become the new Mecca of the southern Texas Gulf Coast.

A few years ago, outside investors paid a lot of money for a big parcel of land north of town. Then they began the painstaking and meticulous process of developing the property for exclusive housing and recreation in the hope of siphoning money from folks up in Houston and rich refugees escaping California's irrational real-estate prices and burdensome tax laws. Californians were noted for paying top dollar for Texas dirt. Nowadays, rural hills and scrub brush suitable for cattle and deer hunting northwest of the line formed between Austin and San Antonio were becoming out of reach except for these elitist immigrants. The character of Texas was also changing.

This paradise on the prairie, Nouveau Estates, was a gated and high-fenced community of homes beginning at the low $200,000s to a million, two-fifty. Over a hundred homes were already completed and occupied along the planned meanderings of the 18-hole golf course. Live oak trees, jogging and bicycle paths, a scattering of small lakes and a high-dollar shopping center were all part of the master plan for 350 homes, which also included stiff architectural and quality controls for every structure built there.

One of the first amenities of the development was the lavish main building and swimming pool of the Nouveau Estates Country Club. The Bay City Country Club and its 9-hole course, which dated back to 1939, was sucking wind compared to this newcomer. The most recent change in the old course was to add a 10th hole to replace the 8th that sloughed off into the nearby Colorado River. Local golfers joked that the old club paid a price for messing with Mother Nature. Out at Nouveau, they quipped that the dress code for their course would not require life jackets.

CHAPTER 4

Nouveau Country Club

The east facing, sprawling, three-story plantation-style clubhouse could have been the film locale for *Gone With the Wind*, except for a few details. There were no tall moss draped oak shade trees, just spindly six-foot plantings of oak 30 feet apart with a promise of elegance two generations away. They flanked a quarter mile, four-lane esplanaded cement-paved street leading to a circular driveway in front of the clubhouse. Large parking lots pealed off on either side of the approach. The esplanade was planted with clusters of short crepe myrtle trees also spaced 30 feet apart.

The front lawn, if you want to call it that, was just now being created from pallets of St. Augustine grass that were trucked in earlier in the week. The grass needed to take hold before the end of May or else things would be too hot for healthy growth. Half a dozen Hispanics from God knows where were efficiently laying the grass panels. They were the landscape contractor's employees, so it didn't matter where they came from or whether they were legal.

Behind the clubhouse was one large 100-year-old oak tree whose gentle arms shaded the walkways and newly laid lawns. A smaller crew was laying additional grass near the golf pro shop on the north end and along the sidewalks leading to the tennis courts. The detached pool house on the other end was already surrounded with newly planted grass and was being lightly watered by the contractor, a black man raised in the Mechanicsville area of Atlanta, Georgia.

Mechanicsville had been a drug-infested, murderous and hope-less slum south of Interstate 20 when Carleton Brooks enlisted in the U.S. Army. Brooks' father, a railroad worker, had died in the crossfire between rival gangs of black youths when his son was still an infant. Raised well and inspired by his mother and her older brother, Carleton had avoided the dead ends of Mechanicsville. His aspiration was to earn a college education through the GI Bill at the highly respected and his-toric Morehouse College on the north side of Interstate 20.

A decorated First Gulf War Special Forces veteran, Brooks found his horizons changing and his attachment to Atlanta waning as his second enlistment was ending. He had been in advanced training at Fort Hood near Killeen, Texas, and liked the openness of the geography and the forward-thinking of people of the state. He enrolled at Texas A&M University at College Station where, three and a half years later, he earned a business degree. A week after that, he married Natalie Robins, a freshly minted pharmacist raised in the Bay City area. Two children later, they were well-established in Bay City. Carleton, by then a Master Gardener, was known as a first-rate landscaper. They were also good friends of Corrine and Dolph Cavanaugh.

Looping around the swimming pool was a seven-foot high stucco wall, painted soft pink and fronted with a new garden. Carleton's peo-ple, a mixed crew of Blacks and Hispanics, were planting shrubbery at the same time as they cleaned up their work area, a hallmark of Brooks' work. Their work was steady and needed little supervision.

If Carleton's clients assumed his Hispanic employees were illegal and thus his jobs were priced lower, that was all right with him although factually incorrect. Brooks insisted that all of his workers be legal U.S. residents and speak good English. He also paid fair wages and required benefits. Taking advantage of poor folks only kept them poor. He believed in, rather than scoffed at, the "American Dream."

The late-morning sun was just coming over the roof of the main building as Corrine and her girlfriends walked out of the pool house toward the umbrella-covered tables spotted around. There were no other members or guests present. It was too early for crowds, and most members wanted to wait a few more days until Carleton completed his landscape work.

"Hey Carleton, it's sure looking good. You ought to be finished by now." Corrine had waived, but kept walking.

Carleton turned the garden hose toward her, but he was too far away to spray her or the other ladies.

"We'll be done when we're done, Corrine. You gonna be at the bank next week?"

Brooks was paying attention to his grass rather than the collection of fine-looking women with her.

Corrine had done a little two-step away from the non-threatening spray.

"Sure. Tell Natalie hello for me." Carleton again flipped the hose toward her in acknowledgement, but said nothing further.

Except for Corrine and Bea Jay, the other women were second wives, having displaced older, presumably now less-attractive predecessors. Mrs. Cavanaugh privately wondered why men were so easily wooed away from the women who often made their successes possible. It was so unkind. However, she kept those thoughts between herself and Dolph. In a town like Bay City, where she had grown up, when you start cutting people off for their weakness, you soon run out of friends. Mean folks were another matter.

Regardless of their social values or backgrounds, all of these women were trophy wives, Maseratis in the driveway. Long legs were made longer by high-bottom swimsuits and stacked-heel sandals, all but for Corrine, whose shoes were flats. For different reasons, all of them had mostly lean, fabulous figures. Eloise Trimmer, three years younger than Corrine, had good genes on her side, while Barbara Piper cycled and watched her diet. Maria Shiprite, a Highland Park High School graduate raised in Dallas, had a little bit of a tummy from kids, but she kept her weight down by eating very little and sometimes drinking a lot. Beatrice Jayne Wynne was just young and had medically inflated breasts.

Only Corrine, the oldest, knew what hard physical work involved. She knew how to sweat and was in top condition. As a young girl, she and her brothers had helped her daddy on the rice farm, and she was a forward on her high school's girls basketball team. When Dolph started traveling so much and the boys were older, Corrine bought an old welding shop east of town. The place had been there for over 80 years, servicing the needs of the farmers in the region. Corrine and her brothers all learned driving by taking a tractor or other machinery over to Helmut's Weldinghaus.

Helmut Stern was a German Jew who fled the Ruhr River valley in 1935. His parents told him to go to America, maybe even Texas to get far away from the insanity gripping his country. In those years of economic depression, jobs using his talents as a machinist and welder were difficult to find. He finally got work in a municipal bus barn in San Antonio, Texas.

When Germany invaded Poland in September 1939, Helmut understood the coming storm and hoped in some way to be a part of saving his family, wherever they were. He enlisted in the U.S. Army in January 1940, and following basic training, he was assigned to mechanized units forming at Fort Polk, Louisiana. Not long after his participation in the North African landings, he was plucked from his medium tank unit and ordered into an intelligence group interrogating prisoners of war. He never saw combat action again, but suffered injury nonetheless. An enraged SS junior officer shouting anti-Semitic curses bashed Helmut's left leg with a folding chair. A guard entered the interrogation room and shot the prisoner dead on the spot. Staff Sergeant Helmut Stern, medically discharged in January 1945, then returned to San Antonio, Texas, with a noticeable but painless limp and, for those days, substantial savings. He bought the shop in Bay City. Corrine's father called him the best welder and mechanic in Texas.

Stern never found his family from Germany, but he soon married a soldier's widow from nearby El Campo. They had no children. He died in 1985 from a sudden heart attack, and his widow moved to Austin to live with her sister. Helmut's Weldinghaus remained unused for seven years when Corrine located his widow and successfully offered to buy the place.

The big, corrugated metal building was in great shape but dirty. Scrap metal of all kinds rusted out in the weed-filled yard and inside the shop, still in the same place they had been when old Helmut keeled over. Engine blocks and tractor bodies rested over the oil-soaked gravel floor of the shop. The little office to the right of the huge double doors into the building was covered in a thick film of dust. Unfilled work orders and receipts hung yellowing from clipboards. All of this was dismal, but Corrine was thrilled. She made a list. The top four items were to take welding classes, fix the overhead lift, clean the place and get a new sign. She honored her memory of the old limping German but claimed the place as her own, changing only the first word on the new sign, Corrine's Weldinghaus.

A warm breeze crossed the swimming pool. The ladies pulled lawn chairs around into just-so positions, fished into their big straw bags for sunscreen lotions and began surveying the work going on around the Nouveau. Just as this activity began, a young Mexican girl in a white waitress dress brought a tray containing a huge pitcher of frozen margaritas, five salt-rimmed frosty glasses, a pile of nacho chips and a big bowl of red salsa. She gestured questioningly and then poured the first round. A second girl then appeared with pressed white cotton napkins, a small bowl of sliced limes and some guacamole dip. The girls retired to the pool house, and the ladies sipped their drinks, for a time in silence.

CHAPTER 5

Changing Pace

Dolph had been eager to get out of Houston and skipped lunch, a rarity. There were a couple of ways to get to Bay City, both involving going somewhere else. This time Dolph chose State Highway 288 down south toward Angleton instead of taking U.S. 59 South to Wharton, a slightly longer but sometimes faster course. Either way, there were plenty of Burger Kings and Whataburger joints to stop at. Corrine always joked that Dolph's idea of a business lunch was a double meat, double cheeseburger and fries at one of those places. The only time Dolph ever stopped at the Golden Arches was to use their restrooms or to grab a sausage biscuit before 10:30 a.m. Otherwise, he passed on McDonald's menu.

He felt a mixture of relief and anxiety. He had been able, with some forethought, to shake the government boy, but this had been the first time any of them got close to his legitimate turf in Houston. This last piece of work in British Columbia had taken two years from conception to execution of the plan, but it had been profitable. His victims had paid a deeply discounted price for Dolph's bearer bonds. The bonds' facial maturity was years away, but their real value was even less. The issuer signatures were the contract work of a man known in the trade only as the Replicator, an excellent forger. From the time Dolph drove out of Vancouver, down to Seattle and arrived in Memphis the night before, the buyers' wire transfer payment of the half million in Canadian dollars to Cavanaugh's fictional identification on the deal had been divided many times and passed through several countries and currencies. The funds came to rest in a Syrian bank account of an import business located in Beirut, Lebanon. Over the next few days, these funds would move out as fictitious vendor payments to various European countries and reassemble with other transfers to an account in Switzerland. Twenty percent of the funds were left behind as processing fees for Syria's and other entities' accommodations. The Swiss account had existed for over 20 years, while the filtering accounts had changed many times depending upon shifts in politics and regional tensions. Dolph was a bottom-line fraud schemer; he knew how much he had stolen and knew that legitimate investments out of the Swiss account had appreciated beyond his expectations. He periodically received a never-repeated listing of three banks with account numbers into which funds could, at his request, be wired. Dolph knew no other details of the elaborate and ever-changing money laundering system, and he did not know any specifics of particular investments. His overseas business associate took care of those details; besides, Dolph focused on doing the deals rather than getting any benefit from all that money, now conservatively valued at more than $23 million in fixed and liquid assets. Dolph Cavanaugh could not easily be written off as all bad. Since marrying Corrine, not one dime ever went into his pocket; none was ever needed.

Dolph's legitimate life in Texas also had been marked with financial profit, but he felt he was losing his edge. He so rarely now got any kind of rush from his elaborate schemes that he was beginning to wonder why he should do them at all. He was a smart guy but not much into self-analysis. Doing deals had been a major part of his life after the

Navy, and because he was good at that line of work, he kept doing them. When he was in the mood, finding the right someone to take down might take six months, and then an additional year to plan the scheme. With that in mind, he concluded there was plenty of time to work out a seamless transition to a totally honest life.

Dolph was also worried about what he called "getting too close to the flames." He had violated one of his few cardinal rules, never to do deals with Chinese confederates or against Chinese entities. They were too unpredictable and certainly vengeful. He liked the more common ethnic generalization, inscrutable. He similarly classified people from South Dakota as too flaky to be partners. Lately, he had added another group to his scheme avoidance list. He couldn't figure out why homosexuals were called gay; they seemed anything but that. He had no problem with anyone's sexual preferences, but when something went wrong or they felt cheated, homosexuals tended to be more upset than most folks. Dolph thought they were smart, creative people, but in his experience, they got too emotionally involved with a deal, crooked or otherwise.

The people he had scammed were Chinese, and part of the fun of the deal was that they represented a Red Chinese government corporation that had been acquiring supposedly outdated aircraft manufacturing equipment and technology. In the name of international harmony with the Communists, old Bill Clinton had approved these deals on the false assumption that none of this stuff would aid China's feared projection of military power, or if it did, participation in the world's economy would restrain their more militant inclinations.

Dolph's philosophical response to this thinking had been unambiguous. His lawyer in Houston had handed him a copy of a Wall Street Journal that included an article dated October 21, 1996, entitled *Let's Make a Deal*. While Mr. Taylor took an incoming phone call, Dolph read the piece. His blood began to boil. When Mr. Taylor got off the phone, Cavanaugh tossed the paper back on the desk and said, "Sir, that's a bunch of 'comminist' bullcorn." Taylor laughed, but Dolph began wondering what he could do to those buzzards. It was not until a couple of years later that his plan came into focus.

Dolph always addressed Taylor as "Sir" or "Mr. Taylor." Only occasionally did Mr. Taylor call him "Cavanaugh." Despite the years, their relationship had at first been defined by those terms of address in the Navy, and they later evidenced their friendship and mutual respect.

Against Dolph's better judgment, he had done the deal with the Chinese and made a bunch of money. They would end up as dead men for stealing from their own government, and that too was satisfying.

Still, there was the question of the boy from the FBI and how and when the kid had picked up on him. Dolph's stomach began growling. He would ponder more on this after getting a bite to eat. He had an internalized homing device working down there, because he could now see a Burger King sign perched beyond the exit into Angleton.

CHAPTER 6

J. Edgar Wouldn't Be Happy

Special Agent Thomas Purdue sat in the Houston office of the FBI. He was on the telephone with his supervisor in the Seattle office. His half of the conversation was unpleasant enough, and his direct flight back to an extended chewing out would be longer than life itself.

"Yes sir, things were fine until we got to downtown. They've got a tunnel complex here that's incredible. He and his pink outfit were gone in a heartbeat."

After a pause, he responded. "No sir. I don't know. For all I know, he's on another airplane munching on a bag of carrots." The young man's frustration was palpable. Two more yes sirs and he was off the phone.

The Assistant Special Agent in Charge, Michael H. Ringer, had let the unhappy agent use his telephone. Ringer was sympathetic but knew these setbacks were not unusual for first-office agents, a term describing the place of initial assignment for a new agent.

"Tell me some of his remarks. I might find them worth using on my new guys." His effort to put the matter in to perspective didn't help. Purdue was disheartened.

"He didn't think much of the tunnel excuse. He told me that was nonsense, that I'd probably lose a tail even if I was sitting in the back seat of the subject's car."

Ringer noted nothing new in that jibe.

"He asked me how I would enjoy Butte, Montana."

Again, Ringer noted nothing new in the comment, an almost forgotten reference to punitive assignments in Montana's hinterlands by J. Edgar Hoover when agents screwed up or displeased the long deceased director. Ringer was losing respect for the unimaginative Seattle supervisor. Since the boy was new to the Bureau, maybe the old lines still worked.

"What were you following this guy for? Had he done anything criminal?" Ringer wondered why the supervisor had sent someone so young and so new for what turned into an extended tail. He wasn't surprised by the answer.

"I'm not sure on either count. My boss got some information from the Canadian authorities. Based on the physical description he gave me, I first saw the man at the Avis rental car return facility in the Seattle airport. From there, this guy took me on a flight to Minneapolis and then to Memphis. He paid cash at all times and used different names as he traveled. So far, nothing has developed to identify the man. I don't even believe the airport cameras got a good shot of him. He kept his head down the whole time he shuffled through the airports."

Purdue sighed. "This morning he left the hotel in Memphis wearing that pink jogging suit. I knew I had him, but then he disappeared on me here in town."

"What kind of cases does your squad handle?" Maybe there was another way to get some useful answers from Purdue.

"My last squad was working fugitive warrants. I've been a floater since then, but my supervisor has an interest in Asian gangs. That's all I know."

Ringer nodded his head. "Yeah, well now you know something else.

When you get one of these assignments, call ahead as soon as you know where you're going. That way we could have helped tag the guy. "

Purdue looked at the floor. "Thanks, I'll remember that."

"Let me know when you need to be out at the airport. I live up that way, and I'll give you a ride. In the meantime, write up a description of this pink rabbit. Maybe our people will run across him."

CHAPTER 7

Poolside Maserati's and Other Models

Small talk and two pitchers of margaritas later, lunch was brought to the table and the chips, dips and salsa remnants were removed. The ladies would claim they had a light lunch; at least the older ones would do so. Corrine ordered jerk chicken salad and a cup of tomato basil soup. Eloise Trimmer, a local banker's wife, had an avocado stuffed with boiled Gulf shrimp nested in romaine lettuce with cherry tomatoes.

Barbara Piper, a stunning, red-haired beauty, snickered at the menu and told the waitress to bring her the seafood salad over mixed greens. What caught her attention was that the seafood included grilled red snapper. Her husband, Roger, called her the Red Snapper when they first met at a men's club up in Houston. She was working there as a dancer. Roger had showed up in Bay City several weeks before Barbara. He rented a furnished and remodeled turn of the century Queen Anne cottage in town.

Maria Shiprite enjoyed further flavoring her bowl of Ceviche with a shot of Grey Goose vodka and Tabasco sauce. She had been the quiet one this day, but the girls thought she was about to speak up.

Bea Jay blew their cutesy dietary image by demolishing a Black Angus, open-faced chili cheeseburger and a large side of waffle fries. Eloise warned that Bea's day would come when youth and energy would turn away from her, but the young woman could manage only to say between bites was, "Oh Mrs. Trimmer, you're so funny." Corrine and Barbara grinned as Eloise rolled her eyes.

Heart-shaped sunglasses covered Maria's eyes, and she did not speak. At this point, none of these ladies had disturbed the pool. A half-hour later, Carleton Brooks' crew was nearly finished with the garden along the wall and completed laying all the grass.

Eloise Trimmer used her napkin to polish the blade of her table knife and then checked her makeup and teeth in its reflection. Her medium-length, straight dark hair, without a single gray strand, lay fashionably forward around her neck, and for good reason. She had some plastic work done on her face in Houston, but her neck and the backs of her arms were now moving toward crepe. So were the insides of her long thighs. She was spoiled and demanding, but the clock was running fast on her. She was bored and brittle, her senses dulled by the tequila.

Speaking to no one in particular, she said, "Baxter works all the time. He gets to the bank early and leaves late. If I didn't know him better, I'd swear he had a mistress."

Bea shot a quick hard glance at Eloise that morphed into a smile. "Oh Mrs. Trimmer, he wouldn't do anything like that. He's at the bank all the time except for lunch and trying to get in more business."

"Maybe you're right, but I'll bet you'd snitch to me if he did, wouldn't you, honey?"

Bea Jay gave a Valley Girl shrug, widened her eyes and accompanied that with an elongated, "Duh."

Corrine wasn't so sure, but kept quiet. Eloise savored what she would do to Baxter if he strayed. In the back of her mind, she remembered that 16 years ago, she had been the other woman he strayed with. She got pregnant, and he divorced his first and childless wife. Baxter and

Eloise had two daughters, and these girls were on the fast track to being spoiled little brats. Corrine understood that some men had reasons other than infidelity for staying away from home.

"If Bax was screwing around, and I found out about it, my next stop would be the courthouse. He could kiss off all the money he's made, the house, and mostly me. I wouldn't want to break him, but it would be nice to see him scared of being broke."

Corrine wrinkled her brow. "I'm sure we've all been broke before or been afraid that would happen, but I don't think I would like to break the buns of the man who got me here." She looked around the country club grounds.

She continued. "I can't always tell you Dolph's business at any one time, and he certainly is out of town a lot, but he's always loved me and kept the credit cards and house notes paid. He's given us two handsome sons and been good for Bay City."

"Honey, I don't want you to think I don't appreciate Baxter. It's just that he's so smug. You'd think he owned the whole oil patch out there and that he was the reason for all the money in town."

Bea Jay needed to defend her boss. "Mrs. Trimmer, he works harder than any man I've ever known. It's like the Devil is after him. He ought to be out here at this club with you instead of me."

"Oh Honey, you're so sweet." Eloise thought of Bea as much younger than her years. Corrine wondered if Bea's knowledge included any biblical context.

Barbara sat up straight, showing off her sparsely covered breasts. She shook her long red hair just enough to fluff it out. "If Piper went broke, I'd go back to one of the clubs in Houston. I wouldn't have to do that very long, just so everybody didn't go broke all at once."

Corrine began reflecting on Country Boy's philosophy about women. He told their sons when they were in their late teens, "There's two kinds of women, long-term women like your momma and short-term women. Don't ever hurt long-term women. You might not deserve them, but they deserve good, long-term men. They will stick with you no matter what, and they're good to the core."

Country Boy, not intending to discourage growth in his sons, always added, "There's nothing wrong with short-term women. Don't hurt them either; they might be long-term for someone else. You just have to remember not to invest too much time or emotion in them." Corrine gained new respect for her husband's insight.

Maria, her bottle-black hair pulled up under a white, broad-brimmed straw hat, removed her sunglasses. As she leaned back in her chair, she folded the sunglasses and paused. In one incredibly aimed shot, she arched the glasses into the half-full margarita pitcher, the group's fourth of the day. The bright sunlight did not bother her aim.

"Bobby Charles and I aren't ever going to be broke. We used to be, but not anymore." Switching from her husband's occasional nickname, she wiggled a bit in her chair, straightened her back and assumed a more formal tone. "Besides, Robert made a deal."

Maria rummaged in her straw bag and pulled out a cigarette and lighter. Holding the two items in one hand, she finished her margarita and then lit up. She then took a big drag and blew the smoke up under the table's umbrella. The others recoiled slightly from the unpleasant smoke.

"You girls want to know how we got rich, I mean really rich?" The ladies were silent.

"Ole Bobby Charles worked hard after he got kicked out of A&M. He'd make money and then lose it. All he could do right was to get me pregnant every couple of years." The women focused. Maria, more as an aside, then muttered, "We even lost a couple of them, too."

The ladies knew that Maria's early teenage daughter was living in Dallas with Maria's mother and that she and Robert had a son just out of college. These women began silently calculating how lost children might have fit into the Shiprite family story. The talk was getting serious, and Corrine thought to change the dynamics.

"Time is getting on. Maybe we should be…"

Maria came back from her thoughts.

"Shut up, Corrine. I've been listening to y'all long enough. Now I'm going to tell you our little secret."

Only Bea seemed disturbed by Maria's tone. She started to say something, but then looked at Eloise.

"We're listening, Maria. Go ahead." Eloise Trimmer folded her arms across her chest.

"One morning eight years ago, I woke up just at dawn. A banker in Dallas foreclosed on our house there, and the movers were coming. Robert was sitting on the bedroom floor staring at me. His eyes were as wide as pie pans." Maria took another long drag and continued. "He told me not to worry, that everything would work out. He'd talked to the Devil and cut a deal. The Devil told him that we'd never lack for money or anything else we wanted."

Barbara thought she had seen a lot of devils in the exotic bars in Houston. These guys always promised everything and rarely delivered. She also recalled that none of them ever claimed to be the Prince of Darkness himself. She wanted to ask some questions, because Piper had indicated he did a little business with Shiprite. Maria moved on.

"The deal was simple. All we had to do was not let the kids go to church, any church. That wasn't tough at all. I was raised on the Church of Christ stuff, and that was all I could handle."

Maria began swaying in her chair. She reached for the pitcher and fished out her glasses. They were still dripping as she placed them over her eyes.

"The rest is history. The mover didn't show up, but the lawyer for the bank did. He said there'd been a mistake and we had plenty of time to work something out. Since then, Bobby Charles has made more money than we could ever spend. And the best part is that we got it from real losers before coming here." Maria looked off toward the landscape crew sweeping walkways near the tennis courts.

"There was another rule. We couldn't tell anyone about his deal. Well, what Robert don't know won't hurt him." The cigarette fell from her hand and her head slowly descended to the table. She began a light snore.

Beatrice Jayne Wynne was the first to speak. "She's sure messed up this time."

Barbara looked over to Eloise. "What got into her? I've never seen her this bad. She's just as creepy as her husband. I'd rather live in equal opportunity housing in east Houston than out here with them."

The Shiprites had bought a house in Nouveau Estates a couple of months after Barbara Piper came to town, and, so far as Corrine had known, the two couples only knew each other socially. Apparently Barbara believed otherwise.

While the older women were content to allow Maria to slumber peacefully, Bea Jay was anxious. "What should we do?"

"Okay Bea, go get those two Mexican girls and have them put her in my car." Fumbling in her purse, she handed her keys to the dutiful young woman. "I'll take her home right now. I want to go shopping before the girls get out of school."

Eloise then looked at Corrine and asked, "Any other ideas?"

Corrine stood and started gathering her and Maria's things. "Sure, next time we do this, we better leave the salt out of the margaritas."

CHAPTER 8

Home Bodies, Bad Boys and Girls

Dolph rolled up to his house a little after 4 p.m. His home was in the mid-range price of Nouveau Estates offerings. Corrine's big new Ford F-250 diesel pickup was in its garage space. Even with the two boys off at college, there were still too many cars in the family. There were Dolph's four, and Corrine had the pickup and a two-year-old Silver Mercedes 450 D. When all the cars were in Bay City, the driveway looked like a parking lot. Corrine gave away her old truck, but that didn't change the crowding. She gave her old pickup to the chunky 55-year-old Mexican housekeeper, Dora, who was there most of the time anyway. Maybe I ought to go in the car business, Dolph thought.

He trudged into the house through the garage, dropping off his suit bag in the utility room. All it contained were a few dirty clothing items for Dora to take care of. His toiletries remained in Houston. In the sunroom he found Corrine stretched out on the couch, still in her two-piece swim suit. He settled down at the other end and began massaging her feet. She opened her eyes.

"You girls must have used up all the Tequila in the county, but I like your tan."

Corrine smiled and rose up on one elbow. She blew out a long breath and smiled at him. "You're right, but that's not the half of it. I'll tell you more over dinner. I've got to pay Dora and get into some more decent clothes."

"You look decent enough to me." Dolph squeezed her feet.

She pulled away and said, "We'll talk about that later, too."

Dolph stood with her. "I'm going back to our room. I need to get out of this suit. It has been a long day." Not much could happen between them with Dora around all the time. "Are we going out tonight or eating in?"

Corrine went toward the boys' side of the house to find Dora. Over her shoulder, she threw back one word, "In."

In their bedroom he hung up his dark gray, herringbone mid-weight suit and put on his favorite Bay City outfit, Dickey khaki pants, size 50-34, Red Wing boots, size 10 1/2 and a 2XL Sears blue denim work shirt. Immediately he felt better. He had the hotel in Memphis box up his other suits and dress shirts for mailing to a dry cleaning place in Houston. The government boy had been too rushed to notice any changes in the bulk of Dolph's suit bag. For obvious reasons, he always traveled light going home. He could reclaim that clothing when he was next in town.

His walk-in closet was a study in immaculate contrasts; a dozen conservative, two-button business suits, all medium weight, only two with matching vests on the right. His dress shoes were all black or cordovan with plain toes. The vests were for times when he wanted folks to think he was a big-time city lawyer. Dolph did not use tobacco these days, but he always carried expensive cigars when he wore his three-piece suits. When circumstances warranted, he gave the stogies away, claiming his cardiologist had ordered him to quit.

The middle of the closet contained some nice sport jackets and plain blazers, several pair of slacks and a few lace-up casual shoes and loafers. He hated tassels, thinking they made guys look like cheap chiselers or pimps. That didn't matter, anyway, because that part of the closet was Corrine's decision, and she picked out all of the shirts.

On the left was the best as far as Dolph was concerned, with more than a week's worth of ironed and lightly starched Dickey khakis. The left also had his work shirts, long or short sleeve of either denim or khaki. Overhead were three Stetson hats, two of which were stained around the brim, and a pile of baseball caps. On the floor were two pair of street-heeled cowboy boots, a pair of old-but-like-new jogging shoes and a pair of black nubby Tevas, the most comfortable foot wear he ever owned. The Tevas were for walking around the pool at the Nouveau. In the back left corner were his hunting gear, waders and shotguns. He refused to touch any rifle. His fishing gear was in the garage and always ready for action. A golf bag and clubs hung out in the garage, but he had not swung at a ball in 10 years.

About the time he was ready to go back to the kitchen, Corrine came in and shinnied out of her bathing suit faster than Dolph could blink. Just as fast, she threw on a long blue cotton shirt with spaghetti straps and began vigorously brushing her hair. Dolph knew from experience that she was freeing up her brain cells for commentary and that he was going to need to sit down near the glass patio doors while she held forth.

As if he couldn't guess, her first words were, "I gotta tell you a few things, Country Boy."

Dolph knew that tone and folded his arms. "Alright, baby. Tell me what you've got."

"First, I love you, but you look like Hell and you're putting on too much weight. You're a good-looking man, but too heavy on me. I'm not going to have you dying in the saddle, and I don't want any of the men around here thinking they have a chance of getting in the Widow Cavanaugh's shorts or our bank accounts. I mean it."

Dolph felt his eyebrows burning but decided to take it like a man. There wasn't any stopping Corrine when her blood was up.

"I was nice to you on the phone this morning, but your butt is staying in Bay City until you start looking better and weighing less. Every time you go on the road, you come home looking all dragged out. And you are gonna stop eating like a 20-year old sailor or one of the farm hands around here. Momma and I have been thinking and talking."

Oh, Lord, Dolph thought. I really am in trouble.

Next to Corrine, Dolph's mother-in-law was the toughest woman he knew. She was neither rough nor mean, but she had convictions about right ways and wrong. She had been raised in a mainline religious denomination, but had recently jumped ship to another for a whole lot of reasons. If you wanted to spend an afternoon and late evening, she could tell you exactly why she had taken her prayers, her membership and her sizeable purse away from her lifetime affiliation. What she had admired as loving tolerance had been corrupted into flexible morality. She believed that spelled doom for our souls. Even if someone could get used to thinking that the Ten Commandments were only metaphors for trying to do better, concocted by a bunch of old Jewish men 5,000 years ago, she knew the church of her birth was selling out to current secular convenience.

What really sent her out the door was a statement made by a visiting minister from Houston. He was a pensive, quiet-spoken fellow in his mid-40s named Dumson. He was speaking in the fellowship hall on the current enlightenment of "the Church", an elitist code for encouraging his audience to feel special and more comprehending than other denominations or, for God's sake, non-denominational evangelicals and charismatics. With respect to scriptural integrity, he opined that we now have a "new understanding of an old tradition." Momma knew revisionism when she heard it. Momma just about spilled her coffee, but remained politely attentive until the end of the man's presentation.

Some folks can't bring themselves to chew out a man of the cloth when they think he is wrong. It's not that they don't want to be rude, but more that they are worried that the preacher has an edge with God. This logic did not prevail with Momma. Quite the contrary, Momma believed that God wants us to speak out when falsehoods are represented as fashionable, even compassionate.

Momma waited until the usual sycophants had gone out to the patio for coffee, leaving Reverend Dumson to gather his few notes. As she approached, the minister flashed a toothy smile and stuck out both hands to greet the old girl. He was so full of himself that he failed to detect a certain set of her mouth and the arch of her brow. Speaking quietly so that only he would hear, her words froze him faster than a blue norther.

"You ought to be ashamed of yourself standing up here spouting out that new understanding garbage. You need to take off that collar and think of a new profession, maybe selling aluminum siding. Your blather ignores the dangers of sin and the healthy virtue in repentance. Arrogant, self-absorbed intellectuality is what's wrong with your vision of church, not the poor struggling sinners like me who come here asking hard questions and searching for hard answers instead of the poop you put out."

With that, she turned and left the hall. She doubted his senses would recover soon enough to say anything meaningful. She knew his kind, no stomach for a fight or a rematch.

Dumson made his second mistake of the day. If he had licked his wounds in private, he would have escaped Bay City without the whole county knowing what she had said. He blabbed almost verbatim everything Momma had said to the senior warden of the church. It was little comfort to Dumson that the warden acknowledged that Momma had her days. The warden repeated the story a couple of times, in confidence, of course.

Momma was lean and wiry and might outlive everyone. She was a university-educated, articulate woman, who despite spending long hours and hard years working the family rice farm and running the local bank, was no uninformed country dullard. Momma gently suffered many fools, but few of the dangerous ones. When Momma got on Corrine's side, it was all over for Dolph. What made it worse was that she stayed out of their business unless she was asked, and even then was reluctant to express her views. She always had an opinion, and the aggravation was that she was always right.

"Randolph, Momma and I have decided that you need to start taking care of yourself. We love you, but your days of eating too much of the wrong stuff and not exercising are over. You'll begin with supper tonight, a piece of fish and green salad will be just fine."

Corrine was smiling inside. Dolph just sat stunned. She had planned how to do this, and it was going to be fun. She almost burst out laughing when she heard Dolph mutter, "Prairie vipers." That was all the fight he had in him that evening. She decided to change the subject.

"Country Boy, I wish you'd been at the Nouveau today or that I'd had a tape recorder." Corrine's tone was gentle again. Dolph knew she was going to tell him what happened.

For the next few minutes, Corrine recited the events at the swimming pool. What really bothered her was Shiprite's deal with the Devil. She didn't like the man and thought his wife had become spooky. Dolph laughed when she told him about Maria's ace shot into the margarita pitcher, but his only comment was, "Defiance."

"Did she have any bruises on her? I guess you would have seen if she did since you girls let everything hang out at the pool." Dolph saw that he had carried his color a bit too far. Corrine clearly didn't like the idea that her husband thought she had anything at any time "hung out."

"No, she didn't look like she'd been hurt, but she was sullen. Eloise got her home, but called me later and said that Maria started crying at her front door. Her maid took her the rest of the way."

Dolph scowled. He hated men who whipped up on women or kids or made them cry.

"How is that tart, Eloise?" He wanted to change the subject, to think a bit about Shiprite and his deal. He had his own reasons for being uncomfortable with the man; Shiprite liked alligator loafers with tassels.

"She's just like always. She worries about Baxter slipping around on her and more that she is looking older than she wants to."

Dolph had a warm spot for Eloise; it was just one of those things. Baxter was a first-class stuffed shirt, but was also so busy trying to get the bank in shape for selling that he had neglected to love his wife, to assure her of his emotional if not physical fidelity. Sure, he showered her with things, but not anything to make her heart flutter. Dolph had seen this a hundred times on the road and a lot in Bay City.

"That little cheerleader he's got up there at the bank, Bea Jay, probably doesn't help much." With a sly smile he asked, "You didn't see any calluses on her knees, did you?"

Dolph wondered if Baxter Trimmer defined marital infidelity to exclude other indecencies, emulating the view of the former chief executive of the United States.

Corrine was flustered and slapped at Dolph's shoulder. He already knew her suspicions. "Come on, let's go to the kitchen."

CHAPTER 9

Hell Comes in Many Forms

That next morning, the first thing to hit Dolph was a pair of shorts and a T-shirt, the next were his New Balance jogging shoes. The clothing fell on his face, and the shoes plopped on his stomach. Corrine was unsympathetic to his groans. She was already dressed for their walk. Shadow boxing at the foot of their bed, she challenged him.

"Come on, big boy. Get your fanny moving. It's almost dawn."

"Oh Lordy, Corrine." He staggered toward the bathroom. Returning shortly, he had to dodge her shadow punches. Obediently, he picked up his shorts and shirt, but tried to delay the inevitable.

"Honey, it's not even light. Can't we go a little later?"

No sympathy. "Dolph, we've got to go now and get back before the little kids start heading for school. If they see you out on the street, you'll scare them."

The morning walk wasn't all that bad. Corrine didn't want Dolph keeling over the first morning. Still, the sweat soaked his shorts and shirt. He grumbled about the breakfast of fruit, dry toast and a boiled egg, but he believed her zeal would pass by the following Monday. He could tough it out over the weekend.

* * *

As they showered and dressed, Dolph's manner was relaxed. He actually felt better for having been out earlier. "What are you doing today?"

"I'm going to the shop. Momma is meeting me there, and we're moving things around for the weekend. Two girls from the high school are coming out Saturday morning to help with our sale. We're opening up at ten and closing at three."

Dolph watched his wife from his mirror. She was energy personified. That welding shop had been a passion for her, one of many over the years. She cared for her mother with a passion when the old gal got sick after Mr. Wilson died. She raised Mrs. Wilson's grandsons the same way. She loved without coddling them after the boys got older. One day, the boys found rainstorm shelter with a sweet lady down the road. The woman loved boys and offered the refugees cookies and milk. As time passed, Corrine became concerned. The lady, a mother of older boys, told Corrine's sons to call home. When Corrine was satisfied that they were safe, the boys wanted to stay longer because it was still raining. Corrine quipped to the oldest son, "Get on back to the house. You won't melt."

In her spare time, she got the shop and scrap yard cleaned, the overhead lift repaired and created low maintenance gardens flanking the crushed white rock parking lot in the front of the building. She took welding classes through a pipe fitters union in Lake Jackson. She learned to cut, shape and weld all kinds of metal. More as a joke, some good ol' boys asked if she could weld a broken trailer tongue or a cracked axel, and then they started asking her to do bigger jobs. She financed all of the shop improvements with the income from these jobs. However, none of that was her real dream. What she really wanted to do was to create decorative things, unique fencing, footbridges and garden arches. She made black iron and stainless steel images of all kinds of animals, big fish and birds, some life-size and some much larger. Folks started buying these works, and she began keeping records of the time she spent creating these pieces. After a fellow from the San Antonio Express did a Sunday spread on her work, a lot of slick-looking, gabby decorator people from there, Austin, Houston and the Dallas-Ft. Worth areas started calling and asking for special designs. She was a hot item and making real money.

Corrine's Weldinghaus was open to the public for retail sales, but only on the third Saturday of the month, and only from April through October. Corrine was no slave to that schedule, and she had a keen sense when business would be light. She spent the rest of her time filling contracts, arranging for project deliveries or dreaming about her next design. It was hard, physical work, but creative. It was one of the reasons she was in top shape. Dolph went out to the shop every now and then. He hung around, avoiding introductions to Corrine's customers so that he could study their reactions to his Gulf Coast iron sculptress. He thought that a lot of the rich women who bought Corrine's works privately bit their knuckles with envy over her good looks.

Corrine's business drive and energy went beyond the shop. She and Mrs. Wilson owned a significant slug of stock in Baxter Trimmer's Matagorda Peoples State Bank. Corrine and Momma were on the Board of Directors. So was Carleton Brooks.

"Well, I'm going to stop by the bank and see Baxter. Then I think I'll drive down to Sargent and see how Hannah is doing." Dolph studied Corrine for any reaction as he finished brushing his hair and checking his khakis. He saw none.

"Okay, Sweetie. You tell Hannah hello for me, but don't say anything about that 15-foot crab at the shop. I want her to be surprised."

Maybe I won't have to hang in there 'til Monday, Dolph thought.

"Oh I almost forgot. Drop by Doctor Merritt's before going to the bank or Hannah's. He'll work you in. I found a program, and he needs to take a look at you first."

Dolph knew well she had forgotten nothing.

* * *

Dolph Cavanaugh worried. Over the years, all his doctors and dentists were older men, and they knew what they were talking about in part because they were older. Now they seemed much younger, except for Doc Etling; it was like they were getting out of school before they needed to shave. Etling was a true codger, but Merritt was one of a new breed. He was married to a charming, high-energy woman; they had two children and a Black Labrador retriever.

When the doctor and Mrs. Merritt came to Bay City a year ago, folks were surprised. Most of the professionals in the county had ties that brought them there. The Merritts were from Georgia and seemed to have picked Bay City as a place for him to open a family practice more on calculation than emotion. Nobody questioned the decision; they were thrilled to have a new doctor in town and hoped they would remain.

Corrine and Eloise Trimmer stumbled all over themselves to make the Merritts feel welcomed and to see to it that folks moving in to Nouveau Estates found out about the doctor and his lovely wife. When it became known that their black lab was a great bird dog, the doctor got more hunting invitations than he could handle.

Dolph had another reason to worry. This kid kept calling him Mister Cavanaugh or Sir. It wasn't his words, but his intonation that suggested Doctor Merritt was addressing a senior citizen.

Dolph got to Merritt's office by 9 a.m. and began thumbing through fishing magazines as he sat in a large, comfortable chair that he later came to learn was known in town as the Geezer's Corner. Neither the wait nor the examination had taken long.

"Mr. Cavanaugh, your wife has asked me to arrange an appointment for you in Houston. Methodist Hospital has an executive health-assessment program that I believe can be a valuable asset in getting you back in reasonable shape for your age."

A crowbar slammed in his face could not have stunned Dolph more than for this kid to use the "A" word.

The young doctor paused; his eyes softened a bit. "You're overweight, and Mrs. Cavanaugh tells me your road trips are tiring. As you know much better than I, she is a determined woman. We need to get you thoroughly checked out, blood tests and all that, before she really starts working you. I've got your appointments set up early next week, I think on Tuesday. Mrs. Cavanaugh has the schedule details and other requirements the night before your appointments. Plan for the whole day. They'll send me the reports in due course."

Dolph sagged at the end of the examination table. Other requirements, he wondered?

"Don't look so grim, Mr. Cavanaugh. She has promised me she won't push you much beyond your day-to-day limits, and I will check on your progress regularly."

His words and the slight smile crossing Merritt's face did not encourage Dolph. This was serious trouble. Dolph hadn't seen that kind of smile since the day he enlisted in the Navy. The recruiting chief in Little Rock had that same smile. Who defines reasonable anyway, he thought.

As he walked to the town square two blocks away, hunger pangs began stabbing at his waist. He ignored the temptation to stop in the coffee shop for a cinnamon roll, and he knew that word would get back to Corrine if he so much as stuck his nose in the K-2 Steakhouse. She had snitches everywhere. Besides, he would keep his visit with Baxter short and then head on down to Hannah's Place. Her gumbo and garlic bread would make his day. Maybe shrimp, French fries and hushpuppies with a couple of beers would make it better.

CHAPTER 10

Good Women Are Everywhere

A crushed oyster shell driveway bears off to the west a hundred feet from the asphalt paved surface of Farm to Market Road 457 south of Sargent, Texas, one of a network of highways designed to facilitate the movement of agricultural products from rural farms and ranches to marketing centers around the state. A parking lot, also surfaced with crushed oyster shell, has spaces for about 75 vehicles, depending on their size. Two 30-foot high creosote-soaked posts pounded into the soil flank a wide wooden stairway. The stairs lead up to a covered veranda of the building perched 20 feet above the ground. Adjacent to the stairway is a ramp with periodic landings as patron-resting spots for those in wheelchairs or with troublesome knees. This building, designed as a possible refuge from storm tides, rests on a big mound of rubble further anchored to deep pilings. A large, faded white sign suspended between the posts proclaims in dark green script the site of Hannah's Place.

The veranda wraps around the entire structure, shading all angles of the sun and enhancing the cooling effects of breezes from the Gulf of Mexico. On the backside of Hannah's Place is a meandering slough that leads to the Intercoastal Canal and thence to East Matagorda Bay and the Gulf.

Moored to a small pier is a 40-foot shrimp boat, nets up and drying, with seagulls waddling around on the flat surfaces or preening in the rigging. On deck, Junior, known by no other name, Hannah's hired hand and operator of the boat, coiled a garden hose he used to wash the boat's topsides. The catch had been good last night. Hannah would have fresh seafood through Saturday evening.

Junior's uniform of any day was faded jeans varied only by an assortment of T-shirts. Some of those were also faded and bore cryptic logos or wise commentaries on the vacillations of life. One shirt had particularly amused Hannah's patrons who were veterans of the war in Vietnam. Oddly, only they saw the humor in "PTSD-Don't Leave Nam Without It". Another said, "I like this color. It don't show the dirt." Hannah made him pitch another one that Vietnamized the spelling of an American obscenity.

His other trademark was a beige baseball cap given to him by the owner of DBP Exploration Company up in the Texas panhandle. The hat covered a thatch of shaggy gray and black hair matching Junior's droopy mustache. Mr. Poole had given him the cap when he fired Junior for drinking on the job, telling him he could have his job back when he sobered up for good. Junior wore the hat day and night as a reminder of what he'd lost and what he needed to do to get his life back. Mr. Poole was always on Junior's short list of good folks.

Junior's thoughts turned to his pre-breakfast beer. When Hannah took him in three years earlier, she told him he could have one beer a day and that was it. The choice of when was his, but if she caught him having more, that was the end of his job.

He had lived all his life on the margins and looked like it. This had been a tough standard for him to maintain, but she had been straight with him so he followed her rule. Maybe one day he would be able to go back to Mr. Poole.

Junior began by hauling two-wheeled dolly boxes of ice-covered shrimp and fish up to the kitchen walk-in cooler. The beer could wait. Hannah's would be open for business in a couple of hours, and Junior could then take his mid-day nap down on the boat.

* * *

Janie Farmer had been walking over to Hannah's from her broken-down trailer house six mornings a week for the last 10 years. Hannah gave her coffee, two eggs, toast or biscuits and link sausage or bacon. "Gave" is exactly the word. Hannah knew that Janie could no longer take care of herself in any meaningful way. Janie and other poor folks in the area always welcomed leftovers from Hannah's Place. Hannah never made a big deal of her charity or allowed anyone's dignity to suffer from it.

Hannah Gregory had just finished raising the windows and adjusting the outside metal storm blinds. The adjustment allowed for an easy flow of air without creating any draft that would scatter napkins or the stack of magazines and area newspapers near the restrooms. Over the pile of reading material was a big, hand-printed cartoon bubble coming out of the mouth of a poster-sized photograph of William F. Buckley, Jr., which read, "These are better than the New York Times, so keep 'em or put 'em back when you're done."

Rectangular dining tables, mostly six-seaters that could be put together for large groups, were spotless, and all of the vinyl-covered chairs were meticulously positioned. She had room for about a hundred guests in one big dining area.

For at least the third time that morning, Hannah was wiping a wide U-shaped serving counter that pointed at either end to doorless openings into the kitchen. Some patrons preferred the few stools at the counter to the dining room for its opportunities for interaction between patrons and the help.

Janie, seated near the cash register at the bottom of the "U", was wearing her usual morning outfit, a blue, cotton house robe and pink, fluffy slippers. Janie too was subject to Hannah's one-beer rule, but it was also conditioned on Janie eating all her breakfast.

"Hannah, quit scrubbin' that counter. Your place is just fine. What's the rush?" Janie was mashing the last of her egg yolk into the center of a thick biscuit. Not getting an answer from Hannah, she went on.

"Hannah, baby, did you hear me askin' you a question?"

"Sure I did, Miss Janie. In a couple of hours this place is going to be swarming with people sucking down gumbo and beer. Looking like a dump on the outside doesn't mean it can't be cleaner inside than the Nouveau Country Club."

Cleaning was Hannah's form of exercise, and she took quick breaths as she talked and scrubbed.

"Girl, you were cleaning things around here fourteen years ago, an' there weren't no Nouveau then."

"Just drink your beer. A lot of things were different fourteen years ago."

"Yeah, my worthless Bennie was still alive and workin' on the shrimp boats."

Hannah, as though suddenly distracted, turned her head back toward the kitchen and yelled, "Seferina, turn that fire down under the big pot. Janie, I ought to run off that girl. She'll burn this place down if I don't watch her."

Janie laughed. "She's just like you when you dragged yo' sad ass out here from Houston. Banging stuff around, actin' mad, never talking. I didn't know how long I could work for you."

Ignoring Janie's recollections, Hannah stood back from the counter and asked, "There now. How's that?"

"Beautiful. Yo' lunch crowd ain't gonna' know the difference. This here is Hannah's Place an' they don't come all the way out here for nuthin' but the food."

Caught for a moment in her own memories, Hannah spoke not so much to Janie, but to herself. "Sargent was the closest place to the end of the world as I could find at the time... and it's been good to me."

"Bennie said you wouldn't last a year; you were too pretty."

"Bennie was right about one thing. Pretty was the first thing to go. The sun burned out and frizzed my blond hair, and salt air rusted the rest of me."

"Girl, back then this was the nastiest place on the water. Bennie and I watched you fix it up by yourself. You were a tough girl."

Hannah reached over and affectionately patted the hand of this skinny, dried up old black woman. Janie's patience had helped her through the early years.

"I was mad about a lot of things, but not anything around here. Are you going to finish your beer?"

"Honey, I was figuring on jes' watchin' you work, but maybe I better move on back to the house." Janie put her Lone Star aside and began climbing down from her stool.

Hannah knew it was time to get on with work. "Janie, I'll come by later this evening. Mr. Cavanaugh is probably coming in for lunch, and I want to be ready for him." To third parties, he was always Mr. Cavanaugh. She respected him about as much as any man she had ever met.

Adjusting her house robe, Janie, almost absentmindedly, said, "He hangs around here about as much as I do. Probably likes more'n your gumbo."

Hannah bristled. "Good thing you put that beer down. I'd take it away from you for talking about my friend like that. Corrine is a friend too, and you watch your mouth. Neither one of them deserve to be hurt by loose talk."

There was no point in explaining Dolph's role in Hannah's life, either before or after she came to Sargent. Janie would think what other people had thought, but none of that was true.

"Seferina," she called back to the kitchen, "get on the phone and find out if the other help is coming in before we open." Janie was right. Seferina was a version of the younger Hannah.

CHAPTER 11

Bankers Try to be Honest

The façade of the Matagorda Peoples State Bank still faces the courthouse square at one of its corners. Housed originally in an old frame storefront, the current structure was built in 1928. It would have been an attractive target for Clyde Barrow and Bonnie Parker if they ever found their way so far south of their usual bank-robbing grounds. Renovations in the 1980s retained the original façade, but they provided a more modern entrance on the Highway 60 side of the structure.

Back in the old days of banking after World War II, bank officer desks were visible on the lobby floor. Bankers were a part of the community and tried to appear available and friendly. In many of today's big city banks, you don't see anyone other than tellers and customers, and some kid out of college might be an assistant vice-president with a private office in the bowels of the bank. Baxter Trimmer tried to hold on to the old ways, but he found advantages in a private office before the bank opened and after the lobby floor closed in the afternoon.

When Dolph lumbered in, Baxter was seated at his lobby desk visiting with a fellow from the local title company. He nodded toward Dolph and discreetly raised his index finger signaling that his discussion would soon end. Bea Jay Wynne came out of the private office and beamed a big smile at Dolph, giving her best high school-cheerleader wave. Dolph became even more convinced that he ought to have a talk with Bax about the high cost of marital infidelity.

Shortly, Baxter stood and shook hands with the title company man, walking him out through the swinging wooden half gate. He then moved toward Cavanaugh. "Good to see you, Dolph. I heard you were back in town. How are you?"

Although he well knew the influence Dolph's wife and mother-in-law had on the bank's business, Baxter's pleasantries were a mixture of sincerity and habit. Dolph always kept a correct distance from these women's financial affairs, but it didn't hurt Baxter to be on the good side of this big man with his own substantial deposits.

Baxter, born in 1954 in Beaumont, Texas, spent two colorless years at Lamar University and lived at home. To his father's delight, he then transferred to the University of Houston. By the time he was draft age, the lottery was in place. Bax had a very high number, and America's disengagement from the war in Vietnam was less than a year away. That was fine with Baxter because he never saw himself as a warrior. He remembered feeling comfortable when the collapse of South Vietnam finally happened in April 1975, signaling an end to even the remote risk of service. Military service, he thought, would have been a less than adequate use of his talents. With a major in finance, Baxter received a Bachelor of Business Administration in 1976. He planned to make his name and a lot of money in the big city of Houston.

Baxter's first job the following September was with First City National Bank, an old line and growing institution on Main Street with a brand-new building. He had a grand title: loan officer. But as a management trainee, he didn't know squat about lending or credit other than to follow as best he could the reams of written policy statements issued by upper management. In a year or two, he could look forward to another title, assistant vice-president.

First City was a good enough bank in those days, but it suffered from one major flaw in its hiring practices: nepotism and its variations. Relatives of senior officers, bank directors and large depositors could always find work there, especially in those years. Baxter's daddy had moved his company's sizeable operating account to First City the same day he found out that Baxter wanted to stay in Houston and seek employment with that bank. Within the Houston banking community and among those who observed the personalities of the trade, including employees who had no connections, the bank was known as First Titty.

Inflation during and after the war in Vietnam made all real estate related loans appear safe and the loan officers look like geniuses. Even with a mini-bust looming about this time with land syndications and real estate investment trusts, young Mister Trimmer felt he had a bright future.

The following year was a blessing in disguise for Bax. For not approving a small loan to the worthless son of a director's second wife, he was fired. For this bit of prudence and Baxter's honorable refusal to back down when word arrived to do otherwise, Baxter's daddy moved the operating account back to Beaumont and sent his son some walking-around money to tide him over until he could get another job.

Two months later, another bank, one block west of Main Street on Travis, hired him. Allied Bank of Texas, located in the Esperson Buildings, was Baxter Trimmer's business home for the next six years. Allied was a great training ground for all the young men, and later women, hired there. He learned a lot about lending and banking operations, something that never would have happened had he knuckled under to pressure before crossing Main Street. It was also a blessing that he often ate lunch at Massa's Restaurant, located in the Esperson Buildings. That was where he met Randolph Cavanaugh eating a big bowl of their special gumbo.

It wasn't long before the two men became friends. Ultimately Dolph recruited Baxter to join the Bay City bank. Allied had welcomed Baxter's departure on friendly terms; it was thought that he might be a useful insider in the big bank's acquisition plans. The trend in those days, favored by the regulators, was for the big banks to gobble up the small independent banks, a means of developing more uniformity of operations of the acquired banks and simplifying regulation by the bureaucrats. Local interests, personal relations and loyalties to the community were remote considerations.

Being acquired was not then on the minds of Peoples' board or shareholders, but growth was. In about 15 years, the bank's deposits went from $35 million to slightly over 130 million, and that happened despite the real estate and banking disaster of the mid-1980s in Texas, a downturn caused by the collapse of crude oil prices. At the time, Peoples had not been heavily invested in property development or the oil patch. Momma and the board of directors had carefully guided the bank and Baxter Trimmer through the difficult times, and they watched the racy and larger banks and badly run businesses fall away. A much stronger Texas economy emerged from all that. So too did little ol' Matagorda Peoples State Bank, ready for the good times. Today, if the ink on the bank's financial statement and the rouge on its reputation didn't run and the price was right, the bank would do well at the market place. These were good times.

Momma snorted and flapped her elbows when politicians claimed responsibility for the good times and accused their opponents for the bad times. Her view was that individual hard work and prudence, along with a heart for the community, gave a better return than tax dollars sent to Austin or Washington, D.C. According to Momma, politicians, regardless of age, office and political party, male or female, became moral cowards and suck-ups to the crowd once they took their oaths of office and the issues got tough, if they had any morality to begin with. Momma hated slick packaging and political handlers disguising candidates and office holders from the electorate.

Momma also didn't like anyone who rolled over at the slightest challenge. She often challenged Baxter, but he had a good record of standing his ground when he thought he was right, particularly when he had time to think about it. At the same time, Baxter always sought to address Momma's underlying concerns with pleasing cordiality.

These days, Trimmer was anxious to please, and his interest in Dolph's welfare was understandable.

"Oh, I'm fine, but Corrine has me on a diet and exercise program that's going to get old before Monday." He paused. "I came by to check on someone. Could we talk privately?"

"Sure Dolph. Let's go to the back office. Do you want some coffee?" Baxter didn't wait for an answer, and, looking at the cheerleader, he raised two fingers. She was off in a flash to get the bank's special monogrammed china and not the Styrofoam cups used for the ordinary folks.

After delivering the coffee, Bea Jay swished out of the private office, saying, "I'll hold your calls, Bax."

Trimmer furrowed his brow, but he said nothing at her informality.

Aw, Hell. That's for another day, Dolph thought.

He decided to get to the point of his visit. Trimmer never handled surprises well. A lot could be gleaned from his initial manner.

"What do you know about Robert Shiprite? Is the bank doing any business with him out of the ordinary?" Dolph's folksy tone was gone, as was the good ol' country boy.

"I can't talk about other customers." Trimmer adjusted his tie with one hand and brought his cup to his lips with the other. The cup wasn't big enough to hide Baxter's anxiety.

Bingo! Dolph thought. Baxter glanced to the side and then down. Translation? Enough and yes.

"Sure you can. I don't much like the guy, but I value your opinion because I might want to do a little business with him." Dolph hoped that Baxter would slide on the slippery slope of flattery.

"Well, he's doing a little real estate here and there, and the bank loaned him the front end money for his house out at Nouveau. He pays notes on time. We're OK."

Dolph knew a shaved piece of information when he heard it, and he caught the plurality significance in the word "notes".

"So the bank isn't doing any other business with him?"

Trimmer's next reply was the clincher, its truthfulness very much in doubt.

"No, not really."

Dolph stood. He had heard enough, but he wasn't in the mood to deal with this today. His stomach was growling. Besides, he wanted to beat the crowd to Hannah's.

He extended his hand to Baxter. "Thanks for the coffee. Tell Bea Jay I appreciated the little extra sugar she gave me. Maybe I won't starve before lunch."

Baxter smiled his smug little friendly banker smile and then added, "Are you and Corrine going to be out at the club tonight? Eloise and the girls are joining me for dinner. Maybe we could all sit together."

"Sure, Baxter; Mrs. Wilson will be with us, and I suppose you can handle that. Just don't give me any grief over what Corrine orders for me."

CHAPTER 12
Salvation in Sargent

Humid salt air and good seafood are a spiritual combination for Dolph, and beginning the weekend with lunch at Hannah's had become a ritual. He imagined himself crawling up the stairway from a famine-possessed wasteland. It was still cool enough in May for open windows and fresh air to move through the kitchen and out onto the parking lot. The subtle smell of chopped garlic, onions and lemons caught him before his Suburban's wheels had stopped grinding on the shells. Dolph's mouth began to water. As he crossed into the shade of the veranda, Hannah came out to greet him. She wore her trademark wheat-colored jeans, clean white tennis shoes and a short-sleeved, dark blue knit pullover. Stitched over her well-shaped breasts in red letters was "Hannah's", and below, in gold letters, was "Place."

Giving him a big hug, she said, "Come on in, Dolph. Lunch is ready."

Dolph felt particularly kingly. Hannah was normally warm and cordial, but today was a little over the top. He was just a hair early and went to his favorite table on the south side of the building, taking a seat so he could see both the front door and the Gulf in the distance. Folks were entering Hannah's in groups of four to eight, mostly men.

Toey, a little brunette girl whose husband was an oil-patch worker, breezed up with a big glass of iced water and said, "Hey there, Mr. Cavanaugh. What are you having today? A bowl of gumbo, I bet. Anything more?"

She sounded like a little songbird with a cute flippy tail, always cheerful. Her Hannah's Place shirt was red with white lettering.

"Sure Darlin'. And bring me a loaf of garlic bread and a draft Shiner's. After that I'll have your grilled stuffed flounder and a mix of crispy fries with hushpuppies."

Pausing a bit to remember his diet, he added, "Maybe a plate of sliced tomatoes would be good, too."

Toey was a short little thing with a sparkle in her eyes. Her husband was a giant of a man who spoke little, but he loved her more than anything.

"How's Big Joe? I haven't seen him in a while. Y'all got enough money saved for that house you want?"

Her eyes softened as she tilted her head to the side. "Nice of you to ask, Mr. Cavanaugh. He's just fine; we're getting there." She turned and was off to place his order.

I'm going to talk to Hannah about helping them out, he thought.

He started fumbling around on the table, moving the salt and pepper, catsup and Tabasco sauce, as well as the napkin caddy. He was looking for the butter packs usually piled in a bowl at each table. He looked up to get Toey's or someone's attention when he saw Hannah coming toward him with a big tray. That was fast, he thought. When Hannah arrived and started placing the food on the table, Dolph wanted to cry with disappointment. It crossed his mind to go over in the Gulf and just drown himself.

Six large, pealed, half-split shrimp spread around the edge of a big bowl containing mixed greens and cherry tomatoes. On the side were a couple of ounces of red sauce and a demitasse cup of olive oil and vinegar. Over the shrimp were sprinkled no more than ten croutons. Beside the salad was a cup of gumbo containing a few grains of rice. Toey walked up behind Hannah carrying a small slice of garlic bread and Iced Tea. Words did not come right away. The two women stood there; Hannah smiled, but Toey looked pained. Dolph spoke first.

"I can see you've been talking to Corrine."

"To be honest with you, we've been talking about this since before you came home. Sorry Dolph, but we're all in this together, even Toey here. Is there anything you really need?"

"Yeah Hannah, could you or this little puppy dog bring me a couple of lemon slices?"

CHAPTER 13

Nouveau Gathering

Dolph took longer than usual getting back home, stopping twice on the drive up from Sargent to relieve himself on the side of the road. He wasn't satisfied, but he wasn't as hungry as before lunch, either.

Hannah often heard things, even a bit about Shiprite. She thought Shiprite was cold-hearted and calculating. Shiprite and Trimmer had come in one day for a late lunch in the middle of last week while Dolph was out of town. Shiprite picked up the check, but then Baxter almost never grabbed the tab when he came in with other men in the community.

Cheapskate, Dolph thought. He's getting my attention. He's supposed to be developing business for the bank, not saving a few bucks at the expense of potential customers.

The admirable art of picking up tabs as a business development cost wasn't bribery or showboating but was closer to genuine gratitude and hospitality.

No one was home when Dolph arrived. Dora was gone, and there was no sign that Corrine had been there since they parted in the morning. Dolph couldn't understand it, but he was drawn to the couch in the den, the same place he found Corrine the day before. He pulled off his Red Wings and was soon asleep. An hour and a half or so later, Corrine kissed his nose, and he was wide-awake.

"How'd you like your lunch?" She sat at the end of the couch.

"Why ask, baby? You've probably got my truck wired, microphones under my table at Hannah's and are taking pictures of me from a helicopter. You have spies everywhere, and young Merritt's middle name must be Mengele. I think I'm defeated and better surrender." Dolph's reference to Dr. Josef Mengele, infamous as a German Nazi death camp physician, went unnoticed.

Corrine smiled. "Good, it will be easier on both of us." She then reached over and stroked his knee. "It's 4:30. Now get up and go get on your shorts and jogging shoes. We're taking a walk before picking up Momma at seven."

Dolph worked up a mild sweat trying to keep pace with Corrine. He became short of breath, mostly because he was trying to talk to her about Shiprite and whether she had any information about his business activities. There was nothing useful there. He withheld his own research. Corrine did not need to see the dark side of how his mind sometimes worked.

* * *

Mrs. Wilson's white, two-story traditional home, built on seven acres, backs up to an 11-acre lake. The lake borders the southwestern side of the Nouveau Estates subdivision. A white wood rail fence, broken by an ungated entry to a gravel driveway, follows the frontage road. The driveway runs 300 feet to a cement parking apron adjoining the house, two small guest cottages and an old, but well-cared for, barn. Sixty-year-old pecan trees line the gravel drive. Both sides of the driveway are carpeted with freshly mowed St. Augustine grass. Little garden plots spilling out with spring flowers surround the two cottages and the main house. Between the house and the lake and extending behind the barn to the west property line are fields of natural grasses. Overall, it is a peaceful setting.

No entry gate is needed; vehicles passing over the cattle guard break a beam of light that also rings chimes in the house. Mrs. Wilson was standing on the parking apron as Dolph and Corrine drove up. She waited on no courtesies, and without assistance, she climbed in the back seat of Corrine's Mercedes.

"Dolph, you're looking fit. I heard you got back last night." Momma was dressed in designer black silk pants, low heels and a cream-colored blouse. She was wiry and aging, but attractive.

"Yeah, Momma, you too. I suppose you and Corrine are having fun with me for a while." Smiling, Dolph looked at her through the rear view mirror. As much as he liked to grumble when the two of them got on a tear, he really loved and respected his mother-in-law, and not just for the wife she gave him. A slight smile crossed Momma's lips.

"Dolph says he's surrendering to us, Momma. I don't guess you believe him any more than I do." Corrine wore black slacks with a red top covered by a short black sequined jacket and matching sandals. She carried her favorite Sharif handbag.

Momma's smile broadened.

Dolph had changed into another pair of darker khaki pants and a Land's End light blue pima cotton dress shirt. His cordovan cowboy boots were a nice change from the Red Wings. Dolph liked changing footwear frequently. Everyone had on what Corrine identified as "Friday Night Nice," a term Dolph never understood, but guessed it was as uninformative as "dressy casual." Then again, he never had to understand these codes. Corrine enjoyed pointing out what she thought would look acceptable on him. That was fine with Dolph, though he knew well how to select clothing for any occasion and was adept at its use on both sides of his office environment.

The club dining room was nearly filled to capacity. Affiliate dining memberships had been offered to non-residents of the subdivision as a means of pumping revenues into the club. Besides Hannah's Place, La Riviera Grille was the best restaurant in the county. As long as the club enjoyed a diverse membership only insofar as the age of its patrons, the club would not have to resort to Wednesday bingo or Trivial Pursuit nights and seniors discounts.

The usual crowd had gathered, but everyone was conscious of the balance between a need for privacy and sociability. Greetings and acknowledgements were exchanged, but there was little cross-table conversation. Only as the evening wore on or as dining parties departed or new groups arrived was there much discussion between tables.

The Trimmer girls were bored beyond description. The attractive 14 and 16 year olds shared little signals and rolled eyes as other guests, particularly the few teenage boys with parents, came in or left the dining room. Eloise monitored these gestures without being distracted from the so-called adult conversation. She was particularly watchful when the young waiters came to their table.

Corrine was grateful that she and Dolph had sons and didn't have the same worries over questions of feminine virtue or the lack of it. She also knew that while the girls were not airheads, she was convinced they were not examples of the supposed elevated maturity of girls over boys of the same age.

Small talk and small portions marked the dining experience for Dolph, who felt detached from the others. He was looking forward to an early bedtime.

"Seems like you were gone for quite a while, Dolph. I hope the business was worth it." Trimmer was finishing his third Chardonnay.

"Well, the whole world doesn't revolve around Bay City. It just seems that way to folks who never leave town." He knew Bax didn't care a flip about what Dolph did or where he went, and Trimmer almost never left town. It crossed Dolph's mind that an early clue to an embezzler's activities is the fact that they rarely take vacations or miss work, even if they are sick. Fortunately for Matagorda Peoples State Bank, the board had insisted that all officers and employees annually take a two-week continuous vacation, during which time they must never enter or contact the bank, a standard urged and approved by government bank examiners. Insider thieves are afraid of time off; the person filling in for them while they were absent might discover the scam. Temptation and the disgrace of embezzlement were reduced by this simple expedient. This was just one of the measures enforced by the board to tighten the internal controls of the bank.

Dolph was in a restless mood. His decision to stop doing deals was right for him and his family. Without knowing the truth about her husband's life on the road, Corrine had correctly identified the physical consequences being wrought on Dolph's health. Dolph nevertheless wondered what he would do to replace the excitement of that other life. Maybe he would just shut things down and tend to his business from Bay City. That way he needn't be away from Corrine and Bay City. He would take the big step tomorrow with one telephone call.

Cavanaugh had listened to Baxter off and on for the last 20 minutes talking about how great the bank was doing, and yet he knew Bax was always blowing a bit of smoke. His agitation did not improve with the food or the half glass of red wine Corrine allowed him. Mrs. Wilson told Baxter she would prefer talking about the bank in the board meetings, that dinner out was a time to relax and enjoy family and friends. Bax knew better than to dispute Mrs. Wilson's social views.

Eloise chimed in that she would really enjoy getting out of town with Baxter and the girls, but Bax could only promise to enjoy a trip after the bank was sold. Eloise was not happy with his alternative suggestion that she and the girls ought to get away during the summer. The girls showed no interest in that either.

Corrine wanted to give Trimmer a piece of her mind, but instead offered another idea. "Tell you what Eloise. You and the girls ought to go with me to our place on Lake Travis. We can spend a couple of weeks there swimming and getting sunburned." She knew Eloise's concept of a Lake Travis outing was sitting on the shady end of the porch with air-conditioned comfort a few feet away.

Corrine had her own wishes. "We could have a wonderful time. Maybe one of our boys will come over from Austin on the weekend and do any heavy work." She laughed at the idea of her sons being camp counselors to Eloise's daughters. Finally, the girls brightened, but Eloise had other visions. Baxter was now working on the remains of his after-dinner Martini on the rocks.

Dolph was about to suggest his own therapy plan for bringing the Trimmer family together, four-way mud wrestling, but at that point two new guests entered the dining room, Mr. and Mrs. Robert Shiprite. Corrine and Eloise spotted them first. Dolph knew that female radars are always working.

Shiprite shook hands with guests at a couple of tables, but Maria's smile was forced. When she saw Eloise and Corrine, she looked as though she wanted to come over and speak. Then Robert took her by the hand and led her to their table. In that one dominating gesture, Robert glanced briefly at Baxter Trimmer. Dolph had practiced reading people his whole adult life, and what he saw in that moment set off all his alarms. Shiprite, a cunning and deadly snake, was appraising his opportunity and timing to strike Trimmer, the nervous rabbit.

Bax may have been telling the truth. Shiprite wasn't dangerously into the bank. He was into Bax some way. Baxter did something stupid and was an ensnared rabbit, Dolph thought; he ought to do something.

Decisions, adrenaline and enlightenment visibly changed Dolph's demeanor. He stood. For the fourth time that evening, he had to go to the men's room. When he returned, he was ready for the short drive to Mrs. Wilson's home and on to his and Corrine's house.

"Well folks, it's been fun. Corrine is going to have this old horse out on the track tomorrow, and I need my beauty sleep. Eloise, you and Bax ought to go to the woods or do a little mud wrestling." Eloise blushed and lowered her head. Corrine and Momma shook theirs.

"Girls, work on your mother about Lake Travis. My boys can teach you everything you need to know about water skiing." The mouths of the two girls broke into beautiful grins, with the braces on the younger one gleaming in the lights of the dining room chandelier.

"Come on, Momma. I'll dance you out to the car." Momma grinned; Corrine smiled and shook her head.

Dolph's mood change infected everyone but Baxter. Dolph thought about buying the bank president a pink jogging suit, telling him to get a life. Corrine wondered if Dolph would tell her what was now on his mind.

CHAPTER 14

First Loves

Pierrette, sometimes known to others as Pete, had a muted wild beauty even now. Short dark hair flecked with natural gray, combed slightly forward on the sides, carefully matched the medium length of her delicate bangs. Genetics and the sun combined to give her slightly lined face a light bronze hue. All this framed her glistening blue eyes and small mouth, which surprisingly could widen into a spectacular smile. She weighed 15 pounds less than the day when her life took one of those unrecognized but drastic turns and changed forever. Men of all ages were charmed by her beauty and yearned to hold her, if only once.

This Saturday morning, she relaxed and sipped tea on the veranda of her seaside villa, on the Maltese coast northwest of Valletta. Despite heavy doses of Cognac the night before, she had not slept well. The violence and tensions in the Middle East were driving her to think of yet another place to move, a change that would include relocating her business affairs. She came to the island of Malta, now an independent republic, from Lebanon more than 20 years ago to avoid escalating sectarian and political violence. She had been one of many Christians then living in Beirut when the Lebanese Civil War began. Until that time, a fragile constitutional balance protecting Christians, Sunni and Shia Muslims alike had fostered a peaceful and prosperous existence for all. That had changed by the time of her departure for Malta. Her personal charm and increasing wealth had attracted friends whose greatest interest was money and the mechanisms to protect it. To them she was discretely known as "The Laundress." An evil madness had taken hold then, and it now was menacing the entire region. Charm and wealth only went so far. She had survived a variety of threats to her existence by learning when to move and when to hide. Now, she thought, was another time to move. Besides, she had become too old to hide.

She was born in 1929 in the small town of Belleville-Sur Mer on the English Channel, about six kilometers northeast from the center of Dieppe. She vividly remembered the surprise English raid on that city in 1942. She and her parents spent the day in their basement monitoring events by the sounds of war and the languages of the combatants, initially English and then German. Her mother and father smiled and looked hopefully to the staircase leading from the stonewalled basement to the heavy door next to the kitchen above. When the German voices returned, her father's face became a darkened mask as his arms reached out to embrace his frightened wife and trembling daughter. In the course of a few moments, those voices too moved away, seemingly following the gunfire toward the shoreline of the Channel.

Not until the next morning did they step outside into the debris of battle. She remembered seeing the corpses of Canadian and British soldiers strewn about the street in front of her house and beyond. The face of one young soldier seemed hardly older than her cousin Maurice, an awkward and slender schoolboy who had visited them in the summer before the Germans came. Maurice was now dead, having fallen near the Belgian border when the Germans came pouring down. When news reached her of Maurice's death, Pierrette cried for days. Her mother, not a particularly sensitive woman, assured Pierrette's father that this was only a consequence of a young girl's passage in to womanhood. Today she remembered both boys with the same painful affection she felt all those years ago. Her mother's view was rubbish.

Following their liberation in 1944 and war's end the next year, Pierrette's father was determined to provide a good education for her. Pete, on the other hand, wanted more. She wanted to go to England for higher education, and perhaps to see more of those English boys. Besides, Canada was an ocean away. She got her wish in 1948.

By 1954, she had enjoyed and divorced two English husbands, and she rejected one very young lover in between. Her daughter was born in 1960 from a casual affair with a Corsican businessman who had been working briefly in London. The birth of this child, Lisette, caused Pete to conclude that her reckless ways must end. The following spring she met and married Judson Meredith, a career British Navy warrant officer five years her senior. In 1965, he received orders to the former Crown Colony of Singapore for a five-year assignment to the Royal Navy base, HMS Terror. The base was situated on the backside of the island.

To complement her life as a dutiful British Navy wife and mother, and to cement her new proper image, she took a part-time job at Barclays Bank. Her first husband had by then matured into his own relationship with Barclays in England, and he provided an easy reference for her at the time of application. The bank paid for rudimentary accounting courses, and she later became proficient in wire transfers and correspondent banking relationships. Full-time employment was her reward. She excelled in these dry pursuits in order to distract her more lusty inclinations. Pierrette was determined to force her life into acceptable bounds.

As she contemplated the variety of her life, the decisions she had made and the impact of a permanent relocation upon her significant clients, the telephone rang. It was Lisette, as expected, inquiring about her mother's health and the conditions in the Eastern Mediterranean. Now safely and happily married in London, Lisette had called her mother every Saturday morning since her last husband's death, urging her to move to safer regions. Pete was weakening.

"Today, I am fine. How are the children?" Pete tried to deflect the topic. "Perhaps I can come for a visit late in the summer." She paused. "You know I'm going to Hawaii this summer. It's so lovely."

More warm deflections later, the conversation ended. Pete needed to make very basic decisions and manage details before disclosing anything to her daughter.Returning to the veranda, she found her place again in the memories.

CHAPTER 15

And Second Loves

Judson was a wonderfully solid mate, a competent lover and decent father to Lisette. When Judson was not at sea, the family spent leisure time dining, bowling or swimming at the Officers' Club on the base. Everyone was cordial, friendly and behaved. Shortly after their arrival, Britain announced its intentions to relinquish the base to the Republic of Singapore. Expectation of new assignments for many and the possible retirement for some, including Judson, were constant topics.

The only other routine topic was the war in Vietnam. Indeed, American Coast Guard patrol boats, 82-foot cutters, had come to Singapore's magnificent shipyards and dry dock facilities for major repairs and refitting. Occasionally, larger U.S. warships also visited for a few days of liberty. Singapore was one of the rest and recuperation sites for the U.S. military fighting in Southeast Asia. R&R, as it was known, consisted of a seven-day break from the war, flying hordes of vital young men and their seniors to Singapore to enjoy the women and other exotic delights without the hazards of being shot at.

British wisdom and persistence in resisting the communist movement in Malaya had prevailed in the 1950's, protecting too the vital city and naval base at the tip of the Malaysian peninsula. This wisdom was particularly British as compared with the attitudes of other colonial powers like the Belgians and the French. British administration, as a matter of policy, encouraged competent civil service structures within local populations rather than looting the economy or exerting overbearing authority, traits common to the French and Belgians. Later, transitions to independence for the lands controlled by Britain were essentially peaceful and businesslike.

British military policy in Southeast Asia was consistent, measured and patient. The accepted view at the Officers' Club was that French administration in Vietnam, both before and especially after World War II, resurrected a very nasty relationship between the locals and their European masters. Americans took over almost a decade later when French domination collapsed in 1954. American pluck and good intentions were admirable, but their presence in Vietnam was not consistent, measured or patient. After all, they were Americans.

When Judson was at sea, however, Pierrette focused on the learning process at her banking job. She rarely enjoyed the club facilities. Protocol required that she and other wives of absent officers be accompanied en masse on social occasions by one of the officers left behind, a duty chaperon.

In early November 1969, Judson was at sea on maneuvers with the Australian Navy, but he expected to be home by Christmas. Pierrette had worked late at the bank that Thursday and decided to dine alone on The Junk, a renovated coaling vessel from the 19th century now serving as an upscale restaurant anchored in Keppel Harbor. Owned by two Reuters News Service employees, one from London and the other from Beirut, the Junk had a marvelous array of international dishes. Since the owners were also bank customers, Pete's solo patronage was considered socially safe.

As she and other patrons boarded the complementary motorized bumboat for the return trip to the old Customs House dock, Pete saw a morose young man, obviously an American serviceman on R &R, seated alone on one side of the water taxi. He was a big fellow, but he looked more like an overgrown barely pubescent schoolboy. He wore a new short haircut, equally new cotton slacks and a short-sleeved, light blue shirt. She took the empty seat next to him and spoke, more out of courtesy than special interest.

"Good evening. Isn't it lovely tonight? Did you enjoy your meal?"

"No ma'am. I mean, yes ma'am." He seemed flustered and that was understandable. Pete had that effect on males. Tones of her French heritage laced her English accent.

"I'm sorry, ma'am. My mind was somewhere else. It's nice tonight, but I didn't eat on the ship."

"For heavens sake, why not? The food is good, and you really should enjoy it while you're here." She then remembered seeing him at the dock almost two hours earlier as she boarded for dinner. The boy kept looking out over the water.

"See here, young man. What's your name? I can't very well pry into your business if I don't know your name."

He produced an odd smile from one side of his mouth. "Ma'am, I'm Seaman Randolph Cavanaugh. I'm in the Navy. I mean, ma'am, the American Navy. What's yours?"

"Some of my friends call me Pete. I live here, and my husband is a warrant officer in the British Navy. How do you do, Randolph?" She extended her hand, and the boy stared at her delicate fingers as if he was afraid to touch fine glass. She reached over with her left hand and grabbed his right wrist, pulling his hand into hers. What surprised him, a memory which lasted over the coming decades, was the strength of her grasp. She was not fine glass.

As they arrived at the dock and stepped from the rocking sides of the bumboat to the stone landing, Cavanaugh went first and then turned to help her up safely.

"Thank you, Seaman Cavanaugh. Since you won't tell me why you haven't had dinner, I insist you follow me right now. There is a little Indian café outside the Customs House. I'll have tea while you eat and tell me about yourself. You do eat Indian food, don't you?"

"No ma'am, but I'll try it."

"Now Randolph, you must stop calling me ma'am. I will call you Randy, and you will call me Pete. Is that clear?"

Cavanaugh nodded.

Shortly, they entered a noisy little hole-in-the-wall restaurant and took a table off to one side. She ordered her tea as well as a sampling of food for Dolph. Within 40 minutes, she had pulled from him just about every fact of his young life. Dolph's understanding of his life was less than its reality.

* * *

Randolph Bedford Cavanaugh was born in Fayetteville, Arkansas, on June 1, 1949, to Army Staff Sergeant Forrest Cavanaugh and his wife, Lucille. Sgt. Cavanaugh had served honorably with the 69th Infantry Division in the closing months of the war in Europe and was discharged in 1946. He returned to his hometown of Memphis, Tennessee, and the auto mechanic job he had left for the Army. The job was the same, but Forrest had changed. He took advantage of the GI Bill, and in January 1947, at the age of 27, enrolled as a freshman at the University of Arkansas in Fayetteville. In his spare time, he continued working as a mechanic.

The following summer he met Lucille at a hamburger joint off campus. She was 19 years old, waiting tables and looking for a husband. Three months later, she became Mrs. Cavanaugh on the representation that she was bearing Forrest's child, a hopedfor boy whom Forrest wanted to name Nathan. Anticipating further financial pressures, he quit school and took full-time employment at a meat-packing plant. It was then that Lucille told him she had miscarried. Forrest never questioned the actuality of her pregnancy or the miscarriage. Maybe it was for the best, he thought. Maybe they needed to save some money before starting a family.

Three events occurred in 1948 that changed Forrest's plans. The Russians began blockading Berlin in June, leading to what became known as the Berlin Airlift. Forrest Cavanaugh decided to re-enlist, retaining his prior service credits and rank. He disclaimed patriotism, but not the need for reliable employment and future retirement benefits, as his reasons for returning to the military. He knew what the rest of the country either knew or chose to ignore, that a mighty conflict with communism was coming. Lucille, however, thought little beyond her daily life and conveniences. She figured he was just taking a real steady job. Finally, Lucille became visibly pregnant.

Forrest was home on leave in September from an advanced non-commissioned officer's course at Fort Leonard Wood, Missouri. He assumed incorrectly that he would be back in Europe before Christmas, and they made contingency plans for Lucille to move into his mother's home in Memphis.

By the time Randolph was born, that crisis had passed, but not Forrest's expectation of deployment. When Dolph was four months old, Sgt. Cavanaugh received and followed orders to Japan for a 13-month tour of duty with the 21st Infantry Regiment of the 24th Infantry Division.

On June 25, 1950, North Korean forces poured over the 38th parallel, beginning a war that was to last until an armistice in July 1953. Within 10 days, Sgt. Cavanaugh was a part of Task Force Smith, fighting a bloody and frustrating delaying action against North Korean mechanized units. Forrest fell in battle somewhere between July 5 and 6, 1950, in the U.S. Army's first engagement of that war.

Lucille told Dolph his daddy died fighting "comminists" and was now with the Lord. She wasted no time or tears finding a new husband and the only father Dolph ever knew, Mr. Jackson, a man who owned a dry cleaning business.

In the summer of 1962, Dolph found a roach-infested cardboard box stored in his stepfather's garage. The box contained some curled and fading photographs of his parents and a stained scroll secured with a decaying rubber band. Dolph never learned the exact circumstances of

Sgt. Cavanaugh's death beyond the implications of the Presidential Unit Citation he retrieved that day. For the rest of his life, he regretted never knowing his earthly father.

Dolph sanded his more recent history, including the fact that an Arkansas judge, before whom Dolph appeared to answer minor charges, encouraged his Navy enlistment. That same year, 1968, Lucille died of breast cancer. Mr. Jackson remarried the month before Dolph came to Singapore.

* * *

Pete, on the other hand, was careful not to disclose details of her life beyond having a daughter and working for an internationally known bank. She knew early in their conversation that she was not going to take advantage of Randy in any physical way; that would be dangerous for her crafted image. There was something bothering him, and learning that was her objective. There would be more time tomorrow.

"Randy, I have enjoyed this very much, but I must be getting home. If you are available tomorrow after 4 p.m., I will call your hotel. Perhaps we can drive across to Jahore Bahru for supper. Oh yes, please give me your telephone number."

Cavanaugh didn't notice her prattling; he was overwhelmed by her manner and attractiveness. He fumbled for the hotel card as she raised her hand and beckoned the waiter. Standing, she pushed cash into the waiter's palm, turned and patted Dolph on the shoulder saying, "There now, finish your meal. I'll call tomorrow."

She was gone before he could stand or even speak any sort of thank you or goodbye.

* * *

Cavanaugh spent the next morning on a tour bus and enjoyed a lunch of fish and chips. He was freshened up and ready for Pete's telephone call by 3:30. She completed her day's work shortly after noon, arranged for Lisette's evening care and reached her home east of downtown by 4:15.

"Seaman Cavanaugh, I hope I haven't kept you waiting too long. Did you have a pleasant day?" Not pausing for his answer, she continued. "I should like to pick you up in front of your hotel at 6:30. Would that be convenient?"

Dolph was charmed by her voice. "Yes," he stammered, "Pete. I'll be in front. May I wear something similar to last night?"

"You started to call me 'ma'am', didn't you? That's fair enough; I should have called you Randy. You looked fine last night. We'll take a little drive north of Jahore before dinner. I think you'll find it interesting." Then she was gone.

Dolph had no idea what to expect. This woman was old enough, he guessed, to have been his mother, and yet she was so unlike his mother or any girl he had ever known in any sense of the word. There was something else about Pete that was unique in his experience; he trusted and admired her.

Singapore was a long way from Little Rock and seemed for now a longer distance from the Mekong Delta. Dolph had pieced together that he had been in Vietnam on Swift Boats about as long as his father had been overseas at the beginning of the Korean War. The coincidence had been gnawing at him for several weeks. Combat patrols became more dicey and threatening. His new boat officer, Mr. Taylor, was a good officer and a quick learner, planning every ambush and raid to reduce the chances of dangerous counter-surprises. Mr. Taylor's teacher and patrol partner was a much younger, combat-savvy ensign from Iowa. These two officers and the combined experience of their crews represented Dolph's best chance of going home alive.

Still, Dolph had a mental image of a bullet from nowhere smashing his brain or a B-40 rocket propelled grenade detonating against his body and shredding the life from him. Dolph's general quarters station was a mounted 50-caliber machine gun at the aft deck, a position seemingly more exposed and attractive to return fire than any other on these 50-foot patrol boats. Convinced his time was ending, he visualized that the only shield between him and sudden death was his machine gun.

As always, the presence of the American military and its abundant supply system encouraged black-market activity by servicemen and civilians alike. Off duty, Dolph's specialty had been bulk sales of stolen stereo equipment. He was a commission salesman between the military thieves and the Vietnamese marketers. He never saw or took possession of the goods, and he very rarely saw either his stealing clients or their buyers. His cardinal rule was that payment had to be in large demonination bills of U. S. currency rather than Military Payment Certificates, the only lawful American money in Vietnam. To Dolph and his suppliers, Vietnamese piasters were worthless and, on occasion, so were the MPCs. Periodically MPCs were declared redeemable within a short period, say 30 days, to discourage hoarding, fraud and counterfeiting. Of course, Dolph checked all American currency for genuineness.

His other cardinal rule was never to become greedy or too eager for a deal, both traits coloring better judgment. Following these rules dictated careful planning, reliable partners and absolute control over the execution of the plan. This good ol' boy from Arkansas had done quite well, acquiring during his non-duty hours almost $15,000 in American currency. His premature death would render this worthless too, at least to him.

Getting his stash out of Vietnam and into Singapore had required tedious work re-sewing the lining of a cheap, medium-sized travel bag. His calculated risk that baggage inspectors would be too busy to be thorough given the large numbers of horny travelers in line proved worthy. Maybe now he could find some other way to convert this money into more transferable value.

Its only money, he thought. My life is more important than that.

* * *

Pete pulled to the curb in front of his modest hotel and honked lightly. Dolph was a little surprised to see than she was driving a battered, 10-year-old, dark blue Renault Dauphine with inoperable air conditioning. She barely allowed him time to sit and close the door before throwing the car into gear and zipping into the traffic. As she approached the low causeway to Jahore in bumper-to-bumper, fast-moving traffic, she suddenly honked and jerked her wheel to the right, careening over two lanes and into the driveway of a dilapidated gas station.

"My petrol gauge doesn't work, and I don't remember when I last filled," was spoken over her shoulder as she got out of the car.

"Stay there," she commanded. "This won't take long."

She was clothed in a short, dark evening dress with black sandals. Three minutes later she completed the fill, paid the equally dilapidated Malaysian attendant and jumped back into the Renault. After trying twice to restart the car, she finally under her breath muttered something in French, jumped out and slammed the door. She walked to the front of the car, standing somewhat back and raised her right foot. She did not kick the car, but rather stomped on it two times.

Returning to her seat, she twisted the ignition switch, and the car politely purred to life.

"That's more like it," she said to herself more than to Dolph, muscling the car into gear, roughly engaging the clutch and lurching into position near the teaming traffic.

At that point, she flashed him the most wonderful smile, one that shone in his memories for over 30 years. She then dove into a brief space between two other cars. A virtual symphony of horns and screeching of brakes announced the traffic's displeasure. Her reply through the driver's side window was a feminine but assertive flipping of the bird.

For the first time since leaving the hotel, she softened and focused on her passenger.

"Randy, isn't it a lovely evening? We'll drive through town for a while and then north along the coast road. I'm sure you haven't seen this before."

Once in the countryside, while the people and circumstances were different from Vietnam, the terrain was very similar. Dolph avoided speaking those comparisons, simply commenting on the quality of the roads and the beauty of the land. An hour and a half out, she pulled off the highway and onto a dirt road that ended at a low bluff overlooking the sea to the northeast. For a time they sat in silence.

Pete then rummaged in her purse, retrieving a pack of Rothman-filtered cigarettes and lit one without offering one to Dolph. "Of course, you don't smoke, do you?"

"Well, not since I got to Singapore. I don't know that brand."

"They're English and much better than Gallois." She laughed and joked in a mock deep-voiced French accent that all Gallois tobacco was guaranteed to have been rinsed in the sewers of Paris.

Dolph's smoking habit had been formed within the past two months. Mr. Taylor and the Gunners Mate had got him started. They only smoked after an operation. Besides, a carton of cigarettes was cheap in Vietnam, under $2.00.She turned and offered her cigarette to him. He declined.

"Good," she remarked flicking the cigarette out of her window onto the packed sand. "One day I'll quit those things."

A salty air blew across the jungle and along the shoreline. Dolph could smell that same Asian scent of charcoal, soy sauce and fish that seemed to permeate the Mekong Delta. He wondered how long they would remain parked.

"You see the water out there; eventually it washes the shore of the English Channel near my parent's house and maybe it finds its way into a rainstorm in Arkansas. Isn't it interesting to think of that? In a way aren't we both near home just looking at the bay out there?"

"I really haven't got a home. If I get to go back to the States, I don't know where I'll go." He made this statement as raw fact rather than an exercise in self-pity.

"I can't say that I will ever see the English Channel again, but I do know this; there is a world out there to enjoy. That's true for both of us."

Dolph was uncomfortable talking about his personal thoughts. He had never done that, never thought about his future or even that he had a future worth pondering. He was embarrassed that she didn't seem to worry about anything and was uncomfortable, feeling that she could read his mind.

"Are you afraid of being killed? I have seen young men die. I should think you would be afraid. Doesn't that keep you alert?"

He felt peppered with questions. All he could manage as a reply was to the first, "Yes, I'm afraid."

"Well then, be afraid if you must, especially if it keeps you on your toes, but I believe you will be just fine. One thing you must not do is to worry or fret. A long life is too short for that. Remember, even serious matters ought not to make you unhappy, and I have seen you unhappy."

She plunged ahead. "You're probably unhappy now because I haven't fed you as promised. Let's go."

She fired up the Renault, turned and drove back to the highway toward Jahore. Dolph regretted leaving that quiet little spot of beach; he wanted to listen more to her. He also had become acutely aware of her very mild perfume.

No one had ever spoken to Dolph this way with such confidence and without seeming to have any other purpose or agenda. He knew he could trust that confidence and Pete's judgment.

* * *

In Jahore they parked on the street and walked a short distance to a moderately shabby hotel. Once inside they took an elevator to the 10th floor that opened onto a rooftop restaurant called "The Garden". She spoke to the maitre d briefly, who lead them to a table near the window looking south over the causeway and the lights of Singapore. It was 9:42 p.m., and they were the only guests.

Pete remarked that this was a nice, out-of-the-way place. What she did not explain was that "out of the way" for her meant being away from the social haunts of the Navy base families. She could flirt with her old ways and not be hurt.

The waiter brought drinks, a gin and tonic for her and bourbon with cola for Dolph. She proposed a toast to "enjoyment," using that same beaming smile she flashed at the gas station. As she sipped from her glass, her attention turned to a band area on the other side of the dance floor. No one was playing any music. Her eyes narrowed as she spotted a small man in a seedy tuxedo dozing on a folding chair near a piano.

"Excuse me, Randy. I'll return in a moment. Perhaps we can dance before dining."

She was off in a straight line and marched toward the sleeping musician.Dolph knew that this man was about to get a come-to-Jesus talk from Pete. Her body language said it all; first her right arm went into the air in whipping gestures, and then the left hand came up waving back and forth to the empty band area. Her head moved sharply to the right and then the left. The little guy almost fell from his chair at the verbal assault. He stood stiffly before her nodding as her hands and head repeated her clear message. Finally her back relaxed, and the hands came down just as she executed one quick nod of satisfaction. The fellow disappeared into full-length drapes behind the bandstand as she began walking back to Dolph. Just as she reached their table, the band emerged onto the stage and struggled into its too slow version of "Up, Up and Away." Without sitting, she took a swallow from her drink and announced that the music was not scheduled to begin until 10 p.m. when other guests would arrive.

"That was nonsense, Randy. My reservations were for 9:30, and I expect music with my dinner and …some dancing." She then wiggled her fingers at Dolph, commanding that he arise to her.

For the first time in his life Randolph Cavanaugh was intoxicated, not by alcohol, but by the smell of this woman's hair and her manner. His hands could feel her skin beneath the soft fabric of her dress, and that too was a first for him. Her age was nothing to Dolph. He would do whatever she said, and he had his hopes.

His mood changed, however, with the discordant sounds of "Proud Mary." He hated that music. The song reminded Dolph of sweaty nights in the dank bars across the road from his patrol base at Cat Lo, and his seamy, contrived, brief couplings with young whores. He had to put those memories behind him and separate them from this beautiful and exciting woman. He could never have imagined a woman so wonderful. His emotions were getting the best of him. Only briefly, tears formed and then stopped with the music.

As they returned to their table, the waiter brought Thai-beef salad, chicken curry and fried spring rolls. With every bite, Pete chattered about how she liked the food and how she found this place one night with her girlfriends. She told him that she really enjoyed her work, but that play was just as important to her. She hoped that Randy would find time, even during the war, to enjoy life despite the danger. There was no other good way to live. As she paused to inspect a last morsel of curry, Dolph spoke quietly.

"May I sleep with you tonight?"

She froze momentarily and then smiled slyly. "No, dear Randy, that's not what this has been about. You're going away soon, and you must find your way back in America after the war. When are you leaving, anyway?"

"Early tomorrow afternoon. Why not?" It was a simple question with some tenderness and without hostility or disappointment.

She put her fork down, dabbed her mouth with a napkin and looked at him for a moment.

"It's about loyalty and self-respect. I'm no alley cat, at least not in a long time. My husband has been good to and for me. When he comes home I can look him in the eye and feel no shame. That's what I hope for you, that some day you will find a girl to share loyalty and mutual respect."

He stared at Pete for maybe 10 seconds studying her face. He wanted to remember this instant. He then took a deep breath and smiled.

"Okay, Pete; I'll do that."

He stood and walked to the maitre d station. Pulling out some cash, he pointed back to the table. When he returned, he announced that he had ordered two brandy freezes for dessert and paid the bill.

"You won't get to play last night's trick," he said. "May we dance again?" On the dance floor, joined by other guests, she sensed a change in his whole manner. He was still the very young man, but no longer morose, uncertain, compliant and withdrawn. He led her with author- ity and for just a brief moment Pete felt she was giving way, just one delicious moment. And then he laughed. "Let's eat the freezes and leave. I have something to give you, but not here."

* * *

Out in the car at the curb he asked for her business card. "I won't write to your home or cause any embarrassment at your office. I just want a way to contact you later, if I can."

She produced her Barclay's card and carefully printed her direct line number on its back.

"Why do you say, if you can? Of course you can and will, I hope."
"Pete, you're the one who asked all the questions about me being afraid of dying and telling me I was going to be fine. Maybe you're right, and I'm planning on it. But if you're wrong, I want you to know that not hearing from me won't be because I forgot you."

The Renault obeyed her first command. As she wove out into the night's traffic, she saw him struggling with his shirt and trousers. Looking to her right and then to the causeway traffic and back again, she saw him pull out a money belt and dangle it to allow its straps to hang free. She frowned in confusion.

"I've got something here for you. I don't need this now and don't care what you do with it. There's almost fifteen thousand American dollars in here in large bills. I can't say I came by this honestly, but if you are wrong about my future, there's not anyone I would want to have this but you. Will you take it?" This was the only time in their relationship that she was stunned and speechless. She swerved the car from an oncoming Mercedes limousine and a barrage of honking horns. As soon as she could maneuver out of the flow of traffic, she stopped against as curb, still at a loss to say anything.

"Like I say, I'm not especially proud of how I got this money, just some black-market earnings. It does me no good, but might help you. What do you say, Pete? For loyalty and respect?" casually offering her the belt as though it was a double D bra pulled from a laundry dryer. This time he had the big, radiant smile. When she let him off in front of his hotel, she watched him saunter towards its front door. He tucked in his shirt and straightened his pants as he walked. In his last steps he ran his thumbs back from his belt buckle to eliminate any wrinkles in his shirt.

He certainly looks a bit more trim and fit than when I saw him last night, she thought.

CHAPTER 16

No Rest for the Weary

Corrine was at it again that Saturday morning.

"Get movin' Dolph. Dawn is coming, and I've got to get over to the shop." Jogging shoes and shorts plopped on his chest.

"Oh me. I'd argue with you, sweetie, but I know it's no danged use. You don't own an ounce of mercy." He stumbled toward the toilet.

"Quit your complaining. I meant what I said Thursday. Come get me in the kitchen when you're ready. We won't take an hour." She was already dressed in her exercise outfit.

Before leaving their bedroom, Dolph went into his closet and fumbled around in one of the built-in drawers. Finally, he retrieved a prepaid long distance phone card, placing it next to his money clip. These cards could be purchased for specific dollar amounts, depending upon the anticipated usage. Dolph had been buying these cards ever since they hit the market, mostly at convenience stores and gas stations. By dialing a listed 800 number and entering a code from the card, you could roll into a dial tone. Selecting an area or country code, you were then off and running for an untraceable call. Sometimes the cards worked, and sometimes they didn't. Still, it was an important investment for the times they actually worked.

Not finding Corrine in the kitchen, Dolph went out to the driveway apron. Corrine was already stretching. "Dolph, it's about time. Do a little stretching before we take off." Despite Corrine's tough talk, Dolph knew this girl loved him and wanted him safe. A few grunts and groans later, they headed down the street toward Nouveau Boulevard and the massive ornate stone and metal sign identifying the community. Half a mile later, wheezing to a stop at the gatehouse and giving a wave to the uniformed guard, Dolph bent over to catch his breath.

"While you're resting, tell me what happened last night when the Shiprites came in. I saw you eyeing him. What have you found out?"

"Baby, I'm not resting; haven't got the wind to talk," he gasped. Two deep breaths later, he said, "You sure got a habit of asking questions when I can't say anything."

She laughed. "Country Boy, if you'd spend your time answering my question instead of making excuses, things would go a lot easier for you."

Have I married a cop or an old Navy Chief's daughter? She doesn't cut me any slack, he thought.

"Alright, what little I do know is that I don't like the guy either, that his wife is unhappy and Trimmer is holding out on me. Now before you go charging off and getting Eloise involved, I want you to stay out of this and let me handle it my way and in my time."

Finally Dolph was able to stand upright. Looking skyward and breathing deeply, he continued. "I mean it, Corrine. You can kick my starving butt around working out day and night, but you've got to back off on this business with Shiprite except when I ask you specific questions." He paused for effect. "Are you ready to jog some more?"

Corrine looked at him and smiled approvingly. As she started back down the boulevard, she gave her little buns a wiggle, a sign that she would comply with his conditions. Dolph fell in behind her like an old overweight black lab.

Back at the house, they ate fruit and dry cereal and then showered. As Corrine was dressing, Dolph threw on some shorts and skimmed the Houston Chronicle. His only focus was on the local news, obituaries and the sports section. He didn't like the Chronicle reporting beyond that. Corrine was used to his occasional editorial mutterings, such as "elitist liberals" and "comminist jerks." These were terms Dolph reserved for their bedroom, kitchen and the few times he actually read things printed in the newspaper's first section. Most people in Bay City regarded the Chronicle as blatantly biased and an untrustworthy carrier of news.

When Corrine had finished the very little make up she normally used, she grabbed her purse and asked, "What are you going to do? I'm out at the shop most of the day."

"I don't know quite yet, baby. I think I'll make a couple of calls and shuffle out to Hannah's for a salad." He smiled. "Actually, I want a little think time."

He tabled the Chronicle and asked, "We're still planning on Hawaii, aren't we?"

"Sure, honey. By then you ought to be able to jog up that road past Diamond Head."

As she disappeared from the kitchen, he yelled after her. "Woman, I hope you're having a lot of fun killing me."

Ten minutes after Corrine's departure, Dolph retrieved his phone card and cell phone.

CHAPTER 17
Voices

Three rings. He thought to hang up after two more rings, but then she answered.

"Pete, this is Randy. I hope I haven't interrupted your evening."

"Oh Randy, what a dear surprise." Her voice always lifted his memories and spirits.

Cautiously she assured him that his call was no interruption. "It's mid-afternoon Saturday here. I have been thinking about you today; hope you too are relaxing." It was her way of asking where he was calling from.

"Yeah, me too. I just went for a jog with my wife."

So, he's at home in Texas, Pete realized. Momentarily she conjured up the unusual image of Dolph actually exercising.

"Look Pete, I've been thinking about your plans the last time we met and think its time for you to go ahead.

Will I see you later this year?"

"Of course Randy, your call is very timely. By the way, your last letter arrived safely. Give my best wishes to your family."

"You too, ma'am. Goodbye." Dolph understood that the money from the Chinese deal had passed through her system.

Over two and a half decades, their occasional telephone conversations rarely lasted longer or were more detailed. Once a year, or sometimes less often, they met at a vacation destination agreed upon at the previous meeting. Corrine always accompanied Dolph, but never knew, met or saw Pierrette. The last business meeting had been in Hawaii, and they decided to repeat that location this year.

Their meetings, always private and always efficient, began and ended with a long hug and not a gavel. There were no paper reports, lists or balance sheets, and there was no other physical contact. They were friends before their business relationship matured and would remain so after her plans were carried out.

They had agreed that this telephone call would trigger Pete's sell orders and other measures to close down Dolph's account with Pete. This year's meeting would review the steps she had taken to carry out her liquidation plan for Dolph's foreign assets, not something done overnight. What Dolph did not know was that the Laundress was also ready to retire.

CHAPTER 18

Hannah's Place

Dolph entered precisely at 11 a.m, heading for the sit-down counter that in the evening constituted Hannah's lightly stocked bar. Seeing Thurman, he knew Hannah was away.

J. Thurman Birdwell was Hannah's occasional café manager, more often in the colder months when patronage was lighter. Thurman didn't handle stress well; his management style was normally suggestive rather than commanding or authoritative. His angular patrician features had faded, so too had his once carefully groomed blond hair, which was now a shabby gray. He always wore dark trousers and a pressed, white, long sleeve dress shirt, buttoned at the cuffs but not the collar. Appearing older than his middle 70s, he was fragile and studiously timid.

Thurman's one apparent passion was hand washing and drying the bar's glassware. No machine could duplicate his removal of debris, smudges, clouds, prints or lipstick.

"Good morning, Mr. Cavanaugh. Miss Hannah is not here. Would you like some fresh coffee?" Thurman's cultured voice was clear and strong with a patina that only comes with too many years of too much alcohol and too many cigarettes, indulgences Thurman abandoned in his early 30s. Despite his fetish over bar glass, Thurman seemed unaware of the small patches of paper on his face, torn toilet tissue covering razor nicks on his chin and neck.

"Thanks, Birdie. That'd be great." Folks around the area always called Thurman "Birdie." He never minded the nickname and correctly assumed it was spoken with more respect and genuine friendship than in his former lawyering days in Houston.

Dolph liked Thurman and watched as he carefully poured the coffee. Birdie had a slight tremor in his hands that always seemed to steady up at critical moments such as pouring or writing. For some reason, shaving was not one of those events.

Looking around for Toey or the other wait staff, Dolph thought to test how far Corrine's conspiracy had spread. Hiding his guilty purpose behind the cup's steaming surface, he asked, "How's the food today?"

Fragility and timidity barely concealed a sharp mind. "The food, as usual, is superb, but I'm afraid that Mrs. Cavanaugh's instructions through Miss Hannah are quite specific. Perhaps you would enjoy a small salad and a few sautéed scallops."

Birdie produced a kindly smile. He wrote a note, placing it on the pass-through counter into the kitchen. Then, finding a dirty shot glass cowering behind an unopened bottle of Famous Grouse scotch, Thurman Birdwell resumed his meticulous cleaning routine.

The old boy is enjoying this too, Dolph thought. He decided to change the subject.

"When you stopped practicing law, what kind of law were you doing?"

The answer was always the same, and the subject was dropped.
"I did a little of this and that, Mr. Cavanaugh; that was a long time ago."

Dolph had made inquiries though Sam Taylor and already knew the answers that Thurman avoided.

Thurman had been what Taylor called "a gentleman's commercial litigator", not in the courtroom on even a weekly basis, but enough that he was known and well-respected. His cases were always over big dollars, but they stimulated almost no passion. Thurman's collapse in his profession had been as sudden and complete as was his private life. His wife Clarice, a gentle lady devoted to Thurman and their modest social life, died very quickly from pancreatic cancer. Thurman and Clarice had no children, meeting and marrying in their late 30s. Their extended families lived in Ohio and California. Thurman's law practice suffered with him; he lost all desire to focus on clients, his small staff and the courts. The last day he appeared professionally in any court was before a visiting judge from Wichita Falls, Texas, a noted and gratuitous grouchy jerk.

Sam Taylor knew the whole story. Thurman showed up with his client for a Friday trial docket call covering the next two weeks. His was the second case on the docket. Also appearing was a new attorney willing to substitute for Thurman and try the case if it could be set off until the Monday of the second week. The courtroom was jammed with other lawyers, colleagues of Thurman's who knew his personal tragedy and his efforts to wind down his practice, circumstances that escaped the visiting jurist.

The judge railed against the untimely substitution, the inconvenience to the court, the parties and the witnesses. Taylor said that was all crud since the lawyers, the parties and their witnesses were more than willing to delay trial for a few days, especially since settlement seemed possible. The judge's rage was unstoppable. Seasoned hands concluded that the judge was putting on a show for the rest of the lawyers to demonstrate that he was going to be tough on all of them if they tried to wiggle off the docket without an announcement of the sudden death of a party or settlement.

Then, just as suddenly, the judge became coldly calm and said, "The substitution is granted. Regarding the status of the case, the clerk will contact the counsel of record by Friday next." The judge paused and then concluded, "Mr. Birdwell, you are a disgrace and are excused from any other responsibility for this case."

Trembling, Birdie gathered his few papers and small briefcase and left the now silent courtroom. Once back at his office, he instructed his assistant to complete the transfer of his other cases to other firms as agreed, issued two-week severance checks to his remaining staff with the request that they take care of further details to close the office. If there were any problems, they should call him at home.

What Thurman may never have known was that a firestorm of protest erupted from the other lawyers present at the docket call. As cases were called and announced and client's interests were preserved, the attorneys gathered outside the courtroom to discuss the judge's appalling conduct and slander of a respected but severely wounded member of their community. The group selected a delegation to go to the administrative judge for Harris County and inform him of the morning's events. They asked that he do something.

As Taylor related the story to Cavanaugh, he remarked, "Mind you, Dolph, that delegation was not composed of a bunch of wimps. On any given day in trial, they wouldn't hesitate to metaphorically, but professionally, cut off an opposing counsel's balls. They had been stunned by the judge's behavior, but being mindful of their own clients' interests, remained silent until leaving the courtroom."

The administrative judge handled the problem, first by excusing the visiting judge from further duties, second by ordering a transcript of the matter from the court reporter and finally, by reporting the matter to the Judicial Ethics Commission. All this was too late to restore Thurman's demolished self-esteem. No one could remember seeing him in downtown Houston in years. Not until several months ago, when Dolph contacted Taylor, did Taylor learn that Birdie was now a sometime café manager and occasional bartender at Hannah's Place.

* * *

Birdie brought the salad, oil and vinegar dressing, one slice of dry French bread and a heaping plate of grilled scallops. Flatware and a crisply folded white table napkin followed.

"I know I suggested the scallops be sautéed, but thought you might more enjoy them grilled." He raised an understanding eyebrow. "Mrs. Cavanaugh has left us some latitude."

"Birdie, thanks for latitude. Do you have some time to visit?"

"Of course, Mr. Cavanaugh. Besides, this is a light Saturday."

Dolph had given up on getting Birdie to be less formal. It seemed to be his way of maintaining a safe distance.

"I'm interested in Robert Shiprite. Hannah says he comes in with Baxter for lunch every now and then, but do you know anything else?"

Birdie pitched his soiled bar towel, finding a clean replacement. His practice had been to avoid discussing Hannah's patrons. Dolph was different, not a gossip and certainly not a man to ask idle questions. Miss Hannah had also told him that if there ever was any trouble, Mr. Cavanaugh was the go-to man.

"She's correct. Mr. Shiprite occasionally lunches with Mr. Trimmer although, as you know, my hours are irregular."

"You ever see him with anyone else?" Dolph knew to take this slowly.

"Mr. Piper. They generally come in the mid to late afternoon, well after the lunch crowd. They mostly take that table over there." Birdie pointed to a two-seater in a corner, far from the windows and the usual flow of Hannah's patrons.

"Do you have any idea what their business is?"

Birdie smirked slightly. "I couldn't swear to anything, Mr. Cavanaugh, other than that Mr. Shiprite has claimed to be a private investor, and I think Mr. Piper is in a mortgage business."

Dolph caught the smirk and decided to press on. "Do you have any other observations or personal opinions about either of those gentlemen? I'm curious."

"I can tell you are. They're careful to avoid mingling with our regulars. They never come in together, Mr. Piper always being the first to arrive. Mr. Piper stands when Mr. Shiprite approaches, but they never shake hands."

"Who picks up the tab?" Dolph was still smarting over Trimmer being a cheapskate.

"That would be Mr. Piper."

"I guess you're saying these boys aren't having a social time."

Birdie refilled Dolph's water glass and said, "Have the scallops been rewarding?" The interview was over.

Standing, Dolph laughed and put $20 on the counter. "They sure have. Tell Hannah I came by. Y'all won't have to tell Corrine what I ate. I'm going to the Weldinghaus and will confess straight out."

* * *

Dolph needed the fresh air. The tingling along his spine began to fade. He assessed what few people were meant to know. Robert Shiprite and Roger Piper were somehow working together, and Bob was the boss. Reflecting on Shiprite's eye contact with Trimmer last night at the country club, he concluded that the snake's shadow partner was Piper. That's usually the way these things go.

Thurman is an observant old boy, Dolph thought as he turned onto the road to Corrine's shop.

CHAPTER 19

Old Time Religion

When Dolph and Corrine met as students at the University of Houston, Corrine had always been a church-going girl. For her and Momma, church was an expected and necessary part of life. Mr. Wilson felt the same way, but was known in his later years to find God on his fishing boat or on a golf course. Church, at least for the women in the Wilson family, was a time for spiritual refreshment to withstand the cares and stresses of life for the rest of the week.

Corrine never pressed Dolph or made him feel guilty for not having the same inclinations she had grown up with, but eventually they struck an unspoken deal. Their sons would go to church regularly with Corrine and Momma, and Dolph would show up about once a month. In recent years at Momma's former church, the preachers had become less devoted to substance than to platitudes dressed as incisive understandings of man's relationship with God. To Dolph, one Sunday a month wouldn't hurt him, but it was a stretch. He rationalized his attendance by thinking it might look good to a judge if he ever had to face up to his wrongdoings.

Three events changed the deal. First, the boys grew up and went off to school. Second, Momma fell out with her old church and started attending another where the pastor seemed better equipped intellectually to deal with Momma's standards. The third event was Dolph's reading a thick book about the history of battleships. He was especially attracted to the career and accomplishments of Sir John Arbuthnot Fisher, First Sea Lord of the British Navy, informally known as Jacky. Fisher's solid claim in history is that by force of his leadership, he renovated and modernized the British Navy in time to meet its greatest challenge with Imperial Germany in World War I.

Fisher too was a church-going man, daily and sometimes more on Sundays. All this was not because piety demanded it, but because he liked to hear sermons. On learning that Fisher had listened to four sermons in one day, a cleric warned him against "spiritual indigestion." Dolph was impressed.

Since then Dolph and Corrine modified their deal by going to different churches in the area at least once or twice a month. Denominational variety caught Dolph's attention, not because of any religious conversion, but because God apparently inspired his preachers differently. Dolph was only an observer.

Today Mr. and Mrs. Cavanaugh were Southern Baptists. As the sermon began, the pastor talked about the history of the Christian Bible and its translations. The preacher gave a short but interesting chronology of the compilations of the Old and New Testaments and their ultimate unification into what we know today as our Christian Bible. He segued into the trend of recent years to modernize the language of the Bible into what he called colloquial versions. He was especially disturbed by the changed wording done by editors who were supposedly motivated by the desire to make the text more understandable and less archaic to modern readers. He opined that these editors probably had day jobs at USA Today or were scriptwriters for Entertainment Tonight. In this process of their claimed innocent revisions, long accepted, carefully studied understandings of the deeper meanings of biblical text were subtly but often dangerously altered to the spiritual peril of the reader.

The preacher, in an offhand but matter-of-fact manner, said that it is man's sinful nature that estranges or separates us from God and puts us at odds with our creator. Along the way we become at odds with one another, almost hopelessly entangled in joyless evil. We make excuses for our bad and destructive behavior and will go so far as to rewrite the rules, even the Bible, in order to avoid infractions. In the guise of secular progress, we explain away our bad behavior by denying biblical authority and asserting science as a basis for questioning biblical relevance. We claim that portions of the Old and New Testaments are lacking in conceptual authenticity because supposedly sexist Middle Eastern Jews of ancient times wrote them. We further insinuate that subsequent religious commentaries are flawed as having been written in the Dark Ages by those whose descendants conducted or approved of the Spanish Inquisition. In this country, the preacher urged, we wrongly cite the U. S. Constitution as a basis to ignore religion in our schools and public places, all in the effort to avoid coming to grips with our failed personal relationships and with God.

Should we be complicit in our own destruction, the forfeit of our souls, he asked. Of course not, he replied. There is such a thing as reconciliation; some theologians identify that as atonement with God, he explained. Reconciliation between God and humanity is affected by repentance and then sacrifice, originally in the Old Testament Hebraic sense of sacrificing animals to turn away God's wrath.

Still later, as set forth in the New Testament, it was God's sacrifice of his Son, his earthly incarnation, which cleared man's sinful slate of all guilt. It was the death of Christ on the cross, and later His resurrection that made reconciliation of man with God possible for those who believed, then and for all time, in Him. God's grace and eternal salvation are the open invitation to those who believe in Him, who repent and pledge to abandon wicked ways.

In a few minutes, the pastor had drawn Dolph deeply into traditional though often watered-down Christian theology, and then in a gentle and pleading voice, he pulled the congregation's focus to the simple point of his sermon.

Anyone truly professing to be a repentant Christian or inquiring about the meaning of faith needs to study carefully an accurate translation of the Bible for its crucial insights and not rely on so-called modern versions. Studying and understanding in solitude needs deepening in groups. "Amen," he concluded. Several members of the congregation affirmed his message with strong Amens.

Dolph wasn't the only person in the church impressed by the preacher's message. When the church music director announced the closing hymn, there was a universal immobility in the sanctuary. Only the introductory notes played by the organist stirred folks to grasp pew hymnals and rise to sing. Fumbling for the correct page in the hymnal, Dolph's first conscious thought was, I'd bet Momma would like this guy. He barely noticed the moisture clouding his sight.

Cavanaugh's deal with Corrine had become consequential, more than a domestic convenience or a community convention. Dolph didn't know it then, but he had been touched as much by the message as the apparent candor of the messenger. There was no blinding epiphany, no sudden awareness of spiritual peril. There were, instead, fleeting questions.

What if this preacher is right? He seems like a smart guy; why would a smart guy believe these incredible assertions if they were not true?

The questions faded in the social clamor of the departing flock. Corrine spotted a former high school classmate and dragged Dolph back three pews to meet the woman. She had returned to Bay City to pack up her father's belongings for an anticipated move to her home in Edmund, Oklahoma. She looked 20 years older and 60 pounds heavier than Corrine. Dolph thought, I'm blessed to be married to my little fox.

Now, however, Dolph was also distracted by other conditions. The sermon had only been a temporary relief from the nagging concern about Baxter Trimmer's involvement with Shiprite. Dolph needed to have a straight talk with the banker. The other distraction was the constant muscle and joint pain Dolph was experiencing from Corrine's exercise regimen. Finally, he wondered if he could talk Corrine into a real meal; he was hungry.

CHAPTER 20

A Day of Rest, Sort Of

Hannah's Place was closed and the K-2 Steak House was off limits, but Corrine's mercy was measured. On the way home from church, she and Dolph stopped at the H.E.B. grocery store and bought a hot rotisserie chicken and a large assortment of green cooking vegetables. Dolph decided to track down Baxter before lunch to give him plenty of time to worry over Dolph's intentions. Eloise answered the phone.

"Hey, sugar, is your boyfriend around? I want to talk to him for a minute. You two can jump back in bed when I'm finished." Dolph's opening lines to Eloise were often colorful and sometimes lewd. She always laughed and he suspected her spirits were lifted.

"Sure, Dolph, he's in the kitchen reading the Chronicle. I'll get him."

"Darlin' you better rip that paper out of his hands and get him studying you instead of the sports section."

A minute later Baxter picked up the phone with his more relaxed weekend greeting, "Hello Dolph. Whatcha got?"

Dolph didn't waste words. "Baxter, carve out time for me tomorrow around mid-morning. You and I need to talk about Shiprite. I'll swing by the bank and pick you up about 10 a.m. Got a problem with that?"

Trimmer was silent for a few seconds, and then, after realizing that Dolph couldn't be put off, he cleared his throat and replied, "Sure Dolph. How long do you need?"

Cavanaugh ignored Baxter's implication that Trimmer was doing him a favor. Good, Bax's defenses are already crumbling, he thought.

"Ten minutes is enough for me," he said, "but you may want to take longer. See you in the morning."

After lunch, Corrine gave him permission to take a nap. Later she decided to join him.

CHAPTER 21

Blue Monday

Twelve seconds before the appointed time, Dolph eased his Suburban alongside the curb at the front of the bank. He switched off the radio and unlocked the doors just as Baxter came out. They exchanged one word greetings and drove off, circling the courthouse square before going north on State Highway 60, past the entry to Nouveau Estates.

The silence of the drive provoked Baxter into small talk.

"They executed Timothy McVeigh this morning."

"So I heard. The guy deserved it." Dolph's tone shut down any further comment on the bombing of the Federal Building in Oklahoma City. Dolph had other priorities.

"Bax, I've known you for almost 25 years and seen you through some tough times." Baxter knew that Dolph had not been happy with him chipping around on his first wife, but Cavanaugh also had been cheerful and supportive when he married Eloise, the chippee. Baxter's personal life, however, was not Dolph's initial drift.

"I got you out here from Houston because I thought you were a good banker and could protect Corrine and Momma's interests in the bank along with those of the other shareholders. Until the other day, except for letting your zipper loose for Bea Jay, I had no doubts about you, but..."

Trimmer interrupted. "Dolph, is this about my sex life? That's none of your business."

This was just the point that Dolph hoped they would reach.

"Let me tell you what is my business, you little jerk. I don't care if you think sheep are pretty. You're doing some kind of business with Robert Shiprite, and you lied to me and fuzzed up your language about him. I don't like the guy, and I think he's a dangerous person to have anything to do with. Along with my selfish reasons, I happen to have your better interests in mind as well." Although his anger was palpable, Dolph's voice never got above a conversational tone.

Baxter first defiantly folded his arms, but then his hands fell to his lap as his chin slowly drooped toward his tie. Dolph, now out in the country, slowed the Suburban and pulled over to a wider shoulder of the highway.

"Bax, I'm going to give you a choice. You either come clean with me, or I'm going to suggest that two of the women in my life take a better look at you at the Wednesday board meeting. I know they will do what's right, but I can't imagine that it will be very pleasant for you."

Trimmer sunk within his business suit. Dolph without resistance could have shoved him out of the truck like a sack of potatoes. Now it was Cavanaugh's turn to wait and listen.

"I bought some water-district bonds from him about eight weeks ago; I mean personally, not the bank. I gave him $200,000 dollars for what seems to be a pretty good deal. The bonds came from a new subdivision he's interested in developing. He needed a little walking around cash, but I would buy them back later at a good profit whenever I wanted."

Trimmer could not see Dolph's eyes rolling toward the headliner. Dolph thought, the snake is probably paying his monthly banknotes with Bax's money. Trimmer's shame from Dolph's verbal thrashing and hearing his own lame explanations completed Baxter's submission.

"Where'd you get the money? That kind of transaction is going to pop up on any examination, isn't it?"

"No, I've got a little account over in Lake Jackson, and I wrote him a check."

Dolph's eyes rolled again. "I suppose he didn't deposit it in your bank, did he? I guess he's got a little account somewhere also."

Baxter was cringing. "No, but I can find that out from my cancelled check?"

Now, with less anger and a small amount of compassion, Dolph brought a weak smile to Trimmer's face. "You are one dumb sucker. That little account of yours, is it a rat hole for the day when Eloise finds out about you and Bea Jay?"

"I don't know, Dolph. I've been going nuts these last few months. We need to get the bank sold; Eloise is unhappy, and the girls are starting to act just like her."

This was more than Dolph had expected, but he needed to plunge ahead.

"You won't find any credentials about me being a family counselor, but it seems to me that a lot of this clears up by paying more attention to your marriage vows and recognizing that Bea Jay is just a young tart who doesn't need an older man playing with her. You're not the first man to make these mistakes, but you can clear that part yourself. But let's talk about the bonds and the bank. Have you told me everything about Shiprite's business with the bank?"

"Yeah, that's it. The bank is well-secured."

Dolph's mind had been processing and planning at warp speed.

"Good. Now I want you to call Shiprite and tell him you need to take him up on his buyback offer; you have marital problems that won't go away without costing you. Tell him to forget about the profit and suggest discounting it another 5 percent just for his trouble so soon after your having purchased his bonds."

Trimmer was puzzled. Dolph went on. "If he seems reluctant, tell him you have an investor buddy in Houston that you were going to offer them to. Tell him you met the guy when he was a bank examiner years ago. He did you a favor when a senior officer at one of your prior banks was screwing with the books; you want to return the favor. That should do it."

"Why are we going through all this hoop jumping? I really do have friends up there, and I could sell this to any of them in a heartbeat."

"They'd be just as dumb as you are. I'll bet you half the discounts right now that those bonds are phony or stolen. Either way you or your friends would be the losers. Shiprite probably thinks no one could be as stupid as you've been and will worry that your former examiner friend will snap to the problem and tell you. And when he tells you, then Shiprite is going to need to explain himself maybe to the FBI or somebody."

Trimmer was in no position to argue. He had never seen Dolph so authoritative, so analytical about anything. He was seeing Cavanaugh for the first time in a new light.

"Bax, I'll bet you the other half that if you call him this morning, Shiprite will accept the offer, waive the discount and promise to have you a check by Thursday. When he says that, you tell him you need certified funds. Get me a copy of the bonds, both sides of your original check, and his repurchase check that you immediately deposit in your rat hole account. Don't mess with me Bax; do exactly as I tell you. If this all works out, as soon as Shiprite's check clears, close that account and reopen one in Austin or Houston. Entitle it as a college account for the girls. Shiprite now knows where you secretly bank, and you want to close that door as quickly as possible. Also you will be able to explain the money to Eloise as a surprise you'd been planning for her and your little treasures. That should get you out of the rat hole problem with Eloise. She'll buy it because she wants to and because she wants you to love her as much as she really loves you."

Dolph could not remember the last time he spoke at such a personally emotional level with anyone other than Corrine and Pete.

Trimmer's feeling of awe was now supported by respect for Cavanaugh's thoroughness. Dolph was pulling him out of the fire in most respects. His only concern now was Miss Wynne.

"What do I do about Bea Jay?"

Dolph laughed. "Let's keep you out of jail and the divorce court first. Also, in case you haven't realized it, keep your pants zipped and stop working late. Got any other questions?"

"Yeah Dolph, what kind of diet does Corrine have you on?"

"Like I said, Baxter, don't mess with me. I'm in no mood for it. Just do as I say and keep me posted. I have a doctor's appointment in Houston tomorrow, so call me tomorrow night." Dolph was privately smiling as he put the Suburban in gear and turned back toward Bay City.

CHAPTER 22

Doin' What You're Told

That evening Corrine served what Dolph had come to call rabbit food, only this time there was a mere starvation portion of leftover chicken. She told him that was because he was going to have a bunch of tests in the morning. The doctor's instructions called for no food after 7 p.m. and no water after midnight. Complaints were useless.

The morning jog was out of the question because they had to get on the road early to get to the 8 a.m. appointment in Houston's massive medical center. Dolph felt like a kid being dragged to the pediatrician by his mother. He knew, however, there would be no sucker at the end of the day. Corrine dropped him off at the Fannin Street entrance to the Methodist Hospital complex, telling him that he was old enough to find the executive health program without her help. As he got out of her Mercedes, she cheerily advised she was going shopping for the rest of the day.

The day went beyond his expectations. No examination in the Navy came close to what he experienced that morning. After blood and urine samples were taken, he was given a bottle of water, a lukewarm, plain, scrambled egg burrito and a small glass of orange juice. He was then poked, jabbed, stuck, weighed, pinched, pressed and stressed. In a pair of hospital provided gym shorts, they had him wired variously to a treadmill, a stationery bicycle, a rowing machine and a universal weight machine. Close to noon, a friendly nurse and two doctors just stared at Dolph as he turned slowly on command, like a roasting chicken on a vertical spit. They took notes. He was released for lunch with instructions to return by 1:30 p.m.

At 2 p.m. the friendly nurse and one of the doctors breezed into the examination room. They were all smiles. The doctor held a report about a half-inch thick.

"Mr. Cavanaugh, I'm sending a copy of this to Dr. Merritt in Bay City for his use in your rehabilitation. I just got off the phone with him, and he suggested I be blunt with you. The good news is that despite your appalling excessive weight and general flabbiness, your numbers are manageable. With the regimen I understand your wife has already instituted and Dr. Merritt's assistance, you should be restored to good health within, say, six months."

Dolph listened intently, gasping inside at two words, rehabilitation and flabbiness. Trying to seem unaffected by those words, he asked, "What's the bad news, Doctor?"

"Apparently your wife is more committed to your recovery than we usually see here. It is unprofessional for me to say this, but some of these women have more to gain from their husband's bad health than otherwise. You're a lucky man."

The nurse, no longer smiling, was gravely nodding. The doctor's formality down shifted another gear. He was older than Merritt and had more seasoning.

"Let's put it this way. I see that you served in the Navy years ago. So did I. Your wife may be tougher on you than boot camp."

The nurse's smile returned.

CHAPTER 23

Business

"Drop me by the office for a few minutes. I want to go check the mail and see if I have any messages. If you don't mind, I will be up there for only 10 minutes."

Dolph was true to his word and anxious to return to Bay City for Trimmer's call. He got back in the car with a couple of magazines and a few pieces of mail he said were unimportant. Unmentioned was one call slip that his girl had left him from the day before. A Mr. Gwinn had come to the office in the afternoon. She had let him in the waiting room and taken his name, as she understood him, and his cell phone number. He wanted to discuss an investment, but did not elaborate. She thought it might have been a cold call. None of that bothered Dolph. What did catch Dolph's attention was the final sentence of her note: "He was well-dressed, and I think he was Chinese."

When they got home, there was a brief telephone message from Baxter. "Hey, Dolph, I just want to let you know, the check is in the mail. I'll tell you more after the board meeting tomorrow. Thanks."

"What's that about? Is there a problem with the board meeting?" Corrine was fussing with her day's purchases, but she had heard the message.

In addition to the business of the meeting, there was a special occasion. Some sixth graders were coming to the bank for a field trip and an introduction to what a bank does and looks like. These kids were coming to the boardroom for part of their tour. Both Corrine and Momma had been material in this invitation, as they had suggested to the primary schools that they have such field trips as the school year was drawing to as close.

"Naw, baby, just a little business Bax and I are working through."

CHAPTER 24

If Momma is Happy...

Albert Wilson, Corrine's great grandfather, along with other farmers in the area founded the Matagorda Peoples State Bank before the First World War broke out in Europe. His son, Amos, succeeded Albert as the Chairman of the Board, a position he held well into his 80s. Corrine's father, Andrew, never cared much for the business of banking, preferring the uncertainties of rice farming and protecting the land from the hazards of oil drilling and pumping units on the family properties in and beyond the county.

That being the case, Andrew's wife, Elizabeth Jean Marshall, now Wilson, who had worked in the bank initially as a teller, later as a combination trust and loan officer and finally as the executive vice-president, was asked if she had an interest in becoming the president and board chairman when Amos stepped down. There was never any doubt of her answer.

Old man Amos never stepped down; he fell off a tractor hitting his head on the shredder he was pulling late one Saturday afternoon. He had been mowing a small pasture that had a great view of what they called Big Lake. Amos was anticipating a family and neighbor gathering the next day after church. He wanted the pasture presentable. The back lawn of the Nouveau Estates Clubhouse is the location of that pasture. The week after Amos' funeral, the board confirmed Momma's new position.

Mrs. Wilson was never an example of the worst consequences of nepotism. She was always informed, politely aggressive in developing business and forward-thinking. She encouraged smart business practices by the bank's customers and tried to stay ahead of the hazards for rural, closely held banks. The bank's profits grew steadily, and its loan failure rate was always on the low side of the region's range. When Andrew, her husband, died, Momma decided to look for a younger man to come in as president so that she could become more involved with the family's rice growing and their oil properties. Randolph recruited Baxter Trimmer, but Momma was the final authority and moving force behind the bank's health and growth.

A long oval table at one end of the boardroom on the bank's third floor could seat up to 50 people. Mrs. Wilson often used that room for gatherings of community interest, such as United Fund drives and presentations by agro-business interests. The 12 board members were representative of the people who lived in the county. All of them were financially secure and behaved without the pretensions found in most urban boardrooms. Momma sat at the head of the table and steadily moved through the agenda items. Baxter responded to questions and comments from board members and Momma with equal courtesy and respect. Of chief interest to them were Baxter's remarks on efforts to market the bank.

While the board members were pleased with the health of the bank and its profitability, they also recognized that banks in the big cities of Texas, mostly owned and controlled by banking companies in even larger financial centers, were paying top dollar for established institutions in smaller communities. For now, the sale of the bank was not a certainty, but it was the board's direction.

One item on the agenda concerned the bank's potential purchase of a package of real-estate mortgages from an area brokerage firm, Red Fish Mortgage Company. The bank had previously bought an earlier package and was considering another and larger set of these mortgages. Baxter asked that this item be deferred until the board's next meeting. Trimmer promised to report to the executive committee when he completed his more detailed review of the package.

Mrs. Wilson was happy with matters so far presented and was anxious to conclude the meeting. Today she was more interested in the sixth graders. A few minutes after her concluding remarks and a freshening of the members and the room, the kids were ushered in.

Corrine and Carleton Brooks whispered to each other about the special demeanor and odor of sixth grade students. At various speeds they were racing into hormonal conditions that provoked all kinds of amusing behavior, or what Corrine called fidgeting.

Momma introduced the board to the teacher and students. One of the boys told his grandfather hello, and a scrawny little girl waived to her Uncle Bob. Momma asked if the children knew what banks did and how they made their money. One boy said he thought they got their money from the government and another said they got it from an Army fort. Cox, he thought. When the laughter subsided, Mrs. Wilson answered the questions. While the American government prints the cash and makes the coins, depositors actually put the money in the bank from what they earn in their jobs or whatever work they do. The bank earns its own money in part by lending some of that money back to the community and charging a percentage of the loan as interest. The more depositors a bank has, the greater is its ability to loan money to people and businesses. It helps communities and families grow as long as the government bureaucrats don't meddle too much.

One boy whose clothes were in an uncertain order asked Momma how they kept people from stealing the bank's money. Momma replied that the first thing to remember was that the money belonged to the people, that the bank held the money as a trust and that they had an obligation to make sure that people were honest with the bank. Of course, if someone tried to rob the bank, we all hoped the police caught the bad guys.

About this time, the kids began to fidget more than before, and Momma figured they had heard enough. She and the other board members thanked the kids for coming by. They filed out, some whispering or occasionally poking one another. The odor followed the students.

Bea Jay Wynne had slipped in during Mrs. Wilson's dissertation. She and Corrine took the stairway down rather than the elevator. Bea Jay seemed impressed by what Mrs. Wilson had said.

"Gosh, Corrine, your mother is wonderful. I never heard banking explained that way. She must really be smart."

"She is, Bea Jay. She is."

CHAPTER 25

Reporting as Ordered

"He carped about certified funds, but you called it right. He waived the discount. I said it just as you told me. He was reading your script. I thanked him and that was it. He said he would come by Friday morning. Dolph, you're incredible."

Trimmer was excited, almost breathless. He could not believe the accuracy of Dolph's predictions. Dolph's precise directions elicited exact confirmation of Robert Shiprite's true character and intentions. Cavanaugh remembered one of Sam Taylor's maxims; keep your eye on the endgame.

"Thanks Bax, but this isn't over. Right after he leaves you, call the certifying bank and confirm the check. When you have done that, get over to Lake Jackson and deposit his check in your account. Tell your bank officer over there to expedite presentment. Pay whatever fees, if any, are necessary to get that money into your account quickly. You can move those funds next week, I suggest to Austin. It will look better to

Eloise."

"Dolph, I owe you. I'll call you when this is done."

"Baxter, you owe me nothing. Just do your best for the bank and for my women. By the way, where are you right now?"

"I'm in the kitchen at home, and Eloise is upstairs. She wants to go out and eat Mexican food tonight. The girls are ordering pizza. You know how Eloise likes margaritas."

"You're a regular Prince Charming, Bax. Just don't eat any of that pickled garlic and keep your fingers off the jalapenos."

Cavanaugh was pleased with himself. This deal wasn't quite put to bed, but it was close. This was the part he loved the most; the part where the deal was near and on target regardless of which life he was working from. He hoped Baxter had learned a lesson.

CHAPTER 26

Life is Good, but Not Always

For the first time since Dolph got home last week, he woke up before Corrine; she was in the easy breathing of deep sleep. The girls had cancelled their usual Thursday lunch at the Nouveau pool for a variety of stated reasons. The truth was that they weren't anxious for Maria to give a repeat performance.

Dolph dressed for their morning jog. The soreness was beginning to go, and while he was still pissing like a hound dog every two or three hours, his weight had dropped an amazing eight pounds. He was feeling good. Maybe he could surprise Corrine this morning. He tossed her workout clothes over her face, and she popped up like a cork.

"Good morning, Country Boy; I was wondering how long it would be before you started feeling better. I've been laying here for a good 10 minutes trying to guess how you'd wake me."

They reached the subdivision entry this time without Dolph complaining or wheezing too much; he even managed some conversation on the way out. "Don't be too proud of yourself. That kind of weight comes off easy in the first few days, but it can climb back on a lot easier. Dr. Merritt read your report and gave me some pointers. I'll be picking up the pace next week."

"Y'all are ganging up on me, but I'll get my revenge."

Dolph knew his remarks were just bluster, but flabbiness had cut his ego the deepest. This situation was beginning to piss him off. He tried to put on some steam on the way back to the house. From Corrine's perspective, it was more like a sputter, but she didn't comment. Dolph failed to see her slight smile. She loved her big, lumbering husband and wasn't about to lose him to bad health.

Corrine was off to the Weldinghaus by 9 a.m., and Dolph collapsed on the family room sofa five minutes later. He hadn't run a marathon, but felt like it. The telephone interrupted his sleep at 10:30.

"Dolph, I have the check in hand. Do you want to ride over to Lake Jackson with me? I'll buy lunch."

Through his grogginess, his first thought was, That's a start, and Bax is springing.

"How long before you get here? I need to shower."

"Half an hour. Is that okay? I need to tell you something."

Baxter was early, but Dolph was ready. He wrote a note for Corrine, found Dora in the laundry room and told her where he was going. Dora was a good lady and spoke perfect English just like a Texan. She also liked pulling the banker's pretentious chain. He was standing in the laundry room doorway looking at his wristwatch as Dolph told Dora goodbye.

"Choo gonna have lonch with Meester Baxter? I'll bet he likes dat diet Meese Corrine has for choo. He won't have to pay so much. Choo have a nice day." She gave them both a big toothy smile.

On the way out to Trimmer's car, he muttered, "Does she do that to all your friends, or does she just specially like me?"

"No Bax, she likes you all right; she only does that with stuffed shirts".

Dolph was enjoying the ride. Baxter handed him an 8- by 14-inch envelope containing copies of all the documents he had requested, but he deferred studying them until he got back home. Baxter was always careful about document assembly. Once on the highway, Baxter set the cruise control; Lake Jackson was 45 minutes away.

"I said there was something I needed to tell you. Actually there are two or three things I need to say."

Cavanaugh noted that there was a more serious tone in Baxter's voice. This was not his friendly, banker's, you-can-trust-me voice, but one that was more genuine. Sincere was the word that came to Dolph's mind.

"I've been thinking a lot about what you said the other day, everything about Eloise, the bank and my responsibility to them and really to you."

Dolph was tempted to lighten Baxter's seriousness by telling him not to get dewy-eyed but remained silent.

"At the board meeting, Mrs. Wilson made a little speech to some sixth-graders. She talked about some basic banking concepts, and how the money isn't ours, but that we hold and use it as a trust for the depositors and the community. I know all that sounds corny, but its true and the worst thing is that I had forgotten those basics."

Dolph's only visible reaction was to turn his head away from the passing fence lines and fix his eyes on Trimmer.

"Before she made that speech, I don't know why, I took an item off the agenda, telling the board I wanted to study the matter more. Did Corrine say anything?"

"No Bax, I told you, I don't get into things like that with her or Momma. Where are we going on this?"

"It had to do with some mortgages the bank is thinking of buying. I don't think I want to do that."

"Why not; there's nothing wrong with buying mortgages. I've been doing that myself for a few years. They can produce a good income stream, and my default rate has almost been nothing. Fact is, in the long term, I've even made money on the defaults."

"That's not what I'm talking about Dolph. This isn't an issue of the apparent quality of the mortgages; it's about who is trying to sell them." Dolph turned his whole torso to the left.

"It isn't Shiprite, is it?" A mild dread was creeping into his gut.

"No, or at least I don't know if he's involved. The problem is Roger Piper. He owns a mortgage company, and I think he and Shiprite are friends. Based on my recent experience with Bob, I'm beginning to doubt anybody he runs with."

"Good. He's bad news and so is anyone he works with." Dolph elected not to disclose Birdie's comments. There would be time enough for that later.

"So Bax, this is OK. Just don't buy them; take your time and then kiss them off."

Cavanaugh was really encouraged by Baxter's behavior. This was the old Bax. This was what Dolph had seen in the banker years earlier that provoked him to recommend the man to Momma. This was good.

"I won't, but that's not the real problem. Three months ago, the bank bought another package from the company. So far, they are well-performing notes, payments on time and all of that. The packages appear to be clean. We're in for about $900,000."

"How much is the second package being offered for?"

"A million two." Trimmer began nodding what he knew that Dolph understood; depending on the true character of the first set of mortgages, a substantial loss on these loans could materially hurt the bank and at least injure its reputation. It might not kill a sale of the bank, but would depress the sales price. The second set would cripple the bank.

"Bax, this is bad. Did you have any clues at the time?" Dolph's gut tightened.

"No, I don't think so. We went through all the confirmations, and the documentation was good, so were the numbers. The transaction was well within the regulations and our capital requirements. All I can tell you is that Shiprite is my reason for anxiety. Don't you think I ought to tell the board and call the FBI?"

"I don't think so, Baxter; don't do that yet. I need to think about this. At least you're alert to what may be going on. Get copies of the papers in both loan packages, and let's plan to look at them next week. Maybe we can figure out what's going on. Get Bea Jay to do that, but don't tell her or anyone else your suspicions; just make a duplicate set."

Other than Dolph's stated and obvious personal reasons for not wanting the FBI swarming on the bank, he wanted Shiprite's cashier's check collected and the funds moved out of Bax's present rat hole account to protect Trimmer from any other schemes. One day Baxter might have to satisfy the government boys that he was a victim and a dumb dupe. Now the problem, however, was to protect the bank.

Cavanaugh remained in Trimmer's car while Baxter went in to take care of business. When Baxter returned, he explained that he had also signed off on closing out the account when Shiprite's check fully cleared. Before picking up Dolph that morning, Baxter telephoned one of his banking colleagues in Austin and asked that signature cards and new account information be sent by overnight mail to his home address. Everything should be in place by the middle of next week.

On Baxter's tab, Dolph enjoyed his first beef in over a week, a 10-ounce rib eye at one of the few remaining Steak and Ale restaurants. Lemon juice was the only dressing on the modest salad. The suspicion that Corrine even had informants in Lake Jackson poked his present feelings of nobility.

CHAPTER 27

Sometimes Don't Open The Doors

The restaurant business demands a lot of time and attention. Location is vital, but it's not really everything. The place needs to be open and ready for service, even if nobody walks through the door. Over the years, Hannah had learned when the traffic would be light. Sometimes she took a calculated chance and left matters in Birdie's hands with a light wait staff and kitchen help.

This Friday had been heavier than usual with the luncheon crowd. There were a lot of folks from Houston getting a head start on the weekend and a bunch of locals. As the pressure eased after 2 p.m., Hannah developed a mind-numbing headache. She was unsure of its source, but figured that Birdie needed to come in and take over. He could make the decision later about cutting staff based on what the evening crowd was, but she believed business would be sparse.

Locals were unlikely to come back that night for a second round and instead would do something else, eat home or go to a movie. In the fall, the Friday night mania for high-school football stripped most eating-places by 7 p.m. The school year now was drawing to a close, and some families were beginning to hold back on dining out and other entertainment anticipating summer vacation expenses; a few might also press their kids to study for final examinations. Yes, she was certain that this evening, things would be unremarkable.

Birdie checked in a little before 4 and a half hour later, Hannah had returned to her home five miles away, taken aspirin and gone to bed. True to her expectations, the evening revenues were slight. A little after Wheel of Fortune, Janie Farmer came into the restaurant dressed in loose fitting long pants and an old T-shirt with faded lettering. Over that outfit, she wore her trademark blue robe and pink slippers. One item was missing; she forgot her false teeth.

The light was fading outside, and Birdie correctly assumed she was there for leftovers. When he realized she did not have her false teeth, he asked if she preferred some gumbo or the navy bean soup they had on tonight's menu. Understandably, Mrs. Farmer's dignity was important to Birdie, with or without false teeth. She sat at the bar stool nearest the cash register. They carried on a conversation, of sorts, for a few minutes while waiting on the bean soup. This was only mildly difficult for Birdie; over time, he had learned to interpret her words when her dentures were missing. When the soup came, he moved away to do some other work; he was not inclined to listen as she enjoyed her meal.

Just past dusk, a man came unaccompanied into Hannah's; nothing unusual about that. What was unusual was his clothing for a Friday evening on the coast. He had on a dark blue business suit and tie. The suit was fading from wear over years or perhaps from the man wearing it too often. The tie was drab and plain. The man was slender and graying. His already thin hair was short on the sides, but it had just enough top length to be combed over. He wore rimless eyeglasses that covered his small, dark eyes. When escorted to his table, he sat without removing his coat. He did not fit Hannah's usual customer profile.

Toey, who volunteered to work this slow evening, waited on him. She rolled her eyes as she came back to the kitchen pass through. She muttered as she placed the slip of paper on a spindle.

"A guy comes all the way down here for a well-done hamburger patty and dry salad. Why spend the money or waste our time?"

As quickly as she commented, she returned to the dining area sporting her usual bright smile. Janie continued slurping her soup. When she was done, she asked Birdie for a second helping. About that time, the hamburger patty and dry salad were ready. Toey brought Janie her second bowl, this time with some French bread from which she had carved the dry crusts. Birdie delivered the man's plate, inquiring if everything was satisfactory. The man looked at his plate and then at Birdie; his only response was a nod. Birdie kept his distance from Janie and the man.

Toey glanced over as the man ate. He stabbed everything very deliberately as though he was spearing fish. His mouth would not open until the fork was almost to his lips and then only long enough for the portion to be thrown into his mouth. His jaws worked the food mechanically; his face was expressionless. She thought he was some kind of perverted creature from the Terminator movies. Choosing the appropriate time, she went over to his table and asked if he needed anything else. It was difficult for her to smile, but she managed it. She left his check and cleared the table. Without leaving a tip, he headed for the cash register.

As he stood waiting for Thurman to come out of the kitchen, Janie continued eating her soup and bread. In these circumstances, Janie was not tuned to the negatives of speaking and eating at the same time. They were, as far as she was concerned, compatible activities. The man was repulsed. That was not enough; what Janie said, as far as was understandable, was even less congenial.

"Don't know why any white man would come down here and eat no burger when they's much better on the menu. You might try the gumbo some time." Marketing was not one of Janie's talents.

Anger flashed across the man's face.

"Why don't you shut up, you old bag?" He spoke softly.

About then Thurman came from the kitchen and saw a look on Janie's face that was pure shock.

"May I help you, sir?" Correctly guessing that Janie had offended the man, he added, "Please don't mind Mrs. Farmer; she is an occasional patron here. I'm sure she meant no harm."

Whatever initially bothered the man about Janie immediately passed. As the man tendered cash and change was returned, he asked, "Would this woman, by any chance, be Jane Farmer?"

"Yes she is; may I ask why you are interested?"

"Don't tell this man nothing Birdie. He was ugly to me."

Thurman raised a cautioning hand towards Janie.

Ignoring her, the man focused on Thurman.

Cracking a slight smile, the man reached into his inside jacket pocket retrieving a folded sheet of paper. "And you are probably Mr. Birdwell?"

"Well, yes; why are you asking?" Long dormant alarms began ringing within Birdie's brain.

Now ignoring Birdie, the man turned to Janie. "I want to talk to you alone."

Janie was pulling her robe tightly around her frail body as if shielding against a chill. "I'm not talkin' to you, mister. You're a mother..."

Thurman's hand went up again stopping her response.

"Sir, perhaps it's not a good idea for you to speak with Mrs. Farmer under these circumstances. She's upset and should have someone with her if the matters you wish to discuss are important and possibly complex. I'm sure you understand this."

Studying Thurman, the smile became a smirk. "Are you some kind of lawyer, this woman's lawyer?"

Thurman's body began to tremble. "Well yes, if she wishes me to be."

"That's right. I sho' do," raising her chin towards the man, "Mister Birdie's my lawyer." She gave a proud and abrupt nod. Janie never had her own lawyer.

"Well, Counselor Thurman Birdwell, maybe you and I need to have a private chat as well. Will you step outside with me, perhaps on the front deck?"

Janie saw the two men walk out onto the deck and pass out of view towards the unlighted side of the building. Toey came over and asked Janie what was going on. Just as Janie was about to explain, a scream came from near the ramp that led down to the pier. Janie and Toey froze for a moment. Then, a second scream wailed, and Toey grabbed a telephone under the cash register. As she dialed, she heard another voice; it was Junior yelling up from the dock. She heard running footsteps and Junior's clearer voice saying, "Toey, Seferina, someone call the cops."

By the time Toey got off the phone with the sheriff's office, she heard a car leave the oyster shell parking lot. Junior came in through the kitchen.

"Did you get ahold of the law? Birdie is out there hurt. I can't tell what's wrong with him; he's just shaking all over and kind of curled up. We need to call Hannah. That man had a gun. "

Janie Farmer had remained seated at the counter taking in the drama around her. Confusion and fear marked her face. Finally, it was too much for her, and she began moaning. Crossing her arms on the counter, she sobbed, and then moved her hands to catch her bowing head, "Oh Mr. Birdie, please don't be hurt. Oh God, please help Mr. Birdie. He's a good white man."

Thirty minutes later, sheriff's patrol units arrived at Hannah's. Hannah Gregory beat them by 15 minutes. In the span between Toey's second call and Hannah's arrival, the few remaining patrons had paid up and cleared out. Not unlike other parts of the nation on Friday nights, folks around Sargent avoid interviews with law enforcement representatives. Toey had also called the Cavanaugh home and spoken to Corrine.

Junior helped Birdie to a table near where the man had been served. Birdie trembled as tears rolled down his gaunt cheeks. He made no sounds, and his eyes seemed unfocused.

"He looks like he's gone away. Miss Hannah, I don't think he can hear us. We've got to do something." Toey was close to tears.

The deputies fanned out around the property looking for culprits without success. Realizing that most of the lawmen did not need to stick around the scene, all but one car drove off into the night, leaving the senior deputy to sort things out. He might even get a shrimp and oyster po' boy for his efforts.

Deputy Rufus Walton, in his early 50s, surrounded his large stomach with a wide pistol belt cinched in enough to spill fat in all directions. He wore 3X chest protection under his shirt. Dangling from the belt were a .380 Walther PPK, two extra ammunition magazines, a cylinder of Mace, handcuffs, a stun gun and a little radio. All that extra gear added more than 20 pounds to his weight. Typically for Rufus, one cuff of his dark brown uniform trousers failed to fall neatly over his polished dark cowboy boots. His uniform shirt, light tan, sported a whistle, a nametag and what looked to be like a bunch of Boy Scout Merit badges. A generous Stetson, beige, covered his beefy head. Despite the first impression from his regalia, Rufus was a competent peace officer and a good man. Among his friends, he was also known as Festus and sometimes Burl. Tush Hogs around the county called him Mister Walton and rarely tested his patience or authority. Others had regretted doing so.

The deputy briefly interviewed Toey, Seferina and Junior. Seferina knew nothing until Junior burst through the back door of the kitchen. She had been wearing radio headphones and listening to Latin music from one of the local stations. Junior heard the screams, but he could not see what was going on in the darkness of the back deck. He did see a hand holding what looked like a pistol pointing toward the slope of the ramp from the dock. Junior dove behind a stack of empty ice chests; hiding until he heard someone running along the deck. By the time he got to Birdie, the other man was gone. Janie's interview was deferred until dentures were available.

Walton then attempted to speak to Thurman but got no response. He shined his flashlight on Thurman's head and neck, and he then gently unbuttoned Birdie's shirt. The others wondered what the officer was looking for. His meaty hands moved the sides of the shirt away from Thurman's body. Birdie showed no reaction to this probing. Just as deftly, Walton re-buttoned Thurman's shirt.

Turning to the group, he asked, "How many screams did you hear?"

All of them said two, although Janie waited to give her answer after the others.

"Has anyone been able to talk to him since this happened?" Everyone shook their heads.

"Birdie has two red marks on him; one under his left rib cage and the other on the edge of his left jaw. It looks like he was pinched in both areas, more like clamped. My guess is that he was brought to his knees by the first and held in place by the second. I think old Birdie just got a taste of some darker tricks of martial arts."

Hannah was the first to ask, "Who in the world would to this to Birdie? This sweet old man would never hurt anyone. What should we do?"

Deputy Walton, speaking to the group said, "Anybody know who this fellow was?"

Everybody shook heads.

"Ma'am, I don't think he needs medical attention, but someone needs to watch him for a while until he gets himself back together. Maybe we can interview him later. Without a better idea of what happened and a vehicle description, there's not much we can do except file a report."

As Deputy Walton was making notes on a pad, Dolph strode into the restaurant and made straight for Hannah.

"What's going on Hannah? Corrine said Birdie was hurt."

Hannah told Dolph as best she could what had happened. Toey contributed her views and concluded that the man was a bum for hurting Birdie. Dolph walked over to Janie and, placing a gentle hand on her shoulder, asked if she was all right.

"I'm okay, Mr. Dolph. I just pray that Mr. Birdie is gonna' be better. And I hope they get that…" she rolled her eyes. Everyone knew what she wanted to say.

"Don't you worry about that Janie. Festus will get him; you can count on that."

Toey answered the ringing telephone. "Mr. Cavanaugh, it's for you."

When he took the phone in hand, he thought it was Corrine calling for an update. No, it was Momma. He gave her a brief description of the events,an assessment of Birdie's situation and then listened.

"Sure enough, Momma. I will take care of that. Don't worry. I'll see you after a while."

As he returned the phone to Toey, he looked at Hannah and Deputy Walton and said, "If you don't have any better ideas, I'm going to take Thurman to Momma's. She has a little guest cottage across the driveway. Thurman can stay there until things settle down."

"Dolph, that sounds fine. Hannah, if you'd check on him with Mrs. Wilson and let me know when he can talk, I'll get right out there," Deputy Walton concluded.

"Well, if we're done here, let's close up. Toey, you get on home to Big Joe, and thanks for being here. Festus, do you want a little food for the road?"

Walton smiled, and Dolph looked a little hopeful.

"Not you, Dolph. My deal with Corrine still stands."

CHAPTER 28

Uncle Buddy and Other Family

"What's this 'Charles' stuff? I'm looking for Uncle Buddy, or is he too lazy to work on Saturdays?"

C.W. Rogers had inherited his father's initials and the nickname of Uncle Buddy. No one in his hometown of Muleshoe, Texas, ever correctly knew what C. W. stood for, and Dolph never asked. He and Dolph had done deals in the old days, but Uncle Buddy had dropped that life and was now selling cars and trucks at the Ford dealership in Portales, New Mexico. Dolph knew the voice over the telephone and now learned CW's first name.

"You want to buy a car or talk about family names? I've got a brand new Ford F-250 with a heavy suspension just right to haul your big butt." He was already chuckling. In their long friendship, telephone cordialities never prevailed over gentle insults.

A year after Dolph's discharge from the Navy, Uncle Buddy came onto his path. C.W. had completed nine months of credits in three years at a junior college in Levelland, Texas, and was once again nearly broke. In Arkansas, Dolph's veteran status did him little good in getting a real job given the attitude about Vietnam vets in those days. He didn't even have a stash of money from other pursuits.

When he got back to his patrol division after R&R, he shut down all of his part-time commission business and focused on his duties as a Swift Boat sailor. Good thing too, because no sooner had he returned to the 59 Boat than they and 14 other boats went on a very bad raid on the Song Bo De that got a bunch of guys killed along with a whole mess of NVA. Mr. Taylor and the Ensign on the 37 Boat, known as Double Bourbon, brought both crews through unscathed. Dolph never once thought he would die. The morning that the operation ended, their two boats made the sad journey back to Sadec with the 37 Boat carrying the corpse of one of the other boat officers.

Still, Seaman Cavanaugh went to Mr. Taylor and thanked him for bringing them through. Taylor was surprised at the comment. Cavanaugh had never made a personal remark to him by way of praise, gratitude or complaint.

"You're welcome, but we did this together. That's the only way we get by. You seem almost happy, Cavanaugh. What gives?"

"Well Sir, it's like this. I have been scared to death for the past two months, and I'm over that. Dying isn't the worst thing that can happen to me, but being afraid of life's dangers is."

* * *

Being broke isn't any fun, but you might as well enjoy what you can. That was Dolph's mantra when he met C.W. at a truck stop in Levelland. They were both pumping gas into their cars. C.W. had $98 in his dirty jeans pocket after buying half a tank for his old Chevrolet pickup. Dolph had $182 and a full tank for his dusty 1967 Chevrolet El Camino.

"Where you going today?" C.W. asked. He saw baggage in the back.

"I'm driving straight through to Las Vegas."

"You don't need a tank of gas to get there; it's just 150 miles away."

"Naw, man, I'm going to Nevada." They laughed and then finished gassing in silence.

"You want to park that piece of junk and come along with me? Maybe we can win some money together. It'll cost you the next refill." To this day Dolph never figured why he extended the invitation.

"I guess I ought to go along just to see that you don't stop in Las Vegas, New Mexico. Besides, there isn't anything there." He paused, looking around. "Shoot, there isn't anything here either."

Dolph followed Uncle Buddy about six blocks to a run-down, unpainted, one-room, little stucco-covered house surrounded by nothing but a lawn of dirt and dried tufts of weeds. C.W. pitched some things in a little bag and was out the door. He didn't even lock the door; there was nothing worth stealing.

Las Vegas in those days was a real deal. You could check in to a big hotel, eat and drink cheap and lose every dime you had in a heartbeat. This wasn't the case with these boys. By the end of their first night, they were up nearly $4,500 playing Black Jack. They bought some nice clothes and paid for their room in advance for three more days. Finally, they stuffed another $500 each in the El Camino's glove box.

The second night ended at 5 a.m. They were up only another $1,800. They woke up a little after noon and sat around the swimming pool talking about their past and their intended future.

C.W. had been kicking around the Texas Panhandle ever since graduating from Muleshoe High School. He kept enrolling at the junior college, picking up a few hours in the process, but he always wandered off. His family gave up on him, at least financially. At that time, he had an ex-wife and daughter living in Plainview, Texas. The ex-wife had her own issues; drugs, he thought, and C.W. gave up on her. C.W. confessed that he believed his highest and best career employment would be in the livestock feedlots dotting the Edwards Plateau. Military service had never been an option since C.W. suffered from asthma. Asthma hadn't stopped C.W. from hard work or play. Tall and lanky with a flat tail and a slight beer belly, C.W. was one of those cowboy caricatures you find in drugstore greeting card humor sections.

Dolph thought he was listening to another version of himself before the Navy and before Singapore. What C.W. needed were some victories in his life.

From C.W.'s point of view, his attraction to Dolph was founded in admiration of a cousin, Ronnie Lee, from New Home, Texas, who was killed while piloting a helicopter for the Navy. He was convinced that if Ronnie Lee had lived, the two of them would have been lifelong friends and C.W.'s life might have been very different. Being around Dolph was like being with Ronnie Lee.

That night, they went up an additional $2,500, and Dolph decided to turn in a little after 2 a.m. At 6:15 a.m., CW returned to the room excited and happy. Dolph rose on one elbow to hear the good news.

"Dolph this has been the greatest time of my life. In the last two hours I've lost every cent we have."

"Even the money in the glove box?" Dolph asked, now wide-awake.

"I forgot about that." He grinned. "Besides, you have the keys anyway."

C.W. pulled up the mini-blinds flooding desert light into the room. "Man, I feel great."

"Feel great later. Get some sleep now. I'm going to the pool. We'll check out of here this afternoon."

* * *

"Corrine already has one of those loud trucks; don't need a second one." He paused while C.W. snorted. "I really called to talk. It's been a few years, Uncle Buddy. How's your health?"

"I've got a little blood pressure problem, but I'm fine otherwise."

"And your family?" Dolph knew that Uncle Buddy had re-married some years back, a good German girl from northern Colorado. She didn't know his past, but she helped him find religion. Uncle Buddy actually always had a lot of religion, without understanding what any of it meant. Time and that good German girl made the difference.

"Trudy passed two years ago; they said it was an aneurysm."

Dolph was stunned. All he could mange to say was, "God."

C.W. was silent for a moment. "My daughter from that first marriage graduated from Texas Tech with a degree in chemistry. She's working for an oil and gas company in Midland and married a lawyer. I'm glad I was able to help her along the way. I even have a grandson."

There was one of those quiet moments when both men knew the small talk was at an end. Cavanaugh sensed that C.W. wanted to move on.

"If you're available, I've got a little work for you down here in Bay City. I need you to do some things that I can't do without raising questions."

"Country Boy, you know I've given up on all that. No more deals. I promised myself that a long time ago."

"Did you give up on honest work, or do you just like schmoozing old farmers into new trucks? I didn't say this was one of my deals because it's not. If you come down here for a few weeks and hang out, I'll pay your expenses plus ten grand up front and ten when we're finished. You can quit any time, no questions asked and no refunds required."

"This must be serious, Dolph. You're talking real money and honest purposes at that?"

"C.W., this is serious bidness. Someone is messing with my town and my friends. I don't know what to do, but we'll be on the other side this time. Can you help out?"

C.W. did not immediately answer. "Let me see what I can arrange. If I'm in, I'll be in touch. Otherwise, I hope things work out for you."

"Fair enough Uncle Buddy. I'll be looking for you."

"Yeah."

Cavanaugh had a feeling his old friend would show up in a few days. The spark in C.W's voice had been absent in the early part of their conversation, but it returned with the prospect of doing a deal, even if it was righteous.

They would have one or two meetings at first and then probably not see each other again, if at all, until the work was completed. Despite being tired from last night's action with Birdie and staying up late with Momma getting Thurman settled in, Corrine had rousted him out for a jog and light breakfast. After speaking with C.W., Dolph realized that his muscle pains were gone.

CHAPTER 29

Rules to Live By

After leaving Vegas, Dolph and Uncle Buddy tried a little of everything but dope and dirty women. In Los Angeles they sold advertising for phony police association magazines; they worked boiler room operations in Tulsa and Oklahoma City selling oil development interests to out-of-state investors. These promotions weren't effectively regulated by the state authorities and were only casually monitored by the U. S. Securities and Exchange Commission. Such investments fell below federal and state radar screens. In those days, doing securities scams was easier if you could find a gap between what was regulated, by whom were they regulated and how strongly existing rules were enforced. The best deals of all were those that took advantage of differences in the regulatory philosophies of the Feds and the states. Nothing lasts forever.

The boys, little more than well-paid telephone operators, always sensed when the time came to quit their jobs and move on. Their employers always stayed until the doors crashed in and indictments fell like hail on a tin roof. In one year the boys had nothing to show for their efforts but two new cars, some nice clothes and decent tans.

Dolph actually had a little something mostly non-perishable to show for his efforts. In their travels across country, he looked for real-estate parcels in economically depressed small towns. If he found one on good terms, he would buy it on a contract for deed that meant he was at risk only if he failed to timely make payments. For many folks, that is risky business, but for Dolph, it was perfect. His down payments in shady cash only went to the seller's hands or maybe a bank, and were always less than bank reporting regulations. He never missed payments and often paid off the relatively small notes on an accelerated basis. Until the seller's deed was signed and delivered to Dolph, nothing was recorded.

In that single year, Dolph took title to an old vacant hotel in Jerome, Arizona, and five acres of raw land on the north side of the highway leading into Clovis, New Mexico, from Muleshoe. He had contracts working on two other parcels in eastern Colorado and western Oklahoma. These deals were better than savings accounts; his money was stuck in the land and could not be withdrawn unless the property appreciated. He might have to wait, but it would be worth it.

Dolph was the first to speak about ending their adventures out West. They were passing through Denver staying at the Brown Palace.

"C.W., we're getting nowhere. We need to make some changes, get some real jobs and stop this stuff. I've had a lot of fun, but it's time to grow up. What do you think, Uncle Buddy?"

"Suits me. I'd just as soon stop in Lubbock. Doing all this conning ought to be worth something in a real job. Maybe I could finish college at Tech."

"It has been a good run, but I agree. If we do this much longer, we're going to be dead men or wearing white uniforms, and I want nothing of that. I've still got my GI Bill. I'll head on to Houston. I hear the town is growing like crazy and the University of Houston is easy to get into. Getting a real education and real jobs is better than this."

Later than evening, after they had eaten dinner and were sitting in the bar, both men felt they had turned a corner but were looking back.

"Suppose we decide we want to do another deal?" C.W. asked.

"I was thinking that same thing. Maybe we ought to think up some rules, stuff that we keep to ourselves." By the end of the evening, two duplicate cocktail napkins contained their contract with one another and the future:

Work only on big deals, not small ones.

Don't get greedy or repetitive.

Quit on the vote of one.

Take no associates; uninformed subcontractors are okay.

Do deals only to those who deserve it.

Have a plan going in and coming out of a deal.

Never mess with the military or their families if we can help it.

Don't abuse or overuse identities.

Don't abuse the help, tip well but not excessively.

Always be polite and good-natured.

Confide in no one.

Never brag.

Never do deals in the home state.

Never do drugs or dirty legs.

Never cheat on a spouse.

Never involve family or friends.

Have no social contacts with one another.

Do no violence.

Quit when it's no longer fun or gets dangerous.

Enjoy life.

Live otherwise regular and separate lives.

It's only money.

CHAPTER 30
Fire in the Hole

One summer three years later, C.W. contacted Dolph and wanted to talk about a plan he had to separate a bunch of cash from some dope heads in Santa Fe. C.W.'s ex-wife, Crystal, was living there with their daughter. She worked at a motorcycle shop and had fallen in with some bad people, he learned. C.W. had driven from Lubbock to Crystal's Santa Fe apartment to pick up his little girl for a court-ordered two-week visitation. Until then he only had suspicions about the extent of Crystal's drug use.

When he arrived, she was all whacked out. She had lost weight and was chain-smoking cigarettes. Trying to act normal, she was failing miserably. Maybe she was bragging or just dreaming, but she told him about going with her boyfriend a couple of nights before to get something from an old frame house she described on the east side of town. Nobody lived there, but while he was in the bathroom, she wandered around. In a back bedroom she saw a green plastic sheet covering what appeared to be a double bed. She pulled back the plastic, intending to wait on the bed for her boyfriend's usual demands. Instead she saw Chiquita banana boxes arranged carefully to simulate a bed's dimensions. According to Crystal, when she looked in one of the boxes, she saw a bunch of money carefully packed in baggies. Before she could look in the other boxes, her boyfriend was slapping her back-handed and front as he told her to forget what she thought she saw.

C.W. told her that was good advice and that she ought to pack up and go back to Lubbock with him or to Plainview where her parents and a brother lived. She refused. When he left her apartment with their little girl, Vicky, he vowed never to return the child to those conditions. He would go to the Hale County Court in Plainview to get full custody of Vicky. He hired a lawyer there to file a motion and got out of state service on Crystal. She never appeared or contested in any way the change he requested.

C.W. went back to Santa Fe on two occasions, the first time to get things belonging to Vicky. He heard from Crystal's brother that she had lost her job and moved in with some guy, a truck driver for Walmart. By the time C.W. located her and Vicky's things, she was really looking sick and malnourished. It was clear that in time, Crystal would pass permanently out of Vicky's life.

Then and later on the second trip, C.W. set up a modest nighttime surveillance of the doper's old house. It sat at the back of a dead end dirt road on about two acres. It had been a farmhouse maybe a half century ago. Barbed wire fencing around the place was torn and ineffective. Three hundred feet beyond the dead end, through some scrub brush and weeds, was East Zia Road that ran up a hill and parallel to the property. From the top of the hill in daytime, one could see the house and its surrounding grounds. So far as C.W. could see, whenever he passed that way, there were no daytime visitors. C.W. parked his pickup a quarter of a mile away on Zia and made his way into the brush over three consecutive nights the first time and two nights the second time.

Sure enough, true to Crystal's recollections, a lone motorcyclist would drive there and remain inside for no longer than 10 minutes.

One night, two men in a beat up van with what appeared to be Mexican license plates pulled up in the weed- choked driveway and carried a small suitcase in and four boxes out. CW was convinced that the house was a storage facility for cash and dope. His plan was to go in, take the money and destroy the dope.

"C.W., that sounds like a mighty dangerous situation. We have no assurance that the place still has anything worthwhile in there. For all we know, it's wired or something. How do you think we can do this?"

"We won't. The power company will. My white pickup will do just fine with some borrowed New Mexico plates and one of those removable plastic signs on the side. We'll just drive down the road in broad daylight, break into the house and haul away with what we can in less than 15 minutes, just like bad guys."

There wasn't anything slick about this job, no flim-flam, no smooth talking and no safety. It was nothing more than a daylight burglary and theft, but Dolph was in because it was in a good cause.

The deal went off without a hitch. When they broke through the back door late one afternoon, they found approximately 23 boxes of bagged marijuana, a variety of colored pills and capsules, also separately bagged, and a suitcase of white powdery stuff in small zip lock bags. All this was in the bedroom described by Crystal. A further search of other rooms disclosed three banana boxes containing loose and bagged cash in a hall closet.

Interestingly, the bathroom medicine cabinet contained personal use quantities of all of the merchandise, kind of an employees' snack bar. There was also a box of 9mm ammunition and a Soviet Markarov semi-automatic pistol. They dumped the contents of the cash boxes into two big duffle bags they carried and threw into the back of the pickup. The contents of the suitcase and the rest of the banana boxes were piled up in the middle of the living room floor. Time was running short; a more detailed search of the house was not possible. As they left the house, C.W. turned on the gas heater in the bathroom, and Dolph did the same with the kitchen range. Dolph ejected the Markarov's magazine and emptied its contents and the other ammunition onto the top of the pile. He then stuffed the empty pistol into the center of the pile. Dolph's last act before walking out the front door was to leave a burning cigar propped in a box of kitchen matches near some old curtains in the dining room.

They were 20 minutes away when the house blew up. The only sign of anything odd when the fire trucks arrived were fresh tire marks through the scrub brush and some muddy tracks up onto Zia Road heading east. Down a few hundred feet, C.W. had made a careful U-turn back to the west and U.S. Highway 285 South where it connected to Interstate 40 East. In subsequent years, Santa Fe's sprawl would obliterate the scene. There was one hitch, however. The dopers' cash was mostly in the small denominations. When they got back into Texas, it took them almost two days to count and sort the cash. They split $648,000, but it took almost two years to convert those little bills into effectively spendable bank notes. Dolph never spent his take; he just shipped his by DHL to the Laundress in a box marked "school supplies."

Dolph spoke to C.W. a week after their deal. He said the Santa Fe New Mexican, the town's newspaper, reported a suspicious house fire accompanied by gunfire east of town, and that authorities were seeking to find the owner of the property. In an unrelated report, killings among some particular motorcycle gangs had dramatically increased. When Dolph asked about Crystal's health, C.W. fell silent for a moment.

"Well Dolph, her brother told me she's dead now. He said the cops told him she had been a truck-stop whore for quite a while. They're still investigating her death."

CHAPTER 31

Doin' the Lord's Work

Another deal was a little less risky. By then Dolph had married Corrine, and they had their first son on the way. He was still putting his spare cash from his real-estate commissions into distressed properties in little towns and occasionally, acreage. By then he only bought dirt that also conveyed the mineral interests. While they were living in Houston, they spent a lot of time in Bay City with Corrine's parents. Mr. Wilson was a fine father-in-law who enjoyed goose and duck hunting and fishing on Big Lake and occasionally along Matagorda Bay. He got along well with Dolph.

Mrs. Wilson in those days was more cheerful, but she knew even then what she liked and what she didn't. One Saturday afternoon, she mentioned that a college girlfriend of hers who now lived in Long Island, New York, had been victimized by a preacher fellow up there and had lost over half a million dollars to this gigolo in clergy clothing. The woman had never married and presided over what amounted to about a $15 Million inherited trust fund. The loss was more significant to her soul.

Bitterness and the pain of unfulfilled emotions in her spinster years had weakened her defenses to the kind of sharks that are ever-present and circling the wealthy. In the guise of professed love and affection, this clergyman had induced the poor woman to make a charitable donation and a modest bequest in the event of her death to a non-profit, feel-good seminar outfit of which he was the sole employee. This was a sideline to his well-compensated pastoral duties at the ancient establishment church the woman attended.

Of course, he promised to divorce his wife of 30 years, but only after his retirement in order to avoid the unnecessary tongue wagging that would compromise his position and, of course, his benefactor's reputation. Retirement and its consequent benefits came, the wife remained and the preacher fled with his non-profit company to the pleasant and verdant hills of western North Carolina.

Mrs. Wilson's old girlfriend was then sinking into her final sad months of life, having been recently diagnosed with advanced lung cancer. This caused Mrs. Wilson to speculate that an unhappy life filled with suspicions and disappointment were as much a factor in the onset and success of diseases as anything.

The story left Dolph seething and contemplating a good revenge. By the middle of the next week, he had identified the preacher by name and found his residence in Asheville, North Carolina. He recruited and briefed C.W. about their next noble cause and set about planning how they would take this man down and what roles he and C.W. would play to do so.

This scheme too was simple, and while it had risks, they were limited. Dolph posed as a bookish, fumbling IRS compliance auditor whose limited duties were to verify the propriety of non-profit, particularly charitable, organization expenditures. Armed with a fraudulent but official-looking identification card and badge and an equally fraudulent Notice of Examination, Dolph quickly gained access to the preacher's books and records. He even used the taxpayer's copy machine to make a complete set of those records, including his check register. Dolph left cash to pay for the paper he used. Compliantly pleasing people had been the preacher's particular talent to induce trust. No less so had he treated this Internal Revenue Service functionary. Dolph left the man with assurances that everything appeared to be in order and that a letter so stating would be forthcoming. Among the items in Dolph's briefcase were the back two sheets of checks removed from the victim's book, 6 in all and a conveniently retained copy of the clergy's signature card when he opened the account.

Almost immediately a forged check for $50,000 was cashed by C.W., dressed in preacher clothing and collar and cosmetically posing as the man himself. The other five checks were made out in liberal amounts and mailed to various organizations for abused women and children leaving a little over $100 in the account. All of those checks fluttered in and cleared within the next few days. The preacher was peppered with effusive thank you notes and phone calls for his fine contributions. When his bank statement arrived, confusion was replaced by embarrassed outrage. He had been had.

When he went to the bank and protested the transactions, they said they would investigate the matter. The teller clearly identified him as the person who cashed the $50,000 check. When he went to the IRS local office on Patton Avenue in Asheville to report the fraud of their employees, he was ushered into an interview room where two IRS Criminal Investigations agents questioned him. There was something unexpected in their demeanor. Soon they produced a large mailing envelope containing the records copied by Dolph along with a carefully typed but unsigned invitation to look very carefully at the preacher's contributors and expenditures. The writer suggested that the preacher's frauds were far greater than those who exposed him. With unconcealed smiles, the agents suggested that he should retain counsel for what they anticipated would be a long engagement.

Over the next few months, the minister's lawyer, originally retained to keep the preacher out of jail, had to sue the bank and the five charitable recipients. Document examiners in the civil case reaped lovely fees arguing over the validity of his signatures to the point of a nice division between them being genuine or perhaps forged. One examiner even expressed the view that the check made to cash was genuine, but intentionally crafted to look forged. The preacher settled his lawsuits, getting only enough money back to pay his lawyers.

The final and lasting humiliation was a weeklong set of news articles in the Asheville paper. Even worse for the preacher, *The New York Times* picked up on the story, savoring every confused detail of what they titled "Clergy Scam", including wild speculation about the identities of the persons who wrecked the preacher's life. Needless to say, the hierarchy of his denomination was not inclined to discuss the matter or to acknowledge that his was not the first situation to come to their attention in recent years. The preacher also got his divorce, but not as he had promised. Unfortunately, Momma's friend had already gone to glory. Under the circumstances, the preacher gave up any claim to the decedent's estate.

Less expenses out of the $50,000, C.W. and Dolph again divided their winnings and disappeared. As always, Dolph mailed his take at a book rate to the Laundress with a phony return address. After all, it was only money.

CHAPTER 32

At Loose Ends

Despite the early morning workout and talk with Uncle Buddy, Dolph's energies were fading from last night's trip to Hannah's and getting Birdie bedded down. And yet there was just too much going on for him to nap. He figured to go over to Momma's and check on Birdie and then out to Hannah's to see what was going on.

About mid-morning, his Suburban rumbled over the cattle guard onto Momma's property. As he swung into the parking apron, Dolph saw Momma and Birdie sitting on two wooden Adirondack chairs out on the shaded lawn. They were drinking coffee. Mrs. Wilson was dressed in jeans, a denim blouse decorated with embroidered little red flowers mixed with bluebonnets nesting in grass blades, and what she called her garden clogs. Birdie was still in his slacks from the night before, but now he was wearing a fresh khaki shirt buttoned at the cuffs and collar. Dolph recognized Mr. Wilson's trademark work shirt.

"Randolph, I'm glad you're here. I was about to call you. Mr. Birdwell has decided he needs to go back to his apartment."

Birdie began to rise. "I don't want to impose further on your kindness, Mrs. Wilson."

"Nonsense. I was fixing to put on my tennis shoes and take him to the Weldinghaus." She turned to Dolph. "He'd enjoy that, but if he insists, you can drop him off at his place."

Dolph was pleased to see that Birdie looked better than the night before. He noticed some stacked breakfast dishes on a tray covering a little slatted table between the two chairs and was glad that someone had a hearty country breakfast. Corrine gave Dolph yogurt and fruit.

"Well, it's up to you, Thurman. I'm at your disposal. I'm calling Hannah in a few minutes and might run down there. You can come along if you're up to it."

"I appreciate your offer, Mr. Cavanaugh, but perhaps we could visit here a while."

Mrs. Wilson took the hint and rose from her chair. Gathering the tray and dishes, she headed to the back door of her home.

"You men take your time. I'm going to put on a little more color and be out of here. Perhaps I'll see you again, Mr. Birdwell."

"Thank you Mrs. Wilson. I'll return the shirt later, if that's all right." Birdie got no reply. Elizabeth Wilson was already inside the house. Dolph and Birdie stood there for a while; it was a bit awkward for both. Finally Dolph gestured to the chair that Birdie had used and took Momma's place. Birdie rubbed his face with one hand. Dolph could see that he was put out with himself for not being clean-shaven that morning.

"What do you have on your mind, Thurman? And by the way, I appreciate your formality with me, but I'd be more comfortable if you'd call me Dolph or Randolph as Momma sometimes does."

"Your mother-in-law is a fine lady; I've never met her before last night. You must feel blessed."

"Thanks Thurman, but perhaps you're unaware that she has been known to show another side."

Birdie looked at his lap for a moment and slightly smiled. "We all have other sides that we don't often show. Sometimes it's for the best, but in Mrs. Wilson's case, I see a person entitled to great respect."

Dolph didn't feel exactly chastised, but knew that J. Thurman too, was a person due respect. There was another moment of awkwardness.

"Randolph, please accept my gratitude for your help last night. I felt very small and impotent. As age advances for us, I believe we are less able to recover from physical violence or verbal assaults to our self-image. I was lucky that you and Miss Hannah were there to get me through."

Dolph now was embarrassed and at a loss as to what to say. Men, he thought, didn't talk this way.

"Come on, Thurman, we did what anyone would have done."

"That's not always true, Randolph. Anyway, thank you."

Mr. Birdwell eased back in his chair and continued. "I know that Deputy Walton and you want to know what I remember from last night. I remember a lot. I'll call Mr. Walton when I'm ready, but because Miss Hannah thinks so highly of you, she would want me to brief you first."

"Thank you, sir."

Birdie spent a few minutes relating events Dolph had already pieced together, and, knowing Janie Farmer as all did, realized that she had unwittingly triggered the man's bad temper. Thurman, always sensitive to situations, but often silent or subdued in his responses, had tried to calm things down for the customer as well as Janie.

Something altered the dynamics that Thurman only realized just before dawn in Momma's guest cottage. The man knew names, not just informal forms of address, but complete names as though printed on official documents such as legal citations and birth certificates. He had a list, a typewritten list in his jacket pocket that Thurman only saw obliquely. When Thurman cautiously suggested more appropriate circumstances for Janie's interview, the man seemed to know even Thurman's name and prior occupation. That was when the man suggested going to the veranda for a more private discussion. Thurman had debated whether to go with the man, but decided it was better that Janie be separated from the man's hostility. Outside, things moved very quickly.

Once outside in the darkness, the man did most of the talking. He said he was a United States Postal Inspector working on a case and that he would tolerate no interference by anyone, particularly a crooked lawyer. He suggested that Birdie might want to get his own counsel, but that things would go harder on him if he did. He said the same thing was true for that "old Nigger" in there. When Thurman protested his innocence and the slurs about Janie, the man grabbed Thurman's ribcage and squeezed. Birdie fell to his knees and the man said, "You've not been paying attention, old man. I said no interference." He then took another grip on Birdie's jaw and pulled him upright. As he did so, he shoved something in Thurman's back pants pocket and said, "We'll talk later."

Birdie remembered hearing Junior's yells and the man running away. He apologized to Dolph for not speaking up last night, for not talking to Deputy Walton. He was too disappointed with his weakness. Dolph saw tears forming in the Birdie's eyes.

"Are you all right now, Thurman?" Birdie nodded.

"What did he put in your pocket? His card?" Dolph correctly guessed.

"Did you see or remember any other names on the list?"

"Yes, besides Mrs. Jane Louise Farmer and my full name, I saw Seferina Lopez and Dora Gonzales. Isn't she your housekeeper? I also saw the name of that fellow that cooks over at the KC Steakhouse; it escapes me for the moment. You call him Hubey, but his first name is Herbert."

"Good," Dolph added.

"That's right, Herbert Good. What does all that mean, Randolph?"

"I don't know about you, Thurman, but these other folks aren't high rollers; they're just working people. Can you guess about the number of names on the list?"

"Yes, I would say more than a dozen."

At that point Birdie pulled the man's business card out of his pocket and handed it to Dolph. It bore the golden symbol of the Great Seal found on dollar bills above which were written, "United States Postal Inspection Service." Beside a Houston street address on Franklin and phone numbers was a name: Culver Foxmon.

"Mind if I hold on to this for a while? There's someone I want to talk to first."

Thurman studied Dolph's eyes and understood that he should wait to disclose this piece of information to Deputy Walton. Hannah had said Dolph was to be trusted. "No, I don't mind."

"Something else, Randolph." He paused, pondering just how to express himself. "Unkindness," he paused again, "even the best of us inflict unkindness on people often without realizing it. But Mr. Foxman did this to me willingly, intentionally, and he meant to hurt me, to hurt Janie and anyone who stood in his way."

Birdie seemed to sit more erect in his chair; his chin moved forward as his shoulders came back.

"That man uncovered another side of me, one I put away years ago before I met my wife: anger. I want to get the man. Will you help me?"

"I'll try, Thurman; I'll try."

"Thank you, Randolph. You're a good man; I know you will."

Dolph's own anger had been rising. For this gentle old man, I need a plan. I need C.W., he thought. Thurman's proclamation of Dolph's goodness struck him deeply and in an unfamiliar way.

Just then, they heard the garage door lifting, and a few seconds later Momma fired up her five-year-old Cadillac and drove away, giving two hoots crossing the cattle guard.

"Admirable woman," Thurman muttered.

"I'm going in the house to call Hannah. I'll be back shortly."

The line was busy on the first and second attempts, but Hannah answered quickly on the third call.

"Dolph, I've been on the phone all morning, and I'm opening shortly. So, what you got?"

"Just been visiting with Birdie. I think he's going to be fine. What have you been on the phone about?"

"Let's talk later, but I'm checking on security lighting and cameras. I can't afford to have people hurting my help or my customers." Hannah was not in a gracious mood.

"Mrs. Gregory, perhaps I could stop by after the crowd subsides. We need to talk."

"That's fine Dolph. Sorry I'm a little short. You come on down anytime; I'll get over this in a while."

Outside, Birdie was still sitting in the chair, but he rose when Dolph approached.

"Thurman, I think I'll just run you by your place. Hannah isn't in the mood for company. Let's not get Festus involved quite yet."

*   *   *

Hannah's Saturday crowd was much larger than normal with mostly curious locals and regular weekenders. Word of last night's activities had spread quickly through law enforcement officers' wives and girlfriends. Patrons from last night, while not keen on police interviews, were more than willing to blab to friends and neighbors about what they had seen. Hannah had been peppered with questions since she opened her doors. By the time Dolph arrived, the patrons were sharing their new insights with each other as they ate.

"Dolph, you'd of thought the mayor got shot or Peoples' got robbed given all the fuss being made here today about poor old Birdie. Seems everybody is putting an interesting twist on things. Birdie is a hero; he distracted the guy from hurting Janie and took the abuse himself. You said he's going to be fine. Is that true?"

"Hannah, I picked him up at Momma's and took him back to his apartment. He's going to need some time to get his bearings. You might want to stop by and prepare him for his hero status. It can't be long before someone over at the Tribune decides to contact him."

The Bay City Tribune claimed to have been serving the county news needs since 1845. Dolph kicked himself for not thinking of that before dropping Thurman off at his place.

"Could you call over there and tell him you talked to me and that I said for him to decline interviews?" Dolph saw that Hannah was puzzled that Dolph didn't make the call. "Mrs. Gregory, I've got to go to the head; this diet that you and Corrine have me on keeps me going."

Hannah smiled and took the telephone near the cash register as

Dolph set a course for the men's room. When he returned from nature, Hannah had already set up a mixed greens salad topped with grilled Tuna strips and croutons for him at the counter. No separate bread or butter. She also had poured him a Lone Star beer in an iced-tea glass. They exchanged looks as Dolph sat.

"Now Dolph, enjoy your salad and don't forget to drink your tea. You need to keep hydrated." She and Dolph exchanged conspiratorial grins. Cavanaugh's guilt was overcome by gratitude for this deviation from Corrine's plan, but he decided not to push his good fortune. They visited as she had time to talk.

"How's Janie? It hurt seeing her so worried."

"Oh, she was over here as usual for breakfast and seemed in good spirits. She asked about Birdie and said she had prayed for him."

"You know, Hannah, Thurman may be a hero after all. Old and frail, he did get that fellow away from Janie and for that matter, Toey and Seferina."

Looking around, he could see at least three mini-cameras strategically mounted inside the place.

"Are all these operational?"

"No, the guy has just mounted them for now for show and will put more on the outside. He's going to start the wiring on Monday and should have everything hooked up by Tuesday evening. He says sticking those cameras up today will have a deterrent effect."

Dolph nodded approvingly.

"I've cleared a space for the monitoring equipment in that pantry next to the kitchen. It's got two entries, that over there and one from the kitchen. When I first used that for an office, I had air conditioning duct work run in there, and the guy says it will be just fine for his purposes."

"You going to need any help on the cost? You're going top of the line. I'd like to contribute a little something from the Special Account if you'd agree to turn off the unit looking at my table."

She threw her head back and laughed. "You can't bribe me, Dolph; I've got enough in my operating account to cover this. As for keeping a camera off you, Corrine and I have a deal. We love you to death, and we're not going to let you angle your way out of this. Just so you know, Corrine told me I could sneak you a beer."

Dolph stood and reached for his money clip. Peeling off two twenties and placing them on the counter, he smiled. "I love y'all too. Keep the change. I've got to go to the john again. See you."

Cavanaugh got home around 3 p.m. He wasn't inclined to nap, but instead got on his jogging clothes and left the house. Something was going on with his body, and he sensed he would feel better if he worked out for a while. He set out at a slow but steady pace, pondering how cluttered his life was becoming in Bay City.

He ranged around the subdivision until his second pass by the gated entry, where he turned for a slightly faster trot to the house. Lost in his thoughts and pride over this solo flight, he failed to see or hear Corrine's truck rolling up behind him. Trotting into the driveway, he nearly fell over on the grass when she hit the horn with one long blast.

His marathon effort got him no relief Sunday morning from either exercise or church. This time they were Presbyterians. That afternoon he made a call to Baxter urging him to get the papers copied, to Thurman checking on him and to Mr. Taylor at his home.

Sam Taylor answered the phone with a little gruffness in his voice, but when he realized it was Dolph, he became more cordial.

"Mr. Taylor, I'm sorry to bother you on a Sunday afternoon, but I was wondering if you could make time to see me tomorrow. I'm OK, but I need your advice on something."

"Dolph, you come on in around 11 and we can have lunch if that's on your schedule." Taylor understood that Dolph, like many clients, had an aversion to discussing substantive details over the telephone.

"Well that would be great, but Mrs. Cavanaugh has me on a diet. It would have to be something light. How is Mrs. Taylor?"

"I'm shocked, Dolph. I never thought I'd see you on a diet, but I'm also happy to know you're getting after it."

Despite the years since Vietnam, Taylor and Cavanaugh never really escaped their officer/enlisted man relationship. They were nonetheless also friends.

"How's Mrs. Taylor? Corrine will want to know as well."

Sam Taylor paused.

"Becky's in the hospital again, but her spirits are just as good as always. I just returned from seeing her. When I go up there tonight, she'll be pleased that you asked about her."

Dolph knew how painful this was for Mr. Taylor. He also knew how hard it would be if he had to face the same prospects with Corrine.

"Sir, you let me know if there's anything I can do."

"Thanks. I'll do that. See you at 11."

Dolph felt a swelling in his throat as he put down the telephone. He then called into the family room.

"Corrine, I'm going up to Houston in the morning. I need to see Sam Taylor. Becky is back in Anderson. This is the second time this year. I don't like that news."

M.D. Anderson Cancer Center, a University of Texas teaching hospital in Houston, is a renowned cancer research and treatment facility. From the kitchen Dolph could see Corrine first shaking and then bowing her head.

CHAPTER 33

Uptown Lawyers

The offices of Lindsay & Taylor, LLP were on the 14th floor of Two Houston Center, a black marble and glass obelisk connected to similar office buildings jutting up on the east side of downtown Houston. Three banks of six elevators each serviced blocks of floors in approximately 10-floor increments. Houston's skyline was brilliantly growing eastward.

The firm occupied a significant portion of the floor, but it was becoming crowded with the addition of two new associates and three paralegal assistants. Business was good.

The receptionist cheerfully greeted Dolph and advised that Mr. Taylor was expecting him. Unnecessarily, she gestured to the hallway leading to Taylor's outer office. It was guarded by Sam's legal assistant, an air-brushed term for secretary. Dolph, in light gray slacks, a blue blazer and an open-collar dress shirt, breezed up to the Lakota Sioux Indian assistant.

"How you doin', Doe Eyes?"

With mock deadpan grimness, Jacqueline Martin drew her right index finger across her throat in a cutting fashion. Her large dark eyes were a beautiful but now menacing centerpiece framed by her straight black hair and longish face. Finally she softened and smiled.

"Can I get you some coffee, Dolph? I'll be at lunch when you two louts finish, so tell Corrine I miss her."

Dolph gave her thumbs up and a smile as he turned to Sam's open door. Mrs. Martin, in her early 40s, was fiercely loyal to Taylor. One Christmas, they exchanged gifts. His was a certificate to a local high-dollar ladies spa for an all-day beauty and massage treatment. Becky and Sam signed the card. Her present was a razor-sharp, heavy skinning knife, serrated on the top front three inches of the blade. She proclaimed its utility for buffalo carving at summer Sundance gatherings in the Dakotas.

As he unfolded the blade and admired its lethality, she murmured, "Put it on the table at partner meetings. Mr. Lindsay will just love it."

Taylor's large corner office was cluttered with stacks of expandable red-rope folders, labeled file boxes and large exhibit tubes. The tubes might contain maps or other graphics, and they were all carefully grouped according to particular litigation matters.

There were also two client chairs, a dark leather sofa fronted with a large glass topped coffee table, and an 80-inch wide burl wood parsons table that served as Taylor'ss desk in front of an equally wide matching credenza. A computer flat screen, keyboard and mouse, some family photographs and a couple of files that Taylor had just reviewed topped the credenza. Except for his telephone and inbox-outbox trays, Sam's desk was clean.

A distinctly prominent sidewall contained naval service unit plaques, an 8-by-10-inch photograph of Sam's Swift Boat underway, his professional license from the Supreme Court of Texas and other court admissions.

Taylor moved from his chair to greet Dolph and took one of the client chairs.

"I haven't seen you in a while, Dolph. You been gone?"

Settling in the other chair, Dolph replied, "Yes sir, I have. Just taking care of a little pressing business. That's not what I came to see you about. Besides, I think I'm going off the road for good. It's too ... ah, strenuous shall we say."

Despite their long relationship as commanding officer and crewman, lawyer and client and friends, Sam Taylor never knew the dark side of Randolph Cavanaugh's life as an occasional fraud schemer and confidence man. What he did know was that Cavanaugh was an immensely successful real-estate investor and occasionally a financial backer of down-and-out, but deserving, entrepreneurs. Dolph sent him a lot of these small-business owners for corporate and tax work as well as estate planning.

Dolph's investment philosophy was guided by a belief that otherwise smart and talented folks who were broke and being chased by the IRS were good risks for incremental but controlled financial help. In these situations, Taylor had often negotiated payback arrangements with their creditors or quietly filed missing back-year tax returns. Once free of the demons behind them, these people were ready for a good future. This work for Cavanaugh was all very different from Lieutenant Taylor's estimation of his crewman three decades ago.

Dolph had very literally prayed that he would never need Mr. Taylor's criminal law skills to get him out of a jam. Cavanaugh could never suffer the embarrassment.

Jack, as she also was known, brought in the coffee and a glass of club soda for Taylor. She swirled out of the room with noticeable jingling of jewelry. Today she was into her Native-American-silver-and-turquoise mode. Both men laughed.

Over the next several minutes, Cavanaugh outlined the events at Hannah's Place, one of Dolph's financial backings that had paid off handsomely. Hannah Gregory had also become a client and owned the cafe free and clear. Taylor came to know her brokenness when she arrived in Sargent, but he never discussed those facts with Dolph.

As Cavanaugh related the facts, including Trimmer's foolishness and

Dolph's concerns about Shiprite and Piper, Taylor remained silent. He resisted asking the 'who' question concerning Thurman's assailant and allowed Dolph to go at his own pace. Finally, Dolph got to the point.

"This guy said he was some kind of postal inspector, a turkey named Culver Foxman." Dolph was shocked as he said the last two words, because Mr. Taylor spoke those same words in unison.

"Mr. Taylor, how do you know this man? How'd you know he was the man I was talking about?"

"Well, Cavanaugh, your physical description was a pretty good clue, but frankly, I had a similar run-in with him years ago. Stink rarely leaves a turd like Curley. By the way, he hates being called Curley."

Taylor leaned back in his chair, folding his arms behind his head and stretching out his legs. Dolph settled in for a bit of a story.

"Back in the 1950's here in Houston there was a good old boy, a country musician and singer, named Curley Fox. He and his group played all of the old favorites. They were on the Saturday television broadcasts when I was a kid. He had a songbird named Miss Texas Ruby. She was a mature-looking gal with too much make-up, frizzy hair and big tits. She always wore a cowboy hat, a beaded western blouse with fake mother-of-pearl buttons and a frumpy skirt. She sang with a deep voice. I said she was a songbird, but she looked and sounded more like an old painted parrot. Rumor had it that Curley had discovered her after she got out of Goree Prison for murder. I don't know or care if that's true; they seemed like good folks, and I liked their music." For just a bit Sam was lost in his thoughts.

"Apparently, I was not alone. Years later after the Postal Service deposited Foxman on the community, one of his co-workers jokingly called him 'Curley'; Foxman slugged him and almost lost his job. Apparently he didn't like being compared with country folks. Behind his back he's still known as Curley. I would have sent him to a shrink; Culver Foxman has always been bad news."

"Well Mr. Taylor, if he's so bad, why hasn't the service canned him?"

"I don't know; it has always seemed to me that the postal service had a lower ratio of bad apples, and I would say that often their inspectors are more dogged and creative in their work than some of the other federal agencies."

Taylor's legs drew up and his back straightened. "When an agent is delivering convictions on a consistent basis and he has gotten away with bad behavior, also on a consistent basis, and retirement of the jerk is just on the horizon, a supervisor whose retirement may also be looming has to decide if disciplinary action is worth the hassle. The call gets down to this in all of the agencies."

Dolph's chin sank to his chest for a couple of moments and then rose.

"So what you are telling me is that it would take something pretty enormous to overcome what you just described."

"Afraid so, Randy. I've got two more things to say. First, let me do some checking around. Be careful yourself; you don't need an obstruction-of-justice claim. That's one of Curley's tricks. Second, since old Thurman was his latest victim, I think I know some people who will be more than interested in making things right."

They both stood. Dolph nodded. Taylor smiled.

"Pocahontas got a call from Corrine this morning reminding us of her scheme to get you in shape. You look like it's working; your clothes are hanging loose. Maybe I ought to get on Corrine's program. No Coronado Club for us today, but I'll take you to a new salad bar down the street."

"Why am I not surprised?"

CHAPTER 34

Maintenance Matters

After lunch, Dolph walked to his office. His girl had just left. She typed a note saying she might not be in at all for the rest of the week because of final examinations. That was fine with Dolph. For a moment, he thought of more than leaving the road. He didn't need an office in downtown just to pay bills on his properties and projects or make income deposits. Without things happening beyond the back door, he sure didn't need the front door. Bay City would do just fine. Not that he could eat there, but he did know a good storefront office down from the KC Steakhouse and an old building owned by a dentist.

He took care of his usual business and then focused on the call slip from Mr. Gwen. The "Sweetie," as he always thought of these college girls he hired, had said he was Chinese. Dolph had a passing concern that his latest Canadian activity had somehow been compromised, perhaps by that FBI agent who followed him from Seattle.

Although Gwen's number was local, Dolph dug out one of his phone cards and dialed. Caller ID was a hurdle overcome by phone cards. Two rings and a man answered in correct but Asian-accented English.

"I'm looking for Mr. Gwen. Are you Mr. Gwen?"

The man laughed. "You Americans never know my name. Yes, I'm Mr. Gwen, but it is more better to spell it as N-G-U-Y-E-N. I'm Vietnamese. Are you Randy Cavanaugh?"

Dolph had relaxed from the man's hello. The tone was familiar and special to Vietnamese speech. It had become more obvious as the man replied to Dolph's question. Dolph too laughed.

"You bet. What can I do for you, Ong Nguyen?" Dolph asked using the formal Vietnamese term for Mister.

"Oh good. My father-in-law, Ha Shi Dang, trained on American Swift Boats and then served in Vietnamese Navy Swift Boats until he went to re-education camps. He told me about you. He said all Americans on his boat were good men."

The memories were all rushing back to Dolph; the scrawny, tough little 18-year-old Vietnamese sailor had been his friend. When Mr. Taylor had given Dolph the nickname of Baby Fat, Dang had enjoyed the joke as much as everyone else. In those days, Seaman Cavanaugh had rippled rolls of youthful fat around his stomach, mostly from beer rather than mother's milk. When Dolph left the boats and came home, he forgot all about Dang. Seaman Dang was a good guy and not a part of Dolph's black-market commission business.

"Ahn, what are you doing in Houston and what's happened to my friend Dang?" Dolph slipped into the more informal address roughly equivalent to "brother."

"Oh, he escaped and came to California. He's in printing business in Orange County. My parents did too, and that's where I met his daughter. She and I went to grade school together."

"How did you find me? I haven't stayed up with anyone except our boat officer in those days, Trung Uy Taylor." Lieutenant Junior Grade.

"Oh, that's how I located you. Mr. Dang gave me Lieutenant Taylor's name and said he was a lawyer in Houston before Navy and that I should call him. I did, and he gave me your office number. Mr. Dang did not know where you were."

"Again, Ahn Nguyen, is there anything I can do for you? My secretary said you wanted to talk about an investment."

"No, no. I told her I was in investment business. Mr. Dang's daughter and I are now living in Houston, and I wanted to introduce myself and tell you what I am doing. Mr. Dang always said that you and Mr. Taylor were Number One."

"What kind of investments?" Dolph sensed an opportunity for some business.

"Mr. Dang and I are looking for small shopping centers in Houston. California is too expensive and too many people."

"Well Ahn, that's right. Our Asian community is growing fast. You might have some competition."

"Oh that's okay, Vietnamese people like competition."

Dolph's years of caution were not suspended. He lied to Nguyen, saying that he was out of town and was uncertain as to his return to Houston. Instead he got the contact information on the Nguyen couple as well as his old friend, Dang. He was confident about Nguyen's genuineness, but he would first talk to Mr. Taylor and then Dang.

He was excited. He got through to Jack, who verified Nguyen's call to Sam. She transferred Dolph's call to the firm library.

"Say Mr. Taylor, when were you going to tell me about Nguyen's call and about Dang?"

"Slipped my mind and besides, you were gone on one of your extended trips. If you didn't stay away so long, I wouldn't have to be your messenger service."

"Well, okay sir. I have a lot going on right now, but I'd just as soon jump on a plane for California."

"Me too, Dolph. It's really good news to hear about Dang. Hey, I've got to run. Jack's got another call for me."

Dolph decided to wait on his call to Dang. At least it wasn't some Chinese Triad society setting him up for a hit, he thought. Dolph had learned during his latest adventure that these gangs are prevalent in British Columbia and Seattle. They are available for hire even by those who publicly denounce them. He was also aware that affiliated Vietnamese gangs are particularly violent and prone to automatic weapons. For this specialty, the Chinese often subcontract their dirty work. Dolph felt justified in his cautions with Nguyen.

CHAPTER 35

Task Force

Law enforcement isn't the only entity devoted to action language as a way of characterizing a response to a significant problem. War metaphors had long been a hook for uniting the public behind an effort to address just about any crisis--exaggerated, contrived, imagined or real. They were handy words for politicians, social activists and demagogues alike. Pronounce a crisis and announce the means destroy it.

Teamwork is an American way; why not put together a multi-disciplinary group to win out over the forces of evil? The public had long accepted wars on poverty, drugs, discrimination, crime, pornography, hate and other social issues as the indisputable solution. For a society raised on the victories of the Second World War, "Task Force" and "Strike Force" evoked special images. Besides, such thinking clearly labeled "the enemy" for public attention and elevated force members to warrior status. The effectiveness of these verbal contrivances, for politicians at least, was at most a secondary consideration.

In federal law enforcement circles, such groups were mostly composed of talented representatives from various agencies. They brought to the table their angles of attack without necessarily trespassing on jealously guarded bureaucratic turf. The FBI, the IRS and the Postal Service were among the permanent members of all such groups. A Justice Department lawyer or some senior prosecutor in a local U.S. Attorney's office coordinated or at least advised these groups.

"Thanks for returning my call, Mike. Are you still heading up the Major Frauds Task Force?"

Mike Charbonneau was one of the old hands in the U. S. Attorney's office, a man who valued his relationships in the defense community, especially with former assistant U.S. attorneys. Most former government prosecutors in the Southern District of Texas appreciated Charbonneau's integrity and discretion. Back-channel conversations often accomplished more objective and reciprocal justice than all the posturing harangues in the courtroom or strident quips to the media outside on the courthouse steps. Charbonneau knew he was being tapped for a purpose.

"Yes, of course, why do you ask?"

"A mutual friend of ours, I suspect is on your team. He's up to his old tricks, and I thought you might want a heads up."

"What's Curley doing now?"

Charbonneau and Taylor worked together on a case several years earlier. Foxman was their case agent. Taylor's particular run-in had been later after he went into private practice. Each incident had involved claims that Foxman had been overly forceful with people he interviewed. While Foxman's behavior had compromised the government's cases, an oral reprimand was the only action taken by the postal service. Charbonneau required no guesswork. Foxman was the logical culprit.

"My source is not the victim, although he got his information from the victim. I don't believe my man would have anything to do with whatever you're looking into. I've represented this guy for years in business and commercial matters, and he was one of my crewmen."

Sam was mildly concerned that he had given too much information if he was talking to anyone other than Mike. It wasn't relevant to mention Dolph's other suspicions or to name other possible bad guys. His job was to pass on information about an agent's possible wrongful intimidation of witnesses.

Mike laughed. "I suppose none of your crewmen could ever do anything wrong."

"I didn't say that, you suspicious bureaucrat." Sam too laughed. "I think he's just interested in the victim, a guy that Curley got too physical with. Anyway, you know the victim; I do too. J. Thurman Birdwell."

Mike Charbonneau remained silent for a full 10-count. He felt cold-cocked. The lawyers who worked in the pit of litigation broadly knew Thurman's ill-deserved disgrace.

"Sam, you don't represent Thurman, do you? Where'd this happen?"

"Mike, if I need to, I will represent my long-time client, but I don't think he needs to be in the loop." He paused. "This happened in Sargent. I hope this is enough for you to look into the matter." This was Taylor's way of bringing the discussion to an end.

"I'll do what I can. One thing I can tell you is that Curley has had his second strike."

"Mike, I appreciate that. Call me if there's anything I can do."

As Sam started to say goodbye, Charbonneau spoke.

"How is Becky? News gets around."

"Thanks for asking. She's cheerful, but I think we're getting near the end. I'll just deal with things as they come. I'll tell her tonight that you asked about her. She always thought you were one of the good guys."

* * *

Dolph called Baxter to pester him about copying the loan packages and was satisfied that he and Baxter could begin the analysis tomorrow. It had been a good day seeing Mr. Taylor and Jack. Despite Sam Taylor's disturbing report about Culver Foxman, Dolph felt cleaner just being around the lawyer and his secretary. Cavanaugh had just shredded and bagged his trash, locked up his business checkbook and locked the door to his private office when the telephone rang. For just a moment, he thought of letting the caller leave a message.

"Glad I caught you, Dolph. I've talked to someone, and I want you to listen to me very carefully. Do you understand me?"

"Yes sir, I do."

"I expect you to back off on any personal efforts you might be thinking of concerning Thurman. Something must be going on in your neck of the woods. I feel it in my bones. I want you to let things take their course. You call me if you learn anything relevant. My goal is to keep you out of trouble. Are we clear?"

"You bet, Mr. Taylor. That's music to my ears. I'll keep a low profile."

"It's hard for me to imagine you in a low-profile mode, but do the best you can."

Dolph chuckled. "Thanks for helping me out."

CHAPTER 36

Seed Money Ain't All for Farming

Taylor's call had reminded him of business he had to take care of anticipating Uncle Buddy's appearance. He picked up the telephone dialing Hannah's Place.

"Darlin', this is Corrine's starving sex slave. You got a minute?"

"Dolph, you're a bad dog. Good thing she has you on a leash." Behind Hannah's laughing voice, Dolph could hear customer sounds and the ka-ching of her cash register.

"I need you to get something for me when you make your next deposit."

Hannah Gregory understood that Cavanaugh wanted her to remove something from the large safe deposit box she kept at the Wells Fargo Bank in Bay City. She ran her operating account and kept a significant certificate of deposit at that bank as a back-up for her restaurant. She maintained her personal accounts and other assets down the street at Matagorda Peoples, where she also had a box. The Wells Fargo box was a favor for Dolph and not an inconvenience to her. Although the box was in her name and Dolph was authorized to enter the box, he had never done so. Whatever was in the box upon his death, she could do whatever she wanted, but he hoped she and Corrine would enjoy it.

"Get me two of those white envelopes, not the big ones, just the white."

Hannah knew the sealed envelopes contained cash, but she had no idea of the denominations or how Dolph got the money. For that matter, she didn't care. Every now and then she would put envelopes in the box and get some out on other occasions.

On one such occasion, she withdrew a white envelope and delivered it to Dolph. The next thing she heard was that some preacher at a black Baptist Church in Wharton was claiming that God had answered their prayers for enough money to fix their roof. God had been overgenerous, however, when a 'fat envelope' containing $10,000 in cash and a note were left at the preacher's home very early on Sunday. The unsigned note said, "Stop talking about fixing the roof. This ought to cover a new one." The Wharton newspaper was careful to observe that God didn't mince words when providing time came.

Despite all his good humor and openness, Dolph had a very private side. She thought his good-old-boy folksiness was a cover for a certain kind of shyness. You could fuss at Dolph all day and he took it like a man, but he always squirmed when she or Corrine praised him. The fact is that she and the Cavanaughs respected the dignity of the poor and frail, but they would have been embarrassed if anyone blessed their way of helping them.

It had been a big day. As soon as Dolph hung up with Hannah, he left the office. He decided to take U.S. Highway 59 south back to Bay City; once beyond Sugarland he could make better time. Besides, he was hoping Corrine would be home and ready for a jog.

CHAPTER 37

Clocks Don't Move Faster with Worrying

Corrine knew there was something going on with Dolph. He was falling into a pattern different from earlier years. Each morning he was dressed and ready for stretching, a few calisthenics and an ever-lengthening jog. While at first she had forced him into second workouts in the late afternoon, he no longer needed urging. When he got home from seeing Sam Taylor, he was preoccupied. He said he needed to return to Houston in a few days to check his mail, pay some bills and most significantly to her, talk with the building management about possibly abandoning the lease. They would be thrilled, he advised; the rate on his old lease was ridiculously below market value. The other oddity was the way he was eating, sensibly and without complaint. Maybe he really was serious about leaving the road, or maybe he was serious about something else. Or maybe he was bluffing. As to another possibility, he might be cheating on his diet. Corrine discarded that option; she would be able to smell cheeseburgers and other fat pills on his breath and clothing, or at least Dolph believed so.

The next day Dolph reviewed copies of Baxter's utility district bond purchase. They were each for $70,000. How convenient, Dolph thought, for Shiprite to illustrate the discounted value to Trimmer. Carefully reviewing the form and the substance of each document was easy; the language was appropriate, but then his attention was drawn to a seemingly minor flaw. The corporate secretary's signature was illegible, something not unusual in the legitimate trade. But something jumped out at Dolph like a barking dog. The preprinted form misspelled the word 'secretery.' No respectable corporate issuer, no professional printing house, retail or mail order, would tolerate such an error, much less those seriously engaged in the business of making worthless paper look authentic; pride of workmanship drove them all. Not so with the quick and dirty cons; their type figured that greed and gullibility coupled with laziness would blind their victims to any obscure printing or typographical errors. While not conclusive evidence of fraud, Cavanaugh felt confident in his rescue efforts for Baxter; Dolph was learning more about Shiprite.

Before Corrine returned from her daily gallivanting, Trimmer telephoned to report that the copying of the mortgage packages was now complete. Dolph knew that the girls were resuming their usual 11 a.m. poolside margarita tasting and lunch the next day, giving the two men almost four hours to review the papers. Dolph's home office was large and well-equipped. It also offered privacy. Dora mostly worked in the other parts of the house where she could listen to Spanish-language television.

They agreed that Baxter would make some excuse at the bank about a long lunch and arrive at Dolph's at 11:30 a.m. With luck, they would be done before Corrine got home for her expected nap. True to the schedule, Trimmer arrived with a large, black leather briefcase; it looked more like a small suitcase with a flip top. Sam Taylor had one of these in his private office. He called it a trial box. Baxter also brought a supply of legal pads, pencils and colored-marking and highlight pens.

They reviewed the sets of documents backing up the loans now owned by the bank, dividing the work in two stacks. Before long, Trimmer had completed his examination. Observing that Dolph was still plowing through his pile, Trimmer commented.

"I've finished looking at my stack. These are just fine. What about yours?"

Somewhat annoyed by the interruption, Dolph replied, "I'm not just looking, I'm studying."

After a pause, he straightened in his chair. "Tell me, Bax, what are you looking at to be satisfied that these loans are worth buying with the bank's money?"

It was Baxter's turn to be a little annoyed. On the other hand, he felt his pride welling up at the opportunity to explain to his non-banker friend just how these reviews are conducted. Dolph missed neither reaction.

"I take two or three of the files and look to see that all of the forms from different sources are there and that they are in the proper or logical order. You understand, like the Promissory Note, the Deed of Trust, the Title Policy, Appraisal and Credit Report. There were two of the loans on raw acreage, and I looked to see that they had surveys. On the top of each package is the Closing Statement showing disbursement of funds from the buyer and the original lender."

Trimmer took a deep breath, warming up to his lecture.

"Next I review all of the documents for signatures and dates and date-time stamps on the recorded documents. Sometimes I find a little mistake and put a yellow sticky on that page for later correction before we take on that particular loan. Also, and this is important, I review the credit report to see that the borrower has credit appropriate to the amount being loaned. These representative or sample loans were well-supported by the credit reports."

"Oh really?" Dolph observed.

Taking that as encouragement, Trimmer further expounded. "Yes, yes. These weren't like the stuff being acquired by the big lenders. Fanny Mae and Freddie Mac have been arm-twisting regional lenders, especially in the big urban centers, to provide loans to substandard borrowers. You can't loan money to people who can't pay it off. It's a "taint fair" situation; lenders lose their money, and poor folks lose their dreams."

Dolph only had a passing awareness of the two quasi-governmental corporations established by Congress to encourage broad home ownership. He was also aware that their chief function in recent years had been to buy votes in minority enclaves. Political proponents could crow about how they were taking care of poor folks while the opponents cowered in noticeable silence. They were in fear of being ambushed at election time as racists and mean-spirited if they criticized the lending, accounting or regulation of these corporations. He thought the whole thing was the biggest fraud scheme ever done in his experience, the government's way of doing a Ponzi.

"I'm glad we're not a part of that, Bax, but let me see if I understand your review process."

Trimmer drew up his posture, anticipating his student's new comprehension.

"You review the files to see if everything is there that you expect to be there."

Baxter nodded.

"Then you make sure that all the dates and signatures and so forth are there, as well as a good credit report. You don't go look at the property or make any inquiry outside of the papers given you. Is that about it?"

"That's it, my friend. That's the way it's done."

"Well, my friend," Dolph's tone remained congenial, "I have a couple of more questions. Do you ever compare one loan with another or with several others?"

Baxter nodded vigorously. "Why yes, in a sense. You see, I told you I reviewed two or three files personally, and then I turned over the remainder to Bea Jay with explanations about what I am looking for. She then goes through the rest of the packages and makes a chart for me to speed up the process. She checks off each point; the chart on this set is at the top of my stack, and then there is a similar chart on the set that's not yet accepted. I can then look at these charts of all the other loans and verify that they are all appropriate. Pretty thorough, huh?"

Trimmer missed that Dolph's eyes went half-lidded as he nodded at the banker's acumen. He also missed Cavanaugh's weary intake of air.

"Perhaps I was unclear. Do you ever look at the other loans to see if there is anything that jumps out at you, big or small, that says the bank is being deceived or manipulated, anything tell tale?

"Why would I do that? These are different borrowers and initial lenders, and besides, the appraisals and surveyors are different. There would be just too many people involved for that to be a possibility. So the answer is no."

Dolph had not shared the results of his review of the bond documentation or his convictions about Shiprite. He had not wanted to infect Trimmer's mind until after they studied the mortgage packages. Apparently Trimmer's mind was immune to infection. Dolph's anger rose, though, at the realization of his friend's incredible arrogance and stupidity. He spilled this all in one fierce chewing-out.

"You lazy toad. Don't you think someone trying to steal the bank's money with these papers is going to show you exactly what you expect and want to see? Don't you realize that studying this stuff doesn't mean just looking at it? When you compare documents in other packages, you might see a clue, some little something that triggers further inquiry." Dolph took and then blew out a long breath.

He continued. "Your crowning stupidity was turning over this review to that young girl's inexperience just because you were too lazy to do it yourself. I ought to take you outside and whip your butt."

A beating would have been preferable to Dolph's verbal thrashing. Trimmer was imploding within his clothing; his face went pale. He was a grown man, and no one had ever spoken to him that way, not his father, not anyone. The fact is, he couldn't remember his father ever speaking harshly to him.

"You idiot!" Dolph spit out the assertion. "Don't you see that none of your reviews and charts tell you whether these loans were good or bad when what we are trying to find out is if there is any fraud on the bank, two different concepts?"

Trimmer was unable to answer.

Dolph's anger began to subside with the realization that he still need-ed Baxter's cooperation if he expected to work through all this. Perhaps a temporary reprieve was in order.

"Get back over to that chair now that you know what we're searching for. Let's do this right and then decide what we do after that."

Trimmer wordlessly complied. Dolph was likewise silent except for a noticeable restoration of his normal breathing.

Ten minutes later, Baxter, more to himself than to Dolph, muttered "Uh, oh," and then he shuffled other papers. Finally, he spoke one long "Good Lord."

"What do you have, Bax?"

* * *

The packages were complete fakes except for the letterheads of so-called third-party providers. The letterheads belonged to known busi-nesses in the region, but were on stolen or reproduced stationery. An inventory of signatures of borrowers, lenders and third-party providers such as survey reports revealed an interesting consistency. Regardless of the various women's names, the feminine hand appeared to be the same. Of course, these documents were photocopies and not originals, but Dolph and Baxter concurred on the obvious conclusion: one wom-an had signed all of the female names.

There was more variety in the masculine hands; six took turns sign-ing the seller and buyer documents, while it appeared that three other masculine hands signed for the lenders and third-party providers. Pro-fessional document examiners would establish further confirmation of these opinions. Dolph knew the results would not change. There were many ways to acquire cheap, cloudy-minded accomplices who saw a good wage in signing other people's names without asking questions.

Documents recorded as official public real-estate records are stamped with a distinctive impression that portrays the identity of the office of recording, a sequential filing number and the date and time of filing. Jurisdictional requirements and local practices may vary, but essentially all recording references identify where, when and with whom a document is filed together, with the sequence number on each page of the document to distinguish that paper from all the others. Several recorded documents in unrelated loans bore the same or similar date time stamps and sequence numbers. In three of the dissimilar loans, recorder notes in long hand bore the same feminine characteristics as found earlier on other papers.

As he and Baxter completed their analysis and notes, Dolph commented, "These people have a lot of cojones in putting this together, and they worked to give facial authenticity to their product. They got lazy turning out this junk on an assembly line. Once we focused on comparisons, the patterns were obvious."

Dolph's eyes narrowed. "We didn't recognize any of these borrower or seller names, and that leads me to think that other banks elsewhere might have loans involving some of our local folks."

"Do you think I ought to get on the phone and check around the region?"

"Not so fast, Bax. I need more information and time. You told me that all of the loans continue to be current." Trimmer nodded.

"Yes, we get checks twice a month from Piper's mortgage company. They service the loans and send us one check every couple of weeks listing all of the borrowers and their payments. All we have to do is to look at the list to see if anyone didn't pay."

"The shelf life on this junk is defined by the amount of money the bank paid to buy these loans and the cost needed monthly to keep the loans current. They'll continue servicing until they've collected all they expect from larger sales of fraudulent mortgage packages. It won't take long for this to collapse after the first default, maybe days, maybe weeks. And if there are other banks involved, you're going to see a big slide in banking confidence."

"What do you want me to do?" Trimmer had visions of a regional banking calamity.

"Let me know if one of their checks is even a day late. Tomorrow morning, you call Piper and tell him that you have finished your re-examination of the second packet and concluded that everything is fine. Tell him you'll take your findings to the executive committee in the next two or three weeks and get the board's approval next month. Apologize for any inconvenience and thank him for his patience. Got that? I'll rip your face off if you tell anyone else about this."

Baxter gave his best attempt at a salute.

They reformed the stacks in good order, gathered their notes and repacked the briefcase. Despite the office supplies Trimmer had brought, they had not marked one page in the documents. Guided by his healthy paranoia, Dolph reconsidered the contents of the briefcase.

"Baxter, let's unload that box. If you don't mind, I'll keep those copies here and the notes. I've got a good place for them."

Dolph had built a doghouse for old Sid, their black lab. It had a lift-off insulated composition roof with a small ventilation fan to draw in outside air in the summer. He ran a power cord into the garage and plugged it into a timer set to go on at noon and off at seven in the evening. Both Dolph and the dog were proud of that house. Sid would lie up in the heat of the day enjoying the power driven breezes. It was better than digging holes in the garden, ruining the plants and making Corrine mad at the two of them. Sid had enjoyed his house for two years and then died. The veterinarian said it was spine cancer that took him. Dolph kept the house, but he could not bring himself to get another dog. Sid's house was clean and dry.

"I have some old hunting and fishing magazines I don't seem to get around to reading and a bunch of Corrine's Southern Living we can put in the case. On the way back to the bank, stop at Prosperity Bank. Carry that briefcase with you when you go in. Chat with one of your buddies there and then leave, still carrying the case. Don't take it back in when you return to Peoples. We've got to be diversionary and very careful now that we know what we're dealing with."

Dolph saw that Baxter's hands were trembling as they removed address labels and loaded the magazines.

"Dolph, you don't suppose anybody would try to hurt us or anything like that, do you?"

"Don't worry, Bax. Mostly these people avoid violence; I'm more interested in folks seeing you carrying around this box and wondering what's in it. I never saw you lift anything heavier than a glass of wine or a newspaper; I figure nobody else has either. Piper and Shiprite have people working with them; we know this just from what we've seen today, and you're the chicken they're trying to pluck. So it stands to reason, one way or another, they're watching you."

Trimmer was following Dolph's analysis, but he was hanging on the word 'mostly.' He clearly understood that people were watching him. He looked out the window toward his car parked in the circular driveway. Dolph read his mind.

"Look Baxter, this is the perfect solution for you. Just have Eloise start the car for you every morning." He smiled. "If she's well-insured, you get the girls and a chance to find another woman to raise them and put up with you."

For the second time that day, Baxter's color drained. As Dolph had hoped, Trimmer was sufficiently frightened to abandon his arrogance and mental indolence, at least for a time. Also for a time, Baxter would follow orders exactly.

"How do you know all this stuff, Dolph?" Trimmer was justifiably puzzled. "You're not anything like I ever saw you."

"I've kept my eyes and ears open going through life; seen a lot of folks trying to cheat other folks." Of course, he did not say that he was the cheat-or and they were the cheat-ees, but the answer satisfied Trimmer. Dolph resisted invoking the mystique of so-called lessons of "'Nam."

Shaking his head, Baxter went on, this time to himself rather than Dolph. "How could I have been so stupid?"

Dolph was happy for one last chance to stick it to Trimmer. "I don't know, why don't you ask your parents? I pray this is just genetics and not contagious."

Baxter was out the door a good half hour before Corrine returned home. Dolph heard her car keys hit the silver tray on the hallway credenza. He had already changed into his work-out clothes. Intercepting her as she headed for the sunroom couch, she saw he was winding up for a smart remark. She was right.

"Corrine honey, I know you're liquored up a little, but could you put more clothes on to go work out with me?" He summoned a cheery voice.

She flipped him the bird, kicked off her sandals and settled on the couch. To close the opportunity for any further discussion, she rolled on her side facing the back of the couch.

In his life of doing deals, he would have headed to the refrigerator or a restaurant as a way of coming down off of intense mental activity. Now, he headed for the streets of Nouveau Estates. He might not be up for conversation while running, but he could do some thinking.

He developed an agenda. When it got dark, he would put the mortgage papers in a plastic trash bag and move the bag into old Sid's house. Tomorrow he would call for another appointment with Mr. Taylor and then try to find out what was holding up C.W. He knew C.W. would give him grief over being a fussy old maid, but he was anxious for his friend's arrival. The prospect of seeing the Laundress in Hawaii was dimming. Perhaps he could change their travel plans.

As he turned back onto his street, he realized two achievements. First, he was not particularly winded, and second, he had trotted every major and side street within the Nouveau subdivision, a distance he knew to be 5.7 miles. Maybe, he thought, I'm ready for real roadwork. Maybe I could make it to town and back.

CHAPTER 38
Kitchen Talk

By Dolph's return, Corrine had dinner ready and was again dressed in her long blue T-shirt. Dolph showered and returned to the kitchen in a pair of shorts and one of his favorite 3X T-shirts. On the front it depicted a grinning hayseed farmer framed by the words, "I luv farmin' cuz it's fun." The back showed the same farmer without the grin and his overall pockets are turned out, saying, "They're ain't no other explanation."

Corrine stirred a pot of green beans and then carefully placed servings on each plate next to some steamed yellow squash and meatloaf. As she did so, she eyed the shirt, now beginning to fade.

"You're fixing to need to get rid of that shirt. I'd tell you to give that thing to Junior for his collection, but that one would hang on him like a cheap dress."

"Darlin' don't be so generous with my stuff. I have plans for this shirt and one or two others in the closet."

"What plans would those be, shop rags?"

"No, baby, I think with all this trimming down I'm doing, there ought to be enough room for you to get in here with me some evening."

"Well, tonight is not the night. Let me tell you about today."

She put their plates on the bar counter and moved around to his side and sat. Corrine talked while Dolph ate and muttered comprehending grunts and chuckles. She picked at her food.

All the girls turned out, this being their last luncheon of the school year. School was ending on Friday, and they knew their privacy at the pool could not resume until early September. Bea Jay had to leave at 1 p.m., but the others continued to visit. Maria didn't dive totally into the first pitcher of margaritas and declined Grey Goose in her shrimp cocktail. She was neither angry nor unhappy. She was subdued, Corrine thought, because of her performance the last time. Barbara Piper, always pleasant, brushed her dark red hair and made sure she used lots of sunblock. She also made good progress on the margaritas.

Eloise was a surprise. She was cheerful and uncomplaining about Baxter. He was coming home earlier and had recently taken to long hugs, 'and more,' as she put it. For the first time in a long time, she expressed concern for Baxter; he was really trying to be kind. She wondered if he needed to see Dr. Merritt.

"Dolph, I think you might have had something to do with that. Momma and I know that Baxter listens to you."

"Don't give me any credit. Maybe Bax is growing up. What else happened?"

"The club grounds around the pool are beautiful, and we need to start going there to work out. I found out they have a running track that goes down to and along Big Lake and an exercise room with a bunch of gym equipment. This will be great in the cold weather."

They had already discussed running in the Texas Gulf Coast winter; when it is humid and only in the 30s, the cold can cut right though you. Dolph didn't want to think about the cold.

"How many pitchers did you girls destroy?"

"Only two, but I think Barbara and I had more than our share."

Dolph grunted.

They finished their meal, and as they were cleaning up, Corrine's face darkened.

"The boys called while you were out running. They won't be coming home until late August." She was downcast, not one of Corrine's frequent moods. Dolph turned, but he awaited further explanation.

"They both have jobs in Glenwood Springs, Colorado, until about August 15. Bedford is going to drive a bus for a whitewater outfit, and Forrest is wrangling at a dude ranch."

Dolph grinned. "Those boys are gonna meet a lot of pretty women, but they'll be OK. You taught them right from wrong."

Their mother was not impressed.

"I know. I just don't want them tested in Colorado. Can't they be tested down here?"

With that same grin, Dolph wagged his head.

"Like I said, Randolph, tonight is not the night."

CHAPTER 39

Sister Kissing Results— Almost

He was on the telephone by 9 a.m. Jack said Sam Taylor was in trial the following week, but if the case folded, she would call and work him in. The second call was even less promising. The man answering for the Ford Dealership in Portales said, "Charles Rogers is no longer with us."

"What do you mean? Is he dead?"

"No, Sir. He up and quit last Saturday. Said he was going to Midland for a while and thinking about selling units in Lubbock."

"Was he living with anyone I could talk to?"

"Oh, so far as I know, he resided by himself."

"Thanks, good buddy. By the way, do you actually sell cars there or do you just answer the phone and talk about selling units and where folks reside?" Dolph was ticked.

"I sell units, I mean cars and trucks, and assist customers in the service department. My father actually owns the dealership."

"No kidding. Let me give you a little advice: Why don't you consider thinking and speaking workingman's English like a real car salesman? Work at it; I'm sure your daddy will see the difference."

Is old C.W. scamming Daddy just to escape having to put up with his son or is he covering his trail down here, Dolph wondered. Maybe he really is going to visit his daughter and head up to Lubbock to sell 'units.' Maybe he wants nothing more to do with me. Dolph hated not getting the answers he wanted.

The third call put him a good mood. Digging out his phone card as he closed his office door, he dialed Pete's number. She picked up after the first ring.

"Pete, this is Randy. Do you have a minute?"

"Things have been a little hectic today, but yes, I do have time."

"I'm afraid I'm not going to make it to Hawaii this year. Do you think you could fly to Dallas instead, same date for the same period? I think you'll be impressed with the Mansion on Turtle Creek."

"Yes, I'm sure I will; I've read about it. It's a Rosewood property; they are wonderful. I can make my own arrangements. This is special good news for me. I have wanted to do something different, and surely Texas is different."

Dolph alerted to her somewhat hurried voice. "Is everything all right?"

"Of course, Randy. You needn't worry. I'm a big girl."

Dolph remembered how he felt about Pete all those years ago; it was a feeling in his chest; he always looked forward to simply holding her. He loved Corrine more than life itself, but he loved holding this never aging woman. He was one of many who felt that way.

"I'll see you then? I may even come early."

"Yes. Thank you, Pete."

Whether he was driven by guilt over his feelings for Pete or the need to affirm his love for Corrine, he found her in the breakfast room pouring over a new design for a bullfrog. The frog was the first of a special contract to fabricate four main menu items for a Cajun restaurant in Beaumont, Texas. The others were a shrimp, a crawfish and an oyster.

The oyster was going to be a challenge. She persuaded the owner that he didn't really want an alligator or a snake in this artistic display. Women and children might feel uneasy. It was one thing to see these items on a menu and be able to shudder or wince, but it was quite another to see such big replicas out in the decorative swamp surrounding the parking lot.

"Corrine, could I invite you to supervise my lunch at Hannah's? I'd appreciate your elevating my behavior."

Ever since they met at the University of Houston, Dolph had a way of saying and doing the sweetest things. She was charmed then and now.

"Sure, I'll be ready in 10 minutes."

CHAPTER 40

Bad News in Good Surroundings

Dolph was always treated like royalty every time he showed up at Hannah's Place. But when Corrine came with him, there was no doubt she was the queen and he a mere footman. She and Hannah, and even little Toey, exchanged hugs and laughs. Seferina came out of the kitchen drying her hands on a cup towel. The normally scowling Mexican woman was beaming.

Cavanaugh never understood the dynamics of women who were so different at one level, but became loving, giggling schoolgirls and sisters at another. Men didn't seem to share that versatility.

He had to stand back as the reunion ran its course, a move hastened by the departure and arrival of other paying guests. Finally, as the women deplaned from some other planet, Hannah laughed and escorted Corrine and her boyfriend to one of their special tables. Toey brought water and unsweetened iced tea. Corrine ordered for both of them.

The place was crowded, but the noise was courteously muted. Soon,

Toey reappeared with salads and bread. Dolph cleared his throat and told Corrine he had some disappointing news. Corrine already knew that when she heard him lightly cough.

She smiled. "You didn't need to bring me out here just to tell me bad news."

"Sweetie, I know that, but I didn't say it was bad news, just disappointing."

"I'm not going to be able to do Hawaii; can't afford to be that far away from town for the next few weeks. There's a lot going on in Houston and here; I just wouldn't be comfortable."

Corrine wasn't curious about the details; she just saw them as irrelevant to the ultimate decision. She did, however, pay attention.

"What do you mean by 'that far,' and what would make you comfortable?"

"You're a tough customer, my dear. I do have an alternative. You've never been to The Mansion on Turtle Creek in Dallas. It's supposed to be a real nice place."

Dolph hadn't stayed there either, but a few years back he had arranged for some Florida investors to overnight there before flying them up to meet him in Oklahoma. The purpose of the trip was to see, from the air at least, the properties Dolph had under lease. As a longtime Oklahoman, Dolph, known to his victims as Mr. McDade, said that he had a theory that had proven correct about 80 percent of the time. You see, when the big boys in the oil "bidness" decide to lease up and explore in one direction, say from Farmer Brown's place northeast to Rancher Bob's spread, McDade explained it would be a good idea to lease up the mineral interests on either end of the of the anticipated play. This amounted, he said, to several thousands of surface acres. He intimated that he had inside information on the details of a particular lease plan and expected exploration and testing to be happening coincidentally during the time his Florida boys were visiting. Sure enough, as they flew low over the land, a seismic vehicle and trailer was parked at a gate leading into some property. On top of the truck and trailer, big letters read "S.E.C." and on the doors, barely discernible, were the words Seismic

Exploration Company. Dolph thought the name to be unimaginative, but often you've got to spell things out for folks. The hard hat helmeted worker down below looked up and waived as he turned to fiddle with the gate lock. Dolph's pilot waggled his wings and flew on.

C.W. waited until the aircraft was out of sight before backing the truck and trailer onto the paved road. He drove back the way he had come, past the rancher's house and toward the highway to Oklahoma City. The rancher had earlier spotted the seismic truck and guessed the driver was lost, a fact he would realize soon after he passed from view over a low ridge. The rancher decided to wait a few minutes and finish his coffee before going to investigate. The faint noise of an airplane in that area caused him to set aside his cup, grab his Winchester and head for his pick-up. But then he heard the straining of the seismic vehicle's engine and transmission as it took the backside of the ridge. Soon the truck appeared and left the area. This was not an uncommon occurrence in Oklahoma's outback, truck drivers and pilots lost on the same mission, trying to find a particular piece of property. Common or not, ranchers just about anywhere are alert to protect their land and cattle. Dolph and C.W. had known their timing had to be precise; they couldn't afford for the rancher to shoot a trespasser or to take a bead on the airplane. Anyway, that led later to a big payday for the boys.

That was the second time they had worked that scheme; the first being to show a city banker in Colorado how many cows they were able to feed on a new kind of grass. The banker had no idea how to read a compass or to orient himself to any landmark. That time C.W. was the rancher seeking the bank loan, and Dolph was the waiving ranch hand. Dolph had the hard job. He had to change shirts and hats and race the pick up to another part of the pasture before the pilot's next pass.

Corrine's voice brought him back from his memories.

"Country Boy, I don't mind missing that trip; we were there last year. I could do a little shopping and see some customers in Dallas. What will you do, though?"

"They have a health spa. Maybe I'll work out and listen to Fox News; it's becoming a popular network"

CHAPTER 41
Night Crawlers

Saturday mornings were special for Dolph. He and Corrine might throw on some clothes and go into town and have the country breakfast buffet at the KC or head over to Momma's for coffee, eggs, grits and homemade biscuits. Since the diet and exercise routine had begun, that sort of food was out; fruit, yogurt and dry toast were in. The problem this morning was that Corrine kept sleeping. Last night had been the night. Dolph decided to let her continue to do so. He could read and cuss out the Chronicle in peace.

About 8:15 the phone rang. It was Baxter.

"Dolph, are you awake?" This was Trimmer's odd way of saying good morning.

"No, Bax, I'm having a wet dream. What's going on?"

"Somebody broke into my car last night, actually the trunk. All they did was dump out the contents of the briefcase. I got out here to pick up my newspaper and saw the trunk was open with all the magazines scattered on the driveway. Should I call the police? Maybe they could lift prints?"

"Baxter, you've been watching too many cop shows. It'd be a waste of time for them to play forensics. Go ahead and report it anyway. Why didn't you hear the car alarm? Were you lost in the loving arms of Eloise?"

"What alarm? Eloise kept setting it off accidentally and couldn't remember she only had to put the key in the ignition to turn the thing off. I had it disconnected."

"Smart move, turn off the security system rather than teach her how to fix the problem. At least we now know you're gaining attention. Assuming they had prior knowledge of the original contents of the box or guessed that it was other than a bunch of waiting room magazines, they have to be wondering when and where you made the switch. That's good."

"Are you kidding? Are they going to break into my house or yours?"

"I don't know, Bax, that depends. It's one thing to pop a trunk offering a limited search area, but it's another to plunder our big ol' houses. Even if a burglar could blow past the security gate and our alarms, they wouldn't know where to look. All their options are risky business."

Trimmer said he was concerned for Eloise and the girls, but Dolph thought he was more worried about himself.

"Look, Bax, go ahead and report this, but play it light. They'll ask you what was in the case, and you tell them magazines. They'll ask about suspects, and you tell them you don't have any idea. I'll take care of this next week. Trust me and stop worrying. This is starting to be fun."

"Maybe for you Dolph, but..."

"Gotta go, Baxter. Sleeping Beauty just came in the kitchen. She needs coffee. I'll talk to you later."

CHAPTER 42

Up and At 'em

Around 10:30 Monday morning, Pocahontas called and said Taylor's case had settled. Dolph could come up to Houston anytime that day or Tuesday. Dolph elected to get on the road. Before leaving, he got the bag out of old Sid's house.

When he got to Jack's desk, he handed her the bag of mortgage documents except the notes he and Baxter had prepared. He requested that she send the papers out to the firm's copying service and put the cost on his account. As he completed these instructions, Sam Taylor walked up behind him.

"She works for me, Cavanaugh. What are you doing assigning her duties?"

Jack smiled. So did Taylor.

"Well sir, I thought you wouldn't mind since I'm here to give you some bidness and make you rich beyond your dreams."

"Cut the bull; let's have coffee."

Settling in a client chair, Dolph began his recitation.

"I'm up here to find out if you can represent the bank and Baxter in the stuff I'm about to tell you. Those papers out there establish that a fraud scheme has been worked on the bank and pretty much who did it. They also show those people are trying to do more."

He summarized their research process and findings, handing the notes to Taylor. Dolph watched his officer. As Taylor did 35 years ago back on the boats before they quietly drifted into an ambush site or began a raid, he softly whistled the opening bars of *Dixie*. It was a signal that matters were ramping up.

"Sir, I figure that I can suggest that Baxter talk to Mrs. Wilson and maybe another director on the executive committee about his preliminary conclusions, but that he wants a good lawyer experienced with this kind of stuff to guide him."

"Who's the other director? We don't want the whole board in on something like this. Not yet."

"Carl Brooks, a straight-up guy, an educated Gulf War vet with his head screwed on tight. He can cut three centers, and he's one of us, Mr. Taylor."

"I hope we don't need any snipers. He's fine." With men like Sam Taylor, the assurance that any person is "one of us" goes beyond all other tributes.

Taylor was pondering priorities. "Is there any reason you just can't have Trimmer call me before he talks to your mother-in-law? As president, he doesn't have to get her permission to hire outside counsel; but I understand she doesn't want to be the last to know. She can decide whether to inform the rest of the board's executive committee." He paused to make the point of limiting early disclosure.

"You're right; Momma's a cagey old girl when it comes to serious business. She likes Brooks, and there's another board member she might tell early on. His name is Shelton; he lives in Bay City and owns a marine engineering firm in Freeport. Mr. Shelton doesn't talk just to hear his own voice, so I think she'll get him involved early on."

Still pondering, Taylor nodded approval.

"Sir, there something else you need to know: a VC broke into Bax's car Friday night or early Saturday morning looking for our stuff. We sneaked a switch, and I kept the papers instead all weekend. I think I need to get them back to Trimmer's possession so they can be properly stolen. That's why I asked Jackie to copy them."

"Randy, sometimes you scare me; you almost think like a crook."

Inside, Dolph cringed. "Aw shucks, boss, thanks for the compliment."

"Let's do this right." He called for Mrs. Martin.

"Jackie, do what this guy asked, but make four exact duplicate sets and tell them I want those copied and stapled in the same way as the original. They are to re-staple the originals through the exact holes when they were first prepared. Separate the original from the four copies and arrange to get the original back to Mr. Cavanaugh ASAP. Use one of the law clerks if that's what it takes to get the original set back in his hands."

Martin nodded with each major point. She had done this many times in the past. She knew the drill.

"I want two of the copies clean and the other two Bates stamped. There's supposed to be two different packages of mortgages in there. Randy tells me it's obvious where the packages break. I want separate Bates numbers on each package. I'll use those when the time comes."

Bates stamping is a procedure where sequential numbers are mechanically stamped on each page of each document as a means of further identifying a document. Litigators do this as a means of protecting reams of discovery from tampering. Some members of the bar and their clients have been known to interleaf a benign or malignant page or two in a document to be entered into evidence. Good lawyers keep Bates copies of everything they produce. Copy costs escalate, but tampering risks drop.

Jack returned to her desk and picked up the telephone.

"How are you going to handle the original set?" Sam was decelerating.

"I thought I'd get those papers back in the leather box along with some unsigned note saying that the writer had reviewed the loans and they looked dandy. That way they can steal a bit of disinformation."

"Randy, are you sure you're not a lawyer in disguise?"

Ignoring the remark, Dolph said, "Mr. Taylor, for personal reasons, I want little or no profile in this. Trimmer is a dummy, but he'll follow your instructions 'cause he's scared and he means well. I don't think you're going to need me, anyway. I'll stay in touch by phone."

Dolph stood and looked toward the door to Mrs. Martin's work area.

"Corrine knows almost nothing about this. I just don't want us to be around when the shooting starts. Can you help me on this?"

At several levels, Sam Taylor would honor the request. Dolph was always a lucrative source of business, a good man in disguise and a friend.

"I'll do the best I can." Sam Taylor decided not to delve into Dolph's motives for avoiding public awareness of his activities. "I assume you'll have Mr. Trimmer call me?"

"Probably tomorrow morning."

Taylor then stood and clapped his hands. "I'm hungry; how about you? I want a red-meat lunch, and I'm buying."

Pulling on his suit coat and walking out past Jackie, he spoke two words over his shoulder, "Coronado Club." Just before the elevator opened, he muttered four more words, more to himself than to Dolph, "We'll get these people."

* * *

Returning later to the Esperson Building, Dolph was in a good mood. He went up to the management office to discuss his lease. Hazel, the good-looking woman who managed things for years, was no longer there. Some called her Witch Hazel, but nothing was further from the truth. She had been a first-class manager and a stunning, mature woman. Dolph regretted her departure.

The rib-eye steak, green beans and two Martinis at the Coronado Club had prepared him for the skinny dork now handling the affairs of this classic building. The young man offered Dolph fresh coffee, at least.

The meeting went better than expected. Yes, he could end the lease whenever he wished; he just needed to give them 30 days notice. Because he had been such a loyal and long-term tenant and they stood to make a lot more money after he left, they would pick up the moving tab for up to 250 miles.

Dolph was ecstatic. Maybe the man wasn't a dork after all.

CHAPTER 43

Rocky Roads

Dolph was getting with the program. He told Corrine about the red-meat lunch and Martinis with Sam, and his evening run had been followed by a very light meal, chicken soup.

The next morning, Corrine passed on jogging again. This time she had a headache, a real one. Dolph warmed up and trotted up to and past the security gate. The guard gave him a friendly waive as he turned right onto the highway and crossed over to the left-hand shoulder. The traffic was light; school was out, and mothers were sleeping in. Most of the residents of Nouveau weren't early risers, and working people had, for the most part, reached their morning destinations. Dolph noted the time as 7:22 for purposes of measuring his time, distance and pace.

Jogging on the mostly level and firm shoulder, Dolph occasionally stepped up on the pavement to avoid trash or uncomfortable slopes. He made good time considering that the last occasion he had trotted like this for any appreciable distance had been at Mare Island, California, during boat training for Vietnam. He had to run in formation then while wearing jungle boots and his green uniform. It made the time pass as he remembered those youthful days and all the life that was then ahead of him, including speculating about whether he would come home walking or in a body bag. Mr. Taylor had been a big part of making sure he came home walking.

He swung into town, proud of this halfway mark of achievement, and headed for the courthouse square. He passed all of his former breakfast spots, including the KC, and the hardware store. Two of the farmers walking out of the store recognized Dolph and poked each other, grinning. Dolph waived back but kept going. The same thing happened as he made the turn and reversed course to home. By then, some of the good old boys had gathered to watch Dolph lumber by. This spectacle would be good for two or three days of chuckling and spreading the word, the male form of gossip in Bay City.

Dolph was proud of himself. His friends and associates might laugh at him, but he was confident that they respected his efforts and knew this was all part of Corrine's broadly known program. Some worried that their wives were tempted to copy Corrine's example.

Former Seaman Cavanaugh was jogging on automatic, breathing evenly; he felt he was running in the zone he had heard about. They said it is when your body and your senses are cooperating and your mind is allowed to relax and ponder great or trivial things. He was a quarter of a mile from the subdivision entry, again facing oncoming traffic, when he recalled that a fire from a mobile office trailer had fried the southbound shoulder. Although the fire had happened last week, debris was still partially in the shoulder, and the asphalt had crumbled. His cooperating senses and body directed him across the highway easily without disturbing his pace. He continued to jog.

Thirty-six seconds later, a sound registered behind him. In that instant of recognition, he stepped to his right to try and get into the grass. He was too late; he was struck on the left side at shoulder height. Whatever hit him spun his body around, and he pitched sideways, sliding into the grass and gravel that lined the outer limits of the shoulder. Disoriented, he rose momentarily and saw a flatbed truck speeding off in the distance. He then laid down to collect his thoughts and decide if he was injured.

He was unable to enjoy the peace and fog of that moment because of another sound, also coming from town. This time he recognized a diesel driven vehicle and the grinding of its wheels over the rocks and grass to his left. The vehicle came to a stop. A few seconds later he heard the truck door open and close. Footsteps followed. Then a voice penetrated his fog.

"I'll be danged. This is a heck of a way to find your sorry tail. I've been eating at every greasy spoon cafe in this town for five days trying to bump into you. I didn't want to make it obvious, but then I saw you plodding around the square like some old plow horse. Figured I ought to catch up with you just so you'd know I'm here."

C.W. didn't much care for Dolph's pained laughter; he was seriously unhappy that he had to eat some of the café food that Bay City offered its inhabitants.

"I could have eaten bad food in Portales instead of driving all the way down here," He paused and looked down at his friend.

"Are you all right, Dolph? I saw that truck hit you. I was hanging back when that buzzard barreled past me and took a bead on you. You must have known something was up. I saw you move right just before his extended mirror clipped you. Stop laughing and tell me if you're all right."

"Why don't you stop complaining and help me up?"

C.W. reached down with two hands, taking Dolph's right arm. He gently pulled as Cavanaugh slowly regained his footing. His left arm was scraped from the elbow to the wrist, as was his left thigh when he had sprawled down and off the shoulder. He was not freely bleeding, but both scrapes had opened his skin.

"You need to get that taken care of. Can I run you to a doctor?"

"No C.W., I'll let Corrine fix me up. Where are you staying?" He grimaced, closing his eyes briefly. "I'll come by tonight if I'm feeling OK. We'll do some planning." In shock, he still did not feel the pain.

"I'm at the Bay City Inn, room 206. Look, you're feeling tough now, but you took a real tumble. I'll be there tonight, but I'd rather you show up tomorrow night. Can I take you to your house?"

Dolph headed toward C.W.'s truck, noticeably limping and trembling as he opened the front passenger door. When C.W. climbed in, Dolph spoke.

"We can't afford for us to be seen together. One of the bad guys lives in the subdivision. Just let me off at the gate. I'll be OK. I'll cool down as I walk home."

When Dolph passed into the safety of Nouveau Estates at 9:15, he waived off the security guard's concern and kept walking. He entered the house through his garage and pulled off his jogging shoes with his toes in the kitchen. As he headed back to his bedroom, Corrine turned the corner from the hallway. She gasped.

"Baby, what's happened to you? Have you been in an accident?" She was shocked by sheathes of bloody skin on his arm and leg.

"I fell" was his only explanation.

"I'm calling Dr. Merritt's office right now."

* * *

Merritt's receptionist instructed Corrine to go directly to the Emergency Room of Matagorda General Hospital, and he told them to expect Dr. Merritt there shortly. He called ahead for them to expect Dolph and to begin cleaning up his wounds. Two hours later, they returned home. Dolph had on light bandages and was significantly sedated. Merritt had no better luck at getting information out of his patient, but after noticing the bruise on his left shoulder and the length of the skid marks on Dolph's skin, he knew there was more to the story. The two men exchanged comprehending looks, and the physician elected not to confront the issue or discuss his opinions with Corrine. Besides, none of that had anything to do with treatment.

Corrine was armed with a prescription for pain and antibiotic pills, and she also had instructions about frequently changing the bandages, bathing and activity. Dolph's training for the Boston Marathon was put on hold. She kept him doped up and in bed until the next morning.

CHAPTER 44

A Bad Patient

The morning started with a piss fight between the two lovebirds over whether he was getting out of bed and going to town or whether he was staying in the house with his nurse. Fists jammed to her hips, her head wagging from side to side and her chin jutting in defiance, Corrine won. But a compromise was reached. Dolph would have free use of the telephone and privacy on demand, and he would only take the pain medication when he could no longer handle it.

What set off the tiff was Corrine's outrage over Dolph's solo trip into town without consulting her. Even the ER people knew of his jog through town before the injury. Dolph's other mistake was trying to defend himself. He was in no mood to back down, but Corrine wasn't going to get off his neck until he did.

These two never slammed doors or threw objects, precious or otherwise; name-calling was kept to a minimum, although certain crude terms and their common variations were acceptable. Normally, it was a toe-to-toe, bare-knuckles form of verbal assertions and counterclaims. When they both had their say and got things off their chest, they made a deal and retired to other pursuits. They agreed early that two strong people make a strong marriage. That morning Dolph thought it wasn't a fair fight.

Dolph's first telephone call was to Baxter Trimmer, describing the incident as accidental. Bax didn't need the additional worry. He asked Baxter to stop by at his first opportunity. They needed to talk.

His second call was to the Bay City Inn.

"I knew you wouldn't make it last night. I found a really good eating-place. You ever go to Hannah's down the road?"

Ignoring C.W.'s question, Dolph got right to business. "Look, I'll try to sneak out tonight, but the prison guard I'm married to takes her responsibilities seriously. Let me say this, do you remember our deal in Casper?" This was a reference to a scam using half a dozen phony financial statements. The files advertently peeked from a file during a business meeting with their victims.

Dolph went on. "Think of some variation on that deal."

"I understand. You do what you can, and I'll see you when you're able. I won't mind going through Hannah's whole menu."

Cavanaugh's third call was to Jackie Martin. He told her the truth about the incident and asked when that package was arriving.

"Kemo Sabe, my scout ought to be skulking in your front yard any time. Maybe I need to send your woman my poultice recipe of dried buffalo dung, Aloe Vera and red ant paste?"

"Poca, anything but the Aloe Vera; have some mercy."

"Seriously Dolph, Sam is going to want some of his goons around you. What do I tell him?" Sam represented a private investigative agency composed of former FBI and other agents. The owner was known by others as "the Spook," a term covering his general demeanor.

"Tell him no thanks. Anybody wanting at me is going to have to go through Corrine first. These people are cowards anyway. Just trying to scare me." In reality, Randolph Cavanaugh preferred to take his chances and wanted nothing to do with any Feds, former or otherwise.

CHAPTER 45

Visitors

Years ago, while Dolph was a student at the University of Houston, one of his classmates invited him to his apartment to drink beer and to watch his two Siamese cats mate. Apparently the male had nailed the female several times over two days. Rough sex was an understatement. When Dolph was handed his Lone Star beer, the female was sitting and backed into a corner of the living room. She wanted no more of the male's attention. She snarled as the male approached. When he feinted to his left, she darted to his right but was too late. He lunged, biting the top of her neck behind the ears and immobilizing her. Her eyes rolled with more snarling as he mounted and banged away. When he was finished, she was released. She then made a low crawl to another corner.

Dolph had not thought of that incident for years until Corrine and Dora entered the bedroom to change his bandages. There was no feinting or snarling, and Dolph couldn't move to evade either woman. Corrine worked quickly as Dora softly cooed Mi Dios and other Spanish words that Dolph might have understood but for the pain.

When they finished, it was Dora who slinked away. Corrine proffered the pain medicine and water, but no sympathy.

"There now, you rest a bit." She actually patted the top of Dolph's hand.

"Yeah, baby. I'll do that. Remind me later to tell you about Siamese cats."

Corrine, puzzled, smiled. "Baxter is on his way here. I've told him to make his visit short."

* * *

"You look terrible." Baxter gazed at Dolph's bandaged forearm and thigh. Cavanaugh was stretched out on his right side. "How long are you going to be down?"

"Not any longer than I have too, Bax. I meant to call you yesterday, but I had a little interruption. Have a seat over there. I need to tell you some things."

Dutifully, Trimmer settled into the armchair near the patio doors. Dolph sailed a Lindsay and Taylor business card over to Baxter.

"Bax, give Sam Taylor a call or speak to his secretary, Mrs. Martin. You'll get an appointment; they're expecting you. I want you to hire him for the bank.   Tell him everything and let him guide you with the executive committee and the authorities. Don't say or do anything without talking to Mr. Taylor first. Do you understand me?"

Trimmer blinked a couple of times. He was in too far over his head, but he had no other options. Seeing Dolph laid out on the bed, Baxter knew he would have to do all this alone, at least until Dolph recovered.

"Sure, Dolph. I'll call him this afternoon." Seeing Dolph's spreading anger, he amended his reply. "No, I'll call him when I get back to the bank. What about the documents?"

Dolph relaxed. "I've taken care of that; you just do as I've asked. There's one other matter. Corrine and I are going out of town late next week. We'll be back the following Monday." Cavanaugh saw angst creeping over Trimmer's face.

"Bax, stop worrying. Taylor is going to take care of you, and I'll check in from time to time. Now, get back to the bank and keep your mouth shut."

As Baxter stood to leave, Dora came in the bedroom and informed Dolph that a young man had left off a box for him. He asked that she bring it in to him. The box was unlabeled, but sealed. Dolph gestured for Trimmer to open the box and told him that those were supposed to be the two sets of original mortgage packages. He also wanted to confirm that there wasn't any extraneous note from either Taylor or Mrs. Martin. Randolph then reached for a sealed envelope on his nightstand.

"Alright Bax, this next step is important. This envelope contains a note written by someone who says that all the loans, original and proposed, look fine. You return both sets to your filing system, but leave this envelope in that leather case. Leave it on the front seat of your car; be careless with it. I don't care if it gets stolen or not. Just do as I ask, and we'll see what happens. And if anyone, anyone at all, asks about the loans, just say they're fine."

Banker Trimmer knew he was up to his ears in a conspiracy, but he felt incapable of understanding where all this maneuvering would lead. He hoped it didn't lead to the jailhouse for him. He was also unaware that Mrs. Martin had penned the note after Dolph and Taylor returned from the Coronado Club. It never occurred to Baxter to ask Dolph who the "someone" was.

Bax hadn't been gone 10 minutes before Dolph drifted off to sleep.

* * *

Smells and sounds penetrated the fog of his sleep. He thought he imagined gumbo, garlic and soft whispers, but it was not a dream. At the foot of the bed stood Corrine, Momma and Hannah looking down at him, smiles forming on their faces.

"Hannah brought you lunch, more like an early supper. You better sit up and eat before it gets cold."

He hoped they weren't going to gang up on him to change the bandages, but he decided to take Corrine at her word.

"You ladies didn't need to come here, I'm all right." His attention was already turning to the steaming soup and garlic bread on the tray held by Corrine.

"Of course we did, Randolph," Momma pronounced. "We needed to judge for ourselves how long you would be at our mercy. We've even agreed to take turns keeping an eye on you so Corrine can get some rest." All were smiles.

Dolph, however, had other thoughts. *These vixens are grinning. Why do women take such delight in seeing a man down? I best keep eating or I might say something I'll regret.*

Momma had no better luck at prying a coherent story out of Dolph than Corrine or Dr. Merritt, but she too avoided a direct confrontation. Dolph saw that she wasn't buying the slip-and-fall version. Worse yet, he knew that she knew that he knew that, too.

Only Hannah was loaded with sympathy and compassion.

"Our crowd was lighter than usual, and I left Toey in charge. She sends her love and cried a little bit when she heard the news of your accident. We had been laughing that day when one of the farmers came in for lunch. He told us about your run around downtown, and about that time, Dr. Merritt's receptionist called to ask if we'd heard the news of your accident. That's when Toey teared up."

"Hannah, you ease up on the part about Dolph showing off in town. I'm still thinking about rubbing salt on his wounds for not telling me what he was going to do."

Dolph dusted breadcrumbs off the bed sheet. "You girls leave me out of this. Thanks for the gumbo, Hannah. Y'all don't need to stick around. I'll be a good boy."

As the three women left the room, a plan began to form in his head when he heard Corrine say in confidential tones, "Good boy, my fanny. I'll give him one of those pain pills, and he'll be out like a light for the rest of the evening. Momma, I'll be over around six. I need to run up to the H.E.B. first."

CHAPTER 46

Deception in a Good Cause

Dolph listened carefully for the diesel rumble of Corrine's F-250 Ford truck as she pulled out of the garage. Palming the pain pill had been easy, as had faking sleep. Now was the hard part, getting out of bed and dressing. But not even climbing into his Suburban truck was nearly as bad as getting out at C.W.'s motel and climbing the stairway.

C.W. answered on the second knock.

"Well, well, well, I wondered if you'd show up this evening. You're looking pretty rocky, but better than the other day." C.W. was grinning.

"Have you got some coffee? Corrine has had me so doped up, I'm probably not legal to drive."

A few minutes later, Dolph's mental dashboard began lighting up. Over the next hour and three coffees, Dolph told his friend the whole story. He described all the relationships as well as his impressions of the bad guys, added that there probably were women in the mix and provided an overview of the possible scope of the scheme. He gave him an update on Sam Taylor, whom C.W. already knew as a lawyer to contact if he ever got into real trouble. Sam, who was also convinced of the Shiprite/Piper conspiracy against the bank, was going to make the decision of when to call the Feds. But C.W. was to make sure that Sam never saw any connection between the two old friends.

Over the next half hour, C.W. outlined his general ideas while Dolph provided some tweaking. C.W. essentially intended to play the role of a newcomer to town. He would be a small-time promoter of sorts with a little money and a lot of investor contacts. The idea was for him to appear not quite as sharp as Shiprite or Piper and to gather information.

Dolph, it was decided, would remain in the background, only being the contact man between C.W. and Baxter Trimmer or Sam Taylor. All that having been decided, Dolph gave C.W. an envelope containing $10,000 in cash. He delivered it with his left hand as they shook right hands, almost as if he was awarding a diploma. The men knew that they would not see each other again for sure until the deal was completed, and maybe not even then.

Time for Dolph was running out. Corrine would be leaving Momma's any time now, and he had to beat her home. It was going to be close.

Three minutes was too close. Dolph had rushed to get his clothes off and put away, and he hurriedly redressed in boxer shorts and a T-shirt. He got under the bed sheet just as he heard the Ford diesel reentering the garage. He prayed that Corrine wouldn't decide to touch the warm hood of his Suburban. She could be a suspicious tart, and he would consider this one of his great victories if he pulled off this outing without getting caught. His vision of success quickly faded. As she came through the bedroom door, he realized that he was sweating profusely and that his truck keys were on the dresser instead of the first drawer where he normally kept them. Genuine fear gripped him until she spoke.

"Aw, darling, you never looked like you had a fever, but it must have just broken. That's good. Now let me look at your bandages and see if they're okay."

CHAPTER 47

Travel—A Refreshing Experience

Before the following Saturday, Dolph returned to Dr. Merritt's for a check up. He was told he could resume mild exercise, but only if Corrine accompanied him. Dolph was put out with the restriction, but he realized that he had to be more careful about his safety and that of Corrine's. The thugs he was dealing with were more dangerous physically than most fraud schemers. They were more corrupt and prone to violence. They were a new breed. In the old days, a good schemer knew to disappear when the heat got up. This new bunch just killed those in their way and never had real friends. Everyone was expendable.

During Saturday's slow jog, Dolph had pondered another reemerging, less violent phenomena: ordinary and generally honest businessmen turning crooked. Their pants came down during dramatic sustained rises in the interest rates, when borrowing funds becomes more expensive. Eventually they get so leveraged for operating cash that they can no longer sustain the cost. They loot their employees' withholding funds, kite checks, and cheat on their taxes, all in a vain hope that something may save them. That path dead-ends at disgrace and the jailhouse door.

If an inflationary economy has its serious dangers, so too does the deflationary situation. The dramatic cooling of an overheated or inflated economy exposes everyone, especially investors and money managers whose greed, groupthink and ego blind better judgment. What was easy before, especially with other people's or borrowed money, now becomes impossible. At that point, no crime may have been committed. Bankruptcy, embarrassment and civil liability may be the only consequence. Knowing when to fold is a talent, but for ordinary mortals, it is easier to ignore the truth of failure. They ride the descending arc into the ground and again lie and cheat in the hope of some way out.

These players cannot cash out or withdraw from the game fast enough to avoid the rocky bottom. Against falling values of assets, their naked failure becomes public. What was genius one day transforms into depraved criminality the next. Investors whine, the press shrieks, and prosecutors grimly promise investigations. All the while, politicians adjust their disguises from willing accomplices to outraged protectors of the people.

Within any of these market conditions, a professional schemer like Dolph finds profit in these amateur crooks' fears of loss and exposure. His mind briefly recalled selling fictitious offshore cashiers drafts to the owner of an on-the-ropes aircraft brokerage company. The man used the drafts as collateral for further loans from one of the banks he was kiting. When the collapse came, it hardly mattered that the perpetrator had also been a victim of fraud.

In those days, Dolph suppressed his conscience with the belief that he was stealing from thieves. Now he saw the danger of that rationale and the damage of his other life in a different light. He was not proud of his past.

How, he asked himself, can he make up for this? Surely he hurt a lot of innocent people, just like Shiprite and Piper were trying to do to Bay City's bank, its shareholders, depositors and employees.

For a brief moment, he studied the tea leaves and imagined turning himself in, wondering if anyone would believe him or if anyone would care. He was not going to suppress his repentant conscience, but he was no fool. He certainly wasn't going to have that quiet inner-voice drive him behind bars.

Randolph Cavanaugh had just a glimpse that Saturday morning, but he saw bad times coming. He needed to change his legitimate investment practices, and he also needed to abandon the life on the other side of his office door in Houston. In that morning's trot through their subdivision, Dolph had become more committed to change. He would begin by meeting with the Laundress for the final time and closing of his offices in Houston.

But what do I do with the money, he thought. Corrine interrupted his pondering.

"Dolph, why have you been so quiet? You're breathing fine, so I know you're thinking rather than struggling. Do you want to tell me about it?"

"Honey, I don't want you to get alarmed, but I think I'm finally growing up. I've been thinking about Shiprite and the kind of person he is. There's a lot I can't tell you right now, if ever. But trust me; it's going to be really interesting."

In silence, they walked a little farther to cool down. Corrine sensed something new in her husband, and she loved him for whatever it was.

"Corrine, why don't we talk about Dallas next week? I'd like to go up on Thursday and come back on Monday. That could be a nice break."

She stopped and stretched. He loved what he saw and felt blessed that she had come into his life.

"That's fine, big boy. Let's go back to the house."

* * *

Early on Thursday morning, they drove Corrine's Mercedes to Houston's Hobby Airport and took a Southwest Airlines flight to Dallas' Love Field. Dolph picked up a rental car, and they went straight to The Mansion. Settling into their two-bedroom suite on the ninth floor,

Dolph announced he was going to take a nap and then would head to the exercise room.

"Well, you're no fun. I'll go shopping instead." Corrine anticipated this and had made some client appointments for that afternoon and the next day. Dolph seemed to need more rest since the accident. And whenever they traveled anyway, Dolph always kept to himself for a couple of days before feeling any urge to see the sights.

Going on the road and doing deals was always stressful for Dolph, so when he and Corrine traveled together, he made himself consciously relax a while to enjoy the rest of the vacation.

"I'll be back by 3 or 3:30. We can have drinks around five and an early dinner. You might even charm me tonight."

Corrine was gone in a flash.

Perhaps a half hour into his sleep, a knock on the door brought him up from the couch. He saw through the peephole that it was the hotel bellman.

"Mr. Cavanaugh, I've been requested by one of our guests to deliver this bottle of wine to you and your wife. There's an envelope she asked to be given only to you. Shall I open the bottle now or would you prefer to wait?"

"That won't be necessary; just put that on the coffee table, and thank you." Dolph gave the bellman $5, locking the door as the man left.

"Dear Randolph… Please enjoy this with your Corrine. Perhaps I'll see you tomorrow or the next day. I met a gentleman here in the hotel, and he's invited me to a baseball game this afternoon. Imagine, my first American baseball game! This is exciting…. P."

Dolph studied the slightly fragrant envelope. He had opened it with his index finger, creating a jagged tear. On the inner side of the sealing flap were three numbers, 816. He knew that to be one of the master suites on the eighth floor.

A smile crossed his face, and he shook his head slightly.

That 'gentleman' has no idea what he's getting into, he thought. Like me, even if he never sees her again, he'll always remember her and the feeling she causes at the top of a man's chest.

It never occurred to Dolph to worry about whether this gentleman or any man would take advantage of Pierrette in her advancing years. Under her spell, they were powerless to do so.

Dolph tore up the note and envelope and then tossed them into the trashcan next to the writing table. The fragrance clung to his hands. He'd save the wine for the weekend. He then headed to the gym.

* * *

The next morning, Corrine and Dolph worked out and took a jog along Turtle Creek. She left the hotel for her appointments after breakfast, and Dolph returned to their suite to think about his meeting with Pete. He made some notes, and then, as was his practice for these meetings, he dressed nicely for lunch. He wore a light blue seersucker jacket. dark blue trousers, a crisp white shirt without a tie and cordovan loafers. Corrine had made these purchases to keep up with Dolph's weight loss. Much of his clothing back in Bay City was to be boxed up for the charitable resale shop she supported in Houston.

He made one phone call.

"Can I come down in about 10 minutes? Is that convenient for you?"

"Certainly Randy. Everything is ready."

* * *

"Randy, you look wonderful. You know, I don't think I have ever seen you looking so healthy."

They hugged. She was swallowed in his embrace, but only briefly.

"It's Corrine; she has me on an exercise and diet program, and I guess it's working. I feel better. Thanks for the wine; we'll enjoy it tomorrow evening."

Smiling broadly, she gestured to a small dining table where she had arranged a light lunch provided by room service. Over the years they had established this ritual of dressing nicely for a pleasant and private lunch. He removed his jacket and took his seat. Business talk was deferred. Pleasantries and catching up on each other's families were preferred.

Dolph spoke at length about Corrine's creative design business, her appointments in Dallas, and their sons' plans for the summer. Pierrette outlined her summer travel. It included seeing her daughter Lisette and her family in England and a visit to her parent's graves near Dieppe. She briefly mentioned that she was thinking of leaving Malta for good.

She returned the dishes to the room-service cart, poured steaming coffee for them from an elegant silver pot and then pointed Dolph to the sitting room. Cavanaugh always felt better of himself in these meetings with Pierrette. They never openly discussed the ways Dolph had acquired the money he periodically sent to her. That was irrelevant to her function as the Laundress. This was her practice with all of her clients.

"Randolph, you've mentioned that you want to liquidate the assets you've entrusted to me. Tell me, after all these years, why you have chosen to do so now?"

"Pete, I think I'm growing up. I'm certain that I'm growing older, and I'm not entirely happy with what I have done with my life. It was never about the money; I'm still trying to figure the why of it all."

Dolph was confessing his deepest personal feelings. Not even Corrine had seen him this introspective.

"I always reserved a part of myself from Corrine, and maybe that wasn't good for either of us. I want to change that, and I cannot make that change without ending our business."

The Laundress studied her client. This man was now so altered from the young sailor she met in Singapore. Most of her clients were dark-hearted men who never seemed to struggle with their souls. She did not know what had touched him so profoundly since their last meeting a year ago, but his words resonated with her. What mattered now was that he was saying what she had been feeling for several years.

"Randy, quite apart from your particular situation, I have already changed your liquidity. You may be pleased to know that was accomplished before I left Malta, and your funds are positioned for movement." This was her usual practice when she sensed or learned that a client was cashing out. Such matters could not be accomplished overnight. She paused to refill their cups.

"Now tell me what you want to do with your funds, or more specifically, what arrangement do you want me to make?"

"Pete, I never asked you what you did with this money in the past; I never looked over your shoulder about the wisdom of anything you did. I won't start doing that now, but I have some thoughts."

He retrieved his jacket and pulled out his notes.

"This is a list of things I want you to do with whatever I have accumulated with you. I've made some special notes. I need no reports, no confirmations, and I really don't care if you decide to keep all the money yourself."

With that, Pete's head flew back in laughter, so rich with joy and understanding of what must be going through Dolph's mind.

"Oh Randy, that won't be necessary. I have done quite well over the years and taken my normal fees from your account. You can be assured I will follow your wishes."

Dolph stood, bringing an end to any discussion about money. It was no longer his money, if it had ever been. Maybe the coffee agitated him, but he walked to the window and gazed at the view of downtown, thinking for a moment of the wealth and world reputation of Dallas. He wanted very much to return home to the simplicity of Bay City. Wheeling about, he returned to his chair.

"Mrs. Meredith, now tell me what you are planning for the rest of your life. What's this about leaving Malta?"

Pete stared at Dolph. She saw him now as a friend, a very dear friend, but not as a confessor. She was beyond confessing anything, but still she could share some things in a general way.

"Randy, I have had a good and lucky life. It has not always been fun, but it has been interesting. You called me Mrs. Meredith, but actually I had other names before and since you and I first met. For all practical purposes and my British passport, I remain Mrs. Meredith."

Dolph raised his eyebrows not in surprise, but in intense interest.

"There is a malevolent spirit running about in my part of the world, a hatred and dedication to violence that worries me daily. I am seeing a spreading and renewed Islamic militancy similar to that of the first millennium. I cannot remain in Malta any more than I could in poor Lebanon to be devoured by that evil."

Dolph had never heard the world condition described in those terms.

Privately, she often thought of the militants as bullies for Allah, but the greater shame for her was that many of her clients were funneling their laundered money to the bullies. It was one thing to help her clients move and protect assets from unfavorable situations or governments, but it was an altogether different matter to have any role in funding violence. Her shame did not fully obscure her awareness of another personal hazard. She had become the central, although hidden, instrument of transfer for the bullies and their benefactors. If her business identity as The Laundress was even slightly compromised, her remaining life could be calculated in hours.

She went on. "My British passport allows me to go to many places that are relatively safe, and I am wealthy. Few civilized countries will question the suitability of my presence as long as I am wealthy."

Her eyes glistened.

"America and Canada are and shall remain the safest nations in the world. It is such a pity that your people do not see the beauty of all that it means to be here as a citizen."

She paused, regaining control of her emotions. "Halifax is a very pleasant city and convenient for flights to London and my daughter, but I haven't settled on any particular place."

Dolph again was enchanted by her manner, her careful English words tinged with a never lost, soft French accent.

"Improving your liquidity has tracked my own efforts. You, in fact, are my last client. It is rather fitting since you were my first."

She leaned toward him and smiled her small smile, not the dazzling beam she had shown on the causeway to Jahore. That was her way of ending the discussion.

"Will I see or hear from you again?" he asked.

"Perhaps, I need to resolve some other business here before going to England."

As Dolph stood, so did Pierrette. The meeting was over. He put on his jacket and they embraced. This time they lingered.

* * *

Two rings to Baxter Trimmer's back line at the bank passed before Bea Jay answered.

"Mr. Trimmer's office. May I assist you?"

"Sure, Bea Jay. Is the president around? This is Dolph Cavanaugh."

"Oh, Mr. Cavanaugh. He's down the hall, if you know what I mean. Can I have him call you right back?" Dolph wanted to slap the girl silly.

"No, I'll call back in 10 minutes." He hung up without further comment.

Later, on the first ring, Trimmer answered.

"Don't talk, Baxter. Just listen. Go to a phone outside the bank and call me here at the hotel. You have the number. I'm in Room 919. Are you clear?"

"Yes, I'll take care of that."

There was something odd about Trimmer's tone.

Seven minutes later, Dolph's telephone rang. It was Baxter.

"Where are you now?" He could hear background noise.

"Dolph, I'm in the KC Steakhouse, their old phone booth. I've got some things to tell you."

"Good, that's what I called about. First, what's this with Bea Jay answering your private line and telling me you were down the hall? If she was down on her knees , I'm gonna kick you all the way to Freeport." Dolph's anger was barely controlled.

"Hold on, Dolph. Nothing like that was happening. I was out in the lobby with Mrs. Wilson. She was telling me how pleased she was to meet with Sam Taylor." He paused. "Look, I'm strictly business with Bea Jay. You've got me so scared I don't trust anybody. I don't know why she answered that phone; she normally doesn't."

Cavanaugh's temper began to subside.

"Was she in the office when I called back?

"Yeah, I didn't want to say anything to you with her or anyone around."

Dolph was satisfied that he had misread the situation.

"What has been Bea Jay's reaction to your new found marital fidelity?"

"She has made a couple of runs at me, but I've told her that I don't feel right about any of that. Then I start talking about how good Eloise has been, and she backed off. I gave her a raise, too. I guess some day I'll have to face the music or get sued for sexual harassment."

"Don't worry about that now. We've got bigger problems to tackle. Tell me what's been going on."

"Sam Taylor and I met yesterday afternoon at Momma's house and let her know what was going on with the mortgages and what Sam's plans were."

"Good, how'd she handle that?"

"Dolph, she's a tough old bird. She said for Sam to run with the ball and to report only to her or me. She said she would talk to Carleton and Mr. Shelton, but she wanted this kept close for now. Taylor said he's putting a package together for some friend of his in the U. S. Attorney's office. In the meantime, I'm supposed to complete the paperwork for the second series of loans, but I am to do so slowly. Those were his words, 'slowly.'"

Cavanaugh understood that Sam Taylor was methodically preparing for an ambush; he wanted Shiprite's greed to keep him in Bay City.

"Good, good, good. Anything else going on?'

"Naw, Dolph. I just wish you and Corrine were here. We could go to the club and drink. I'm sure going to need a lot of drinking when this is over."

"Calm down, Bax, you're doing fine. You do a lot better when you're scared." Dolph laughed.

"Don't laugh, Dolph, this is serious. I never thought I'd have to be dealing with gangsters."

Dolph imagined Trimmer flipping his hands up and down, dithering like a frightened schoolgirl.

"Mr. Trimmer, I advise you to seek comfort in the mature and loving arms of Eloise. You'll both feel better for it." He heard but ignored a dissatisfied grunt from the banker. "I've got to go. I'll stop by the bank Monday afternoon or Tuesday."

Dolph then called the Bay City Inn and left a message for Mr. Rogers in Room 206. "Call at your convenience and leave a message for your friend in 919."

He thought about the morning's events and his talk with Baxter. He was confident that C.W. would call when he had something to report. For now it was more important for him to enjoy the rest of the weekend with Corrine. Maybe they could take in a baseball game.

CHAPTER 48
Camouflage

Several times since arriving in Bay City, C.W. had driven by the two-story office building located near the Municipal Airport off of FM 457, about four miles southeast of town. It was on the way to Hannah's Place. The airport had no tower and two runways. He speculated that the building, 20 or more years old, had been constructed on a bet that Bay City and its little airport would thrive more than it did. Hanging on either side of the structure were large banners proclaiming offices for rent and a phone number for inquiries with a San Antonio area code. It was just a curiosity until Dolph's briefing the preceding week.

Roger Piper's business, Redfish Mortgage Company, was located in that building. C.W. called the number in San Antonio and found that the building was managed on behalf of a bank that had foreclosed on the property two years earlier. The bank had tried to find a property buyer without success and decided that rentals would at least minimize building deterioration. A mortgage company leased the first floor, but six smaller spaces on the second floor were available for long- or short-term lease at favorable rates. C.W. asked when he could see those offices, and the man on the other end told him anytime. He said the people at the mortgage company had keys for the second floor and agreed to let folks in to see the spaces. The San Antonio management representative seemed bored by C.W.'s call.

That same day, C.W. drove to Houston, and with a portion of Dolph's $10,000, rented a new Cadillac DTS for 30 days, bought some appropriate clothing and accessories and left his truck in long-term parking at Hobby Airport.

At mid-morning the next day, he rolled up to the Redfish offices in the rented dark blue Cadillac, wearing what could best be described as West Texas agro-business flash: highly starched, tight-fitting Levis, and an equally starched form-fitting, long sleeve white dress shirt open at the collar, street-heeled, deeply polished, stove pipe cordovan cowboy boots and a pristine beige Stetson hat. His other accessories were a wide cordovan leather belt held in place by an oversized pewter buckle. The buckle depicted a bucking bronco. Two glittering rings adorned his pinky fingers. One was gold and the other silver, but each was studded with little stones, diamonds on the gold and turquoise on the silver. C.W. had bought enough such outfits for about two weeks, mainly in shirt varieties.

Except for a little stomach paunch, time had been kind to C.W.'s slender frame and narrow face. This old boy's crisp appearance was enhanced by neatly cut, graying hair and a carefully trimmed, salt-and-pepper mustache.

Removing his hat and smoothing the hair on his temples as he entered the reception area of Redfish Mortgage, he saw two men standing in a back office and talking with a tall Mexican woman. One of the men was burly with a rough looking face. He wore black 6-inch military/law enforcement boots, dark gray slacks and a light gray blazer over a maroon knit shirt. He was not the executive type.

The other man wore a cheap polyester blue suit and ill-matched tie. He was a little overweight and looked like he would faint after climbing one flight of stairs. His most striking feature, however, was his beady, darting, non-committal eyes. It would have been a tough order to trust this man on first impression. C.W. thought familiarity would not have seen an improvement.

The Mexican woman was a different matter. Trustworthiness would not have been among any of her top qualities. C.W. was reminded of those paintings on black velvet he saw back in the old days when he and his feedlot buddies would run down to Mexico to drink and chase whores. The senorita, maybe in her late 20s, had black curly hair hanging down her back and over her shoulders, but she was fully clothed in a dark green, shape-conforming business suit and high heels. Her full lips and long fingernails were carefully dipped in bright red. This was not a girl you took home to your mother - or even your brother.

The trio stopped talking as C.W. came in. The senorita turned, smiled and walked toward him. The big guy walked out of C.W.'s line of sight, and Beady Eyes sat at his desk and began fumbling with papers.

"May I help you, sir?" Her voice was like silk.

"Yes ma'am. My name is Charles Rogers, and yesterday I spoke with the building's management company in San Antonio and they said I should see you for keys so I can look at the offices upstairs." C.W.'s neck was getting in a bind looking up at this woman and her painted face.

"I'm new in the area, and I'm looking for office space."

Senorita bent her frame slightly at the hips, pulled back her hair over one shoulder and crooned, "What kind of business are you in that you need an office way out here in the middle of," she hesitated, considering her next words, "wherever this is?"

"Well, ma'am, you might say I'm in the milking business. Up in my part of the Panhandle there's a bunch of feedlots, but lately investors have been putting up big dairy operations. Tree-hugging Lefties and West Coast environmentalists have made the dairy business tough going. So they've come to Texas and New Mexico."

The proximity of her face to his was distracting; he fumbled a bit with his hat. He could tell she was used to men fumbling.

"Mr. Rogers, you don't look like any milkman I ever saw. So what do you really do?"

"I don't think I'm serving up my resume to you, ma'am, but I find land for sale or lease, my investors put up the money, and I build the dairy operation. I need an office for my stuff and for my folks to visit. You going to give me the key … ma'am?"

C.W. had seen cagey interrogations in a lot of forms and places, but never from someone like this senorita. Besides, he'd already seen what he needed.

She straightened and shrugged. She studied his face for a moment and then reached in a drawer, tossing him a ring of keys.

"They're numbered; be my guest, Mr. Rogers."

During this exchange, Beady Eyes sneaked glances at Senorita and C.W. Just before C.W. left the reception area, he saw that the goon had returned and was badly pretending disinterest in either C.W. or Senorita. No man could keep his eyes off of her.

CHAPTER 49
Dispatches from the Front

On Sunday mornings in Dallas, if people aren't sleeping in, they either go to church or sit around high-dollar sidewalk cafes drinking lattes and eating pastries. During the week there's a hardness in the city that needs a break on Sunday, a distraction from the town's incredible emphasis on fashion, propriety, status and business. Significant sedatives are Chardonnay and Merlot, beginning on Mondays and with hard liquor added from Thursdays on. Dolph observed that there were more sunglasses being worn on Sunday mornings at these cafes than he would see in a week in Bay City in the middle of a dazzling and baking summer.

This Sunday, Corrine was trying out for the sleep late title. Dolph trotted down to one of the many Starbucks in the area and got a regular American coffee. For a few moments he sat at a little wrought iron chair and table and tried to look reclusive and bored like the rest of the people. Initially he tried to remember the lyrics of "Sunday Morning Coming Down," written by Kris Kristofferson and performed famously by Johnny Cash. He then thumbed through an abandoned Dallas Morning News, muttering to himself that this newspaper only pretended to be as bad as the Houston Chronicle. It might be a little better. Then he spotted an enclosed phone booth a hundred feet down the street.

Phone cards are a wonderfully convenient invention, he thought.

"Wake up, C.W. You're burning daylight. I gave you 10 grand to do a little work, and I haven't heard squat from you. Are you getting old and lazy?"

C.W.'s initial response was to direct Dolph to self-copulate. The fact of the matter was that C.W. was heavily into obscenities that morning. Dolph held the handset away from his ear while C.W. vented and awakened from a sound sleep. Dolph had forgotten that C.W., when disturbed, could curse more colorfully coming out of a sleep than anyone wide-awake.

When C.W. finally got his brain in focus, Dolph spoke more gently. "What's going on down there, my friend?"

"What do you mean with that 'friend' comment? You've done it to me again. You really know how to get me involved with bad folks, and the last time, I got shot at and dang near died. That's why I quit this bidness, you jerk."

Dolph waited.

"Let me tell you what happened; these are mean, dangerous and evil people. I found that flatbed truck that ran you off the road. It's parked over at Redfish Mortgage. Its right extended mirror is busted."

C.W. described his first visit to Redfish and then his impressions.

"Dolph, that office ain't no real office at all. You can't imagine how tall that Mexican girl was. Her legs ran all the way to her shoulder blades. She had fingernails so long she couldn't possibly type her own name. The thug that probably tried to kill you was there too. He disappeared while I was talking to the senorita, and I think he was checking out the car. He's mean and ugly, but he's also dumb. The car was locked, but I left an accordion folder on the front passenger seat just so somebody like him could read the label. It said 'Investors'. I figure the guy can read simple words. They had a desktop computer, one old manual typewriter, a photocopy machine, a shredder next to that and a couple of telephones that I could see. There was also a huge table with stacks of papers on it. I got the impression I was in a printing shop rather than a business office. What really hit me was that I saw no filing cabinets; just file boxes on the floor and that stuff on the table. More stuff could have been in some other space I didn't see, but if that was the case, files were not where they'd be convenient. Back in the day, you and I could have done a first-class phony mortgage company dead drunk."

"C.W., did you go back?"

"Of course. I called the people in San Antonio and rented one of the pieces of crap on the second floor. Overnighted him a postal-money order for two months, got the key from the senorita and moved my stuff in the day before you left for Dallas. It took exactly two nights before they snatched my investor file, copied and returned it. On Friday that tall girl came upstairs and was wiggling her tail around, telling me that her boss wanted to meet me. She said he might be able to find some land for my people."

"C.W., it's a shame they're so few real professionals around. So, what's going on now?"

"I told her that would be fine, but I wouldn't be available until later in the week. I didn't want to be too eager."

"Anything else?"

"Yeah, she's a bad girl. She offered me some quick sex. I think she may be a little crazy."

"I share your disgust, Mr. Rogers. The world is going to be a better place when we get those folks out of town. Did this Latina Tart have a name?"

"Get this, Country Boy; they call her Cherry, Cherry De Los Santos."

"What about her offer?"

"I told her thanks, but I never mix pleasure with business."

"Good idea; you never know where her body has been. Hey, I'll get back with you."

C.W.'s way of saying goodbye was again to suggest self-copulation.

As Dolph dialed the hotel to see if Corrine was up, there was a tapping on the booth. A twit was standing outside wanting to make a call. He had on his appropriate urban running attire and was rolling his eyes editorially. He nearly dropped his Latte Grande when Dolph shot him the bird.

CHAPTER 50

Interim Reports

The Southwest Airlines flight from Dallas began its final approach into Hobby Airport. The flight was so short that Corrine and Dolph barely had time for coffee and juice.

"Baby, you've got two choices. You can drop me downtown and go back on your own to Bay City; I'll get one of my cars later. Or you can go with me to see Sam Taylor. I also need to pick up some things at the office. I'll call Sam's office when we get on the ground. What's your decision?" He already knew the answer. She was also worried about Becky Taylor.

"I'll stick with you. Are you going to need some business time with Sam? Jack and I can gossip about you two for a while."

"I'll need about 10 minutes. Depending on his schedule, maybe we can have lunch."

Corrine sensed Dolph's growing preoccupation. The weekend had been an escape, even an adventure of sorts. They went to a Sunday afternoon baseball game. In their entire marriage, Dolph never once indicated an interest in baseball. Something is going on, she thought.

When they arrived at Sam's office, Dolph was again relegated to chopped liver status as Pocahontas and Corrine gushed. Even Mr. Taylor went over the top about how good Corrine looked and how if she ever needed a lawyer to kick Dolph around, he'd give her a cheap rate. He pulled Dolph into his office and closed the door. Both women knew that the group social time was on hold.

"Sir, lots of stuff has been happening. I spoke to someone who took a swing by the Redfish offices. I don't want this person involved by name, so let me just give you the essential information."

Taylor never took his seat; he folded his arms and listened with deep interest as Cavanaugh described the interior of the Redfish offices, the sparse appearance of the place, the apparent absence of filing cabinets and the three incongruous persons working there. He nodded almost as if he expected what Dolph was telling him until the recitation focused on the tall Mexican woman known as Cherry De Los Santos.

"Son, this is getting interesting. So far as you know, has anyone ever mentioned this woman being in town? She would attract attention. Same question about the muscle. Guys like that don't exactly fit in Bay City."

"Mr. Taylor, that's what I think, too. I don't get around now to my usual spots in town. You'd be surprised what a fellow can learn at the K-2 Steak House or the Shipley's, but I haven't heard anyone talking about a big ugly or Chiquita Banana." Dolph loved graphic metaphors.

"There's something else. My source thinks the flatbed that tried to run me off the road is parked in the office lot."

Taylor's eyes narrowed.

"The Mexican girl is trying to arrange a meeting between my contact and her boss, Shiprite. I don't know if I want that to happen. These people are bad actors. Anyway, my person is going to stall for a while."

"That's good. I'm going over to the U. S. Attorney's office early this afternoon. I've got Trimmer's package of documents to give to a friend of mine. I'll give him a little presentation and this new information.

Maybe he can put the dots together. Let's stay in touch. Start thinking about some place you two can go for a while, two weeks or so, at the most."

"That will be easy. Offering a trip to Corrine is like feeding sugar cubes to a pony. She'll pack her bags in a heartbeat."

Dolph's face darkened. "What about Trimmer and his wife, Eloise? I don't want them hurt."

"Don't worry. I'll take care of them. When this thing goes down, they'll be in good hands. Trust me. Besides, I'll bill the bank." He smiled.

Dolph nodded acceptance of his officer's unsupported assurances.

Sam Taylor represented some private people: ex-FBI, military intelligence and contract company men who, for a fee, could be available for discreet protection.

"Poca said you and Corrine wanted to take me to lunch. I've got to pass."

"Sir, I understand, but could you let Corrine spend a little time with you? She's worried about Becky. I know it would help her to express her concern. We know this is a tough time. I'd just like you to let her say all that."

"Thanks, let's see if we can pry her loose from Poca."

CHAPTER 51

A Cooperative Effort

Sam Taylor and Assistant United States Attorney Michael Charbonneau went back a long ways. They had been young prosecutors then, and when Taylor, following his naval service, went into private practice, he hoped that Charbonneau would soon join him as a law partner. Of course, that never happened; each had made their life choices, and their paths diverged. Taylor had made a lot of money, but then he had wasted a lot of it, he thought. He longed for the feeling that he had made a difference, that somehow his work would endure beyond the sterile obituaries in the Texas Bar Journal.

Not surprisingly, Charbonneau felt the same way. To him, putting bad people away provided job security but hazy fulfillment. Maybe fulfillment was less important than being a part of the chase and the capture. If for Mike carefully building a strong case was the goal, the defense attorney's job was to find the weak points in the structure. When each side does its job professionally, the result is normally just. The exceptions draw headlines, but the norm is fair and appropriate whether the prosecution wins or loses.

Impetuosity was not Mike's defining quality. He knew that some younger prosecutors thought he was an empty suit, that his carefulness was a substitute for action. Age discrimination takes peculiar forms. Both men understood to the depth of their souls that some old trial lawyers are more dangerous to mess with than young ones, because the old ones are patient and watchful and their hormones don't distort their aim.

Sam settled into one of the two General Services Administration chairs fronting Mike's non-descript desk, placing his big briefcase on the other chair. All of the furnishings were GSA standard except for two categories personal to Charbonneau; family photographs and framed academic degrees and court admissions. Mike had received his undergraduate and law degrees from the University of Texas and was admitted to practice before the Supreme Court of Texas, the United States District Court for the Southern District of Texas and the United States Court of Appeals for the Fifth Circuit. He had no interest in appearing before the high court in Washington.

One framed document that might become a collectible two or three generations down the line was Mike's appointment in 1971 as an Assistant U. S. Attorney. Attorney General John Mitchell signed it. Early the following February, Mitchell resigned to run President Nixon's reelection campaign and became involved in the Watergate scandal, which led to his conviction and imprisonment for perjury and obstruction of justice. He was not alone in disgrace. That scandal ultimately resulted in Nixon's resignation, a presidential pardon and retirement from constant public attention.

Mitchell had also signed Taylor's Certificate of Appointment. On a scale of scandalous attorneys general in the past three decades, they agreed that Mitchell's signature was more prized than that of Janet Reno. Her flaws and failings occurred while she was in office and resulted in needless deaths in the raid on the Branch Davidian sect compound near Waco, Texas, not so with Mitchell.

One evening at the Old Capitol Club in the Rice Hotel, years later and well into the whiskey, Charbonneau and Taylor chatted after dinner about the old days and various famed and flawed judges as well as other politicians. It was a cordial and candid bipartisan reflection. As coffee was being served, Taylor observed, "We all have feet of clay. I pray that mine don't find their failure point before I die." That comment was the high point of the evening for both men.

"Filling in on my telephone call to you last week, I represent the Matagorda Peoples State Bank down in Bay City. Their president contacted me when he became suspicious of loan packages being offered to the bank. They did buy the first set but are stalling on a decision on the second. I have encouraged him to give me time to present this to you and time for you to decide how you want to proceed."

Charbonneau rocked back in his government issued-executive chair and laced his hands behind his head. Taylor had made similar presentations in the past on behalf of victim entities. He never showed up without a careful written analysis and documentation.

"I've brought you some light reading." Taylor reached into his large briefcase and pulled out copies of the two sets of loan packages Dolph brought to Taylor several days earlier.

"My client retains the originals for now, but I thought you would like to go through these preliminarily just to get a feel for what I think is happening. I also have here a summary, including some names, for your review. These are likely very bad people. I smell career crooks."

"Tell me, Sam, how'd this guy in Bay City find you? You're not exactly a good-old-boy country lawyer with cow poop on your boots." He smirked.

"C'mon Mike, I've got a Houston business client who lives down there. The bank officer confided in my client, who recommended me." Taylor decided to needle Charbonneau and deflect any further inquiry as to the referral source. "Besides, Mr. Charbonneau, if you ever spent any time in private practice, you would know and understand the strange paths people follow seeking advice."

Charbonneau, ignoring the jibe, returned to a sitting position and began thumbing through the stack of papers. Taylor could read his mind.

"Mike, I called because you're one of the old hands. Read the stuff yourself. Don't pass it to one of the kids just yet. I promise, you read this, and your tongue will get hard."

Charbonneau grinned. "That good, huh? Not much gets my tongue hard these days."

"Yeah, and there's more. Somebody happened to go by the offices of the mortgage company. It's called Redfish Mortgage Company. You won't find them registered anywhere, including the Secretary of State's office in Austin. They don't show up locally in assumed name records, either. They're in a nice enough building near the little municipal airport, but Redfish is the only tenant. In addition to the two men l listed in the summary, they have a goon out there and a tall, big-titted Mexican girl who probably does more than typing and filing. She goes by the name of Cherry De Los Santos. The visitor says that the place doesn't look like any office he ever saw."

"You want to tell me who the visitor is, or do I need to know?"

"Now Mike, I'm just giving you the lay of the land and some documentation. This other information is simply a heads up on what your people might find if they happened to discretely stop by."

For just a moment the two men were silent. Charbonneau understood Taylor's plea for discretion. No point in doing anything that might make the bad guys nervous.

Then Charbonneau spoke. "I'll give you a call in a day or two."

Sam stood. "Fair enough, Mike. I'll look forward to your call."

As Charbonneau walked Taylor out to the reception area, he paused at the security door.

"Sam, I took care of that matter about Curly. I don't think we'll have any more problems with him."

Taylor knew this wasn't an occasion to ask for details. He just reached out and shook Charbonneau's hand and said, "Thanks, I appreciate that."

Out on the street, Taylor reflected on the meeting. He and Mike Charbonneau had just engaged in a common dance between a prosecutor and an outside lawyer presenting a law violation. Prosecutors hate being used or manipulated. They don't mind being invited to take a look, but they want to make their own investigations and conclusions. Sam had given the government just enough solid documentary evidence to justify further investigation. The rest was up to Charbonneau. How strongly enticed he was depended on the quality, clarity and accuracy of the material submitted by Taylor.

The Redfish visitor's information had not been procured at the instance of the government, but it rather was obtained before the government became aware of the possibility of a crime in Bay City. In other words, Taylor knew the kind of information that would stimulate real interest from Charbonneau without having to disclose Sam's sources or become entangled in allegations that the visitor was an instrumentality of the prosecutor's investigation.

There was another significant happening during the meeting. Sam had almost missed it. When mentioning the goon and the Mexican girl, Charbonneau was impassive, too impassive considering Sam's graphic description of the lovely and charming Miss De Los Santos. The problem was that Sam couldn't tell if Mike was carefully not reacting to the goon, the girl or both. As he got close to his office, he softly whistled the opening bars of Dixie.

At that moment, Mike Charbonneau had just completed scanning Taylor's summary. He picked up his telephone and dialed.

"ASAC please. Tell him Mike Charbonneau is calling."

'Hey Mike, what's going on?" The FBI's Assistant Special Agent in Charge of the Houston office, Michael Harold Ringer, thought this might be a social call.

"Hal, I think we've just had a break. Could you get over here this afternoon? God is good."

"I'll be there in 30 minutes. I want my coffee black."

CHAPTER 52

Paths Apart

Special Agent Ringer was born in early 1949 in Hazard, Kentucky, in a small house on the edge of town. He was the third child of the Ringer family. Dreary described that January day, the town, the surrounding mountains and the opportunities for folks in the area, including newborns like Harold. People there lived an existence near the shadows of ignorance and poverty. The mountains of Appalachia, brooding sentinels, isolated Hazard from the glories of America's westward expansion and the high-minded achievements and rhetoric of the late 19th and early 20th centuries. Until 1912, when the railroad punched through into its valley, the only way out was a two-week trek over the mountains or a 45-mile journey down the North fork of the Kentucky River. That was Hazard's western boundary.

Coal mining, the railroad and two world wars brought prosperity to the valley for a time, but by Ringer's birth, Hazard had not shorn its atmosphere of mind-numbing isolation. Ringer's mother and father made ends meet on Mr. Ringer's wages as a railroad worker.

Harold and his siblings shared one great blessing, the wise love of their parents. These children were encouraged to look beyond the mountains. They endured the limitations of local schools and sources of employment, but only until graduation.

That day for Harold came in May 1967. His dream had been to attend Berea College a hundred miles to the west. There, a good Christian-based, four-year education could be obtained tuition-free. Dedicated to providing access to higher education for students with limited financial resources, Berea and its work-study program was the ideal opportunity for Harold. That dream would compel a life's allegiance to the region. Competing with that dream was another vision he did not share with his parents.

The town of Hazard is situated in Perry County. Both were named after the Hero of Lake Erie, Oliver Hazard Perry. In the War of 1812, Perry's fleet successfully defeated the British in the Battle of Lake Erie. In reporting the victory to his superiors, Commodore Perry, a Rhode Islander, wrote, "We have met the enemy, and they are ours..."

Ships and heroes at sea, even on one of the Great Lakes, were a compelling image to Harold, and that image was certainly well beyond the mountains. Harold ignored his other dream and the fact that a nasty war now was being fought on the other side of the world. Only vaguely concerned that he would be exposed to being drafted into the Army, Harold packed a small bag, took a bus to the Navy recruiting office in Lexington and enlisted the first week in June. To his surprise, he was told to return home until he got orders by mail.

The next two weeks were an agony for the recruit. He had already said his goodbyes to his mother and father. He had written a letter to Berea College withdrawing his application for admittance, and he had expended his small store of teenage bravado in saying farewell to friends and the only life he had known.

Some folks, even veterans of the Korean War and World War II, tested his resolve by criticizing the war in Vietnam and pointing out that protesters were making the news. One of the more common remarks was that at least these old veterans knew the identity of their enemy. Finally, specific orders came, directing him to return to Lexington seven days hence for further transit to the Naval Station at Great Lakes, Illinois, for recruit training. He would not return home for 16 months, and then only for pre-deployment leave. He completed A-School as a radioman, and he took swift boat training in Coronado, California.

Thanksgiving at home with his family in 1968 had been anticipated as a joyful event, but he then internalized the meaning of claustrophobia. It hung on him like a cough he could barely suppress. The mountains obstructed his vision, and the culture of Hazard seemed so remote from the new life he had chosen. Whatever happened to him in the next 12 months in Vietnam, he would thereafter only be a visitor in Hazard.

His mother was ill at ease, realizing she was losing her son to the outer world, if not also to a deadly, foreign war. That was a path they had encouraged without fully appreciating its twists and turns. Privately and mostly at night, she and Mr. Ringer prayed for Harold's safety. God, they knew, had inspired them to send their children beyond the mountains. If God did that, then He must have a plan for their boy.

Within hours of returning to Coronado, Ringer was seized with excitement and anticipation of his new adventure. The lungs of his soul had cleared; his decisions were affirmed.

Harold could not have guessed the dimension of the shadow cast by his decision to leave southeastern Kentucky and join the Navy, nor could his youthful mind have embraced the meanders of the next 33 years.

* * *

Now in his 52nd year, Agent Ringer was a member of Mike Charbonneau's Major Frauds Task Force. Before joining the FBI, Ringer had obtained an accounting degree with a focus on auditing and governmental accounting. As he could over the years, and depending on city assignments by the Bureau, Harold also had earned a law degree from the University of Maryland. His first office had been Houston, Texas, and now he had returned and served as that office's second in command. His next assignment might be as a Special Agent in Charge of an office in another major city.

Ringer always looked beyond the numbers. He wanted to know the whys of a case as well. If other agents could connect the dots and come up with an outline of a suspect, Ringer was more like a sketch artist who filled in colors and shades of demeanor to describe a defendant.

Charbonneau had a mild distrust for bean counters; without supervision, they could identify every tree and never see the forest. They were often unskilled in human dynamics. Harold Ringer was different. Charbonneau told the U. S. Attorney that he needed Ringer on his team because the man was a bean counter with an open and inquiring mind.

In appearance he was a classic product of the Bureau, average height and weight, brown eyes and short, slightly graying hair, physically fit but not especially athletic for his age. He blended well. With friends he was comfortable; with others he was cautious and reserved. A unique characteristic that set him apart from other government agents was his capacity to avoid groupthink. He did more listening than talking in a conference-room setting, but he was clear-headed and articulate in a one-on-one meeting. For him, silence was his private study, his refuge from conference-room babble. For that reason, when he did speak in groups, heads turned not just in surprise, but also with the assurance that he was going to say something important.

"Thanks for the coffee. What's the break?"

Savoring this moment, Mike Charbonneau leaned back in his chair, clearing his throat and smiling.

"The elusive Shari may have turned up as Cherry." Charbonneau distinctly spoke the final word. He brought his chair forward and shoved Taylor's report toward Ringer.

"Take a look at that and see if this doesn't light your fire."

Agent Ringer paused at the summary and then flipped back to the section entitled Persons of Interest. Charbonneau had lingered on that same section. He saw Ringer's smile begin to form.

"Actually, Sam Taylor said he is considering changing the title of that section to 'Obvious Crooks.' When you get to know him, you'll see that he writes more formally than he speaks. He's real clear either way."

Deep into the text, without smiling at Charbonneau's attempt at humor, Ringer muttered, "I knew him way back when."

"You mean when he was an AUSA and you were a first office kid?"

"Before that. I met him in the Navy." He never looked up, still absorbing the importance of this development. Finally he closed the report and returned it to Charbonneau's desk. Looking out the window to the buildings across Travis Street, he said, "Funny how things come around. I'll have someone do some very discreet viewing. I'll stay away from the banker for now. You never know. We don't want to flush anybody out quite yet. Besides, you seem to have a good channel open with Mr. Taylor."

Charbonneau saw Ringer's eyes narrowing, his lips tightening and his back straightening. Ringer was thinking beyond the numbers.

"Hal, you let me know when I need to do something. Let's keep this tight. I'll call Ben Olney in the Western District so we're on the same page, but that's it." Olney was Charbonneau's counterpart in the U. S. Attorney's office in San Antonio.

"Mr. Charbonneau," Ringer stood and reached out to shake Mike's hand, "it's been a salutary interruption to my otherwise routine day. Perhaps some Kentucky libation will be in order after we work through this."

Mike smiled. "Whenever it suits you, Hal."

As Ringer was leaving, he turned and asked, "Have you found out who is replacing Foxman? I don't believe we need anyone from their shop quite yet."

"I agree. Things might be a little tense over there. I'll just let them work it out."

Mike Charbonneau had been very bureaucratic about reporting Culver Foxman's behavior. He advised the U.S. Attorney that Foxman needed to be removed from the Task Force and replaced by another postal inspector deemed skilled for the job. The U.S. Attorney had spoken to the postmaster in Houston, and the removal was accomplished without a stack of memos. A few days after Charbonneau's report, a copy of a letter sent to his boss came across Mike's desk, stating, "Postal Inspector Culver Foxman has been reassigned to other important duties and thus can no longer participate in the Major Frauds Task Force. His replacement will be named in due course."

Foxman's career had not been ended nor had it been particularly damaged. Quietly, with as little fuss and paperwork as possible, the system had moved him on, giving him another chance to reach retirement with grace. Whether Agent Ringer or the underground network of investigative agencies knew any of this was not his business or Charbonneau's concern. The matter was closed.

Mike had enjoyed the afternoon's revelations, and, as always, the occasional but quirky way Hal Ringer injected high-dollar words into casual conversation. When he got home that night, Mike thought he might invite his wife to join him in a salutary libation.

CHAPTER 53

Moving On

Corrine drove her Mercedes to the Esperson Building garage three blocks away. Dolph walked. They met and enjoyed a light lunch in the tunnel system, returning to Dolph's office by mid-afternoon.

During lunch, Dolph outlined what he wanted to accomplish before the drive to Bay City. To Corrine's delight, Dolph asked her to plan what he needed to move from his office to Bay City. He told her that he was taking home the critical records, his checkbook and current files that afternoon, but he wanted her to contact a moving company for the other packing. He wanted her to make that happen in the next few days.

"Dolph, you really mean it? You're giving up on being in Houston?" Her tone was anxious.

Corrine was genuinely surprised. She had thought his earlier report, that Esperson management would let him out of his lease and even pay for his move, was just talk. She remembered many occasions that talk was his way of stalling. Now he was taking action, and he wanted matters handled as quickly as possible. She was puzzled.

"There's no point delaying this anymore, Corrine. It's time to do it. The building management will be happy, and I'm happy. I just don't want to deal with the details on this end."

"Baby, you don't have a place to move to yet. What do you want to do with your stuff?"

"Good thing you mentioned that." He smiled. "First, you can put it in storage for when you help me find another office. I want your help on that, too. We can afford to buy a building, and my preference would be one of those old, brick, two-story places near the square. Old Doctor Etling wants to retire, and his place would be just fine."

Lindell Etling had been the Wilson family dentist before Corrine's birth. These days, folks went to him mostly for dental cleaning and not much else. He muttered curses when his tools - or more likely his eyesight - failed him. He was loved in the community, but people were quietly wagering on when he would shut things down.

Cavanaugh now was grinning. His excitement was almost boyish. He had probably already spoken to Dr. Etling and must even now be imagining his renovations.

"Don't you understand, Corrine? The best part of my life is in Bay City and not here or anywhere else."

Until that moment, Corrine never considered that Dolph would give up the special ambiance of Houston, its dynamic heartbeat that rewarded business risk and achievement but disdained snobbery, that honored hole-in-wall eateries and burger joints as much as high-dollar, white-linen restaurants downtown and on the west side, that reveled in its wide choices of ethnic and cultural foods all over the city and its suburbs. These qualities signaled deeper, more positive attributes of this city.

When she ordered him to go off the road, she assumed that he would continue to commute into Houston for two or three days a week to take care of business and to free her for her pursuits at the Weldinghaus, the bank and the Nouveau Country Club. Besides, she and Momma had their special activities.

While Dolph hated the R word and never used it in referring to himself, she realized that leaving Houston for downtown Bay City was about as close to retirement as her husband would ever get. She remembered and inwardly shuddered that some of her older girlfriends complained about their retired husbands being under foot and driving them crazy. Some of the old widows remarked about that phenomena at the same time they longed for the insanity.

All these thoughts rushed across Corrine's mind as she munched on a dry Turkey sandwich. Dolph had set aside the bread on his Reuben sandwich, and he forked its contents as he listed items for her attention. He wanted his mail forwarded to the post office in Bay City. She needed to get him a box. He needed his business telephone to roll over to their home number; he thought for at least three months. She was ahead of him on all this, anyway. She heard his words but now was indulging darker thoughts.

Corrine wondered if her husband was going through some sort of late onset of the middle-age crazies or whether he was eaten up with guilt over a secret affair that had recently gone awry. Her mind wandered over the possibilities that she had seen with other couples, such as husbands staying late at work like Baxter or taking long business trips.

Ohmigosh, she thought. *That was the biggest clue that she had missed.*

In the past few years, he always came home off the road looking worn out, exhausted. She attributed this to his excessive weight and the stress of air travel, long meetings and rich food. Only now did she wonder if some woman somewhere was responsible for that exhaustion.

The harlot! She should burn in Hell, Corrine mused. *She deserves that for hurting my big boy.*

Oddly, she pulled back from the anger in her mind. There weren't the other confirming clues: an unanticipated new fur coat, diamond necklaces or the big trip to some fabulous resort. Going to Dallas and The Mansion didn't qualify; a long weekend in San Antonio might be better, but still, these were not destinations for guilty husbands with cheated wives, at least not given their financial status.

Mrs. Cavanaugh finished savoring her doubts about Dolph, concluding that all the evidence was not in and that, for what it was worth, she had rescued him from the clutches of whatever vixen was endangering her husband's health and their marriage. She would soldier on.

They returned to his office. She listed furnishings and decorations and the contents of file drawers. She called the building management office to ascertain freight elevator availability for movers and preferred moving times. She also got a couple of recommendations of companies that seemed to do better work than others. Dolph filled a file box with things to take back to the house and pecked out a nice letter to his part-time secretary who was now on summer vacation from Rice University. He told her that he was closing the office and thanked her for her work. He also enclosed a check paying her through the end of the year.

When this was done, Dolph locked the office, handed the keys to Corrine and loaded the box in the Mercedes. The drive back to Bay City was pleasant enough; the couple chatted about details. Corrine reminded him of a follow-up appointment with Dr. Merritt in the morning and that Momma was having dinner with them that evening. Corrine was outwardly cheerful, but her heart was not. Soldiering on isn't easy.

* * *

Late that afternoon, Sam Taylor left his office for the drive to M.D. Anderson Center, where Becky was spending her final days. The short drive constituted the only part of his daylight hours that Sam did not have to keep up a front as an upbeat and focused trial lawyer. He was a sort of juggler keeping all the balls in the air while planning his next strategies for the big case or a calm counselor guiding clients to the right choices while being sensitive to the emotions of those around him. Later at the hospital he would join Becky in their masquerade of good cheer. They avoided, at least for now, talk of the approaching end. They both knew a time would come for final kisses and goodbyes.

The 15-minute drive south on Fannin Street was a straight shot to the Medical Center without the usual demands of Houston's busy traffic. It was a time for Sam to relax and to weep.

CHAPTER 54

Far Vistas

After Cavanaugh's 9 a.m. appointment with Dr. Merritt, he walked over to Peoples Bank to visit with Baxter and to accomplish another task. Baxter was busy with customers and Bea Jay was nowhere to be seen. During a break in Trimmer's duties, they spoke briefly.

"Where's your little cheerleader? I noticed you were fetching your own coffee."

"She called in sick. That's fine. I've got a lot going and don't need her today. Do you want to visit?"

"Sure, but not right now. You're busy. Do you have a phone and desk I can use? I'm planning a little surprise for Corrine, and I want to make the arrangements without her getting wind of it."

Baxter pointed to a cubicle office in the corner of the main banking floor that was used for small loan closings. It was not assigned to any particular employee, but it did have basic supplies, a telephone and a phone book.

"Use line 6 over there. I'll catch you when things slow down."

Randolph fished a phone number out of his pants pocket, an Arizona resort's 800 number he had obtained from Poca at Sam Taylor's office the day before. While Corrine was visiting with Mr. Taylor about Becky, Dolph had told Poca of his plans to take Corrine away when things got nasty in Bay City. He also spoke about his idea to make inquiry as to how flexible Canyon Ranch could be for his schedule. He was going to splurge.

Ever since the Navy, Dolph had realized he had a thing for telephone voices, especially women's voices. Obviously Pierrette's voice had been the first to enchant him, but Corrine's was the second. Her vibrant and confident South Texas accent was wrapped in soft cotton. They had been introduced over the telephone in their university days. Dolph still remembered first falling in love with her voice. As the years passed, Dolph played a game with women's telephone voices. He conjured up physical, ethnic and cultural images to go with those voices, comparing them with movie and entertainment stars.

He had his favorites, but did not, however, find today's young voices particularly charming; they seemed light-minded and inattentive, revved up and hinting at mechanical. He thought of them as chirpy.

Yes, he loved analyzing voices, and today was no different. One of those chirpies initially took his call to the Canyon Ranch Resort on the northeast side of Tucson, Arizona. She referred him to Ms. Steiner, whose distinct Minnesota accent immediately charmed him.

Of course they could work with his schedule and that of his wife depending on the season of their travel and whether the resort was fully booked or not, she said. She explained that they offered a wide range of accommodations for either a four-, seven- or 10-night stay. Of course they had exercise, fitness and dietary programs that could be tailored to their guests' needs. Of course, since privacy and confidentiality were hallmarks of the resort's philosophy, they would do all they could to discourage intrusions from the outside. There was a unique melody to Ms. Steiner's voice. It was at once instructive, authoritative and welcoming.

When Dolph expressed concern about the heat of the midsummer in

Tucson and the potential that they might want to book there in the next two weeks if his schedule would permit, Ms. Steiner's voice bloomed with assurances. The next two months, July and August, were some of the most beautiful times in Tucson, she said. It was the monsoon season for Arizona. Great shows of lightening against the Santa Catalina Mountains in the afternoons followed by horrific downpours were an unforgettable treat. Professional photographers came in droves to film the drama of that special season. And as for guests, there was plenty of time in the mornings for outdoor activities. Once you got onto a schedule in concert with the weather, you would not trade that time for their high season. She became almost mystical describing the smells following the rains. Best of all, because only a precious few understood the incredible beauty of Canyon Ranch in monsoon, the resort had their lowest rates of the year.

Cavanaugh was stunned by her soaring descriptions. He was ready to snatch Corrine away that afternoon and go to this paradise that he knew only by Ms. Steiner's words. She asked if he wanted to know the rates they were offering. He actually didn't care, but he knew that response would sound false. To his credit, he only mildly gasped at the per-person charges; for two people for 10 nights, he could come close to buying a new, fully-loaded pickup.

"Ms. Steiner, I'm ready to get onto a plane right now, but could you let me make arrangements for an open arrival date? I can give you my American Express number."

"Please hold for just a moment while I research something. Keep talking."

"Yes ma'am, My problem is that I am moving offices sometime next week. When that's done, my sweetie and I can be out of here."

"Mr. Cavanaugh, it is refreshing to hear a man speaking so fondly of his wife." She paused, and he thought he heard her say softly, *you betcha*, and then she said, "Yes, I have booked you and your wife first for four days and then again for seven days. That way you will be able to use our cancellation policy to your advantage. You see, that gives you the ability to tailor your arrival for just about any time after you have completed your move."

Efficient, organized, straightforward and charming, he thought. *Where does America find such women?"*

After getting his home address for mailing confirmations and other materials, she asked if there was anything else she might do for Dolph and his wife.

"Yes ma'am. Please don't lose your accent."

* * *

Dolph sat for a moment, dreaming of the delights of Canyon Ranch and thinking that he had never enjoyed such a place with Corrine. Expensive resorts and hotels in his dark past were trappings in many respects. They were signs of business success, of deserved personal indulgence intended to disarm and dull the senses of his victims, turkeys stuffed with so much dressing. Such stays never exceeded two nights and were carefully planned as a part of the budget for any particular scheme.

Canyon Ranch would be different. He would eat sensibly and avoid alcohol altogether, both of which were hallmarks of his scheming days. While Corrine hardly needed any of the specialized dietary and exercise programs, he hoped she would join him as he became more disciplined in self-care. Cavanaugh had no guess where this new life would take him, but he felt some long-lost spirit was returning to him. As he attempted to reach back through the years to find the origins of that lost spirit, Baxter Trimmer knocked and entered the cubicle's opening.

"Sorry to interrupt, pal, but do you want to get some lunch?"

"Sure, Baxter. But first, I've got to move some money out of savings for a little trip I'm planning for Corrine. I'll tell you more over lunch. Where do you want to go?"

* * *

For about 10 seconds, the diners at the K-2 Steakhouse fell silent in waves as Trimmer and Cavanaugh made their way through the noon-day crowd to a just-cleaned booth. Raejean West had almost scrubbed the varnish off the table and was placing napkin-wrapped flatware and water glasses for her new guests.

"Long time, no see, Dolph. What'chu boys gonna' have?" She dealt menus like a croupier. Ms. West had on blue jeans and a tightly tucked, denim short-sleeved shirt. The ballpoint pen in her left shirt pocket was shoved out on the ready to write orders.

As she stood waiting, Trimmer ordered a cheeseburger and crispy fries along with iced tea. She jotted her usual code and then turned to Dolph.

"And yew, Dolph? Yew gonna have the same thing?" Her eyes narrowed to slits.

Her gum chewing came to a full halt.

"Yeah Raejean, except I don't want the bun, the cheese and any dressing. Instead of fries, I want you to double up on the tomatoes and bring me some extra pickles. Oh yeah, have Hubey back there blot the grease off the patty."

The waitress rolled her head back on her shoulders and laughed at the ceiling.

"Raejean, you didn't think I was that dumb, did you? You're one of Corrine's top spies, and I hope you report everything to her just like it happened."

Trimmer shook his head and smirked. He admired Dolph for walking into this den of cholesterol and corpulence and for not succumbing to its attractions. What he didn't know was that Dolph nearly gagged on the grease smells that met him at the restaurant door.

A few minutes later, Raejean brought the food. The last item she placed at Dolph's left hand was a small bowl of cottage cheese.

"Corrine says she's proud of you, but thinks you ought to have some of this as well." Not waiting for a retort, she put the lunch tab down and went off to check on other patrons.

Dolph, not actually addressing Trimmer, said, "That's another good woman."

Trimmer attacked his burger and fries while Dolph methodically peppered his tomatoes and cottage cheese. He then began eating slowly.

"Bax, I'm taking Corrine out of town for the next few days, maybe as early as some time late next week."

Trimmer slowed his chewing.

"My guess is that stuff could hit the fan any time after that. You talk to Mr. Taylor and get your instructions from him, but I'm sure he has a plan to take care of you, Eloise and the girls."

Trimmer laid his burger on the plate and wiped his lips with a napkin. Silent for a change, he listened.

"For my own reasons I don't want to be around when all this happens. Besides, I'm not needed. If you must get in touch with me, do so through Mr. Taylor. Corrine and I are going to Canyon Ranch Resort in Arizona, but do not try to contact me there. Taylor is the only way to get to me."

Baxter was attentive.

"Taylor has some men; I believe they are heavy-duty security types with military backgrounds that he will have for your protection. Don't worry. When this goes down, it should be over quickly. Between now and then, just do business as usual, but be ready."

Trimmer finally spoke. "Why do you need to be gone?"

This question called for a half-truth answer.

"These old boys have already tried to pop me. I think they believe for some reason that I am a threat. If I'm gone, they might relax until it's too late. At least that's my opinion."

Dolph studied his friend for a moment to see if he bought that partial explanation. Apparently he did.

"What do I tell Eloise?"

"You can tell her that I'm going to a fat farm with Corrine, but don't say where. Tell her how serious I am about losing weight and all that, but let her know that Corrine and I are going to be out of pocket. If I were you, I would say nothing to Eloise about this other matter until Taylor says it's OK."

"That sounds fine to me. If I said anything about needing protection, she would go crazy."

Finishing the meal, Baxter grabbed the check. "I'm picking this up, Dolph. You're a real piece of work."

As they left their table, other patrons eyed them. Up near the cash register, one of the good old boys, Virgil Henry, who owned the lumberyard, said, "Dolph, you're looking real good. Some of the boys are wondering how you've done it."

"Virg, I work out, eat right and stay out of this place unless Baxter picks up the check. Then there are Corrine's incentives; she'll whip me if I don't do what she says. Tell your buddies they can do what I do but they can't have Corrine. She'd be too much for them." The good old boys grinned and shared knowing looks.

When they got back to the bank, Bea Jay had also come in and was cheerfully helping customers. As Dolph left the bank, he thought he saw a slight swelling on Bea's left cheekbone.

Trash boyfriends, he thought.

Before going home, Dolph decided to visit Dr. Etling's building. What he liked most about the 10,000-square-foot structure was the raised white tile lettering, inlaid just below the top three courses of dark red brick, that said, "Bedford Building - 1906."

CHAPTER 55

Being Far Sighted

Dolph got home in the mid-afternoon. Corrine had the table prepared for Momma's arrival and had the food ready for cooking. She had been on the telephone and had notes scattered around the kitchen counter.

As Dolph entered she said, "I love having friends in this town. You know Raejean and I went through grade school together."

"I wish she'd been a dropout," Dolph grumbled obediently.

"Aw, big boy, she's a real fine girl. Had some hard times, mostly in bad boyfriends, but she's taken care of her daddy when he was sick, and I think you guys at the K-2 will miss her when she goes to glory."

"You're right; I enjoyed catching her spying on me."

Dolph ambled over to the counter.

"What's all this about?" gesturing to the scattered notes.

"Your movers are packing you up this coming Friday. They'll do boxing in the morning and bring their truck in the afternoon for loading.

After that, they will hold your things in storage at their place on the Southwest Freeway, near Sugarland. They don't charge extra for the first 30 days, but maybe we can get you settled before Labor Day. I'm going to Houston to watch them."

"By golly, Corrine, you're fast on your feet."

She was shredding carrots over the sink.

"And the telephone company will do the rollover tomorrow, but you've got to go by the post office to sign for the box you pick. When you do that, Marilyn says that she'll have you fill out a change of address from the Esperson to the new box."

"You're taking my breath away, Mrs. Cavanaugh. Is there anything else for me to do?"

"Yes, let's change and go for a jog before we get cleaned up for Momma. We're having drinks at 6:30 and dinner at seven."

As they walked down the hall and into their bedroom, Corrine turned at a right angle to Dolph, rolled her left shoulder like a bar dancer and, smiling, said, "Doc Etling said he saw you this afternoon gaping at his building. He said he'd think over my offer and give me a call."

"Give you a call?" His surprise was heavy in his voice.

"You bet. You said you wanted my help; you told me your thoughts, and I acted on them. What else did you expect?"

"What did you offer him?" He hoped for a little more control than she was allowing.

Corrine took the measure of her man. She was competing with a vixen of her own imagination. She elevated her chin.

"I said that we would pay him $150,000 for the building, and he could take whatever furnishings he wanted or we would get rid of what he left behind. I told him that I thought we would remodel the place, anyway."

During all this, Corrine had changed into work out clothes and brushed her hair. She looked impatient that Dolph was not further along.

"I've been thinking, Dolph," always a big clue for him to brace for something he might not like, "if you take the upstairs, I could use the bottom floor as a design shop and photo display of my Weldinghaus work. What would you think of that?"

Dolph wished that his positive reply sounded convincing. He was not so sure that 24 hour togetherness was a great idea. Going to the office had as good a feel to it as coming home, but to dilute the two concepts was a bit much. He decided to let things ride; no sense meeting an issue head-on until you get there, if ever.

"Baby, I think that's a great idea."

When they returned from their workout, sweat and physical release had done its work. The heat was becoming brutal.

"You know Dolph, I love you, but maybe it's not a good idea for me to be a part of this Etling project. It's your dream, and I need for you to enjoy it." *This was a part of soldiering on,* she thought.

God, thank you for this woman. I'm glad I didn't get my back up.

That evening over dinner, Dolph was feeling real joy about the way things were working out and decided to tell Corrine and Momma about his plans for Canyon Ranch as an early anniversary gift. He reported that Dr. Merritt encouraged his progress and approved the idea of going to a place like Canyon Ranch as long as he didn't overdo it. Both ladies were appropriately pleased and excited.

However, when Dolph returned after taking Mrs. Wilson home, he found Corrine in the kitchen putting dishes away with tears streaming down her cheeks.

"What's the matter, baby? Is there something wrong? Are the boys OK?"

Somehow he knew the boys weren't the issue. She turned and in a torrent of tears, half phrases and hot accusations, she spilled out her fears and suspicions about all the changes that were going on with him, the suddenness of it and the sweetness of his attention to her. She imagined that he had a girlfriend on the road or somewhere and that they must have ended their relationship or he would not have been behaving the way he was. She confessed that he did not need to take her away to Canyon Ranch or anyplace else just to make up for whatever he had done. Tears and more tears.

Dolph had first stood and listened, then, as the rains fell harder, he moved in and gently held his wife and continued to listen. Finally, he stood back and said, "Corrine, come over to the couch and sit down. I'm going to tell you as much as I can. I've not treated you right, but it is nothing like you think. My main fault is that I have been playing things too close to my chest for too long."

As he reminded her of her request that he do something about Shiprite, she realized there was a story far different than her rampant imagination. Without creating apparent gaps in the narrative or anything about his dark work on the road, he told her of his discovery that Shiprite and others were involved in a scheme to victimize the bank, that Momma was aware of the steps being taken by Baxter and Sam Taylor to protect the bank, and that Dolph expected matters to come to a head very soon. He needed her to keep his disclosures on their couch; that is, she was not to discuss this with anyone, even Momma.

"And that is only part of the story." She looked at him in silent anticipation.

Cavanaugh then began the more difficult explanation of his new attitude, something she had seen, but was, in his mind, less clear. Her demands that he go off the road to embark on a grand plan for diet and exercise had been a catalyst for him. As a result, he considered a lot of changes he could make in his way of thinking. He said without detail that he had thrown weights from his shoulders, weights that were every bit as damaging to the soul as physical pounds are to the body. For years he had failed to recognize these burdens, and now he was playing catch up on his life with her.

"Now as to Canyon Ranch, you and I need to be out of town when the cavalry comes riding in. That little scrape out on the highway was intended to get me out of the way, and I'm very obliging. I hope you will agree."

Corrine's eyes were red, but now widened. She actively nodded.

"I got Sam Taylor involved so that I could step away. He came up with the idea that we hide out somewhere, and Pocahontas knows all about this too. Baby, just so you know, I'm the one that came up with the idea for Canyon Ranch. I thought you would be thrilled to go to a place like that, even if it costs me another truck."

She flew from her end of the couch into his arms. She offered more tears and apologies for misjudging him. She buried her face in his chest and held him tight.

Stroking her head, Dolph whispered, "Corrine, there's no room in my life or my heart for any other woman. I love you and always will."

They held each other for a time and fell asleep.

CHAPTER 56

Intelligence Reports

Dolph and Corrine slept late the next morning, but they still managed to get in a trot around the subdivision. The Bay City heat and humidity were mounting. Ms. Steiner's glowing promises about Tucson's low humidity, even in their monsoon season, were difficult to believe. Dolph and Corrine were soaked in sweat.

Following showers and breakfast, Corrine was out the door after announcing that she was going shopping. His clothes were becoming baggy, and she thought he could use a couple of casual outfits for Arizona. Dolph cautioned her not to mention the upcoming trip. She also was going to the Weldinghaus to see if there were any urgent orders that couldn't wait until their return from Arizona. Corrine intended to close for a couple of weeks.

By the time she rumbled out of the garage, Dolph was on the telephone to C.W.'s motel.

"Get out of bed and tell me what you've got planned for the day. I've already done a real man's bunch of work. What about you?"

Following commands for Dolph to eat unpleasant things, C.W. settled into a brief report.

"I'm having lunch with Shiprite over in Lake Jackson. I suggested Hannah's Place, but he prefers business lunches out of the way. Said people had a way of snooping when he ate local."

Dolph couldn't argue with that premise, especially when it comes to eating with a relative stranger. Better to hold such meetings at a distance.

"Where are you going? There's a Steak and Ale over there."

"Naw, he says there's a German place he likes. He's picking me up here at 11:30. Hope it's good. I haven't had any decent kraut food since Trudy passed."

"You be careful, C.W. I think things are heating up. Call me when you can."

* * *

Dolph couldn't help worrying about his friend. It had been a long time since they went up against the mean and uglies out in Oregon, a bunch of dope head, phony veterans. He and C.W. had scammed a shrink out there who was selling PTSD diagnoses to these clods, who were in turn scamming the Veterans Administration for disability money. The VA was easily scammed.

Neither he nor C.W. knew that the doctor was into his own scheme. He acted as an informal trustee for their earnings from dope deals, a fact that came out later. All he and Uncle Buddy were doing was a straightforward fraudulent investment deal; it was only money, $300,000, and no cause to get violent. When he realized he'd been taken, the shrink called on his bunch of bearded psychos. C.W. had been the front man on this deal, and the doctor gave his boys a description of C.W.'s rent car, a Chevrolet Celebrity. He correctly guessed that C.W. and the doctor's money were heading south on Interstate 5 to California. They caught up with C.W. leaving Ashland. Four of the bums tried to run him off the road. They were driving a 12-year-old pale green Chrysler Newport that was all junk except the engine, but C.W.'s car was no match. Besides, the bad guys were shooting at him.

Some parents raising kids make a point of never, for any purpose, flying on the same airplane, even dividing their children in case something awful happened. Dolph and C.W. tried to follow that practice in most of their travels, especially when leaving the scene. Dolph was about a quarter of a mile ahead of C.W. and driving a Chevrolet Monte Carlo Super Sport, also rented. It was the oddest car he ever rented. It had little roses etched in the side- and rear-window glass, and its white sidewall tires had skirts over the rear-wheel wells. The deep red velour seat covers matched the car's dark maroon exterior. He felt like a pimp, but he always wanted to drive a Super Sport despite the fact that it inhaled gasoline faster than a car-wash vacuum sucks dust.

In his rearview mirror Dolph saw C.W.'s erratic driving and the old Chrysler pulling up alongside, or at least trying to. C.W. kept swerving to keep them behind him. Instinct informed Cavanaugh of the situation. Dolph searched for some way to relieve C.W. Ahead he saw an exit off to the right and assumed that once he reached the elevated cross road, his direction of travel would continue to an entry ramp on the other side. That was his hope. He adjusted his speed downward a bit to allow the two other cars to catch up. Just before he blew the elevated intersection, he looked back to see C.W. and his friends approaching the underpass. As they cleared the other side, Dolph floored the Monte Carlo.

The maroon beast leapt toward the freeway entrance. Dolph correctly assumed that the bad boys would be too intent on killing C.W. to notice the monster bearing down on them from their right. Being a dope head encourages those types of limitations. As long as the Chrysler essentially maintained its course and speed, Dolph could tune the Monte Carlo's speed to collide anywhere on his target's right side.

In the few seconds it took Dolph to exit and then to reenter the freeway, a long forgotten but familiar and focused calm took charge of Cavanaugh's mind and nerves. Without passion, fear or anger, Dolph foresaw his goal and its consequences. He had not felt this way since he returned to the boats after Singapore.

Moving close to 85 miles per hour, the Monte Carlo's front end French-kissed the right rear of the Chrysler. At those speeds, a kiss was all it took to put the bad folks into a deadly spin. Dolph was prepared for the moment of the kiss, and he countered the Monte Carlo's urge to fall off to the left. He pulled firmly to the right and lowered his speed just enough to gain traction in the left lane. The spinning dope heads were unable to avoid the 18-wheeler parked on the road's right shoulder ahead. Its trailer was loaded with thick steel rebar for highway construction. Between the trailer's deck and the stacked rebar, the Chrysler was blown open at its middle. The bad men's body parts were going to be tough to match.

In his rearview mirror, Dolph's last sight of the Chrysler was its explosion of pieces. Glancing at the right-side mirror, he saw the trucker still running from his vehicle.

Five minutes later, Cavanaugh caught up with C.W. Pulling alongside, Dolph was treated to C.W.'s bird, and Dolph's calm was overcome with fatigue. They continued at lawful speeds into California. A hundred miles later and just before dark, they pulled into a motel in Redding, California. After checking into separate rooms, they rejoined for a damage assessment. Other than a few bullet holes, CW's car was in good shape. The Monte Carlo's front end was a little messed up and could not be driven at night without gaining the attention of law enforcement.

The next morning, again separately, the boys went to two paint and body shops in town to get repairs. They each went with a story to explain the damage, and each wished to avoid the hassle of dealing with angry rental agencies. C.W. alleged that his damage was caused by some irate highway redneck. Redding being what it is, the story worked.

Redding was a pleasant place to rest for a week. While passing the time, Dolph saw an article in The Oregonian, a newspaper out of Portland. An allegedly deranged patient at the Portland VA Medical Center had murdered a noted physician. An anonymous source told The Oregonian that the authorities were examining a bizarre highway auto accident south of Ashland in which four of the physician's VA outpatients had perished. Dolph and C.W. figured they had conned the psychos' money being held in trust, so to speak, by the doctor.

Getting shot at was not high on C.W.'s list of pleasures. That incident ended the partnership between C.W. and Cavanaugh. Uncle Buddy was grateful for Dolph's rescue, but they figured they had come to the end of their run. They didn't speak for two years and then only when C.W. called to tell Dolph he'd married a German girl named Trudy.

* * *

When Dolph returned from lunch at Hannah's Place, he had a telephone message to call Sam Taylor.

"I was out when you called. What do I need to know?"

Both men were in their essentials mode, that is, a pre-operative state of mind. They were in a focus that dispenses with chit-chat and irrelevancies, a mode that moves from a walk to a trot and then to a canter all as a prelude to a mad dash. This state of mind had been familiar to Taylor and Cavanaugh since their days on the boats when snapping flags, crackling radio transmissions and the jacking of 50-caliber machinegun rounds were signals of a coming fight.

"Forget about it. Apparently Piper isn't who he says he is. Piper isn't Piper. Shiprite is an ex-con. He did time at Seagoville for banking violations, serving long enough to meet a lot of bad boys, future confederates. The Task Force is running the records to see who might fit Piper's description and the offense profile."

Dolph could hear papers shuffling in the background. Taylor continued.

"Of course, I couldn't give them a photograph, just the verbal description you passed on. Beyond height, weight, approximate age and coloring, as well as, to quote you, *round faced shifty-eyed subservient type who prefers polyester clothing* may be the clue that narrows the search."

"Sir, I tried my best to describe the weasel and confirmed it in a little light conversation with Corrine. She thought I was dead-on right."

"Got news for you, Dolph. Lots of crooks fit that description. The good news is that when caught, they have no balls and will sing like little birds in the spring. False identities don't change that kind of character. Can you tell me anything?"

"Maybe later this afternoon. My contact had lunch with Shiprite, but he hasn't called in to report. If it's all the same to you, I'm putting him on standby to bail out. I don't want him hurt, and nobody can protect him."

Taylor was silent for a moment. "Call me when you hear anything. If you think he needs to go, that's good enough for me."

"How's Mrs. Taylor?"

"Not good. Thanks for asking."

* * *

Mr. Rogers called at 3:45.

"The German food was good, but not anywhere like Trudy's. I think maybe it might have been the fact that it's the middle of this hot summer and that kind of food is best in the dead of winter."

"C.W.," exasperation dominated Dolph's tone. "I don't give a flip about your views on Teutonic food in any season. I'm more interested in why you were late calling me back. What took so long, and what did you find out?" Dolph thought he heard a little chuckle.

"I was getting to that. I just thought you'd want to hear the most important part first. Mostly we blew smoke at each other for over an hour. We talked sports, weather and women. He was curious about my investors and their level of sophistication. He wondered why I picked Bay City as a place to develop major dairy operations. Told me that if I worked up a spec sheet on the kind of land I was looking for, he might be able to hep' out."

Dolph waited for more.

"Actually, I think he was testing me. For some reason, I got the feeling that he thought I was conning him. Imagine that."

They both laughed.

"Imagine that. How'd you leave it?"

"We didn't. That's my point. We just stopped. The fat waitress brought the bill, he paid and tipped well, and we drove back to Bay City."

Cavanaugh pondered a bit. "You don't think he thinks you're a lawman, do you?"

"No, if I had to guess, he thinks I'm more of a crook than he is."

"Under the circumstances, that's a compliment. C.W., I think you ought to get ready to pull the plug on this. You've earned your fee, and I don't want you hurt. We're too old and it's too hot for us to repeat the Oregon getaway. I still feel bad about you getting shot at."

"Good. I like thinking of you suffering." They laughed, but both men knew how close death had come to C.W.

"You wanted to know why I was late. I hope you feel bad complaining about that, too. When we got back to town, he swung by the Redfish offices, and I took the opportunity to go to my office to see if anything had been disturbed. Everything was OK. But when I came down to get my ride back over to the motel, a Federal Express truck had rolled up and was offloading a big, eat-anything-you-feed-it paper shredder. That can mean only one thing."

"Yup."

* * *

"Mr. Taylor, here's the latest. Redfish got a monster paper shredder delivered this afternoon. I don't know what you think, but to me that means these people are cleaning files. They don't want to have anything that a Grand Jury might want produced."

"Good, I'll pass that on. Jack tells me you're abandoning Houston. Is that true?"

"I'm already gone. Corrine has movers coming on Friday afternoon, and she's going to supervise. As soon as that's done, Corrine and I can hide out at Canyon Ranch. All you've got to do is give me the departure call. Poca has the contact information, and nobody gets through to us except you."

CHAPTER 57

The Plot Thickens

Hal Ringer was not a man to show excitement over interesting developments - good or bad. He was measured and methodical. He showed up unannounced at Charbonneau's office late the next morning.

"Thought you would want to know, we got a hit on Mr. Piper. His name is Robert Harris Carter. He was Shiprite's roommate at Seagoville for about six months. His first fall was for embezzlement from a bank in Conroe. This was years ago."

Ringer lightly tossed Carter's rap sheet onto Charbonneau's desk.

"He was supposed to be a married, church-going fellow who made a tiny little $60,000 dollar misapplication when he covered a friend's check kiting scheme. The kiter covered the loss when he got caught, but Carter still had hidden the fact of the kite from the president, and, of course, the bank board. People at the church he and his wife attended near Rice University wrote nice letters, I think mostly because Mrs. Carter was the decent one in the family. I remember this case for two reasons; I worked a portion of it when Houston was my first office, and the AUSA who handled it made a colorful comment about Carter's wife. He told me at sentencing that she had a 'sad countenance.' I've seen that look many times since then, women who've had their hearts broken by their husband's moral failures." Ringer paused.

"The rap sheet shows three more falls, one for forgery in Oklahoma, and another in Arkansas. The last one was for defrauding HUD on a housing project in Dallas. In that offense he was using the name of Robert Piper, not Roger. He was on supervised release until 18 months ago when he dropped from sight. I've got an active capias on him for breaking the conditions of his release, but thought you would want to talk about larger considerations." Ringer had in mind a grand sweep of all the bad actors.

Mike Charbonneau studied the rap sheet and now was looking out the window. Ringer waited.

"Could you send his photo and that of Shiprite over to San Antonio to see if we get any hits there?"

"Already done that; it's the case out of Boerne. This morning our guys showed a photo spread to the bank employees there, and we have positive identifications on both men. We still don't have mug shots of De Los Santos or the other woman."

"Did Rothgeb get anything when he snooped around the Redfish offices?" Charbonneau was referring to the IRS Inspector on the Task Force.

Both men laughed. Rothgeb looked like an out of work Elvis impersonator. He was appropriately overweight as well. His dark side burns and natural sneer always made people smile.

"He made a pretext stop at their office. He went in and told them he was lost and was trying to find a seafood place called Hannah's. They gave him directions, and he left. He called me from Hannah's saying that a woman fitting the description of Sherry or Shari was in the Redfish offices, and he thought a man in the back fit Taylor's description of Piper or Robert Carter."

"Why was he asking about Hannah's? What's the big deal about that place?"

"Law enforcement has its underground on good-eating joints, and Rothgeb had heard of the place from one of the IRS auditors. That's why he jumped at the chance to slip on down there on business."

Ringer again waited, but not very long. "What do you want to do? We can pop these people any time."

Ringer knew that 'any time' was not the Charbonneau way of doing things. This Assistant U. S. Attorney wanted headlines, not for himself but for the Task Force. Funding was always an issue, and headlines about successful investigations and arrests tended to free up money for more such work. Participating agencies also got to issue press releases; field agents and their supervisors up the line basked in varying degrees of praise for jobs well done.

Charbonneau and Ringer understood that splashy, favorable headlines were as much a part of the enforcement game as media condemnation when investigations failed or went awry or worse, were bungled. You don't waste an opportunity for good headlines.

"Hal, could you get our group together up here on Monday? You pick the time after speaking to the others. Prepare draft affidavits for search warrants on Redfish, the Shiprite residence and wherever Piper is living. Taylor's presentation has that address. Verify those locations from utility provider records. Use those affidavits to back up arrest warrants for Shiprite, De Los Santos and Carter aka Piper. We'll also execute the outstanding warrant on him out of Dallas."

For Ringer, these were all the appropriate steps for a coordinated sweep of bad guys. Charbonneau was simply thinking out loud.

"Also by Monday, sniff around with the Sheriff's and local Constable's offices for some pairs of uniforms to go with our teams, but don't tell them anything significant."

The unstated meanings of Charbonneau's remarks were important. Sniffing meant that Ringer was to identify the best local officers available for simultaneous activities. Sniffing also implied a low-key, quiet inquiry. Uniforms were important symbols of local authority and willing participation in the event. Local police and sheriff's deputies actually enjoyed higher esteem with citizens who knew them than unknown federal agents. Finally, denying significant information to the local help was an understandable security measure appreciated by those who would be kept in ignorance until the last moment. If things went bad, it could not be credibly blamed on local ineptitude or loose talk. When the federals are the only ones by design who have the big picture, then they're the ones with the big responsibility.

"Be thinking about assignments of our people. I don't think Elvis needs to go to Redfish. Maybe he ought to fall on Carter's home, and you take Redfish. Perhaps our new ATF man can take Shiprite's home. We'll sort all that out Monday."

"When do you want to make this happen? Wednesday or Thursday?"

Ringer already knew Charbonneau's views on best news days and that Mike had a bias for Thursdays. Fridays were bad for high-profile arrests because lots of people don't read Saturday newspapers or listen to the news compared with other days of the week.

"Let's make that call on Monday, but I think no later than about 9 a.m. Thursday."

CHAPTER 58
Keeping Clients Happy

"Mr. Trimmer, I apologize for calling you at home, but I thought this would be a better way for us to talk. Do you have a minute?" Taylor was still at his office, having just come from a short meeting with Mike Charbonneau.

"Sure, I'm in my study, and Eloise is fixing dinner." Baxter tried his best to sound relaxed, but he was jittery.

"I believe this thing is going down next week. You'll be at the bank, of course, and I want you to stay there doing business. I made arrangements for Eloise and your girls. Some men will be at the house before 8 a.m. A Mr. Louis will be in charge, and you will introduce him to your wife. She's going to be frightened and have a lot of questions. Just tell her that these men are for her protection and won't need to stay beyond a few hours. They know what to do. Tell her you'll call every now and then. Promise to tell her the full story when this is over."

Baxter wondered how full the story needed to be. Taylor could hear

Trimmer's elevated breathing.

"I know this is asking a lot of you, but this is the best way to protect your family. Dolph asked me to do this, and we're going to get these crooks. Any questions?"

"Yeah Sam, do I pee in my pants now or just hold it until all this is over?"

Taylor's laugh was so hard that Bax had to hold the phone away from his ear. The laughter was therapeutic for both men. Taylor knew that dark humor was a sign that Trimmer was settling down for the tough job of acting unconcerned under very stressful circumstances. For Sam Taylor, it had been months since he had laughed at all.

Baxter had other questions. "Do you know who Carleton Brooks is? I mean, he's one of the board members that knows what's going on. Eloise and Corrine are good friends with Carleton and his wife. Could your Mr. Louis pick him up before they get to the house? I think his being there, at least for a while, will go a long way in settling Eloise down."

"I know more about Brooks than you might expect. That's a good idea. I'll make the arrangements, and you needn't get involved. The less you know of details, the better off you'll be. One other matter, on Monday morning call out to Redfish and tell them that you've rescheduled the second loan package for the next board meeting and you're certain they will approve. Have your assistant type up a draft agenda for that meeting and send it to the whole board."

"I understand; keep them interested. Can I talk to Dolph before he goes to Arizona?"

"No, he's got his job, and I don't want you two talking. As far as I'm concerned, I would not have you knowing where he goes. Do you understand me?"

Taylor honored the concept that clients are to be served, but serving them sometimes involves making hard decisions for them and brooking no disputes.

Acknowledging Taylor's authority and responsibility in this case, Baxter simply said, "Yes sir, I understand."

CHAPTER 59

We're All in Our Places

Law enforcement task force meetings, federal or state, vary in tone and style depending on Martinet and Drama Queen factors, either of which can, if out of hand, make such events farcical or tiresome. The general public's assumptions of task force dynamics are that its members and leaders are dedicated, experienced, fearless and mature professionals. Even the best, though, are plagued by egos, inter-agency jurisdictional jealousies and individual idiosyncrasies. Too much of that impairs the effectiveness of the force.

Houston's Major Frauds Task Force was blessed to match, or nearly so, the public assumption. Coffee and soft drinks were served in one of the U.S. Attorney's conference rooms before the meeting began. Six invitees were dressed in casual business attire, although a new ATF member showed up in starched blue jeans, SWAT team boots, a short-sleeved collared sport shirt and blue blazer.

Charbonneau began the meeting with a briefing accompanied by handouts identifying the offenses being investigated, the individuals who were to be taken into custody and general guidance about persons who should be detained for questioning.

Ringer then chipped in by identifying the three locations that were to be secured and searched. He also discussed his contact with local authorities identifying Matagorda County Sheriff's Deputy Rufus Walton. Walton promised to arrange for 12 uniformed city officers and county deputies to assist.

The Task Force and uniformed units were to meet in the little town of Van Vleck northeast of Bay City no later than 8:30 on the morning of the raid. They were to convene on the parking lot of the elementary school on 4th Street. School being out for the summer made it an ideal location to assemble. From there it would be a straight shot of less than five minutes down FM 2540 to the Redfish location adjacent to the municipal airport. The teams would depart the school in time for all units to enter their assigned locations at 9:30. Once the locations were secured and persons on the premises were identified for detention, Deputy Walton asked that half of his units be released.

Ringer said he wanted to talk about some variables.

"We expect the Redfish team will encounter a tall zaftig Hispanic woman known to us as Shari or Cherry De Los Santos. We don't know her true identity, but she participated in defrauding a bank in Boerne, Texas. Kendall County authorities there have been unable to help us with the identity of this woman whose appearance is by all accounts unique."

As Ringer shuffled his notes, Elvis raised his hand and asked, "Hal, what's this zaf word mean?"

"Zaf-TIG, it means curvaceous, voluptuous, a big sexy woman."

"Oh, that's what I saw when I was there, that's for sure." His sneer evolved to a lewd smile.

"We know there is at least one other woman involved with these men and their scheme, but we haven't been able to get any information on her or them. I say them because I'm told there's handwriting of at least two females on fraudulent documents we have in our case as well as the deal in Boerne."

"Watch out for two possibilities, Mrs. Shiprite and Mrs. Piper or Carter or however she identifies herself. In that regard, I'll have three of our female agents riding with us to assist in any personal searches and initial questioning."

Charbonneau concluded the meeting with a word of caution. One individual, "...a muscular bodyguard type has been seen at the Redfish offices on a regular basis. Take nothing for granted and watch out for that guy. We have no name."

When the others left the meeting, Charbonneau and Ringer reviewed the draft affidavits and other documents needed for the raid. Charbonneau called one of the U.S. Magistrate Judges and made an appointment for late Wednesday afternoon for himself and Ringer to stop by and present the final affidavits for judicial review and warrant authorization.

"So I guess we're going Thursday morning?" Ringer chuckled.

"You've got that right."

*　*　*

"Dolph, this is Jackie. Sam says you and Corrine need a vacation."

"Is he available?"

"No, he may not be here for a while, but he stays in touch."

Cavanaugh knew. "Becky?"

"Yes, he's going to be there as much as possible." Dolph could hear the emotion in Poca's voice.

She cleared her throat. "He said nothing has changed about what you need to do. You and Corrine are to go ahead as planned."

"Alright then, we'll leave in the morning. We can't check in to Canyon Ranch until Friday, but Corrine and I will drive up from Tucson after a couple of nights."

"Why don't you fly direct into Phoenix, stay some place and move over on Friday?"

It wasn't for Mrs. Martin to fathom Dolph's rationale for an oblique travel itinerary.

"Darlin', it's a big ol' world out there; Corrine and I need to see as much of it as possible. I'll call you when we're settled."

* * *

"I've been trying to call you all afternoon. Where have you been?" Dolph realized he was acting like a worrisome mother.

C.W. resented monitors. "Kiss my tail, Dolph. I'm on free time right now, and I don't need my card punched by you at all."

"Getting testy in your old age, are you? I've got some news for you."

Their mutual crankiness would only get worse as the years passed; it was deeply ingrained in their friendship.

"It's time for you to clear out and disappear ASAP. I'm going to drop by your motel early tomorrow morning on our way out of town. I'll leave an envelope for you at the front desk. Give me a call in about a month, and I'll let you know what happened."

"Sounds good to me. I'm ready to go anyway. It's too humid in this part of the country."

"Have you cleared out your office?"

"Sure did. I went over Saturday after midnight and cleaned things up as usual. I poofed."

Poofed was a made-up word to describe their practice when vacating a temporary office. All papers and office supplies were removed and carried later to a dumpster unrelated to the premises. Light switches, phones, furnishings and toilet areas, if any, were wiped down. Except for an empty desk, a couple of chairs and a cheap filing cabinet, the office was left ready for a new tenant.

Poofing was a metaphor for disappearing like a puff of smoke. Landlords never complained, but law enforcement, if it ever got involved, was admiringly frustrated.

CHAPTER 60
Marshalling Assets

Dolph Cavanaugh owed much of his legitimate business success to an uncanny knack for falling into deals. When they picked up their rental car in Phoenix and asked for a nice place to stay for a short time in Tucson, the Avis girl suggested The Arizona Inn. This early Tucson resort consisted of 95 tastefully decorated rooms and suites within several casita style buildings spread over 14 acres. Movie stars and national celebrities 50 and more years ago hung out at the Inn, enjoying tennis, swimming and croquet. This was way before Tucson exploded in population and growth. Now attractive urban sprawl and painted adobe walls surround this intimate garden spot in the desert. Its rates coincidentally were the lowest of the year.

At breakfast early the next morning, Dolph thought, *Arizona could grow on a fellow.* As he and Corrine were enjoying coffee and light pastries in the library, Baxter was telling Eloise that some men were going to arrive shortly with Carleton Brooks to work on some business related to the bank, and that it would be helpful if she made coffee and toast for their guests. Eloise was confused by Trimmer's explanation but was distracted from inquiry by her duties as a hostess.

Carleton Brooks, Mr. Louis and three other gentlemen arrived at the Trimmer residence at 7:45 a.m. Brooks was wearing slacks and a light-weight sport jacket. The other gentlemen were dressed in dark business suits with white shirts and dark ties. One was graying at the temples; another was bald with a gray parson's fringe and a third, younger than the other two, looked like a greeter at a funeral home, courteous but unsmiling. Each of these men presented an image not much different from men Eloise had seen at bankers' conventions Baxter liked to attend from time to time.

Mr. Louis on the other hand looked like a long-distance runner, a Whippet or a Greyhound. His features were aquiline, his eyes intense. While this man was polite and correct in his manner, he was a minimalist in his speech. He was like no banker that either Baxter or Eloise had seen. Only a fool would not think he had a capacity for extreme violence.

Two of the gentlemen ranged around the first floor of the house but did not bother with the upstairs. The girls were up in their rooms playing music; explanations to them could be made when they decided to come down for breakfast.

Predictably, Eloise became alarmed at Bax's introductions and the odd bulges under their jackets, but she steadied up when told by Carleton and Baxter that Dolph had thought it best for these men to be in her home. She knew something serious was going on, but she was assured by her husband that all of her questions would be answered in the next few hours. His goodbye kiss was tender rather than perfunctory, especially in front of these strangers.

She further relaxed when Mr. Louis announced that he would accompany Trimmer and stand by at the bank. It seemed to Eloise that she and her daughters would be safe with the other men and more comfortable without Mr. Louis.

* * *

The federal units, a couple of drab-looking, white, four-door sedans, two glistening black, late-model Chevrolet Suburbans, a faded white Dodge van and one souped-up, red, GMC 3500 crew cab, four-wheel-drive pickup arrived at the school parking lot at 8:10. The gang from ATF rode in the crew cab. These vehicles had formed up earlier in Old Ocean, a few miles northeast of Van Vleck. Local units all marked and clean with uniformed personnel rolled up in caravan exactly at 8:15.

What had not been planned for was the gaggle of scruffy, pre-pubescent boys skateboarding around the lot. When the law started showing up, these kids moved off the asphalt and onto the grass and watched the fleet sail in. They were awed by the display of concentrated power. Van Vleck was their entire world, and everything they understood outside that world they learned from television, simplistic grade-school education, parental discussions or the Wal-Mart in Bay City. Live and in person, these boys had never seen more than one police car, fire truck or EMS ambulance on any occasion. For years they would compare memories of that morning and correct exaggerations with even more exaggerations.

Rufus Walton was the first to climb out of his patrol car. His massive frame was clad with all the brass, silver and matte black splendor of cop gear that could be imagined. He lumbered to the trunk of his vehicle and popped it open. The Federals, engines running, locked their vision on the rural lawman. They wondered what kind of deadly and menacing weapons he would pull from the trunk.

Complying with some unseen signal, the other uniformed officers got out of their units and headed toward the open trunk. The Federals' curiosity compelled them to shut down their engines and join the pilgrimage to the back end of Walton's car.

Across the deck of the trunk were five open boxes of Shipley's Donuts, four of assorted varieties, including fritters and bear claws, and one containing a pile of donut holes. There was also a gallon container of coffee and a sleeve of Styrofoam cups with a carton each of sugar and dry creamer. Men were already helping themselves when Hal Ringer walked up and introduced himself to Deputy Walton.

"Agent Ringer, glad to meet you. My boys don't like to work on an empty stomach. Would you fellows like to join us?"

As Rufus eyed the people behind Ringer, he corrected his offer.

"You ladies are welcome too. I hope you find something you like."

"Deputy Walton, we'd be honored to join you. Thanks for your help today."

The food break ended five minutes later with everyone crowded around the open tailgate of the crew cab. Five minutes after that, the operation had been described, teams formed and assignments made.

Rufus gathered what was left of the donuts and headed toward the kids standing at the grassy edge of the parking lot. They had been gawking and trying to hear conversations. And now this giant of a man was bringing something to them.

"Do you boys suppose you could finish this for us? We've got to get on down the road, and I'd appreciate it if you'd put the empty boxes in the trash." This act of generosity too would find its way into the stories the boys would tell.

As he turned back, two of the female agents came over with paper napkins for the kids. Deputy Walton spoke barely above a gravelly whisper.

"You ladies might want to go to the Country Store up the road over there before we get under way. I'm sure you'll find their facilities appropriate." He walked on.

The two women smiled at each other and got their sister to join them as they drove one of the white sedans to the store. Rufus had surely charmed them.

Agent Ringer got out his cell phone and dialed Mike Charbonneau's number in Houston. Smart prosecutors rarely make themselves unnecessary witnesses by joining officers on a raid. To do otherwise invites recusal motions from criminal defense lawyers.

"We're about to saddle up, as they say here. I'll call you when we have something to report."

Rufus walked up just as Ringer concluded his call.

"Mr. Ringer, I'm going to send one of the units ahead to Nouveau Estates. He's to stop by their security entrance to make sure that Freddy opens the gate when we show up. He's one of my reserve deputies. No point having any delays."

Hal Ringer nodded. The time was 9:12.

CHAPTER 61

Head 'em Up, Move 'em Out

What had been a relaxed gathering of men and women, albeit obviously of one calling, changed to serious business within minutes. Uniformed officers adjusted their gear and exchanged a few words with one another. Because of their familiarity with the area, the local units would take the lead of each group and depart the parking lot at different times to assure simultaneous arrivals at their various destinations.

The federal officers donned protective gear as well as jackets emblazoned with agency names. Handguns and shoulder weapons were checked and ready. Vehicles were restarted and loaded, and the Federals lined up behind their respective leading units. No one would activate emergency lights or sirens.

Everyone on the parking lot had families to come home to, and therefore preparation for the immediate use of deadly force if needed was one element in assuring absolute control at their destinations and minimizing the opportunities for resistance. Cops and crooks, at least those in their right minds, know that these measures are intended to keep everyone physically safe.

One odd gesture signifying readiness was observed by the kids and mimicked by some of them well into their high school years. This gesture was subconscious for the adults. Just as agents and officers were about to enter their vehicles, thumbs of both hands were jammed on either side of belt buckles and slid along the waist to hitch up their trousers and smooth imagined wrinkles. Four minutes later, the first team departed.

CHAPTER 62

With Bright Shining Badges

Elvis and his team had the easiest job that day. They arrived at the Piper residence at 9:29. Uniformed officers fanned out across the empty driveway and side easement of the pretty little cottage, carefully avoiding the flower gardens that were in full bloom. Rothgeb and one of the female agents, Sonja Reynolds, a 5-year veteran of the FBI, knocked on the front door and rang the bell, standing slightly aside from the front of the door. Two knocks and two rings later, Barbara Piper answered.

Peace officers never know what they're going to meet at front doors. Surprise, outrage, violence or cordiality; there's always apprehension. One objective that officers have in mind is to ascertain that there are no immediate or apparent threats to their safety before getting down to business. By training and experience, this assessment becomes second nature within the first few seconds of an encounter.

Barbara was no threat to anyone's physical health; well, that is unless your heart was delicate. She was clothed in the shortest short-shorts Elvis had ever beheld, cross-country running shoes, and a halter top that wasn't holding its own. Her red hair spilled back from the top of a tennis visor. Covering her ears were headphones terminating in a Sony Walkman Personal Cassette player that was jammed snugly into her substantial cleavage. She glistened with sweat and was breathing heavily. Sonja mildly smiled, and Elvis grinned, thinking, *God I love America.*

"What can I do for you?" Barbara yelled.

Sonja gestured to the headphones and drew her index finger across her throat.

Barbara laughed and pulled the phones from her ears.

"Sorry, I was riding my bike. I need to do this every day or ..." Her voice trailed off. "You know what I mean?" She looked at Sonja, who was a pretty fit specimen herself. The police cars in the street and the jacketed federal agents did not faze Barbara.

Elvis was eyeing the living room and asked, "Is Mr. Carter here?"

"Why no, there's no Carter here, I'm Barbara Piper and my husband, Roger, he's at work. You must have the wrong address."

Sonja looked at Rothgeb and pulled a photograph from her jacket pocket. "Is this your husband?"

Confusion crept across Barbara's face. "Yes. What's this about?"

"Ma'am, that photograph is of Robert Carter, his true name; we have an arrest warrant for him, and ma'am, in the past he's said he was Robert Piper." Elvis had stopped grinning.

Unless this woman was a great actress, these revelations were shocking her to the core. Her shoulders slumped, her eyes watered, her legs trembled as she methodically removed the Walkman from its nest, slowly wrapping around it the audio cord. She pitched the instrument on the couch in the living room.

Sonja addressed Barbara. "Before we talk more, can my friend here take a look around the house just to make sure we're alone?"

Barbara nodded. Elvis left the room. Followed by Sonja, Barbara walked down the hallway to an extra large open kitchen. Her bicycle was stationed in a clear area in front of a wall-mounted flat-screen television. Sonja noted that while the set was on mute, Mrs. Carter or Mrs. Piper had the video tuned to HGTV. Barbara retrieved a very large T-shirt from a bar stool and slipped it on over her workout clothes. Sonja correctly guessed that it was a size 2XL.

By then Elvis had come to the kitchen. "We're good. I told the guys outside; we're cool." He also nodded and discreetly formed his right thumb and pinky finger in the shape of a telephone. This signified to Sonja that the uniformed officers had relayed to the other teams that the Piper residence was secure, that the husband was supposedly at work and that the wife was being interviewed.

Most of the time, regardless of what the book says, cops know in their gut when they have an innocent on their hands. One look at Barbara and no one would say she was precisely innocent, but it was very clear that she was devastated to learn about her husband's true identity.

While it was possible that Barbara knowingly might be involved in the crimes under investigation and thus a subject of investigation, just being married to Carter didn't make her suspect, except for poor judgment. Sonja abstained from reading Barbara her rights.

"Barbara, let's talk."

* * *

Arriving at the Shiprite residence, exactly at 9:30, uniformed officers fanned out, one moving down the driveway and side easement toward the back of the house to prevent escape. The lead ATF agent, Thomas Gore, accompanied by FBI agent LeAnn Quan, went to the front door and rang the chimes, clearly audible inside the house.

A few moments later, Mrs. Shiprite opened wide the door, screamed and fled to the interior of the home; Quan and Gore followed.

Maria Shiprite was clad in a bathrobe without slippers. The smell of alcohol had wafted over the threshold. Both agents would later recall that they had the impression that Maria was angry before she opened the door, before she was aware of the presence of law enforcement officers. Again the cops' guts told them that Mrs. Shiprite had been prepared to resume some earlier argument.

But for now, the chase was on simply to detain Mrs. Shiprite and secure the premises. Maria had run upstairs, still screaming. She wasn't difficult to follow. She had run through the master bedroom into a bathroom and slammed the door. The agents could hear her crying. Gore pulled his pistol and started to kick the door in. Quan placed her hand on Gore's shoulder and motioned with her other hand for him to wait. She then pointed around the room.

The king-sized bed was unmade, and women's clothing was scattered on the carpet. Leftover food, some on paper plates, was on both side tables and a long credenza. The smell of alcohol was overwhelming; an overturned wine glass was at the foot of the bed, a wet stain radiated from its lip, vodka.

Miss Quan made a circular motion with her right hand for Gore to check the upstairs to make sure that they were otherwise safe. He complied.

"Mrs. Shiprite, I know you are upset. We're not going to hurt you; we want to talk. Please open the door or better still, can I come in, just me?"

The crying was now moving to keening.

Gore returned to the bedroom and announced, "Clear."

"Mrs. Shiprite, my name is LeAnn and I am going to open the bathroom door. Pleased don't be alarmed. Besides, I need to pee. You frightened me."

The ATF agent shook his head and grinned, but he stood slightly back and to the side of the door, ready for whatever was to happen. This off-the-wall personal plea might do the trick.

Slowly turning the knob LeAnn took a deep breath and pushed the door open enough to see Maria sitting on the toilet, lid down, clutching her chest and sobbing. Quan became erect and entered the room, motioning for Gore not to follow. She opened the linen cabinet and got out a fresh washcloth. Moistening it in the sink and then wringing it, she put one hand on Maria's shoulder and with the other gently wiped the crying woman's forehead and then her cheeks. For the first time, Quan noticed a cut on Maria's lip and swelling. She also saw bruises on her right temple and cheek.

"Maria, can I call you Maria? Let's step out of here."

Quan firmly assisted Maria to a standing position and then led her into the bedroom. Maria needed the help. She was unsteady on her feet. By now she had stopped crying and was yawning. LeAnn put her in a cane rocking chair and returned to the bathroom. She scanned the lavatory and the toilet area for any evidence that Mrs. Shiprite had ingested any pills. Finding none, she returned to the bedroom and leaned over, fixing Maria's eyes to her own.

"Maria, listen to me. Have you taken any meds or pills recently?"

Maria winced and then smiled, "No, no, no, I've just popped a little Popov." She laughed at her bad joke. Her speech was slurred.

"Maria, Mr. Gore is going to leave us for a while. Would you like to get dressed? I'll wait here while you dress."

Mrs. Shiprite nodded.

"Where is your husband, Maria? Where is Robert?"

"Gone. He's gone."

"Maria, is he gone to work?"

"No, he's gone. That's what I'm saying."

"Is he here in town, Maria?" Mrs. Shiprite wiggled her butt and stretched out in the rocker. She shook her head.

"Stand up Maria. Let's walk into your closet and pick something for you to wear."

As the two women headed toward the closet, Quan told Gore to radio for an EMT unit. "Who knows how much Popov she's popped."

Outside, Gore called Agent Ringer.

"Robert Shiprite isn't here. Mrs. Shiprite is drunk. LeAnn says we need an EMT unit here to check her out before we move her."

"He's not here either; Deputy Walton will send the EMTs over there as quickly as they get loose," Agent Ringer said.

Gore replied, "Whoa, Hal, anybody hurt over there?"

"Not on our side."

* * *

The larger third team arrived at the Redfish building at 9:31. Ringer, Special Agent Sadie Gomez and two ATF agents piled from the Dodge van and entered the main lobby of the building, turning quickly to the Redfish entrance. Weapons drawn, Ringer was in first, quickly followed by the ATF boys and Mrs. Gomez.

Ringer loudly announced, "FBI. On the floor. Hands behind your backs."

Gomez repeated those words in Spanish.

Piper hit the floor as though he was experienced with the drill.

Miss De Los Santos, standing mid-feed at a large paper shredder was reluctant to mess up her clothing or ruin her manicure. She looked offended at the suggestion. The labored grinding of the shredder could not prevail over Gomez's authoritative informal Spanish command, "Pendeja, ahora mismo!" De Los Santos darkly complied.

Ringer cuffed Piper and Agent Gomez secured De Los Santos, both with hands in the back.

The ATF men swarmed through the rest of the office space, noting that a back entrance was ajar. They bolted through the door. Gunshots heightened the tension of the moment. Ringer ran to the lobby front door, and Gomez followed the ATF agents out the rear entrance.

As Ringer emerged onto the parking lot moving toward the southeast corner of the building ready for a shootout, he stopped and then relaxed. Standing over the prostrate body of the Redfish goon with a set of cuffs in one hand and a baseball bat in the other was Matagorda County Deputy Sheriff Rufus Walton. A pistol lay 10 feet away. Just then, the ATF agents and Gomez trotted up. The goon had shot at the agents and then attempted to escape to the front parking lot. He was looking back over his shoulder as he rounded the corner right into Walton's stomach high home run. When he fell, his cheek skidded over the asphalt, and the pistol spun out of reach.

"My Louisville Slugger goes to work when I do. I heard this boy's shooting; so Slugger and me didn't want anybody getting hurt. I'll just take him over to one of my units for safekeeping."

The Federals looked at each other as Walton put down his bat, rolled the man over and cuffed him in the back. He then used his grip on the cuffs with one hand and with the other hand on the man's belt hauled the gentleman to a standing position. He then patted him down for other weapons and identification.

Prodding the man in the back with his bat, Walton advised, "Son, looks like you've messed up your jacket. You're under arrest in case you don't know it. I'll bet you the first charge is assaulting federal agents. Don't start talking yet," he cautioned. "I've gotta read you your rights first and get you some medical attention. Now, there is one other thing you need to know. From this point on, you'll address my men and me as sir. You got that?"

Mr. Goon was unable to speak, but managed a nod. He was defeated. One more nudge, and the two moved toward one of the patrol cars blocking the street entrance to the parking lot.

The Federals re-holstered their handguns and began walking back to the Redfish office. Sadie Gomez said what was on all their minds. "Don't screw with that man, don't screw with him."

The time was 10:05.

When the four agents reentered Redfish, Piper and De Los Santos were trading crude insults in Spanish and English. Gomez offered to translate, but Ringer declined. Ordered to silence, Ringer Mirandized both subjects, and Gomez followed with Spanish translations of their rights. Piper was then escorted to his private office for questioning about Shiprite. De Los Santos remained in the front office area to be questioned about the same topic. Search and seizure of records could be done later.

"I'm Special Agent Harold Ringer. I'll get straight to the point, Mr. Carter. You're going back into federal prison to finish out your last sentence. We'll be recommending that these new charges be stacked, and as our investigation develops information on your gunman outside, we believe that you will face enhanced punishment opportunities because firearms were used." Ringer had not completed his recitation of Piper's pending doom when the prisoner spoke.

"You want Bob Shiprite, don't you? You missed him by 45 minutes." Looking over at Ringer's wristwatch, he continued. "I'd say another 45 minutes by now. For all I know, he flew out right over your heads."

"Keep talking. You know the drill."

Three minutes later, Ringer got his cell phone out and called his office.

"Get people out to Hobby Airport, two teams, one at the general aviation terminal and another at the commercial terminal. Focus there on Southwest Airline gates. Notify the airport police and scan ticket sales for Robert Shiprite. Extra mug shots are on my desk."

Looking at Piper, he asked, "Did you say Fortune Air?"

Piper nodded.

Back to the phone, "Check the status and passenger identities of any flights from Bay City, airport code BYY, into Hobby. I'm looking for Fortune Flying Service from Austin. Call me back and get going."

Hal met Gomez midway between the two prisoners.

"What did she tell you?"

"She's big into the blame game and that she was just a secretary. She says Shiprite flew to Houston, had an airplane waiting this morning. Says Piper ordered her to shred everything. She didn't know what plans Shiprite or Piper had for meeting up. After all, she was just a secretary." Sadie smiled.

Hal waited.

"She asked about her boyfriend. He had just come over to get her out of this mess. She had told him how bad Piper and Shiprite were, and he wanted to rescue her and call the cops. He must have been scared when we came in. That's why he ran."

Both agents were now smiling.

"Sadie, these people are amazing. They head for cover and lie so fast, they can't even see how enmeshed they're becoming. You could order them to remain silent, and they'd still try to lie their way out. Did you tell her he did the shooting and that he's lucky to be alive?"

"Yeah, she wasn't happy. Poor Bronco."

"Bronco? Is that his name?"

"Well, that's what she calls him; doesn't know his real name. Piper calls him Dutch. I didn't want to ask why she called him Bronco. TMI."

"I understand. Let's start doing the inventory and packing things up. I'll ask if Mr. Walton can detain these three over at the Matagorda jail until we finish here."

As Ringer started outside, he stopped and turned back to Sadie Gomez.

"What does *pendeja* mean?"

"I'll tell you later, Boss."

CHAPTER 63

I'll Fly Away, Oh Glory

The Bay City Municipal Airport has two runways and no tower. Its asphalt and cement runways are 75 feet wide and a little over 5,000 feet long. Its airport code is BYY.

However crooked Robert Shiprite is, he was a planner. Before this day he researched the size of aircraft that could use BYY and made tentative arrangements for an Austin flying service to be on 24-hour standby with one of their Beech King Air B100 Turbo-prop aircrafts. He learned that they accommodate eight passengers in their pressurized cabins with a flying range of a thousand miles, good enough for his purposes. He also knew the driving time from his home or the Redfish office to the little airport terminal. It was the lease deal clincher that the Redfish premises were close to the airfield. He backed up his flight arrangements with a substantial cash deposit to the flying service to assure attention.

The King Air was on the tarmac at 8:40 when he and Beatrice Wynne arrived in his car. They each had a carry-on bag and were nicely dressed for travel. Shiprite also carried a soft black leather briefcase. They boarded and took off five minutes later. Accounting for the 70-mile flight and the availability of a cab at the general aviation terminal, he planned to be in Hobby by 10 am. What was important was to take the first available Southwest flight out of the area. It hardly mattered where.

Shiprite's sixth sense kicked in the night before, and he decided it was time to run; there was no point in dallying about. They had plenty of cash in hand and elsewhere, enough to live high for a year and much longer if they were modest.

His mind slipped into analysis mode.

They had easily disappeared from Boerne, but he had allowed his greed to lead him this time. The dumbbell banker had changed on Shiprite; he was stringing him out. The other banks had started paying, but he should have been able to reload Peoples State a lot faster. That would have been a killing.

At first, Shiprite thought Trimmer had no balls and just needed time to get comfortable with Carter, the little weasel. After fatso Cavanaugh came home, Trimmer changed. Maybe it was Dolph Cavanaugh's balls that were working. You don't grow those things overnight.

He cursed the incompetence of Dutch Hoeflich. Gave him a big truck, and he couldn't knock off the Cavanaugh problem. Instead of thinking, he was too busy with Cherry. At least the near-miss scared Cavanaugh out of the way.

Maria had become a distraction. She was drinking herself into oblivion every night and becoming uncontrollable. Part of the problem was that she liked her girlfriends, especially Eloise Trimmer and Cavanaugh's foxy wife. She even liked Carter's airhead, Barbara. It was time to leave Maria behind. She and Carter would turn on him like cur dogs anyway, and that spic De Los Santos would easily forget who kept her tits out of the wringer in Ruidoso.

And then there was that cowboy clown, Charles Rogers. He looked like a mobile home salesman, an old one at that. He couldn't be a lawman, and as a thief, he would have been unreliable, an amateur. Shiprite shook his head at the thought that he almost bought Roger's prospects.

Only Bea Jay had been reliable, both in Bay City and Boerne. Her routine worked on bankers every time. She would have been stretched thin if she had to compromise the fellows in Lake Jackson and Angleton along with Trimmer. Servicing three presidents would have been asking too much. Fortunately, De Los Santos was able to fill in.

He was jarred from his thoughts as the King Air grabbed the runway, taxiing to the terminal apron. Taxi service was delayed, but about the time Maria Shiprite was screaming and running away from LeAnn Quan, Bea Jay and Robert were let out on Hobby Airport's upper deck near Southwest's baggage check-in stand. The first flight they could catch was a 10:25 to Corpus Christi. *Not far enough*, Shiprite thought.

How often is it that decisions, even small ones, right or wrong, carefully determined, are completely ignored at a critical moment? Justifications are easily expressed after the fact, but inexplicable demons plague our minds to go from calculated steps to irrational leaps, Shiprite's abstention from the Body of Christ, Corpus Christi, was a huge error. No decision after that mattered.

The next flight was to Jackson, Mississippi, leaving at 10:45. *That will do*, he thought, and he paid cash for two one-way tickets. He and Bea walked to the gate and waited. Passenger screening was casual.

Just as pre-boarding was announced, Robert saw several uniformed Houston Police officers entering the concourse. Men in suits without luggage were briskly walking among them. Dread seized Shiprite's heart. None looked to their right or left. These men knew where they were going. Bea was fiddling in her purse. She heard Shiprite mutter some words to her and looked up.

"It's over. Stay calm."

Out of the crowd of uniforms, a young man in a suit emerged and said, "Mr. Shiprite, Miss Wynne, please come with us. You're under arrest."

A noose of blue surrounded them, collecting their baggage, the briefcase and Bea's purse. A female officer patted down Bea as one of the FBI agents frisked Shiprite. As they walked from the terminal, like a priest accompanying a doomed man to the gas chamber, an agent was chanting words from memory, "You have a right to remain silent, you have a right to…" his speech was interrupted.

Beatrice Jayne Wynne could neither remain calm nor silent. Enraged epithets directed at Shiprite spewed forth. She was allowed to vent until they reached separate vehicles for their trip into the criminal justice system.

CHAPTER 64

All in a Day's Work

"Mike, we've got a full sack today. Shiprite and a woman who wasn't on Sam Taylor's list were bagged at Hobby Airport. We got a briefcase full of money, and the woman is cooperating. Just like in Boerne, she was the bank president's assistant."

"I've called Spook, who was sitting on Mr. Trimmer at the bank, and given him the news." Both men knew that Mr. Louis, a former FBI agent who maintained good relations with the Bureau as well as certain other government organizations, earned the nickname that was never used to his face.

"That's good, Hal. He can take care of reporting to Sam Taylor. What about the other people?"

"We're still boxing up documents here at the Redfish offices and executing the search warrants on the two residences, but Carter's wife appears not to have had a clue about her husband's activities. Our people think she was genuinely shocked that his true name was Carter. She wasn't too happy either to learn that he's still married to the real Mrs. Carter, and that has its own benefits for us. Sonja Reynolds is interviewing her right now and getting handwriting samples."

The marital privilege protects communications between spouses in terms of testifying in a criminal trial, but it will not extend to Robert Carter. He is the bigamist and not Barbara.

Ringer continued. "As for Mrs. Shiprite, because she was so intoxicated at the residence, LeAnn Quan asked for an EMT unit to check her out. We're taking everyone but Mrs. Piper into Houston to the Magistrate Judge for initial appearance. We'll keep looking into Mrs. Piper's background and her story, but we are confident that she isn't a flight risk."

Mike Charbonneau was elated. "This is great. No one hurt, I presume?"

"Not exactly, but everything turned out fine. Dutch, one of the subjects, a muscle, unsuccessfully shot at our agents, who did not return fire. One of the deputies knocked the wind out of him as he ran from the building. His true name is Dudley Hoeflich, and catch this, he's got an aggravated murder warrant outstanding from Ohio. They've got the death penalty up there."

Ringer paused. "I found a set of keys in De Los Santos' desk. They had labels matching the other offices in the building. On the theory that Redfish might have stored records in the other spaces, I looked in each office. With one exception on the second floor, they were all empty. One office had bare bones furnishings, but there weren't any records anywhere but in the Redfish office listed in the search warrant."

"OK, Hal, give me a call when you're heading in. I'll tell the magistrate I'm on standby. Good work." Charbonneau thought, *why is it that thugs don't like the names given by their parents? I guess Dutch sounds tougher than Dudley. In the long run Dudley will meet his maker, and not as Dutch.*

"Thanks Mike, there's much more to tell you later. You'll enjoy it."

* * *

Trimmer rushed into Eloise's arms as he and Mr. Louis got home. She had just fixed lunch, which was declined by Louis for his group. Baxter and Eloise profusely thanked Mr. Louis for his help. Only then did the team leader smile; he gathered his men and departed.

"Eloise, you're never going to believe what has been going on and what happened today."

"Sure I will. Bax, you're a hero. You're my hero. The phone has been ringing off the wall with folks saying that you saved the bank and helped catch the crooks."

Eloise was more animated than Baxter had ever seen. She took his coat and pulled him to the kitchen table. She fussed with the sandwiches she had prepared. Baxter liked the attention, but he felt rushed. He wanted more time to think about his words.

"Bax, is it true that Roger Piper and Bob Shiprite were the bad guys?"

"Yeah, baby, and so was Bea Jay."

Eloise's eyes widened. Her shock made her gasp.

"Yes, and later I'll tell you more about that. Apparently Maria Shiprite was also taken into custody. I don't think we'll see her again."

"What about Barbara?"

"Far as I know, she's at home and hasn't been arrested. Someone said that when the agents left her house, she was pedaling her exercise bike."

"This is so exiting, and Dolph and Corrine have missed it all. I can't wait 'til they get back."

"Tell me about the girls. How'd they handle all this?"

There was something in Baxter's voice, seriousness without anxiety, and confidence without being overbearing. *Manly* crossed Eloise's mind.

"Weird. They came down for breakfast at about 10 and were a little unhappy that they couldn't go outside, but I guess the presence of the men let them know that this was important. They've been upstairs since then watching television or whatever. Normally they would have pitched a fit."

"I'm going up there to talk to them in a little bit." He had decided his girls needed to join the real world. Fit-pitching would no longer be acceptable. He wasn't really hungry, but he ate half of a sandwich anyway to be polite.

"Eloise, I want to tell you some things that I'm not proud of. I've been a fool and want you to know that."

Eloise's eyes fluttered. She knew from the dull pain in her chest that her hero was going to tell her things she did not want to hear. In the past few weeks Bax had changed; he had become more attentive, more loving. She understood in an instant that what he was about to say could never be unsaid.

Men who face up to the music of their infidelities do so in a variety of ways. Some engage in conclusions, statements such as, I had an affair or I fell in love. Others favor detail admitting to sleeping with someone, with or without affection. Much depends on the extent of their dalliances and the degree of true remorse that accompanies their admissions.

Baxter elected to speak from his heart.

"One evening at the office, Bea Jay made advances on me that took me by surprise. I succumbed. We never went to a motel or anything like that, but I got into a situation where I was out of control. Dolph somehow or another sensed this and chewed me out." Further detail was unnecessary; that his sex with Bea Jay had been limited was irrelevant to his shame. Fine distinctions wouldn't wash.

Eloise sat across from her husband trying to breathe steadily, working not to cry.

"He was right. This all came to light when I realized that the bank was in trouble with Shiprite. Out of guilt I became strictly business with Bea Jay, and besides, all this was about to come down on the bank. If it hadn't been for Dolph, I don't know what would have happened."

"Until today, I had no idea that Bea Jay was a part of this whole deal, that she and Shiprite and Piper as well as others were working me and the bank. They did the same thing over at Boerne, Texas. I feel stupid, and I've failed you so much. I'm sorry."

Eloise Trimmer took a deep breath. His explanations and the growing community reactions over the telephone showed her what a trap Baxter had fallen into, not necessarily of his digging. She closed her eyes. She desperately wanted to thank Dolph for fighting for her marriage when they were unable to, but for now she needed to decide what she would say. She kept her eyes shut for almost a minute. Baxter was silent.

"Bax, over these past few months, I've been worried about us, but to tell the truth, I've been more worried about me, about growing old and unattractive and about the girls, too. Maybe this wouldn't have happened if you and I had been talking all along. I spent too much time shopping, and you were working too late at the bank even before Bea Jay came to town. I should have realized this."

Gentleness marked her voice. Her candor pierced the pain he had inflicted. The brittleness, characteristic of her past attitude, had vanished. There at the kitchen table they looked at each other for a moment. Then she reached across and covered his hand, smiling.

"You really ought to eat the rest of your sandwich."

CHAPTER 65

A Good Friday

Baxter had taken the telephone off the hook last night so the family could get some sleep. He had replaced the instrument before 7 a.m., thinking the turmoil had passed. Wrong.

The phone and the doorbell rang at the same time. Eloise got the phone, and Baxter took the door. Standing outside were cameramen and a group of reporters extending microphones. The men and women whose faces he could see were smiling, and, contrary to popular myth, they were not clamoring with questions or jostling one another for positional advantage.

He returned their smile, took a deep breath and spoke.

"I appreciate why you are here, but I'm not going to answer any questions this morning. Let me assure you that Matagorda People's State Bank is safe and sound, that the authorities, I understand, have taken into custody all those persons who've tried to defraud this very fine bank. I also understand that these people may have victimized at least two other banks."

By then, Eloise had moved to his side in the doorway and was smiling. Their daughters were peeking out of the dining room windows, trying to hear what their father was saying. They had gotten up early and dressed for breakfast with their parents.

"Please respect our privacy for now and understand that this has been a stressful interruption to all of us. Now, if you will excuse me, I've got to get ready for work. I hope to meet today with our board of directors to give them as full a report as I can. If you folks will give me your cards, I'll have someone notify you when I can be available to answer your questions. Again, thank you for your interest."

With each card extended, Trimmer said thank you. Out of the crowd, someone yelled, "Is it true that one of your employees was arrested in connection with this investigation?"

"Yes," he said with a smile, "but I'm sure you understand that I must first report that and other matters to the board. I hope to see you later."

With that he closed the door. Eloise was flabbergasted. She never imagined that her husband could have been so polished addressing a gang of reporters before he'd even had a cup of coffee. His girls, for once, were speechless.

Baxter was pleased as well, but more significantly, he wanted to thank Mrs. Wilson. He wanted to let her know that the bank's money had been well-spent in sending him to that blonde, wiry media lady in Dallas who teaches corporate executives how to respond to blitz inquiries like this morning's.

He needed to get to the bank well before opening to caution employees about speaking to the media, even the local paper, until after the board meeting, and then only with his approval, an approval he would not give.

"Who was on the phone, Eloise?"

"It was Barbara Piper. She's embarrassed and wanted to tell me how sorry she was about all this. She had some colorful things to say about her not really husband. I told her I would call back later, that news people were out front."

Baxter nodded.

"If she didn't do anything wrong, I hope this town doesn't chew her up and spit her out. When Corrine gets back, I'm sure we'll be able to do something for her. Maybe I'll go over there later today."

Baxter understood that Corrine Cavanaugh's influence with other women in Bay City would ease the shame that Barbara no doubt felt. Wagging tongues were probably already at work. Soon too, the tongues would lick at speculation on just how Bea Jay had performed her role as a member of the gang. If such speculation were confirmed at all, then Bax's image as a community hero would surely fall. He would deal with that when it came. What mattered to him now was what Eloise thought.

* * *

When Trimmer got to the bank, he instructed the employees on media contact and loose talk at home or elsewhere. He called Mrs. Wilson at home and then asked one of the loan officers to call the other board members to see if they could attend a meeting at 1 p.m. for a full briefing on yesterday's events. He then called Sam Taylor's office.

"Mrs. Martin, this is Baxter Trimmer. Is Mr. Taylor available?"

"No, Mr. Trimmer, he's not. I have been staying in touch with him, but perhaps you don't know that his wife is gravely ill. I have spoken to Mr. Louis and Mr. Cavanaugh. Is there something I need to pass on?"

"Yes, tell Sam that I'm attending a board meeting this afternoon to brief them. After that I am going to arrange a short press conference. If there is anything I should not say, I'd like a call. Tell him also that I regret his wife's situation and asked if there was anything I could do."

"I'll do that Mr. Trimmer. He has told me that he spoke with the government's attorney, Mike Charbonneau, and that Mr. Charbonneau has said FBI agents will probably be in Bay City all next week interviewing witnesses, including you and the bank's staff. He says for you to cooperate fully, but if anyone representing the people arrested yesterday approaches you or anyone working for the bank, you are to decline to talk to them without bank's counsel being present."

She added, "I think that's not going to be for some time." She did not tell Trimmer that agents would also be visiting banks in Lake Jackson and Angleton.

By the time Bax's bank opened, everyone was ready. Local customers poured in for business. What became apparent soon after that was that their business was frequently petty or could have been handled by phone. The tellers and others fielded the questions with essentially the same line: *This has really been interesting, but we're not supposed to talk about this until the FBI has interviewed us."*

This satisfied most of the people, and the few who persisted were referred to Baxter, who alluded to the mystique of the FBI as the ultimate authority on when they could speak freely.

CHAPTER 66

Momma is Very Happy

Regular board meetings had never been so well attended. The arrests were all over local television and the radio stations; even CNN and Fox News had done pieces on bank fraud arrests. Members knew Momma would call a meeting.

Mrs. Wilson began by advising that Baxter had first notified her of the probability that the bank was being scammed. She in turn appointed Mr. Shelton and Carleton Brooks as members of the executive committee to assist her in monitoring events. They approved Baxter's recommendation of a Houston counsel for guidance in just how to proceed.

She then called on Baxter to report. When he got to the point of talking about Bea Jay and her apparent role as an inside mole reporting to the bad men, Mrs. Wilson interrupted.

She said that President Trimmer had acted prudently in bringing this matter to the attention of the board. She went on to say, "Despite our best efforts, evil can walk though our doors posing otherwise. None of us could have suspected that Miss Wynne was an imposter."

Baxter concluded by saying he intended to hold a brief press conference later in the afternoon, but that they could expect law enforcement authorities and media types to be around for the next several days.

When asked about the financial impairment of the bank by these crooks, Momma responded, "We took a hit, but we are not impaired. Also we have reason to believe that we may recover funds that were seized yesterday at Hobby Airport. What is fine news is that we avoided, through Baxter's efforts, losing much more to the thieves. President Trimmer is to be commended for shouldering this burden for us."

The meeting ended with a lot of hand shaking, back patting and hugs. Disaster had been avoided, and those responsible had been arrested. This indeed was a great day for the bank and its shareholders.

Momma asked Baxter to remain behind as the others were leaving. She closed the door and gestured for Trimmer to join her at the conference table.

"Baxter, I meant every word I said just now, and I want to make sure that's what the community understands. To that end, I will be with you at your press conference. You are to let me handle any questions concerning Bea Jay Wynne."

Trimmer's eyes fell towards the table surface and he nodded.

"I've lived long enough to know the ways bad women can get to good men. I consider you a good man, and that's the way it's going to be out there if I have anything to say about it. Do you understand me?"

"Yes ma'am. Thank you." He felt tears might show up. They didn't.

"Good. Now I want you to be thinking in the next several days about what we need to do around here to improve our operations and grow this bank. It's my opinion that we need to go off the market for now and take advantage of the good will we have received as a result of the way this has turned out. We don't want to turn our community over to the big banking interests. It deserves better than that."

Two hours later, Trimmer and Momma joined a group of reporters with cameras in front of the bank. He introduced Mrs. Wilson as the board chairwoman and gave a brief description of the scheme as he understood it, and how he came to observe similarities between certain loans that had been bought by the bank. He also explained that more loan packages were being offered that contained similar peculiarities. With Mrs. Wilson's approval, he sought legal counsel and that attorney informed the Justice Department. The government's response was breathtaking.

When the questions began focusing on Wynne's role, Momma again took over.

"That woman had us all fooled. Every time I went to the bank, she was so cheerful. She played like she was a little old innocent country girl just trying to learn about banking. She ought to be ashamed of herself."

The reporters laughed.

Momma raised her head characteristically, an indication that the afternoon's appearance was over.

"Now if you will excuse us, we have more business to attend to inside. Thank you."

It must run in the genes and the blood, Trimmer thought. *If Corrine can save Barbara's reputation in the community, Momma has just saved mine.*

CHAPTER 67
Arizona Hideaway

That next morning, Dolph called Taylor's office for an update. Jackie Martin reported what was in the Houston Chronicle and focused on the arrest of Dudley Hoeflich, a man who was wanted for capitol murder in Ohio. The article highlighted the high level of cooperation by local authorities, which resulted in a swift conclusion to Thursday's arrests.

"Poca, how are Mr. Taylor and Becky?"

"I spoke with him this morning. He got a little sleep last night. His sons came in and spelled him. This is breaking my heart, Dolph." She sighed.

"He said there's no point in you and Corrine coming back for at least 10 days. He said this scheme got bigger by two banks, and things are going to be hectic in Bay City for a while."

She went on to explain that some of the seized documents indicated similar frauds on banks in Angleton and Lake Jackson. Dolph smiled when she commented that authorities, according to the newspaper accounts, were crediting the quick thinking of Trimmer in preventing further loss to his bank and other banks in the region.

"Dolph, why don't you come back here and bask a little in the limelight?" She shared Sam Taylor's suspicion that Cavanaugh might have a more sinister reason for avoiding Bay City but said nothing further. Neither Sam nor Jackie was going to overtly poke the sleeping dog.

"Poca, it's this way. Baxter Trimmer isn't the first man I've known who needed an opportunity to shine. I don't like people knowing my business or asking me questions that I don't like. My role in this is only that I knew a good lawyer for Trimmer to call. Is that good enough for you?"

"It sure is. I know Sam will agree."

Just before checking out of the Arizona Inn for Canyon Ranch, Corrine had called Dr. Etling to find out what he had decided about her offer to buy the Bedford Building.

"Corrine, soon as you get me a check, I'm out of here. The town has gone crazy. Too much excitement, and I'm too old for that. I've got a place down at Port Aransas that my wife would never let me go to. Well, she's not around to say no anymore." He'd been a widower for over a year.

"Where are you, young lady?"

"I'm in Tucson with Dolph. Why do you ask?"

"Good for you, girl. Stay gone. Everybody's got their britches in a twist over these old crooks that tried to skin the bank, but they caught them. You know about that, don't you?"

"Yeah Doc, I've heard something about that. I'll call you as soon as I'm back in town. You take care."

As she hung up the phone she turned to Dolph, who was carrying out their bags. "You've got a building now."

* * *

Corrine and Dolph checked in to Canyon Ranch that afternoon. A lightning show was already beginning in the Catalina Mountains, and rain was sure to follow. At check-in Dolph reversed his booking from 4 and 10 to 10 and 4 nights. Ms. Steiner was not due back at work until Monday. Canyon Ranch exceeded everything that Ms. Steiner said. Dolph and Corrine agreed to limit their outside calls to one each per day.

CHAPTER 68

The Dark Companion

Betsy Taylor had been fighting breast cancer for two years, and her spirit had won the war . The cancer killed her body, but never her spirit or her love for her husband, their sons and those she called her new daughters. The most important people in her life gathered to say goodbye. Her going was neither less nor more painful for the family than for others who have faced this tragedy. Betsy was gone.

Sam Taylor had been exposed to deaths of loved ones - parents, aunts and uncles - early in his life, and he had seen bodies vacant of souls when he served as a prosecutor in Houston. He had seen it even before the Navy and Vietnam and before Betsy. He never became immune or insensitive to death, but he did understand that the soul was too strong to die with the body. It went away but did not cease. As to where it went, he could not say for sure. What he did know was that the pain he would feel after losing Betsy to that other place would not stop.

From a list of names and phone numbers written by their father on

Saturday afternoon, Jeffrey and Sam Taylor, Jr. took turns notifying close friends and relatives of Betsy's death. While their father tried to get some desperately needed sleep, the sons began their calls at 7 a.m. Sunday morning. Jackie Martin was fifth on the list. Jackie Martin had her own list of names and numbers. Corrine and Randolph Cavanaugh were first.

When Dolph awoke a little before 8 a.m., he noticed the telephone flashing for a message. Jackie had specifically asked the resort operator not to ring but to flash the Cavanaugh room. She did not want to disturb their sleep. When he called for the message, the operator read him the following:

"Betsy Taylor died at 3:15 this morning. Arrangements no earlier than Wednesday are pending. I'll call you later today. Signed Jackie."

Dolph sat in a comfortable leather chair near their bed and watched Corrine as she slept. He hoped the day of their parting was far, far away.

CHAPTER 69
Eulogy

When Jackie finally called Sunday afternoon, there was little to say. A service was to be held Thursday morning at St. John the Divine Episcopal Church in Houston at 10 a.m. in the main sanctuary. Jackie did not pretend to dissuade Corrine and Dolph from attending. Houston was not Bay City, and besides, everybody knew the whole FBI was in Bay City racking up interviews.

Dolph and Corrine caught a Wednesday afternoon flight on Southwest into Hobby and took a cab to the Crowne Plaza Hotel, two and a half miles west of the church. He called Trimmer from the hotel.

"We're in Houston for Becky Taylor's memorial service tomorrow and catching a plane out in the afternoon. I just wanted to see how you're doing."

"Dolph, I couldn't be better. Eloise has been wonderful, and your mother-in-law is in all regards a queen. I'll tell you more when we can visit. Can we do that at the service? I'm driving up early in the morning."

"Pal, I don't think I'm going to be in the mood for business. I need my sprits up before I can enjoy your war stories."

"I understand. Tell Corrine that Eloise is looking forward to her return."

* * *

The church was packed. Except for Baxter and Eloise, who sat on the other side of the sanctuary, Jackie Martin and the Lindsay & Taylor lawyers, Dolph recognized no one in attendance. By the looks of the sea of dark business suits and grooming of the men, Cavanaugh concluded they were nearly all lawyers and other professionals. The women were tastefully dressed and coiffed. Jewelry was modest. Younger people attending were friends of the Taylor sons and their wives. Dolph had not realized the social level that the Taylors ran in. They both were so down to earth.

Despite the dark attire and the somber occasion, guests were greeted in the narthex by large and stunning photographs of a smiling Betsy in her healthy days. Easels holding the pictures were arranged chronologically across the wall that separated the narthex from the nave. They each depicted stages of her life, beginning at the age of eight years. As guests entered and received pamphlets of the Order of Service, gloom and sadness were transformed and hearts lifted. Some pointed to particular photographs, whispered and smiled. Others mildly laughed. It was Betsy's impish smile and sparkling eyes, regardless of age, that marked the life of the one they were about to honor.

Just before the memorial service began, the family was seated. Dolph was struck by Sam Taylor's cadence. He had never seen him weak in his pace, somewhat shuffling. His sons flanked him. Dolph compared this image with the confidant amble of the Navy junior officer of 32 years ago. *Oh I've seen him unsteady on his feet before,* he thought, *but that was off patrol. That was when he and Mr. Boston were carousing together. But then, lots of us were doing that.* Corrine was slowly shaking her head, and small tears marked her cheeks. She nudged him for a handkerchief.

The prayers, the hymns and homily were sweet and thoughtful, but in their detail, not especially memorable. For the rest of Dolph's life, however, he would remember the essence of brief remarks made by an elderly gentleman who preceded the priest's homily.

Dolph did not recognize the man, and his name was not specified in the Order of Service, which simply listed *Remembrances*. The man strode to the podium without assistance or notes, his nicely groomed white hair flecked with black; his dark suit appeared heavier than the season called for. A black eye patch was over one eye. Dolph thought, *He's not from these parts.* He presented an image of a man beyond mortal worry, and that was further evidenced by his measured and sincere speech.

"I was a very young man when Betsy was born to my sister, and over the years I watched her grow. When she married Sam, you could not have seen a prettier or happier bride. And Sam, we all know Sam," the crowd laughed. "Sam was the self-assured tough guy fresh out of the Navy." More chuckles. "Betsy cheerfully took his measure as we all know she could. He was hers, and she never let him forget it. They raised wonderful sons who are here with Sam today. I come to tell you that I never heard Betsy say a cross or hurtful word, quite the contrary. She had other ways than anger to make a point."

"One summer she took a road trip with the boys to see me in Washington. As boys will do, they were squabbling in the back seat to the point of distracting her driving. Instead of yelling threats, she pulled off the highway and began reading a novel. Some time afterward, the boys realized that the vehicle was stopped. When they inquired, Betsy told them that she would resume the drive safely when the boys decided not to fuss. That was Betsy's way."

"I have been blessed to live long enough to realize the hurt and harm I have inflicted on others and myself, some of it minor and others more significant. I have been blessed, as well, with the opportunity to discern my personal flaws and in my own way to attempt amends. Many of you probably feel this too. I was also blessed to know Betsy's example, for she was born understanding, growing, forgiving, helping and loving. Today we say goodbye to Betsy, but not to our memories of her and not to her example."

Only the vise-like grip of Corrine's hand over his kept Dolph from sobbing from the man's personal admissions. Few sermons ever daggered his heart or evoked regret for the dark parts of his life. The words of this stranger, this foreign patrician, became Dolph's guide for his future.

Unexplainably Dolph found his thoughts turning to the deaths of men he knew in Vietnam on the boats. They were good people, and as Dolph measured them against his own self-assessment, they were saints. Why was he here in this time and place and not those decent men?

When the service concluded, the family withdrew to the right of the nave. Dolph again looked at Sam Taylor. Now he was standing tall, smiling and hugging his sons and their wives as they walked away. Later in the reception line following the service, Dolph did something he never would have imagined. He hugged his boat officer.

CHAPTER 70

Back to Business

Eleven days following Becky's memorial service, Sam Taylor returned to his office. Over-solicitous welcomes and pained discomfort respecting his loss were to be expected. His standard reply was, "Thank you, I'm fine now. There's work to be done, and I'm ready to get on with it."

Still, there remained the anguish and emptiness he forced to the back of his mind. *Maybe it will get easier with time,* he thought. *Best to become busy.* He picked up the telephone.

"Hey, Mike, if you're available, could I stop by after lunch and visit about Bay City? I need to get back in the loop, which is my way of saying I need to generate some billable time."

Sam didn't see the humor in his feeble attempt at a joke, but Charbonneau laughed and said, "Anytime. I'm here all this afternoon."

Poca had created prioritized stacks of paper for his attention, and she made them easier by typing notes with recommendations for his decision. She kept an eye on him. Soon he became absorbed in routine, and he nearly worked through the lunch hour.

She went down to the firm's break room and saw that a copy service had delivered one of their low-level bribes for the secretaries, a tray of sliced Subway sandwiches with chips and cookies. Returning to Sam's office with a paper plate of goodies and a soft drink, she interrupted his focus.

"Sam, you don't need to do this all the first day back. Besides, you need some lunch before you go to the U.S. Attorneys' office."

Taylor smiled. "Thank you. You're right." He paused. "Thank you for knowing that I need to pace myself for a while."

Ten minutes later he was out the door. He avoided the tunnel system. It was a hot walk to Mike's office, but it was good for him. The sounds and smells of downtown Houston fostered a form of energy.

Men don't dwell long on another man's loss, even if the other man is a friend. They want to be encouraging without being overly sympathetic. Rarely do they hug or wince. That's just not the way. Mike followed form. A woman might have accused Mike of being callous and insensitive, that his greeting would have been more appropriate if Taylor had returned from a Caribbean cruise.

"Good to see you back, Sam. You're going to enjoy this. Do you want some coffee?"

As they returned from the coffee bar down the hall, Charbonneau closed his office door and began his narrative.

"When you and I first visited and you brought your little package up here, I could tell that you saw my reaction to something in your report. It was the De Los Santos woman. The San Antonio office had been working a bank fraud case out of Boerne. The facts were almost identical to yours. Of course they were using different names and there may have been some hair dyeing involved, but we got derailed; the perpetrators dropped from sight before we could fall on them."

"Then you walked into my office and put the whole thing in our laps." Both men laughed.

"We got a fix on Shiprite, and from that we got the identification on

Piper as Carter, confirming them as the bad guys in Boerne. There was no mistaken identity, either, on De Los Santos by any name; she was the bank president's assistant and was, shall we say, compromising him the same way as Miss Wynne, who was the mortgage office help there. Actually, the Wynne woman played backup a couple of times for De Los Santos. Now that's what I call teamwork."

Taylor took a sip of his coffee and eased back in his chair.

"When we ran the warrants, we got the whole bunch plus two bonuses. They popped a bodyguard with an outstanding capital murder warrant, and we found out they were running a scam on two other banks."

Taylor already knew much of this from Chronicle articles and Jackie's memo on her contacts with Trimmer and the Spook, but he nonetheless enjoyed the presentation.

"Mike, you're letting your coffee go cold. Let me ask you some questions."

Charbonneau gestured for him to go ahead.

"What about deals? Anybody wanting on your dance card?"

"Sam, there's not much to deal on. Because the thug fired a gun during execution of the warrants, we got enhancement potential on the bunch. Everybody has turned on Shiprite, and to one degree or another, on each other. The current conflict is over who recruited and paid the thug. I have really enjoyed this one. By admissions and handwriting analysis, all three women forged various documents, that is, De Los Santos, Wynne and Mrs. Shiprite. She is actually cooperating without asking for any kind of deal."

"The hard case is Wynne. She's made enough admissions to put herself away until menopause, but she keeps dangling the notion that she knows where the fraud money is stashed. I'm inclined to tell her to break rock for a change. There are indications she might have been the co-mastermind with Shiprite."

"I like your colorful imagery, but not so fast, Mike. That's our money you're talking about. Would you consider a little slack if she accounts for and allocates the sources of funds recovered, especially if the banks don't have to waste money fighting over what's left?"

For Sam Taylor, this was like the old days when he and Charbonneau were on the same side, kicking butt and taking names, when cutting deals or not with defendants was a calculated game of cat and mouse, of bluff and bluster with or without enough evidence to make the posturing stick.

"I'll bet the victim banks would appreciate a little consideration extended toward that poor little girl. As a bonus, bank CEOs wouldn't be forced to testify about just how they were lulled into error."

Charbonneau and Taylor grinned at the human frailty exposed in their part of the legal profession.

"What about Mrs. Piper? I haven't seen her name in the papers."

"First, the FBI doesn't think she participated in any of the schemes, that until a few months ago she didn't even know Piper or Carter. She met him in a topless bar where she worked, had too much to drink and married him after a couple of dates. Mrs. Shiprite says all Barbara Piper knew to do was to look pretty. Her handwriting shows up on none of the fraudulent documents, and she was very cooperative with the agents when they executed the search warrant. To quote Sonja Reynolds quoting Mrs. Piper when they started talking, 'You can have the miserable little piece of trash for putting me in this spot.'"

"Sam, she told the agents to search all of his clothes first, because after they were gone, she was throwing everything he owned in the garbage. She said she wouldn't inflict his polyester wardrobe even on Goodwill. I mean to tell you, Hell hath no fury like a scorned red-haired lap dancer."

"Mike, you're a sexist pig, and I guess I am too for laughing."

In the half hour of their visit, Taylor had felt relief. As he was leaving Charbonneau's office, his old friend touched the back of his elbow and said, "Sam, let's have a drink sometime. Any time."

Under the circumstances, that's as good as compassion gets.

CHAPTER 71

Coming Home

After Corrine and Dolph returned to Canyon Ranch, they settled into the routine for which the resort is known. Dolph's once-a-day call was to Poca to check on Sam Taylor; Corrine alternated between calling Momma and checking in with Eloise. It was the middle of August, and things were beginning to quiet down back home.

The charm of the Ranch worked its magic on the couple, and by the time of their departure, Dolph was of two minds. He'd never before stopped to smell the roses. Everything Steiner said about the rains, the smells and the freshness of the air were true. Even Mrs. Steiner matched her telephone image, energetic and attractive; she fell in with Corrine like long-lost friends. They played tennis almost every day while Dolph learned the benefits of a rowing machine, a Concept II. Swimming found its way into Dolph's schedule. But by the end he was anxious to get back to Bay City.

Corrine was eager to see Momma and to conspire with Eloise. They had discussed Barbara's plight and the authorities' conclusion of her essential innocence. Dolph had only two thoughts: he wanted the government out of his town, and he was ready to gut and remodel the Bedford Building.

The first evening home, they took Momma to dinner at the country club's La Riviera Grille. Remarking that the Cavanaughs missed all the big excitement and how great both looked, other guests welcomed Dolph and Corrine back home. After her second Martini, Momma stated her own evaluation.

"Corrine, Dolph is beginning to look hot; you better watch out for him at the pool."

Dolph loved it. "Momma, you better watch yourself; I'll tell the bartender to shut you off."

During dinner they discussed the events of the past few weeks and Trimmer's performance. Momma grumbled about a huge bill the bank got for security services, but given how bad the crooks were and the outcome, the cost was worth it.

Dolph got in a few words about his plans for the Bedford Building, but all Momma said was, "That's nice."

Dolph was abstaining from alcohol; maybe it was the iced tea that was clouding his judgment. Momma's "that's nice" comment should have otherwise triggered alarms. In the past, that statement would have meant that something was up and he would be the last to know the details.

"Corrine went to the bank this afternoon and transferred one of our CDs so we can close this week. Doc Etling had already cleared his stuff out, and I'm ready to get after it."

Momma's second "that's nice" escaped his attention too.

The next morning, Corrine was out of the house by 9 a.m. She went to Eloise's home, and then the two of them drove into town to Barbara's house.

Barbara had been expecting them. She had completed her morning workout and was nicely dressed in white pants and a turquoise top. Decaf coffee, tea and cookies were set out in the living room.

After preliminaries, including Barbara proudly showing off her re-arranged closet and dresser space, they returned to the living room to talk.

"Yes, I got rid of everything of his but the car. That's paid for. Oh, Eloise, did I tell you about Elvis coming to the house?"

Eloise nodded her head, but pointed to Corrine so that Barbara could tell her about the Elvis look-alike agent and how nice he was. After shared laughter, Barbara got serious.

"Girls, I guess I'm the most mortified woman in town. I knew Piper and that evil Dr. No had some kind of business, but not any of that other stuff. Everyone has read the papers, and some still think I had something to do with what's happened."

"That will pass, Barbara. Except for college, I've been here all my life, and folks here have short memories for local scandal. They do, I promise. Now if a politician is fooling around or the president of the country is dallying about, an elephant will forget about it before Bay City will."

"Corrine's right, I'm sure. These are good people here. Don't you worry. But now what about this house?"

"That's one good thing. My former whatever when we moved in paid the rent through the end of the year. All I have to worry about for now is paying the utilities and groceries. I'm not worried about that, at least not now."

"My real problem is that people don't know what to call me; I don't either. I'm not Piper because I can't be, and I'm certainly not Carter, that poor woman. I'm sure not going to use my entertainment name."

Eloise darted her eyes to Corrine. They used that special communication mechanism only women have, the one that requires no words or gestures. No sound at all that affirmed the agreement between Corrine and Eloise that they did not want to know the entertainment name. Corrine spoke next.

"Honey, what was your maiden name? That's a good start."

"Twilly," Barbara said and looked sheepishly off to the side. "People used to make a lot of jokes about my name. You know, plays on the word."

Suppressing a smile, Eloise, with a sense of the reality of her own past said, "Did you have a married name before Piper?"

"Yes, Evans."

"Good. Then there are two questions. What happened to Mr. Evans and were there any credit problems?"

"He died in an industrial accident, and I got a little money out of a settlement and paid all the bills. Fact is, I've got a little of that left for a rainy day, and it looks to me that rain is going to start falling by January."

Again, the look between Corrine and Eloise signaled the next remark.

"Well then, Miss Evans, we'd like to talk to you about a little idea we have."

CHAPTER 72

A Dog Day of Summer

Life in the Bay City area was getting back to normal, sort of. The heat and humidity had been stifling, but the promise of fall was near. Parents and kids were getting ready for the resumption of school. Business had slowed for some but picked up for others, including Walmart.

Dolph and Corrine had closed on the Bedford Building and had been lining up contractors to bid on cleaning out and refurbishing their new property. Dolph got an architect from Lake Jackson, a fellow with a bow tie, to help with the design work; a water blaster entrepreneur to clean the grime and faded paint off the exterior; and an asphalt man to re-top and stripe the modest parking lot in the back. Dolph wasn't sure he liked tousle-haired skinny guys in bow ties, but like briefcases for lawyers, architects always wore bow ties, and they adored seersucker jackets in the summer.

He was so committed to this project that he stopped lunching at Hannah's and instead lived on turkey-sandwich meat and sliced cold vegetables. Corrine pitched another round of outsized clothing. She even had Dr. Merritt tell Dolph to slow down, that he had broken the bad cycle and now should concentrate on maintenance and a sensible diet.

Dolph spent one of his days salvaging some items of peculiar dental equipment to decorate his office. Etling left behind a usable dark leather couch in one of the upstairs rooms. When business was slow and particularly after his wife died, Etling would nap on the couch. Dolph proclaimed that he would do the same. When Corrine admired his decision, Dolph said she could use it too, but he'd charge her a couch-register fee. She tolerated his humor.

Cavanaugh was clear with Corrine and the architect that he pretty much knew what he wanted done to the upstairs, but he was candidly clueless about the big, open floor space downstairs. Dolph personally tore down the first floor partition walls Etling had added poorly several years ago and was stuck in a now-what mentality. Corrine helped him out one Friday morning.

They were dressing for an early jog to get it done before the heat rose. His mind was fresh and ready for the run and another day at the building.

"Dolph, honey, I've been thinking."

Dolph remembered a friend's colorful metaphor to describe a jolt to the senses; *it was like a rush of hot lava to the heart.* In all their marriage, Corrine's thinking predicate meant some kind of trouble, just like this summer began. Could he handle more?

"What's that, my dear?" His hands were frozen at his left shoelace.

In quick order Corrine said that she and Eloise thought he ought to build out a health spa on the first floor, complete with exercise machines and separate shower and dressing facilities for men and women. She was still toying with the thought of steam and hot tub amenities, but the basic idea was for a place to work out and get cleaned up.

"Who's going to manage this operation, you and Eloise?"

"No, we're going to pay to join the spa and so are you. But we want Barbara to own and run it. Oh, you need to know, she's now Barbara

Evans. Anyway, we think she would be perfect for the job and could teach exercise classes for women around here."

He knew she had the answer before he asked, "How's she going to afford all this ownership?"

"Glad you asked, big boy. The bank will lend her enough cash to buy the equipment and some front-end operating money. You and I are going to fund the build out and fold that cost into her long-term lease. I called Sam, and he said he would make us a Bedford Building Corporation and help with the lease and Barbara's business entity. Whatcha think?" She smiled.

"You're talking about spending a lot more money than I had planned, but I'm going to need a separate entrance. I don't want to go to work through all that flabby pulchritude you girls are going to attract."

Corrine shook her head, but she knew that was Dolph's way of saying yes. She had not yet put on her top and walked to the bedside where Dolph was sitting and gave him a memorable hug.

For Dolph's part, the idea sounded great before Corrine had completed her first salvo. He did not want to seem eager.

"Is Baxter on board?"

"Of course. So is Momma."

"Sounds like a done deal."

On the outbound leg of the jog, they discussed added details for the work on the building as well as timing. They took a breather at the main gate and discussed another bright idea the women had.

Bank foreclosure was eminent on the Shiprite house, and Eloise had tracked down Maria's family in Dallas. They, in turn, had contacted Maria's court-appointed attorney. Maria had apparently made a deal to plead guilty and was going to prison for much less time than her husband. Corrine and Eloise had offered to coordinate with Maria's folks in cleaning out belongings that Maria might need when she was released from confinement. There wasn't much, but it might help Maria and would be a benefit to the bank.

"Sounds good to me. Got to maintain the image of the subdivision."

On the backside of the outing, Corrine asked Dolph about some interesting blessings that had been going on.

"Have you heard anything about the anonymous money that's been given to lots of churches and charities around here? That church up in Wharton that got money for a new roof just got a check from some trust fund for $100,000 to renovate and paint their building. They put it in a Wharton bank to pay out as work progresses. And that's just a drop in the bucket."

"Do tell? That's great. I haven't heard this."

"Momma called me yesterday. Her old church got one of those checks. She said there was a condition on the money that the Vestry uses the funds to find and pay a decent salary to a new rector, preferably one that has his eyes on the Bible and not on political agendas. Momma says that the Senior Warden called to see if she was the one who gave the money. She said no, but wishes she had. He then invited her to be on the search committee in light of her long and faithful interest in the church. I guess they want Mamma and her money back. What do you think is going on?"

"I don't know, baby, maybe we just ought to relax and let God sort it out."

Mr. Cavanaugh was amazed at the ease of his response. They doubled the pace.

Dolph realized something that had started at Canyon Ranch. He could actually carry on a conversation while running with his wife.

* * *

Friday evenings at Hannah's Place from mid to late August are a toss-up for attendance. It had not been very hot that day because rain showers had crisscrossed the region. Rain in the summer is not always good for the tourist trade. Mrs. Gregory called Birdie in to spell her. She had an errand to run.

A beautiful sunset was on display, the heat had gone, and the air was unusually dry. A pleasant evening was ahead. Toey and the other girls were taking care of the modest number of guests. She had called

Big Joe to come for dinner and a visit while things toned down. She had been working a lot of extra time, as had Joe: they were saving up to buy a house. It was going to be one of those sweet nights.

Junior was out on the boat cleaning up the deck and the dock, throwing bits of trash fish to the Brown Pelicans. Screeching sea gulls angled for scraps that the lumbering pelicans missed. There was still enough light to work by, but it would be gone shortly. It was close to 8 p.m.

Junior went up on the walkway surrounding the restaurant to take a smoke and watch the fading of the western light. Inside, things were quiet. Birdie had cleaned and re-cleaned the bar glasses, folded some nice cotton napkins he reserved for favored guests and set aside some leftovers for Seferina to take to Janie Farmer after they closed. He felt the pleasantness of the evening. He too decided to step out on the walkway, but at the far corner, opposite from Junior. This moment in life was good.

As civil dusk approached and Junior finished his cigarette, he saw a white, otherwise non-descript 4-door sedan pull into the parking lot. He thought nothing of it as he stubbed out the smoke and walked back toward the dock. He climbed aboard the fishing boat and entered the pilothouse. By habit his hand found a small light over the chart table. He wanted to plan his next morning's fishing trip.

In the instant his brain recalled the white car, he bolted onto the dock, running as fast as his legs would move. He rushed through the service entrance past Seferina and to the bar and cash-register area. He looked around and saw Toey.

"The man, the one who hurt Birdie, his car is in the parking lot. I'm sure it's him." Junior was trembling. "Where's Birdie now?"

Toey did not reply. Quickly she walked into the pantry and then returned to the cash register. She picked up the telephone and dialed the Sheriff's dispatcher. She spoke in a soft but measured voice.

"This is Toey Sonier out here at Hannah's Place. We've got trouble. Come quick."

Not bothering for comment by the dispatcher, little Toey hung up the phone and moved rapidly to Big Joe's table. He had been watching ESPN on the TV mounted in the corner. She whispered in his ear. He put down the television remote and stood.

Outside on the walkway, darkness had descended; the sky remained slightly blue to the west. As Thurman Birdwell turned to go back inside, a hand reached out and grabbed his neck just where it met the top of his frail shoulders. In the next moment he was thrown against the railing. As his body fell to the deck, he was seized by his arm and slapped repeatedly.

A voice, breath laden with alcohol - cheap bourbon, Thurman thought - spoke with increasing menace. "I told you I would come back. I told you no interference. You interfered and have caused me trouble."

The man then reached under Birdie's ribcage just like before and squeezed. Birdie gasped but did not scream. He pulled Birdie closer to his face and said, "Old man, you die tonight."

Praying, Birdie struggled to open his eyes and look this evil man in the face one last time. Finally, J. Thurman Birdwell blurted out, "Kiss my ass!"

The man's surprise that this old coot was still defiant was momentary. The man was bashed against the head, he thought by a large stone. A second rapid blow took him on the other side of his head. He crumpled to the deck. Birdie was lifted out of the way.

As Thurman leaned against the railing while catching his breath, he saw the man on the deck pull a pistol. Before the weapon had cleared the belt, a massive booted foot kicked the gun away into the darkness and salt grass below.

The huge shape of Big Joe reached down and pulled the man up so that his feet could not touch the deck. He pushed the man against the wall, holding him fast with his log of a forearm.

Postal Inspector Culver Foxman croaked, "You can't do this to me, I'm a federal agent."

"I don't care if you're Santy Claus; you can't hurt Birdie, you buzzard."

Foxman passed out when struck the third time.

When the Sheriff's units arrived, Foxman, now inside on the floor near the counter, was bound hand and foot and everywhere in between. Junior had fetched rope from the boat locker. Toey talked to the lead deputy first and pointed to Birdie. She then nodded at Junior and her husband, Big Joe. The deputy eyed Foxman, who was proclaiming his federal status.

"You hush up, mister. I'll get to you when I'm ready." He turned and spoke to another deputy who then walked outside.

Toey motioned for the lead deputy to follow her into the pantry. Three minutes later, they reemerged. About that time the other deputy returned holding a pistol by its barrel.

The lead officer then walked over to Foxman, untied his restraints and assisted him off the floor, helping him dust off and straighten his clothing.

"Sorry I had to leave you there like that; I hope you're all right. Do you think you need medical attention?"

"No, I'm OK. I'll be fine." Foxman was regaining control. Things might work out.

The deputy then requested identification, which Foxman produced.

"Just so I'm clear about this, you are a U.S. Postal Inspector, a federal officer of the law, a public servant, so to speak, right?"

"I am indeed. I'm here on a major fraud investigation, and that brute over there obstructed me. I'll report this to the United States Attorney for charges."

"I don't know about obstruction, but it looks to me like Mr. Sonier whipped the tar out of you." The deputy smiled slightly.

"That's not funny, deputy."

"No, I don't think it's funny. Step over here with me to this pantry. Let's go to the movies." Toey preceded them.

"Do I smell alcohol on your breath?"

"No, I don't think so." Foxman tried to breathe through his nose. He found his glasses and put them on.

The deputy prevented Foxman from fully entering the pantry. A moment later Foxman's gaze was fixed upon an inside wall, and light reflectively flickered against his eyeglasses.

The deputy asked Toey if she could turn up the volume. She could. Then for all to hear, Foxman's words were clear, as were the sounds of his slapping of Birdie. Clear too were Birdie's defiant and uncharacteristic response and Big Joe's comment. The security camera caught it all.

Big Joe's face reddened and patrons chuckled when they heard Joe talking about "Santy" Claus.

Foxman slumped. The deputy cuffed him. As he patted down Foxman, he pulled a set of keys from his trousers and tossed them to the other deputy.

Turning to Thurman, he asked, "Is this the man who beat you earlier this summer?"

"Yes, it is."

"Are you older than age 65?"

"Yes, I'm 74." Everybody but Foxman was grinning. Toey, with tears welling in her eyes, reached out and hugged the old guy.

The deputy sat Foxman down at one of the bar chairs and asked Toey if he could use the house telephone. He moved out of earshot and spoke for a couple of minutes. Afterward he walked up to Foxman.

"You're under arrest for two charges of aggravated assault of Mr. Bird-well, in your case, a felony in Texas. Looks like you might be facing an official oppression charge, not to mention a D.W. I. I've spoken with my supervisor, the chief deputy here, and he is calling your people and an Assistant U. S. Attorney of his acquaintance about tonight's events. Sounds like you need to keep your mouth shut even after I give you your rights."

As he escorted Foxman toward the door, the other deputy returned once more, this time holding up an evidence bag containing a plastic bottle of Four Roses bourbon. He was holding the bag like it was a dead rat. "This was on the front passenger seat."

Contrary to Foxman's earlier visit to Hannah's Place, when patrons vanished rather than be interviewed, all had remained this time to see the rest of the drama unfold. A few of the informed locals told the tourists what had happened before. As Matagorda deputies escorted their prisoner from the premises, the patrons clapped and cheered. Toey wiped her eyes with her fingertips. Big Joe's head dipped and his face turned redder as folks came around and slapped him on the back. He retreated to the TV remote and tried to watch ESPN.

CHAPTER 73
Party Time

Labor Day weekend in Bay City isn't much different from other parts of the nation; it's the last fling of summer, fall is anticipated, and folks expect afterward that work will take on a more serious tone. After all, we are told, everything we earn from then on belongs to us and not the taxman. Football is in the air and maybe, just maybe, there won't be a major hurricane this season.

There are some differences from Labor Day in northern Minnesota or Maine and Bay City, Texas. Up north, the Tuesday following the holiday marks the advent of a short fall. Bay City doesn't begin cooling until October. Significant chill might appear by Thanksgiving.

The Nouveau Estates Country Club directors decided to celebrate the club's first Labor Day and the successful completion of construction and landscaping. They wanted to honor everyone who worked on the project, especially Carleton Brooks. He and his crew had sustained a mighty effort to water the new grass and plantings as well as the greens and fairways of the golf course. Roof catchments from various club structures directed rainwater to intermediate holding tanks around the property, with the excess going to Big Lake. That was Carleton's idea.

The event, to be held on Saturday from 10 a.m. until dark, was not open to the general public. Subdivision homeowners were admitted with homeowner tickets and were given 10 guest tickets per household to give away as they pleased. The club retained 100 tickets for so-called dignitaries and special guests. The anticipated attendance was 800. Attire was to be casual. Casual recognizes a broad spectrum in small towns.

To feed all these folks for free, the directors invited outside restaurants as an advertising opportunity to join La Riviera Grille in offering representative menu items sufficient to feed many but not all of the crowd. The club provided beer, wine and soft beverages. Club management retained overall authority on any issue, but Mrs. Gregory coordinated the food services. Eloise, Corrine and Barbara took turns managing guest lists and a crew of volunteers.

Small pavilion tents with seating and little tables were scattered around the club grounds, offering sanctuary from the sun and opportunities for quiet conversations. As with all such events, not everyone mixed and mingled, with some preferring instead to find their usual group of friends.

The Cavanaugh and Trimmer families showed up around noon. Some bankers from Freeport and Lake Jackson arrived at 1:30 p.m. to pay homage to their hero brother, Baxter Trimmer. After the usual pleasantries, they withdrew.

Chamber of Commerce folks and their wives stopped in to smile and join the club directors in praising anybody they could think of. They didn't stay long because they were also scheduled to eat chili and hot dogs over at the Bay City Country Club later in the afternoon.

On Friday evening, the Cavanaugh sons got home from Colorado. These men were stunningly handsome. Corrine got weak in the knees just seeing her sons. She would not be the only woman to do so. Amos Bedford, the older boy, was rangy, tall and lean. He was named after his grandfathers, while Marshall Forrest, tall and muscular, took his grandmother's maiden name and his middle name from Dolph's father. Corrine worked hard on honoring ancestors, but she'd had enough of the Amos and Andy jokes that were made about her father and grandfather. She would not have her sons similarly burdened.

The high Rockies must have done something to her sons. They had a big announcement. Each had volunteered for Officer Candidate School following college graduation, Amos for the Navy next June and Marshall for the Marines the following year. Corrine was horrified, but Dolph comforted her, as husbands will with the usual stuff about service being easier for officers and how it looks good on résumés. Still, fear clutched their mother's heart.

The next day Amos and Marshall fanned out into the crowd to inspect the women. The Trimmer girls were crestfallen to be abandoned by those whom they had privately named Adonis and Hercules. Eloise suggested they cool off in the pool. Dolph had an attitude similar to his sons. He decided to go tent hopping. His first stop was Hannah's. You couldn't miss the sign, Corrine's gift, a 15-foot wide crab holding a red banner between its claws. It proclaimed Hannah's Place in white lettering. *God I love Texas*, Dolph thought.

Hannah Gregory was about the finest and most cheerful woman in the world, next to Corrine. In her characteristic outfit, she was greeting guests and issuing instructions to the help. Seferina was working on the cooking pots. Joe Sonier was spooning rice into bowls as Janie Farmer, with dentures and a hairnet, was ladling gumbo. Backstopping for Hannah as a greeter was Toey. Junior was hauling trash with another hired hand Dolph couldn't see over Big Joe's bulk.

"Darlin', looks like you've got everything under control." Dolph had on Tevas, khaki pants and a flashy Hawaiian shirt. He was drinking a can of club soda.

"Sure have, Dolph. I couldn't be happier." She put the eye on him, top to bottom.

"Dolph, you're looking pretty tan and flashy today. Corrine and I need to tell the men to lock up their women."

Cavanaugh had never been one of those aw shucks, kick the dirt fellows, but he was blushing now.

"Seriously Dolph, I'm real proud of you. You've lost all that weight, and you look marvelous."

Cavanaugh was about to give over to giddiness when Junior and his buddy showed up, Hannah's Place shirts and all. Dolph had just elevated the club soda to his lips and involuntarily sucked the contents into his lungs and down his shirt. Coughing and retching as Hannah beat his back, Dolph strained to comprehend what he had seen. C.W., Uncle Buddy, Charles W. Rogers, the schmoozing, car dealing, fraud scheming, feedlot worker and ranch hand, was standing arm in arm with Hannah Gregory.

"God, my sins are before me," he thought.

"Dolph, baby, are you alright?" She daubed a towel over his face and the front of his shirt. "I'd like you to meet Charles Rogers. He's been a real help to me the last few weeks. I wish you two had met before. I'm sure y'all have a lot in common."

C.W. looked like a jackass eating cactus as far as Dolph was concerned.

"Cavanaugh is it? I'm glad to meet you. My good friends call me C.W."

The two Academy Awards actors shook hands.

Dolph needed two things, fresh air and a stiff drink. He asked Hannah if there was any real stuff anywhere other than beer or wine. Hannah smiled knowingly and pointed.

"Dolph see that tent over there, the white one under the big old oak tree? Birdie has a little private set-up for certain folks. We call it the Elder Care Tent. It's not for everyone, but I'm sure they'll let you in."

Cavanaugh pitched his soda can in the trash and made for the oak tree. The western sun was angling into his eyes, and it took some moments for them to adjust to the pleasant dimness within the tent. A fan was blowing over a 50-pound block of ice, making the space even more inviting. Dolph smelled whiskey and then saw Birdie on station at a height-adjustable, stainless-steel table. The bar was complete and impressive.

"Randolph, so glad you joined us. What's your pleasure?"

"Gin and tonic, Thurman. You're looking well after your ordeal." That was not just small talk. Birdie was immaculate: clean-shaven without tissue covering nicks, an open collar pale blue dress shirt buttoned at the cuffs, white summer weight linen slacks, and dark cordovan loafers, a gentleman in any circle.

"Thank you Randolph. I almost didn't recognize you. You look 20 years younger. That's good." He handed Dolph his drink.

"Tell me Thurman, What happened out at Hannah's?"

Birdie wiped the preparation area.

"Mr. Sonier and Toey saved my life. Foxman caught me by surprise. If Junior hadn't warned them, I suppose I would be dead now. I thank God and Miss Hannah for putting in the security system. Each outside camera was equipped to record sound and to work in very low light. I'm blessed."

"If it's any interest to you, my lawyer in Houston says Mr. Foxman wasn't a team player and all this business with you was on his own. They also ran a breath test on him at the jail. He failed miserably. Along with the assault, he picked up a D.W.I. and some kind of oppression charges. They can put him behind the wheel with Junior. Imagine that, old Junior is going to be a state's witness in a drunk-driving case." Dolph chuckled, Birdie didn't.

"Foxman won't get probation; the felony cases are too strong, and he's been suspected of this for years. He's already toast with the Postal Service, no retirement."

Thurman winced. "That seems a little harsh."

"Forget about it, Birdie. That man had a chance to pull up and didn't. My lawyer says he hurt a lot of folks before he got around to you."

Dolph was not without sympathy for Foxman's self-destructive path, but he was grateful that he had chosen a different way.

"Glad you're safe Birdie. Between you and Baxter, I don't know if this town can handle two heroes at once."

Dolph turned to survey the rest of the tent and saw Momma sitting by herself at a table for four. He walked over and kissed her on the temple.

"May I join you? What were you doing?"

"Oh, I was reviewing the events of this summer and watching you and Thurman talking." She was nursing a light scotch and water.

"I spoke with Baxter today. He's coming along. I want to thank you for bringing him to Bay City. He's made an admirable admission to me."

Dolph, pokerfaced, waited.

"Most men are afraid to admit inadequacy; even the best of them have limits, but only when they face up to it do they make real progress. Baxter told me that he needs someone to take over operations because he wants to be more involved in developing the bank's customer base. He wants Peoples to be the benchmark of banking strength in this region. He says he doesn't want the bank sold, music to my ears."

"Mine too, Momma. You and Corrine have a lot riding on the bank, a lot of folks do."

"I've been reviewing something else. Dolph, my feelings about you."

Return to deadpan.

"When you married Corrine, I had my doubts, as most mothers do, but over the years I saw how happy Corrine was and how Amos and Marshall were growing into wonderful men. You were successful in your investment business, and I never had a reason to doubt your love for Corrine."

"Thanks, Momma, but somehow I don't think you've quite made your point."

"That's right. Several years ago, you began taking long business trips. Corrine never knew where you were. She didn't complain, but I didn't like it. I started thinking the usual things old mothers-in-law and their daughters think."

Dolph interrupted. "I never had someone else on the road."

"Well that's good to hear, but what I have seen recently tells me more about you than I had ever dreamed. You stopped traveling without Corrine, you left Houston, you got yourself in shape for the long run, and you were the major factor in saving our bank, not Baxter. He was just your instrument. Along the way, you also saved him from himself."

Dolph started to speak, but Mrs. Wilson, almost imperceptibly, lifted her left hand to abate interruption.

"I care not to know the whys and wherefores of the past of your personal or business life or the changes that you've made. It is sufficient for me that you are here and now as you are."

Nobody's words had ever humbled Randolph Cavanaugh until now. His chin went toward his chest and then up.

"Thanks. I love you, Momma."

"I love you too, Dolph."

They sat quietly for a moment. Dolph looked at his empty glass and noticed that Momma's was only ice.

"I'm going back to Birdie for another drink. Can I refresh yours?"

"That would be fine Dolph, but first you need to meet my new friend, a most wonderful lady and so charming."

Dolph stood and turned.

"Mrs. Meredith, this is my son-in-law I've talked to you about, Randolph Cavanaugh. He and I have been visiting. Won't you join us?"

Whatever it was that rushed hotly to his heart, he almost lost his balance in the soft grass beneath the table. His empty glass fell but did not break. His face flushed, but he regained composure.

"Mrs. Meredith, I'm afraid Dolph has been too long in the sun." Momma laughed.

So did Pete as she took the chair in between.

Again, there was that dazzling smile. "I'm sure he will recover; he seems resilient."

"I apologize, Mrs. Meredith. Momma is right. I've had a lot of surprises yesterday and today. I don't know how much more I can take."

"Randolph was about to get me another drink. Can he bring you one, too? You can get to know each other better."

"Yes, Birdie knows what I like. A Pernod Anise and soda, please."

Dolph's eyeballs were burning as he got to Thurman.

"Fix Momma another whatever, and I want gin and no tonic, light on the ice. Mrs. Meredith will..." Birdie interrupted Dolph.

"Pernod Anise and soda with crushed ice. I agree with Pete; it's a refreshing summer drink."

Dolph took Birdie's measure as the drinks of the two ladies were prepared.

"Forget the gin on mine. I'll do only tonic. I've got to have a clear head."

The two women were chatting like sisters, and Pete wasn't much younger in appearance than Momma. Singapore came to mind. When speculative images of Momma in 1969 flickered in his brain, he shook his head to ward them off.

He took the drinks to the ladies. Retrieving his tonic, he excused himself, saying he needed food.

As he walked from the tent he thought, *so it's Pete and Birdie. Maybe it's Birdie and Jean. Whatever it is, Birdie's in for it.* He headed for K-2's tent. He needed a fat pill. The Brooks family and Rae Jean were laughing over something and could only wave at him. The fact was that everyone seemed to be laughing and talking loudly. Dolph needed space and fresh air.

Outside he found Corrine. The crowd and the pressure on the food stations were thinning out. She smiled and told him how happy she was that the day had been so successful. He listened without really hearing. He saw the odd look in her eyes; she knew his mind was elsewhere. Suddenly without saying anything, Dolph pulled Corrine close and kissed her. He continued to hold her. Finally, she spoke.

"Dolph, baby, people are going to think we need to get a room. Do we?"

It was her disarming way of bringing him back to the world.

He laughed. "Naw Corrine, I need you to know I love you."

She smiled. "I'm going to check on Momma. Want to come along?"

"Have you met her new friend?" Dolph was fishing.

"You mean Pete? Oh yes, she's our new neighbor around the corner. Isn't she wonderful? Could you imagine a more attractive older woman? I'm thrilled she's here. Momma too."

"No, I'll pass. I'm going to make another run on Hannah's."

This all was beyond him. He remembered hearing about somebody wandering the earth searching for an honest man, was that it? He felt lost just on the Nouveau Country Club grounds.

C.W. walked up and took him out of his confusion.

"Dagnabbit, I enjoyed seeing the look on your face. I guess we're going to be acknowledged buddies. Isn't that the trip?"

"You scrawny cowboy clown, I thought you left town. Why'd you come back?"

"Hold on there, Randolph. I did leave, but I still heard the call of Hannah. She's worth staying in this sweat lodge you call home. I got back to Lubbock and couldn't get her off my mind. I didn't want to inflict my worthless tail on her but finally decided she could take it."

Dolph listened skeptically.

"Look, you and I are done doing deals. I've pulled up, and so should you. We're not old, but we're too old for that game. You and I both know it stopped being fun a long time ago. The world is changing fast on us. I had trouble finding flight information over the telephone. The automated phone lady was talking faster than I could listen, and then I didn't punch the right number key. It's going to get worse for both of us even if the world stands still tomorrow."

Dolph smiled. His friend made sense. This was the longest coherent, serious commentary he had ever heard C.W. utter. Dolph realized his own pulling up happened the Dallas weekend of his last business meeting with Pete.

Cops, prosecutors and career crooks know what pulling up means, even if they use other terms to describe that time a bad guy irreversibly determines, regardless of the consequences, to stop being bad. Not to be confused with jailhouse spiritual conversions of convenience, pulling up is single-minded and without guile or manipulation; it is real. In many instances, law enforcement, the judicial system and even prison may have little or nothing to do with the decision. It is God's amazing grace, many say, in His own good time, and often the consequences are glorious.

"Dolph, I was good to Trudy 'til the end, and I'll be good to Hannah;

I promise."

"I couldn't ask for more. But, you've got to promise one more thing; don't mess with her menu. I don't want to see any of that West Texas style of New Mexican food showing up at Hannah's. It would give me gas and be a sacrilege."

Before C.W. could jerk Dolph around about his distaste for Panhandle Mexican food, Hannah caught them at the tent entry.

"I see you boys are hitting it off."

C.W. said, "Yup, just like we've known each other all our lives." He then went into the tent. Dolph's eyes went half-lidded.

Hannah looked after C.W. and sighed. "I think he's a good man. I need my own good man. Corrine's got hers."

She turned back and smiled at Dolph. They would always be special friends.

"I think he is too, Hannah. Why don't you go for it?"

Hannah beamed.

"Mrs. Gregory, could you do me a favor? Get one of those big white envelopes out of your box and give it to Toey. Tell her the tooth fairy came to town and heard what a hero Big Joe was. That ought to be enough for a good down payment on a house they can afford."

Hannah reached up and hugged Dolph. Tears welled in her eyes. She then turned and followed C.W. into the tent.

Dolph decided to take the long way around the swimming pool as he went back to Thurman's tent. He had just made the turn at the deep end of the pool when he saw Baxter Trimmer shaking hands with a guy that looked out of place for this environment. There was something familiar about the man's face, but Dolph couldn't place him. He decided to join the two men. Baxter would take care of the introductions.

"Hey, Bax, may I join you?

"Sure, Dolph, let me introduce you to Harold Ringer. He headed the FBI team that arrested Shiprite and Piper or Carter, I guess. He was just telling me about the money. Bea Jay cut herself a deal and told the Feds where a bunch of the stolen money was. Isn't that great?"

In the moment of hands extended for shaking, both men realized their shared past.

"I'll be," Dolph said. "Smaller world than we ever imagined."

"After all these years, but I remember that you were from Arkansas. What brought you to Bay City?"

Trimmer became a spectator.

"The woman I married and the Good Lord." Dolph had never said those words out loud. "She's from here, and we met in college. How about yourself, the FBI is a long way from Sadec?"

"When I got out of the Navy, I started college and decided to give the Bureau a shot when I graduated. Do you ever go to the Swift Boat reunions?"

Trimmer jumped in.

"Wait a minute, you guys. Were you on Swift Boats, Dolph? You never told me that."

"Bax, you never asked what I did in the Navy. Fact is nobody back in the States ever gave a flip one way or another what we did over there."

Ringer, looking at Dolph, but speaking to Trimmer, said, "He's generally right, but the FBI cared, and I guess that's one reason I made this my career. It's good to work with decent men. By the way, isn't it a funny coincidence that Lieutenant Taylor represented the bank?"

Trimmer's estimation of Dolph just went up a notch or two.

"Yeah, sure is. I seem to remember, wasn't he a lawyer before the Navy?" Dolph's deflective response was triggered by the realization that for the first time in his life he was having chitchat with an FBI agent, the last person on earth he would have wanted to talk to, voluntarily or otherwise.

"Well, Mr. Trimmer, I was on my way to Corpus Christi tonight and thought I would find you here. Good news ought not to wait until Tuesday." Turning to Dolph, he added, "You ought to consider those reunions; there's a lot of decent men there."

The men shook hands, and Ringer left.

As he and Dolph watched the FBI agent head to the parking lot, Baxter looked both ways, and then, as if soliciting confidential information, asked, "Hey Dolph, did you ever shoot anyone while you were on the boats?"

"What are you Baxter, some 10-year-old kid? Go find Eloise and your daughters."

On the way to the parking lot, Hal Ringer passed two giggling teenage girls and an attractive woman walking from the ladies locker room area. He loved hearing the laughter but had no idea what had provoked it. If the timing of their passing had been slightly different, Ringer might have paused and wondered more about coincidences.

The girls had been chattering about how buff Adonis and Hercules looked today. Eloise said, "Dolph, looked pretty buff as well, too trim though to wear the pink rabbit outfit next Easter."

CHAPTER 74

Full Circle

There was still plenty of light, but the heat had vanished. Dolph ambled over to Thurman's tent again looking for Corrine. Thurman and Momma were gone. Pierrette was tending the bar. Actually she was surveying Birdie's stock and approvingly found a nice Cognac.

She was dressed in a loose-fitting, attractive yellow and white summer dress. Dolph hadn't seen anything like it in Corrine's closet or on any woman in town.

"Where'd you get that dress, Mrs. Meredith? It's beautiful."

"In Houston, Randy. I was visiting my attorney, actually our attorney. He's a very nice man. You know he's just lost his wife? So sad."

This was too much. Dolph reached across the bar to the Cognac and filled a wine glass.

"You've hired Sam Taylor? How'd you find him?"

"Why in the telephone book, Randy. You have spoken of him so often it was rather easy. Come now, let's sit and wait for Thurman, and maybe Corrine will appear."

In the next 15 minutes Pete related that she had first contacted Taylor some years ago for assistance with a sizeable real-estate investment. Mrs. Meredith, through a company she controlled, had provided interim financing to California gentlemen for the land purchase and development of a residential subdivision: Nouveau Estates. Her organization recently bought out the developers and retained a management company to oversee all further construction, assuring continued quality and exclusivity of the property. Actually, it was Dolph's money that bought Nouveau and then donated all of its assets to a charitable trust. That trust has been executing the items on Dolph's list and would have plenty of money to distribute to worthy causes.

"You and I will have no control over the funds; that will be solely left to the discretion of the Trustee: our attorney, Sam Taylor. I know he is a man you trusted with your life; why not with this money?"

Dolph was stunned. Only Pete could have pulled this off.

"Does Sam know where this money came from?"

"I don't think so, and he probably knows better than to probe. Besides, he couldn't get far."

She finished her drink. "It was, of course, only logical that I should buy one of your homes as an occasional residence to complement another I own in Halifax, Canada. Surely you will be able to adjust to me as your neighbor? I do hope so. Perhaps you, Jean and Corrine will be my guests next summer in Halifax; it is much cooler than Bay City. Your lovely sons, of course, will always be welcomed."

Dolph smiled and nodded.

"Jean and Birdie are really charming, Dolph. I am having fun, and I feel safer here than ever before."

"That's good. I'll be just fine; the truth is I was already missing the prospect of our annual meetings. Your being here is a gift."

"You have certainly had an exciting summer in Bay City. It's not like this all the time, is it?"

"No, this year was special. While life often turns on a dime, Pete, here in Bay City it's normally dull and pleasant."

ABOUT THE AUTHOR

Andy Horne, raised and educated in Houston, Texas, received his undergraduate and law degrees from the University of Texas at Austin. Following three years in the District Attorney's office in Houston, Andy resigned and entered Officer Training with the Navy. The first half of his active duty was on the USS Princeton, a helicopter carrier off the coast of Vietnam. Following Princeton's recovery of Apollo 10, Andy became an Office-in-Charge of a Swift Boat (PCF) in the Mekong Delta.

Andy returned to civilian life where he resumed his professional career again as a Harris County Assistant District Attorney, then as an Assistant United States Attorney for the Southern District of Texas, thereafter entering private practice. During this period Andy was an instructor in International Law at his Navy Reserve Center. In 1997 he became an Assistant Attorney General for the Commonwealth of the Northern Mariana Islands on Saipan. Andy and his wife, Sylvia, now reside in a Galveston, Texas, cottage that survived the deadly 1900 storm as well as Hurricane IKE.

ACKNOWLEDGMENTS

This work of fiction would not have been possible without serious doses of encouragement and reality administered to me by friends and colleagues in and beyond the prosecution and defense of crimes. I am particularly grateful for the critical contributions of Leland Hamel, a highly and deservedly skilled business crimes legal expert in Houston, Texas. Jerry McNeely, a Certified Public Accountant, former bank examiner and retired banker well familiar with in-the-trenches banking personalities and practices, was an invaluable resource. My dear friend, Rosemary Jackson, an Episcopal priest, was my faithful monitor of generally accepted Christian theology unencumbered by denominational nuances. Barbara Kenna, one of a few selected readers for authenticity of female characters, was a constant cheerleader for this book.

Methodist Hospital in Houston, Texas, provides an excellent executive health assessment program. In the interest of brevity, I may have taken liberties in describing Dolph's experience there. The program is far more complete, thorough and professional than I have indicated.

No storyteller can lay sole claim to internal inspiration. My inspirations came from my father and his elder brother, both Texas bankers when banking was believed to be a profession. Jonathan Kwitny's book, *The Fountain Pen Conspiracy,* (New York: Alfred A. Knopf, 1973) an intriguing examination of a dozen or so schemes and their many colorful participants spurred my interest in these crimes and their perpetrators.

I have a great affection for Bay City, Texas, a good example of small towns all over the state mostly filled with good people.

To be sure, I acknowledge the contributions of the many witnesses, clients, victims, prosecutors, defendants and peace officers I encountered in my legal career. The characters in this novel are nonetheless composites and fictional.

One other person stands out as a spur to my imagination in this novel, an unknown thief, clearly a career con man. Spaced by several years, this crafty, intelligent man would fly into Houston, swindle local jewelers and disappear within hours of his crimes. So far as I know, he has never been apprehended for these activities. Perhaps he has been discouraged by heightened airport security in the last decade or the greater prevalence of business security cameras, or maybe he has retired or lost interest. Where did he go and what did he do otherwise with his time beyond Houston? Mixed Company is a story founded in such speculation.

INVITATION

I hope you have enjoyed *Mixed Company*, first of the Decent Men novels. A few common characters loosely connect each story in the Series examining their post-Vietnam War lives. As civilians, they generally lead productive lives. There are exceptions and contrasts, of course.

The women in this series are also colorful and, I hope, credible and interesting.

Soon to be available is *In the Company of Decent Men*, a political action thriller with true heroes.

The story begins in the Mekong Delta as U.S. Navy Swift Boats prepare for action in November 1968. The ensuing events and associated perceptions set the stage to examine the shadows they cast over the next 35 years. I think you will find the characters and their stories go *beyond the superficial.*